PSYCHIC

PSYCHIC

TS Rose

Apprentice
House Press
Loyola University Maryland

First Edition

Casebound ISBN: 978-1-62720-386-9
Paperback ISBN: 978-1-62720-387-6
Ebook ISBN: 978-1-62720-388-3

Printed in the United States of America

Design by Lauren Fallon
Edited by Lauren Fallon
Promotion plan by Hannah Aebli

Published by Apprentice House Press

Apprentice House Press
Loyola University Maryland
4501 N. Charles Street
Baltimore, MD 21210
410.617.5265
www.ApprenticeHouse.com
info@ApprenticeHouse.com

CHAPTER ONE

Alpha Moore hesitated as she crept through the kitchen. Her focus sharpened, and she homed in on the back door. Beyond it she could sense pure evil. She took a shuddering breath, thrust back the dark curtain of hair that had swung across her face, eased open the door, and peered outside into the gloom, dreading what she was about to find.

She blinked in surprise: the only person she could see was little Bruce Pilkington in his Batman pyjamas, his cheeks chubby and his curls dancing in the breeze. He was balancing on his toes in the dull light of the courtyard, rooting around inside an enormous wheelie bin meant for rubbish. He gave a childish giggle as he began fiddling with the bin bags, then drew one out from the overflowing pile. He extracted yesterday's newspaper from the bag and balled up the sheets before stuffing them into the large bin on wheels.

She scrunched up her eyes, peering intently at the young boy. *What the hell is he doing?* Next Bruce pulled a tin from its hiding place. Goose bumps ran up her arms as she read the label— lighter fluid. He poured the contents over the newspaper, placed the tin on the courtyard wall, and took a box of matches from his pocket.

Her stomach lurched as he glanced back at the house. Suddenly she knew exactly why she'd been driven to follow him out here. His thoughts were flashing through her mind in a series of images filled with fire and the stink of burning flesh. Once this bin was alight he was going to wheel it into the utility room, where it would smoulder, fuelled by the laundry. It would send noxious plastic-ridden smoke up the stairs and into sleeping lungs, and it would follow this up with fatal bursts of flames.

She raked at her eyes, digging her fingers painfully into the sockets but the visions of the monster Bruce was growing into wouldn't go away.

No! No way! I can't do it again. But she had to because no one else could stop him. Not permanently.

Bruce struck the match and gazed at it, waiting for the flames to lick his fingers. As he stood there, entranced, she leapt into the courtyard, girding her courage to do battle for the first time in three years. She saw his eyes flicker towards her, but the flame drew him back. She blew out the match, grabbed the matchbox and threw it. With horror she saw it hit the tin of lighter fluid, which slipped from the wall, spraying drops onto her sleeve. Desperate to tear the shirt from her body, she forced herself instead to slide her thoughts into his brainwaves.

The tissue-like barrier that was the outer edge of Bruce's thoughts thinned, then gave way completely as she pushed through it into his mind. Her skin tingled briefly as the torn edges of the protective layer brushed over her, then the barrier sealed up behind her and she was enclosed in another world: a world controlled by Bruce—the inside of his mind. Her vision blurred as her eyes adjusted to this new landscape. It was dark in here— dark and squishy. *Yuck!* Hot black mud was squelching up between her toes. *Why don't my shoes ever come with me into their heads?*

Ahead of her lay a long corridor with dark tunnels branching out on either side. All of it was awash with muck that swirled and boiled, filled with all his pain and pleasure.

She stepped forwards gingerly, almost falling as she sank into mud up to her ankles. Her feet slurped as she ploughed through the mire, peering into every tunnel in search of a glimmer of human kindness. All around her Bruce's thoughts were popping out of the muck with disgusting burps.

Mud splattered onto Alpha's chest as a fat bubble popped, issuing a long, harsh whisper. 'Buuurrrn,' it seemed to say. She felt its heat like an open flame.

Another burst of muck formed a hillock in the distance, before collapsing into waves that rippled towards her. 'Killlll,' they sighed.

Alpha steadied herself as the sickening waves washed past her. Their hot, slimy substance smelled of fresh-dead meat. *I'd hate to live in this dump of a mind.*

The next bubble told her he'd retrieved the matchbox. She hurried on into the darkest corner of his mind where the mud was churning wildly. Her heart fluttered as he lit another match.

Instantly she began pouring words and images into his mind: *'Toss that match and you'll be arrested.'* (Bruce's shoulders twitched as she filled his thoughts with visions of police wrenching his arms behind his back.) *'You'll be put on trial.'* (She created a steel-cold judge sentencing him to life imprisonment.) *'They'll keep you locked up.'* (A cell encircled Bruce's brain. He fingered imaginary bars and backed away from the brutish man she painted as his cellmate.)

With any ordinary boy, these projections would have been enough to turn him, but a thrill of gratification slid through Bruce instead. The match went out—he struggled to light another with burnt fingers.

The mud gushed up around Alpha, dragging her down into it. She fell to one knee, and only managed to pull free with a huge effort. With a sob of regret, she rushed back the way she'd come, moving as quickly as she dared through the rippling swamp. *Got to get out before he sets me alight.*

Halfway towards the exit point she stopped and turned, reluctantly facing the bubbling cesspool she'd run from. *Can't give up now.* She squared her shoulders. *I'll try another way.*

These were Bruce's immediate thoughts and emotions but, to the left and slightly to the rear, if his brain was anything like normal people's, she would find his memory zone. That would give her clues about his reasons. She turned into one of the tunnels leading in that direction and began to plough her way up it. The tunnel twisted unexpectedly, but before she could turn back another mud-filled wave forced her on. She found herself at the edge of Bruce's recollection centre. A misty haze separated her from his earliest memory of his own birth.

Stuff it, I haven't got time for baby years, she thought, knowing that at any moment Bruce would succeed in lighting another match.

But then the memory grabbed her full attention as she saw baby Bruce struggle for air, his umbilical cord caught round his neck, starving his body of oxygen. He was dying before he'd had a chance to live. Suddenly there were bright lights; the cord was unwrapped, and the infant Bruce was gasping for breath.

And now she knew how to stop him. His near-death in infancy had given her that.

She waded back through Bruce's mind towards the darkest part of his brain, wanting to run but knowing that those muddy waves would mean her death if they knocked her down. When she reached the churning muck in his centre of hatred she leaned over and pressed her hands into it. She could feel the mud writhing beneath her fingers like serpents just below the surface twisting together in battle. She fought to get a grip on this essence while currents of the thick, slimy substance battered at her legs bringing her to her knees. The mud rose up to her chin but still, she pressed down. At the same time she sent forth words and images, filling Bruce with the belief that, if he set a fire again or deliberately harmed anyone, his lungs would collapse. Very simply, he would suffocate from the inside out. He would again become the baby he had once been, struggling for air as his umbilical cord choked him to death.

Bruce rasped out a cough, then dropped the box of matches and stumbled back inside.

Alpha felt his head empty of thought now that she had sliced away his pleasure. *Got you!*

Exhausted and dizzy from the mind-changing, she dragged herself towards the exit from his brain, grateful that at least walking wasn't so hard now: the rolling muck had disappeared along with Bruce's evil desires.

She wanted nothing more than to leave his mind (still running on autopilot) to get back into her own body that was patiently waiting for her in the courtyard. As she tore through the tissue barrier at the edge of Bruce's brain her senses prickled in warning: the touch sent a new fear rippling through her. She pulled herself back into Bruce's mind in alarm. *What's that out there?*

CHAPTER TWO

Alpha sent a small probing enquiry out through the barrier of Bruce's mind, too scared of the thing in the courtyard to risk returning to her own body. Information filtered through to her slowly. It wasn't a person; it was a mind that had somehow traced her thoughts. It belonged to someone who could read people's thoughts—someone like her—except that there was no one else around.

One thing she knew for sure: it was waiting to pounce on her as soon as she left Bruce's mind. Terrified, she hovered, butterfly-like, on the edges of Bruce's mind until at last, she felt it go.

———

Back inside her own head, her eyes blurred momentarily, then a wall of dizziness crashed into her, and she clutched at the fence for support, drained by her mind-melding.

Lauren Buttel, her fellow inmate at the Willows care home, peered over the gate leading to the patch of weedy grass they called the garden. 'Hey, it's Poorly Moorly.' She pushed at the gate and spied the open bin. 'What're you doing, you psycho.' Her skinny hips wiggled towards Alpha.

Alpha peered through her hair at Lauren and seethed. *Yeah right, Miss finger-down-your-throat-to-stop-you-getting-fat. And I'm the psycho?* Alpha's bones seemed to be made of melting chocolate—she could barely stand up, let alone deal with Lauren in a bad mood. So instead, she hunched her shoulders, hugged an elbow, and avoided eye contact with Lauren. 'Nothing,' she muttered.

This ploy to make herself look small and defenceless and much younger than her seventeen years had worked before, but it didn't work today. She could sense Lauren's vile thoughts steaming over the boyfriend who'd dumped her. She didn't even need to enter Lauren's mind to gather them—they wove wildly outside Lauren's head, battering at her tired brain.

'Bag lady,' Lauren sneered. 'You smell disgusting.' Her gaze lingered on Alpha's small, lithe body. 'Freak. I'll teach you not to raid the rubbish for leftovers.' She crept up behind Alpha and twisted one of her arms up against her back. Her other hand snaked round Alpha's front and pinched hard at her nipple.

Alpha felt a scream rise in her head, bit it back. 'It was B..Bruce,' she stammered.

Lauren laughed disbelievingly, causing drops of her spit to fly onto Alpha's cheek. Then she twisted Alpha's arm further. Alpha did scream then, and her legs gave way. As she collapsed across the huge wheelie bin she caught sight of Sophie Mitchell from the corner of her eye. For the first time in her life she was glad to see the night carer at the children's home.

Sophie trudged towards them on flat pigeon-toed feet. 'What's going on?'

Alpha sagged with relief, and only the bin prevented her from dropping to the ground.

Unseen by Sophie Mitchell, Lauren's talons sunk into Alpha's behind. Alpha yelped. Only then did Lauren release Alpha. 'Look! She's been raiding the bins. I reckon she's hidden a horde of Skunk in there.'

The carer caught Alpha's eye with a sharp look. 'Are there drugs in that bin?'

'No, I d…don't take drugs,' was all Alpha could manage.

'Hmmm,' said Sophie, her nose twitching. She bent over the bin and sniffed. Then her head whipped back, and she glared at Alpha. 'I smell accelerant!'

A shudder ran through Alpha's body. *She's never going to believe what really happened.*

Sophie's gaze swung towards Lauren, who was now smelling the inside of the bin herself. 'Get out of here, I want to talk to Alpha. Now girl, now!' As Lauren left Sophie stared at Alpha. 'What's the matter? You look as though a breeze could blow you over.' Sighing, she suddenly took pity on Alpha. 'I suppose tomorrow will be time enough to find out what's been going on.' She herded Alpha inside. 'Go to your room, lie down.'

'Thank you, Sophie,' said Alpha, grateful for the stay in interrogation. Maybe tomorrow she'd feel strong enough to fight off Lauren's accusations without revealing her own part in Bruce's change of heart.

She dragged herself up the stairs to the miniature cubicle that served as her bedroom and shoved a folded piece of paper under the door, jamming it as tight as she could, before undressing. The generosity of social services in giving each child a separate space didn't extend to providing locks for the doors.

On her behind two purplish bruises were blossoming over a ring of sharp punctures. Lauren kept her nails long. Not bothering with pyjamas Alpha dropped face-first onto her bed and punched her pillow. *Oh Mum, I'm sorry. I swore I'd never do it again.*

Weakness washed through her as images of her mother filled the space in her head like an old movie. She tried throwing them out, but the one mind she couldn't change was her own.

There was Mum, smiling as she watched Alpha blow out the candles on her birthday cake—five candles. That was when Alpha had first known that she was inside another person's head. Her mother was sending rays of love across the room to her father, the person she regarded as her soul mate. The rays were pretty, each a different shade of purple. They looked like searchlights shooting out from her mother towards her father.

After that Alpha investigated the inside of all kinds of heads. She found the design of a new house in her teacher's mind, ticking round so fast it resembled a spinning top, and she was delighted by the man who cleaned the windows, all the while playing out the lead role in Hamlet on an imaginary stage.

Their family pet, a Labrador called Jake, was the first recipient of her mind changes. Staying within his doggy world of smells she persuaded him to leave his dinner and come to her by making him believe she was holding an invisible piece of steak. But whenever her dad returned from one of his flying trips, Jake was single-minded in greeting him with jumps of joy, refusing to turn for even the make-believe smell of raw meat.

Alpha also came across darker minds, like their neighbour's head that was awash with a simmering stew of anger. His thoughts tallied up with the constant battles Alpha could hear through the walls of their semi-detached house. She knew that his fury would soon boil out of his brain into some violent action against his wife.

But things in the Moore family were good, until the day she touched her father's thoughts and found not her mother, but the image of another woman lodged in his mind—one with skin the colour of the small black keys on Mum's piano.

Her mother seemed to shrink into herself from that point, talking less and less, and then one morning Alpha woke up, remembering a strange, sad dream of Dad saying goodbye, over and over. Later that day a policeman came and told Mum that Dad had suffered a fatal heart attack while he was piloting a plane to South Africa.

After that, her visits inside her mother's head showed that Mum had forgotten her love of music. There was only grey emptiness as she drank vodka from a crystal glass. Months later Mum drank directly from the bottle until she passed out again and again. There was the vivid memory of Mum saying they must move into a crummy little flat, not enough money to live on, but plenty of money to buy those bottles of pale poison. Mum's skin turned yellow as the alcohol ate into her liver. And still, she drank.

Then came that fateful moment when Alpha decided to change her mother's mind—to stop her drinking forever.

She gave a small cry as her thoughts touched on that terrible time that had ended so horribly she hadn't dared change anyone's mind again—until this evening. She could hold back no longer. She sobbed and sobbed, drenching her pillow with snot and tears, racked with grief and filled with guilt until, drained and exhausted, she fell asleep.

———

She awoke abruptly. Someone was in the room.

But the door was shut, and she could see the wedge of paper still in its place, a mousy shadow against the light from the passage. No sound of breathing, no sense of movement, no change in the air.

This was a mind, not a body. Her thoughts rippled through the room, striving to avoid the presence. Suddenly she recoiled, shrinking back into her bed. There was more than one mind in her bedroom—the space around her was filled with hunters moving in for the kill.

CHAPTER
THREE

Sunday peeled the lid off the glue that he'd nicked from Alex's room and breathed in the fumes. The smell made his thoughts drift off. Soon, as he relaxed, he could pick up Alpha's disturbed thoughts.

He fingered a nostril delicately, then smiled. Disturbed or not, he was pleased to have found her. He reveled in the pleasure for a moment. Then, interrupting these feelings, his spindly legs, dangling over the edge of the four-poster bed, caught his attention and he stared at his swinging feet. He wished his legs would grow so he could become a proper South African Zulu warrior. It shouldn't be too long now; he was nine already and boys of his tribe became men at fourteen. *I wonder if I can persuade Dr Scott to hold a rite of passage ceremony for me?*

No! Dr Scott will say it's too much dangerous, Sunday decided after giving the matter some consideration. He sighed, then shrugged. On the whole, things were too much better in this place than back in South Africa. And here he felt much closer to the girl…

That reminded him of her, and he reached for her thoughts once again. He was glad she was still in his head—she'd been popping in and out of it for years now. Mostly it was just the trace of an image: like that time she'd fallen down some stairs and broken her wrist (and he had ached for months afterwards) or that fleeting taste in his mouth when she'd bitten into an olive and almost thrown up. Sometimes he took an olive from the buffet just to remember that moment, though he hated their bitter flavour. He wished he could track her for long enough to find her. The girl reminded him of his mother before…

'Aaaieee! I am not going back,' he cried, as memories of his past rushed into his thoughts, shifting the girl out of them. He felt her go. 'No! Stay with me.'

The loss of contact was painful, as though a knife had severed an artery that extended out beyond his brain to hers. His brows furrowed, eyebrows coming together as he concentrated on drawing her back. It required enormous willpower because his brain was happiest when it was scampering in several directions at once.

It was no good, he'd lost her. For a few minutes he sat breathing deeply, as he'd been taught, then he buried his nose in the glue pot once more.

There! He found a vision of her… and started violently as he realised that she was screaming because another girl was twisting her arm.

He needed Mrs. Hickelroy *now!* He jumped out of bed and hurtled from his bedroom, charging down the main staircase and on towards the door leading to the courtyard.

It was locked.

'Tokoloshe!' he exclaimed, voicing a swear word that named the small demon found under the beds of unwary travellers in Africa.

Suddenly the doors flew open and Mrs. Hickelroy appeared towering over him, her long blonde hair trailing over silk pyjamas. 'Good gracious Sunday, whatever's the matter?' Her eyes softened as she peered into his anxious black face.

Sunday opened his mouth, showing the gap where his two front teeth had not yet grown. 'That girl Dr Scott's been looking for?' he spluttered. 'She's inside my head. She's too much in trouble.'

Mrs Hickelroy turned on her heel and began to run across the courtyard, struggling to tie her dressing gown as the wind caught it, and tried to whip it off her. 'Come on, the principal needs to know at once.'

Sunday sped after her, almost tripping. His mind was too busy with fragmenting images of the girl to control his own feet: she'd pushed herself off an enormous dustbin, head reeling, body in pain and mind in pieces.

Mrs Hickelroy thrust open the door to Dr Scott's private quarters without bothering to knock.

The principal, Dr Michael Scott, was sitting behind his desk, almost glued to the machine that was whirling dizzily in his hands. His eyes jumped to her face. 'Vicky, have you found another one? The Phortometer's going crazy.'

'Not me. Sunday. Come in Sunday.' Mrs Hickelroy drew him into the room.

Hesitantly Sunday eased past the door. His gaze travelled round the room before alighting on a cabinet holding a rather claustrophobic antique diver's helmet, a world globe spattered with stains and a set of books so ancient they might crumble to bits if anyone tried to read them. Despite his concern for the girl, his eyes took them in with interest. Then he remembered that he wasn't fending for himself in South Africa anymore; and if he stole these things he didn't know anyone he could sell them to here in the United Kingdom.

'It's that girl,' stated Mrs Hickelroy.

'I knew it,' the principal said, grabbing Sunday up in his arms as the boy's legs wobbled under him.

'Aaargh!' cried Sunday, as Dr Scott lowered him into an armchair. Sunday shut his eyes and touched his forehead, wishing he hadn't sniffed quite so much glue. The girl's thoughts kept shifting around in his head. She was kneeling next to a closed door. He couldn't work out what she was doing though he sensed her feelings: she was trying to shut everyone out.

'We'd better be quick,' said the vice-principal.

'Details Sunday. What can you tell us about where she is?'

Sunday's glance slid desperately from Dr Scott to Mrs Hickelroy. He'd been counting on her to find the girl. Huge dustbins, bare rooms, splintered images—nothing pointed to where she was.

'Language?' asked Mrs Hickelroy.

'English,' Sunday said, his spirits rising fractionally because he could answer this question.

'Maps, they'll be fastest,' snapped Dr Scott, lifting an armful, but before he could cross the room to deliver the pile to Sunday the glass in the display cabinet smashed and the antique globe came crashing off the shelf. It spun wildly and flew towards Sunday, coming to rest in mid-air just as Sunday extended his index finger to stab at it.

Dr Scott reacted instantly, jumping across the room just in time to detect where Sunday's finger had landed before the globe dropped to the ground and shattered into pieces. 'Fantastic! She's somewhere in England!'

Sunday shook his head violently. 'I'm losing her.'

Mrs Hickelroy grabbed his chest from behind and rested her other hand on his brow. 'Here, I'll underpin you. Is that stronger?'

'No…yes. I can see her. She's in bed.'

Dr Scott slung the maps across the floor then lifted a map of England onto Sunday's lap. Without looking at it Sunday's fingers brushed over it and came to rest on the Midlands.

Flinging that map over his shoulder Dr Scott rustled an ordnance survey map in front of Sunday. Instantly Sunday isolated the area to a patch a few miles wide but, as he tried to find the exact location of the girl on a street map, she snapped out of his head. He looked up at the two adults woefully. 'She's gone.'

'It's OK Sunday, you've done well. Now tell me everything you saw or felt,' Dr Scott urged him. 'Every little detail, no matter how small.'

Sunday tapped on his eyelids, trying hard to recall his visions. He explained how he'd felt the girl watching Bruce, how he'd lost her then found her again... how she was in pain. He described the girl who was hurting her and Alpha's feelings as she fell across the very large rubbish bin sitting on wheels. He was able to add only sketchy details about the grown-up who had barely registered on him. With each sentence he felt worse, certain that he wasn't helping at all until finally, he remembered a name. 'The girl said, "Thank you, Sophie," to the woman just before she went upstairs.'

'What sort of relationship does Sophie have to the girls?' Dr Scott asked, speaking without haste, though his fingers were running furiously through his grey-streaked hair.

'She's ... a kind of boss lady.'

'A relation? A mother, or an aunt?' the principal probed.

Sunday shook his head. 'No, they're not family.' At least he could be sure about that.

'She's in care or at a boarding school,' said Mrs Hickelroy, smoothing down her dressing gown as Dr Scott looked up at her. 'Extra-large wheelie bins, to dispose of the rubbish—it's some sort of communal group.'

'That makes sense. Great work Sunday. I'll get hold of John at once, see whether he can trace a "Sophie" running an establishment like that.' Dr Scott straightened up, reaching for the phone.

Mrs Hickelroy pulled Sunday to his feet. 'It's bedtime for you, Sunday.'

As his head lurched once more, Sunday meekly followed Mrs Hickelroy from the room across the courtyard, up the stairs, and into his bedroom.

———

A brief time later Sunday hid behind the door of a disused linen closet, watching through the air holes as Dr Scott strode down the corridor. The principal stopped abruptly and popped his hand into his pocket, withdrawing his mobile.

'Hello, John,' said Dr Scott, before his phone had completed its first chirp. 'That's great! You've got two addresses for me. I knew your team would find it a simple enough task.'

Sunday could just pick up the sound of John's voice complaining down the line. *How did you know it was me… oh! I wish you wouldn't do that, it's spooky. And no, I didn't use the squad to get the addresses, I got them myself. We can't afford too many questions about you guys.*

After a brief conversation Dr Scott said, '…so a helicopter will be here shortly. Thanks, that'll speed things up. Don't forget the paperwork. Bye.'

As Sunday watched Dr Scott tap the addresses furiously into his phone he heard Mrs Hickelroy's heels click up the corridor. She had changed into a business suit and wound her hair into a tidy French pleat, but she still looked amazing.

'Anything?' she asked the principal.

'Yes.' Dr Scott waved the phone at her. 'There aren't any boarding schools, but I've got the addresses of two care homes housing teenagers in that area. I'll try them both.'

'Can't I go instead?' Mrs Hickelroy asked.

'Sorry Vicky, I've waited a long time for this girl. The last time the Phortometer registered activity like that was three years ago. She's so powerful the needle swung right into the unknown zone. I'm not taking any chances on losing her now.'

Sunday slid out of the cupboard and sidled up behind the principal, just as Mrs Hickelroy opened her mouth to argue. Her eyes swung away from Dr Scott's face. 'Sunday, where did you spring from? You should be in bed!'

'She's in my head again.' Sunday told them. 'She's dreaming, horrible dreams.'

Without a word Dr Scott handed Sunday the phone.

Sunday stood with his legs apart, balancing himself, holding Dr Scott's mobile in his hand. Then he shut his eyes and let his mind reach out.

Mrs Hickelroy stood behind him, draping her arm over Sunday's shoulders. 'He's got her,' she mouthed to Dr Scott. 'Take my hand.'

Sunday barely heard her speak as dark shapes formed below him: a tiny room, a bed, a sleeping girl, strands of black hair wound across her face. He'd watched for only a second when the girl awoke and sat up, startled. Her eyes swivelled fearfully around the room, then a powerful blast kicked Sunday away and he found himself back in the corridor.

The phone gave a tinkle of sound and vibrated wildly. Light streamed from the phone and the words *The Willows* flashed up in blue on the flocked wallpaper before bleeding away until they were unreadable. Sunday's jaw dropped as though gravity had taken an extra bite at it.

Dr Scott grabbed the phone from Sunday. 'She's deleted the rest of that address,' he said, breathing heavily. 'I remember it, The Willows, Wicklemast Avenue. She's got so much power it's astonishing... and she's desperate to hide from us. OK, you win, Vicky. I'll board the chopper, but you and Sunday should catch the next ferry to the mainland. Then take a train to Waterloo Station; I might need your help yet.

CHAPTER
FOUR

Alpha totted up her funds, which amounted to all of one pound eighty-six pence. *Like that's going to get me far!* She packed her schoolbag with the few belongings she owned, shoving them in quickly. She cared about none of them except the wedding picture of her mum and dad and her mother's jade brooch. The brooch was more of a pin with a carved head than a brooch, but it was the only valuable thing left at the end of Mum's life. The reason no one at the Willows had stolen it was that it was tiny, and she kept it pinned to the underside of her jacket collar. In the three years she'd been here even Lauren hadn't spotted it. *Time to go.*

The doorbell rang. Her heart sank—*they've found me.*

———

On the train Sunday placed his half-eaten ham baguette on the empty seat next to him, fully intending to return to it shortly.

'Not hungry Sunday? ' said Mrs Hickelroy.

Sunday stared regretfully at the baguette. 'Dr Scott's reached the Willows.'

'So soon? Goodness, he must have driven like a madman from the helipad.' Mrs Hickelroy fumbled for her phone. As it began relaying pictures of the Willows she held it up for Sunday to watch.

Dr Scott's hand appeared on the screen, pressing the doorbell repeatedly. When a woman answered the door in her nightclothes Sunday stared hard at her, nodding to himself. *I think that's the woman Alpha was talking to.* After a short conversation, the woman wagged her head fiercely at the doctor. 'It's four o'clock in the morning. I can't wake the children now.' The aggressive thrust of her chin confirmed it for Sunday. *Yes,* he decided. *That's Sophie.*

Dr Scott's voice rang down the line. 'I'm sorry, you'll have to. This is an order signed by a high court judge. It permits me to take one of them with me immediately.'

'Which one do you want?'

'I don't know. I need to speak to each of them.'

'That's stupid. Haven't you got a photo or something? Anyway, I don't believe my girls have done anything bad. They're closely watched you know.'

'Who's that guy, Sophie?' a teenager called out. Dr Scott zoomed the phone in on her face and Sunday recognised her. *Aaaiee! This was the monster who had hurt his girl.* Fury fired his blood, and his small fist punched the air.

'Sssshhh Lauren!' said Sophie.

Too late. Doors popped open everywhere. Soon the hallway was filled with teenagers jostling each other. Sunday studied the images on the phone. It was hard to make sense of them; these pictures gave off none of the feelings he was used to getting from groups of people. It was a bit like watching a video without any sound; half the quality was lost.

'Who's the pig?' one girl asked, her mouth taking on a surly look.

A rat-faced pre-teen declared, 'I ain't done nuffin! Get lost.'

The pictures on Mrs Hickelroy's phone disappeared abruptly and were replaced by the text message Dr Scott was sending. WHICH 1 IS SHE?

Mrs Hickelroy turned to Sunday, questioningly.

'None of them,' he told Mrs Hickelroy.

Her fingers texted back at speed. Seconds later pictures returned to her phone.

'She's not in the hall, Miss Mitchell,' Sunday heard Dr Scott say. 'Who else is staying here?'

Sophie shrugged. 'There's Bruce, but he's only a child and Jeremy Unwin, but he's here during the days only, he doesn't live in. Yvonne's on holiday and the temp resigned yesterday so I'm on my own, though what the council will say about that I don't know… '

'What about Alpha?' Lauren called out. 'She's rotten. You know she tried to set fire to the bin.'

Sophie turned on Lauren, her face registering annoyance. Dr Scott interrupted her reprimand. 'This girl, Alpha. Fetch her now please.'

'Alpha?' Sophie queried. She looked vaguely round at the girls. 'She must be too worn out to sleep through all this racket. Lauren, wake her up, will you?'

'She's not in her room, Sophie.'

Sophie went rigid with shock. 'What!'

'Alpha—is she a teenager with long darkish hair?' Dr Scott barked.

Several faces nodded.

'When did she leave?' he demanded.

'Must have been after ten-thirty. I watched the TV 'till then,' said Sophie, wringing her hands. 'You're sure she's not there, girl!' she demanded of Lauren, twisting to peer into the other rooms leading off the hall, in case Alpha was there and failing to find her. 'I've never lost one before. Alpha's such a silent little thing. Heavens, I hope she's all right. I'll contact the police at once.'

'No! I'll find her,' Dr Scott insisted. 'I'm working with the police—she's my responsibility now. Does anyone know where she's gone? It's crucial.'

But Sunday knew that no one would know anything about Alpha. That was exactly how she liked it.

———

Alpha forced down the twist of fear that was threatening to choke her, and hastily revised her plans to sneak out through the kitchen. She eased open the bathroom door and tossed her bag out of the window, then squeezed herself out through it and clambered down the drainpipe, helped by the ivy growing up it. She heard voices from the front of the house, so she slid past the bins, keeping low until she'd reached a neighbour's garage, terrified that her pounding heart would give her away.

She pressed through a hedge, barely feeling the thorns of the Pyracanthas. Any second now and they'd catch her. Her chest thumped as fear lent wings to her feet, and she flew across a large garden onto an adjoining road.

A car passed by, splashing up water, which made her jump. *It's not them.* She concentrated on walking steadily, resisting the temptation to keep running, which would make her too much of a target. *Don't think. They can find me through my fear.* If only she could reach the station before they discovered her, she would catch the next train to anywhere and take herself right out of their orbit.

The roads were wet and glistening from an earlier rainstorm. They threw up images of distorted trees, which made her long for the sparse comforts of the Willows. It hadn't been much of a home but compared to the ghostly street it seemed very welcoming indeed. Fear of the hunters mingled with worries about her future, almost overwhelmed her. Giving a shiver, she pressed on, trying hard to dampen her emotions.

The next car slowed, then screeched to a halt. Alpha swivelled, almost breaking into a run, but then a slurring voice addressed her. 'Do you want to hitch… a lift… somewhere?'

It wasn't them. For a second she was tempted, but then her common sense kicked in. *Not with you!* She could smell the alcohol on the driver's breath from where she stood on the pavement.

'No thanks. My dad will be here in a couple of minutes,' she lied.

'Well… have a 'mashing night… a… hick… smashing sight.' The driver gave a weak wave and pulled away with a shudder.

Relief flooded through her as she realised she didn't have to argue her way out of that encounter, and with relief came the desire to burst into tears. *Don't weaken now, just keep walking.*

————

Ever since he'd learned that Alpha wasn't at The Willows, Sunday had kept both hands on the map on his knee. His baguette fell unnoticed to the floor as he forced himself to concentrate. It was hard work; he closed his eyes and tried not to let stray thoughts enter his mind. He was beginning to think he'd lost her for good when the small finger on his left hand pulsed. He jostled Mrs Hickelroy with his elbow.

'Where?'

He pointed out the spot to her.

Instantly Mrs Hickelroy had Dr Scott on the line. 'She's going west on Waterman Street. That's W… A…T…E…'

'That's the station road,' said Dr Scott. Sunday could hear his voice cracking with worry.

The train was in the station, doors beginning to close when Dr Scott arrived, having driven like a mad man to get there. He abandoned the car, flying up the stairs to the overhead bridge. From there, heedless of the danger, he launched himself over the edge towards the moving carriages.

———

Alpha squashed into a corner in the deserted carriage. 'Go train go!' she whispered as the train began to move out of the next station.

Thump!

What was that? She sent her mind out searching for the source of the noise… *oh no! It's him—the hunter—he's on the roof.*

She sprang out of her chair and ran through carriage after carriage, bathed in a frantic sweat. *He's in the train, he's searching through it.* But there wasn't another soul on the train to help her. *The driver,* she thought desperately, pushing at the seats to speed her flight towards the front of the train. But before she could reach the engine the train slowed to a stop and the doors opened. She swivelled, poised to jump out, but the hunter barged into the carriage and blocked her path to the doors which had drawn open.

'Hello Alpha,' he said. 'I'm Dr Michael Scott. I'm not going to hurt you.'

'Get away from me,' she screamed, backing away, dread dragging at her limbs and turning her legs to lumps of lead.

He took one step towards her, held out his hands imploringly.

She swung sideways, feigning a dodge past him, but suddenly she pulled back and pressed all her energy inside his head.

Get out, she shrieked in the region of his brain that controlled his survival instincts.

His feet stopped working under instruction from his own mind as it filled with the need to flee. He took a few backwards steps, tripped out onto the platform, and fell to the ground. The doors clanged closed once more.

As the train got underway Alpha withdrew from his mind. Without moving a muscle she watched him disappear into the distance. Then she gave a sob, collapsed into the nearest seat and pulled her legs up tightly against her stomach. She felt as though her guts had tied themselves in knots and formed a burning ball inside her middle.

He's gone; I got rid of him.

So why am I still so afraid?

———

London… the train stopped, and everyone got off. *This was it—the end of the line.* Alpha clutched her bag and stepped off the train.

Ticket turnstile… she slithered her body under it then trudged up the ramp. The station was brightly lit, full of little shops and early commuters bustling here and there, carefully avoiding speaking to anyone. She looked round, licking her dry lips and wondering what to do next. *I don't know anyone here. I don't even have enough money for a meal.*

Toilets… She felt pressure build in her bladder, so she walked towards the sign.

Her glance slid over the man standing in the middle of the station. A motorbike helmet hid his face, and he was dragging an enormous, wheeled suitcase. While strange, this man was not nearly as weird as the young groupies of the band X-tra Lean, who wore matching blonde wigs with pig ears sticking through them. They caught her attention, so she watched them for a moment before moving on, rubbing her eyes and wishing she had a place to put her head down safely for a few hours. She was too tired to sense that the tall man wearing the helmet had sidled up the passage behind her. Just before he reached her he opened the suitcase.

The light around Alpha dimmed as a shadow crept over her.

Run! As she stumbled forwards, something caught her round the neck, pressing hard into her windpipe. Pulled from her feet, she tugged at the obstruction, struggling to breath and desperate for air. Suddenly she was pushed face down towards the ground and a dark shape snapped shut around her.

Darkness… a silky material closing in on her. She screamed, but the fabric filled her mouth and slid into her bruised throat, smothering her. Her heartbeat frantically, her lungs cried out for air. She clawed at the fabric but that only made things worse as the material wound itself around her fingers rendering them useless.

Eventually she regained enough control to hold still. She forced the cloth from her mouth with her tongue, made herself breath evenly, and then tested the space with tiny movements. She could shift only an inch or two in any direction, but this was enough to allow her to cup her hands in front of her face and clear a little pocket of air.

Where am I? She tried to fill in the blanks, but mad thoughts filled her mind. *What's happened? Has a bomb gone off? Have I been buried alive?*

Immediately the space seemed to close in even further. She began to pant.

Stop it! Concentrate on physical things—work out what's going on.

She was lying on her side unable to stretch out her legs or her arms. Her stomach lurched as she realised that she was being propelled forwards. A burst of sound banged against the casing and the vibrations filled her head with pain. *I'm in some sort of container. I've been shut in—they're carrying me away.*

'Help!' she screamed, but the fabric absorbed the sound. Panic rose once more, and it threatened to send her into insanity. She tried to box her way out but only ended up stubbing her fists.

Finally she clenched her teeth and tethered her panic, though it fought like a wild beast.

Use your mind, you can stop him...

... but beyond the container she could find no trace of her attacker's thoughts.

Help! she cried mentally, trying to reach anyone in the station, pushing the message out as far as it would go. *Help! I'm being kidnapped.* She broadcast the same words over and over, terrified that no one would hear her.

CHAPTER
FIVE

Sunday felt anxiety gnaw at his guts. He bit on a knuckle, oblivious to his teeth marks. Confinement was flashing through his mind, making him feel trapped, although there was nothing but a large open station around him. He could vaguely feel Alpha's presence, but it was muffled, just as though a barrier had been placed between them.

Suddenly people in the station seemed to go mad. A lumpish young woman, soon to be a mother, began a headless chicken run from one side of the station to the other. 'Help her,' she implored to everyone and no-one, neck bobbing backwards and forwards, arms flapping wildly.

Several people were staring about in a bewildered way while others began confused dialogues with fellow commuters about a kidnapper. A flashfire of hysteria leapt through the station as panic and misinformation (the abductor had somehow turned into an armed villain) were passed from person to person. People began clogging up the exits.

'Lots of scared people here,' Sunday told Mrs Hickelroy.

'Sunday, concentrate on Alpha, will you.'

Sunday's head swayed like a roused python. 'Over there,' he said, darting away.

'Where? Sunday, come back!'

Sunday ignored her cry and ran up the platform. Mrs

Hickelroy chased after him, puffing. For all his small stature, Sunday could run like the street thief he'd been not that long ago.

'Wait! Dr Scott will be here any minute. We've got to let him know,' cried Mrs Hickelroy.

Ahead of him Sunday saw a man wearing a motorcycle helmet making a rush through the crowd using the suitcase as a battering ram. As the man broke through Sunday shouted, 'Stop him. Stop that man with the too big case.'

'Sunday, come back,' Mrs Hickelroy demanded. 'This looks dangerous.'

Taking no notice, Sunday twisted through the crowd. He barged into the man with the helmet and punched him with all his puny strength, which seeing as he was so small, did not affect the larger man. But a burly station worker caught on quickly. He aimed a powerful punch at the man's body.

The man ducked, let go of the suitcase, then landed a cracking blow to his attacker's temple before running off, leaving the suitcase behind. Several people chased after him, while others stayed to help the collapsed hero.

Sunday swivelled towards the suitcase and flipped open the latches.

Alpha lay inside, her body twisted, her face frozen with terror.

He stared into her fear-filled eyes and reached for her thoughts.

You called for help. I found you.

'Get out of my head!' she screamed at him.

A hurt look crept into Sunday's eyes, but he backed off obediently, raising his hands in protest at her words. 'You've been inside my head long enough. Why won't you talk to me?'

CHAPTER SIX

His dark face pulsed in front of Alpha's eyes. She stared at him in horror. *He's one of the hunters in my bedroom.* Adrenaline rushed through her and she pushed herself out of the case. A hand gripped her wrist and an arm pinned her across her chest—a woman, owner of the third mind who'd been in her room at the Willows. Alpha bit hard into the fleshy part of the arm and kicked backwards, freeing herself from the woman's hold, but as she set off at speed the final hunter, the large man she'd pushed from the train clasped her shoulders, stopping her in mid-stride.

'Trust me,' the man who called himself Dr Scott begged. 'Look inside my thoughts, see for yourself, I'm not going to hurt you.'

Alpha shook her head wildly. She was picking up his emotions—he was spilling concern for her like warm water overflowing a bath. *Damn you, let me go!*

She twisted from his grasp but before she could take a step away the man's thoughts swamped her, and she found herself inside his head.

——

She sprang round desperately trying to get back into her own mind, but the exit from his brain had disappeared. All she could see were rows of memory banks, neatly labelled, which went on and on, trapping her in Dr Scott's recollection centre. The rows were like a discount shop filled with televisions piled six-deep, each flickering with the events in his life. She ran down the row, seeking a gap, found one, but this only led to another row, then another. She twisted, this way and that, skittering between the flickering walls, but the screens continued on either side of her as far as her eye could see.

She slowed, breathed, and a small portion of her fear subsided; the mind was her territory—no way he's going to trap me in here. She knelt down until she was facing one screen at floor level. The hard surface of glass melted as she pushed through it and clambered inside the box…

Now she was surrounded by a memory of Dr Scott's in which he had been lecturing statistics to a bunch of university students. Surprisingly only a few of them looked bored out of their skulls… *A math teacher huh! No wonder he's such a neat freak. Well, that doesn't mean he isn't also a mass murderer, or something just as bad.*

She crawled on leaving that memory behind, only to find herself between another two rows of memory banks. Crawling straight ahead she blasted into another memory… here Dr Scott was opening a door with his name on it, followed by the words PARANORMAL STUDIES, whatever they were? Lodged within this memory she felt his years of frustration because only a few people believed that the paranormal even existed.

As she climbed out of this memory she found herself in another dimension, an electric space that was all flashing colours—his emotional centre. This was deadly dangerous—she could easily get sucked up into his feelings. If that happened she might never be able to get out of here. Moving fast but cautiously through the emotional discothèque, she found that one feeling stood out beyond the others: it was flashing a brilliant green and it spoke to her saying, *'come with me… I want to help you… for your sake, choose to come with me…'*

What does he mean for my sake? And why does he want me to choose? While I'm in here he can do what he wants with my body.

She steered clear of the green flashes and had almost reached the calm at the back of the brain when the flickering images in another memory snaked out of their box and wound themselves around her ankle. She tripped, and his feelings came at her in a tidal wave of colour but, just as she thought they would smother her, the memory pulled her into its heart.

Then it unveiled itself around her giving her an enormous shock… She was staring directly at the face of Britain's Prime Minister. *What's he doing in Dr Scott's memories?*

'Good to meet you, Dr Scott,' the Prime Minister said, oblivious of her silent observation. It was like watching a film while standing inside the set. 'This is John.' He waved casually at another man standing next to him before extending his hand to shake Dr Scott's. 'I'll come straight to the point. We want you to head up Britain's new task force on paranormal activity. Your mandate is to develop psychic ability to enhance the security of Britain.'

'P…pardon?' Dr Scott said, rendered almost speechless by the Prime Minister's words.

John patted Dr Scott on the back. 'Look Michael, we need an edge. Terrorists have targeted our transport systems, our entertainment venues, our people, our tourists, our policemen, our social media, and even our cyber systems for too long. The next attack could be just around the corner. And not only that—we're spending so much on protecting Britain it's crippling our economy. As a nation, we've no idea what we're going to face next. You cut off one limb, and two grow back in their place.'

The Prime Minister interrupted then, clearly impatient to get the results he needed. 'We're looking for predictions from you; precognition I think you'd call it. Or indeed anything that will help us fight the next threat, whatever it is.'

To Alpha it seemed that the Prime Minister was desperate, but Dr Scott's shoulders lifted in subtle refusal. 'I'm sorry. I don't think I can help you. I lost most of my ability years ago, and anyway, precognition was never my forte.'

'We know,' John said, wearing a smile that suggested there was very little he didn't know. 'But that doesn't mean you can't train others. You won't be the first. Back in the 1960s, the KGB in Russia used psychics quite successfully. Nowadays the FBI employs them to solve murder cases, the CIA has a unit of psychic searchers to find important missing people and we understand that the Chinese have several task forces dedicated to precognitive dreamers.'

'B-but it couldn't be a task force,' Dr Scott stuttered. 'The best psychics are young, usually teenagers. If paranormal ability isn't actively worked in the teens, it fizzles away on maturity—like mine did, years ago.'

'Then, Dr Scott,' the Prime Minister ordered, 'open a school.'

… The memory flickered and died, leaving Alpha in turmoil. She shook her head to clear it, the implications of what she'd just witnessed were incredible. *How many more are there like me?*

But Dr Scott gave her no time to think. He whisked her through his brain in a mad roller coaster ride and she was transported into another set of memories… here the woman she'd bitten, a Mrs Hickelroy, joined Dr Scott, and together they sought out young psychics, persuading their parents to let them attend a very special school.

One parental pair were concerned about their child's bizarre behaviour. They were pleased to find experts to help…

… next Alpha saw one man push his son towards Dr Scott as though shoving away a pile of stinking rubbish. 'Take him,' the man told the doctor. 'He bears the evil mark.' The boy cringed, turning from his father, and Alpha noted the strawberry birthmark on his forehead…

… onwards through the memories and Alpha saw that another boy's mother was persuaded by the quality of the school, which provided the best education money could buy, especially when she learned she wouldn't have to pay a penny…

Then Dr Scott flipped her back into his emotional centre and placed her right inside a custard-coloured emotion. As she breathed in, two distinct tastes filled her mouth, vanilla and bitter lemon, and she could experience this emotion herself: like a clucking swan protecting her cygnets from a storm she felt his dreadful concern that these precious young people would be misused. She could taste his worry over them, and her shoulders bowed under his burden of love and the sense of responsibility he felt for every one of his students.

She ploughed out of that emotion—it felt like a great weight had been lifted from her. To her relief the roller coaster finally slowed, and the bursts of emotional colour parted in front of Alpha, showing her a clear path back to her own body.

Oh no! I'm not leaving yet. Instead she floated towards an earlier set of memories and found some that were very small. Their flicker was so faint it was almost non-existent. She tried to enter one of those screens, but it remained solid, blocking her. She dug in deeper… forcing with her mind.

Dr Scott allowed the memory to soften. She pushed her way in though it still resisted her—it was like entering a world of molten glass.

Inside it she found that he'd had a twin called Helen. As children they talked without words directly into each other's brain… Alpha followed their relationship into other telepathic memories that carried them through their teenage years…

Suddenly she felt like an intruder… In Dr Scott's last memory of Helen his sister was falling. He gasped as he saw the badly anchored piton spinning loose above her, forced to watch as his twin crashed into a rock face...

Alpha's breath caught in her throat when Dr Scott's pain flooded through the memory. She dived away as the emotional turmoil burst upon her, but she couldn't avoid the blast entirely and it catapulted her into another row of memories.

… This one was of a more recent time; he'd been comforting a sobbing girl whose long ginger hair was tied in bunches. He held her hand, passed her a handkerchief. She sniffed, blew her nose, then wrinkled her freckled nose. 'You're not bizarre—be proud of what you are. Your psychic talent makes you special,' Dr Scott told the girl…

Proud? Of being weird? The idea startled Alpha, and she jerked out of the doctor's head.

———

She stood in front of Dr Scott; her thoughts confused yet filled with the beginnings of wonder—he was different from other people. He understood, he'd also been weird once, although he'd said that he'd grown out of it. But more importantly he believed that these strange abilities were something to revere.

Unused to trusting anyone, she stood indecisively, until the small black boy who'd released her from the case came up to her and rubbed her arm.

'Who are you?' she whispered.

'I'm Sunday, the somebody who saved you.'

She almost pulled away from his calloused little hand, but it seemed oddly warm and welcoming.

'Well, Alpha? Will you come with us?' Dr Scott asked.

He was offering her a new future. *No more running; no more hiding from everyone around her. And most of all, no more shrinking away from what she was. Yes. Oh, yes.* Slowly, with blossoming hope, she nodded.

CHAPTER SEVEN

In spite of trying not to, Alpha fell asleep on the train to Portsmouth. She awoke to find Sunday leaning against her shoulder, gently snoring. Her first instinct was to push him off, but it seemed a pity to wake him, his body looked so young and small. She peered sideways at him. His head was a mass of tight curls, he was very thin, and it seemed likely that his bones would snap with the slightest push. *He doesn't look like much of a threat anymore.*

She shut her eyes again, marvelling at the way Dr Scott and Mrs Hickelroy had stemmed the chaos at the station with a few simple words. Their air of calm had caused the onlookers to melt away.

Dr Scott and Mrs Hickelroy began talking together quietly. Alpha pricked up her ears, but kept her eyes closed.

Dr Scott wasn't calm now; he was filled with concern; to Alpha it felt like boulders were tied to his shoulders. 'I'm very worried, Vicky. Alpha's abductor must have known about her abilities. I wish he hadn't escaped—I think he's got inside information about our school.'

Alpha's eyes almost flew open at his words.

Mrs Hickelroy's voice was puzzled. 'Why would you think that?'

'It's too opportunistic... John warned me to be on the lookout. There's this group he's got wind of... the FBFBA.'

'The who?'

'The FBFBA. John doesn't know much about them yet, only that they have terrorist links, and some loose connection to one of the paranormal TV channels broadcasting from the Middle East.'

'Mmmm. I doubt it.' She paused. 'It's much more likely to be a random act. Paedophiles prey on children everywhere. She's a cute little thing, traveling alone. And she looks younger than she is, being so tiny.'

Alpha cringed… I hope she's right. I'd rather a weirdo than some terrorist organisation coming after me.

'The minute we find Alpha, someone else finds her as well? It's too much of a coincidence,' Dr Scott argued.

Mrs Hickelroy considered his comments, without rushing to reply. To Alpha she seemed more of a thinker than the volatile Dr Scott; the perfect foil for the man whose emotions bubbled just under the surface. Finally she said, 'No one else knows about us, unless you think there's a leak from John or the MI5 crowd.'

MI5—wow! This school keeps high-profile company. Alpha allowed her eyelashes to flutter open a crack and she saw Dr Scott shake his head firmly.

'The Prime Minister is extremely anxious that the press doesn't find out about us until after the next election. He won't risk his reputation on us becoming public knowledge until we deliver the goods—if we deliver them! It's only Sunday's work at reading the mood of the Cabinet that's stopped him withdrawing finances and closing us down already.' He sighed. 'I don't understand it. I was sure the Precogs would have something tangible by now. We've been open nineteen months already.'

Mrs Hickelroy stroked her chin. 'Would it be such a bad thing if they stopped paying for the school? We'll get private funding.'

'Except that anyone willing to pay our expenses would demand too much from our young people: they'd be spying on competitors, predicting market swings, and even getting involved in messy custody cases and divorces. Who knows what we'd be asked to do? We'd find it impossible to protect them. No, that's not the answer.'

Alpha's eyes slid to Dr Scott's face. Lines of worry were pulling at his mouth. 'Sometimes I think we should close down, but without us many of our students would come to a bad end.'

Mrs Hickelroy covered Dr Scott's hand with her own in a comforting gesture. Dr Scott's internal reaction to her movement came at Alpha in a blast of warmth—*Woooh! He really fancies her—and no wonder, she's gorgeous.*

Mrs Hickelroy's reply was calm. 'You're right, we can't close, our students would be devastated. Paranormal ability is so difficult to live with, remember how hard it was for Janna and Alex? Alex's father was trying to get him declared legally insane.'

Embarrassed by these secrets, Alpha gave a big and obvious yawn.

———

The train journey was followed by an exhilarating hovercraft ride to the Isle of Wight. Alpha sat near the edge of the craft and breathed in the sea spray, allowing a frisson of excitement to fill her mind as the island's multi-coloured cliffs came into view. She wondered what her new home would be like.

After disembarking, Dr Scott led the way to the car park, then drove them along a route that followed the coast. They left the town, then passed through open countryside. Eventually Alpha noticed that they drove past a high wall that seemed endless.

Finally he pulled up sharply at an entrance framed by wrought iron gates. Beyond them she could see a long, tree-lined drive.

The gates creaked open as though pulled by invisible hands. 'Welcome to Krakow Bond, Academy for Psychic Students,' Dr Scott said, driving up the curving avenue. 'We named the school after the man who trained Nostradamus, but like him we don't advertise what we are, so we avoid signs on the gates.'

Alpha had never heard of anyone called Krakow Bond, but she knew a bit about that Nostro-guy—he'd lived centuries ago, and wasn't he the guy who'd predicted the atom bomb and even 9/11 that had happened a few decades ago when terrorists flew into the twin towers in the USA? She peered around, anxiety building, and caught a glimpse of the gates closing behind them. Already she felt locked in.

A wood, thick with trees, sat to their right, edged with a riot of rhododendrons. To their left lay acres of neatly mowed lawn. Mrs Hickelroy glanced back at Alpha and smiled—it seemed she didn't hold those really rather bad bite marks against Alpha. She pointed across the grass. 'That leads down to our private beach. We're very isolated here, no one can get in unless they climb the wall or the gates.'

'And then a rather unpleasant shock awaits the unwelcome visitor,' said Dr Scott. 'We run electric current all around the estate. Be careful not to climb any trees near the edge of the walls.'

This place is a fortress!

Alpha's eyes widened as a mansion came into view. On the roof, minarets jostled for space with gargoyles, and much of the building was painted an extraordinary pink. *Heaven help me, is this going to be home?*

'This monstrosity used to be the private residence of an eccentric baron,' said Mrs Hickelroy. 'His architect must have been mad.'

Dr Scott grinned, apparently restored to good humour by the sight of his school. 'An eastern palace with gothic overtones, but it's perfect for our requirements.' He drove smoothly through an arch in the centre of the great building. This led into an internal courtyard, complete with a stone fountain depicting a life-sized lion wrestling a water buffalo.

'I'm so hungry, I could eat an elephant,,' said Sunday, as though the statue had reminded him of dinner.

Immediately Alpha picked up a vision of the boy, wearing a traditional South African skirt of fur, yielding a long, patterned spear against a beast of great stature. *Sunday,* she thought, *fancies himself as a warrior.*

'Never fear, Sunday—I guessed that three or four sandwiches weren't going to be enough breakfast for you,' said Dr Scott, smiling down at the boy. 'I phoned ahead and asked Chef Andreyaz to put on brunch. It'll be ready in twenty minutes.'

He took them into an enormous hall split into levels across the grand arch they'd driven through. Staircases meandered in all directions, a minstrel's gallery ran the entire length of the room, and stained-glass windows high above them filtered patterns of light across the stairs.

'Blimey,' Alpha muttered thinking, *there's enough space right here in this room to house all the kids at The Willows and six-dozen more.*

'Welcome home, Alpha,' said Mrs Hickelroy, putting an arm round Alpha's shoulders and patting her lightly.

'Biddy, our housekeeper, will join us in a minute,' said Dr Scott. 'She'll show you to your room and give you a chance to have a wash before you eat.'

Biddy, descending from one of the staircases, didn't look like a typical housekeeper. She was dressed in a string vest and wore boots that reached up above her knees. A mop of curly black hair cascaded down her back and her green eyes twinkled as she saw them. 'Come on me darlings,' she said in an Irish accent. 'You look half-dead. Bit of serious R & R needed here Doc.' She winked at them both.

Biddy led them up two flights of stairs then down a long passage. Sunday stopped off at a door marked with a brass tag that said, "The Venetian Room." He gave her a double-handed wave and said, 'See you soon.'

Alpha caught a glimpse of a four-poster bed.

'Yours is the next one,' said Biddy.

There was no sign on her door. Biddy thrust it open; Alpha stepped into a room at least sixteen times the size of her cubicle at the Willows. It smelled of new paint and was light and bright, in shades of yellow and blue. She could look down on an apple orchard outside. Voile curtains danced round the window and draped the double bed, hanging from a central circle on the ceiling.

She eyed the bed suspiciously. *Who else shares this room? All this space can't be only for me.*

Biddy put her worries to rest. 'The good doc ordered this room especially for you. Apart from Sunday, the other students are below on the next two levels. Come down to the hall when you've finished. I'll take you on from there. After you've eaten, I'll give you the grand tour. That'll be a bit special,' she promised.

Alpha felt cheered by the welcome she'd been given. Suddenly she was so tired her legs gave out and she plonked down on the bed, tempted to put her head on the fresh-smelling pillowcase and sleep.

To stop herself from dropping off she made herself stand up and walk over to the wall of cupboards lining one side of the room: *how many belongings do they think I have?* Her backpack would barely fill one shelf. She pushed at the middle door and through this she discovered a bathroom with a shower big enough for five. *Fantastic! A quick shower will wake me up.*

She dropped her clothes on the tiled floor, stepped into the shower and pressed various buttons. Water sprayed from hidden holes and steam filled the room, forest rain drenched her then mountain spray spat something so icy she was more awake than she wanted to be. *This isn't a bathroom; it's a walk-in Water Park. Luxury city!*

Realising she'd spent too much time in the shower, she slung a towel round her shoulders, slid her jeans up over wet legs, then fished on her shirt. She dashed to the door leading into the corridor and pulled it open, still doing up her buttons. Instantly mind-thoughts bombarded her from every direction, floating just outside her consciousness, there to tap into if she wanted.

She stepped back into the bedroom and closed the door, which shut with a clang. The seething turmoil was gone. She couldn't remember a time when that buzz of spillage didn't surround her. Alarm bells rang through her brain—*they've made this room thought-proof. Why didn't I notice that before?* Her mind had been on other things, she realised, like who might be sharing with her, and she'd been so tired. Then the shower had been wonderful…

She slammed the door behind her and left the room that only a few minutes ago had seemed so inviting but had the ability, she realised, to steal her access to the outer world.

'There you are,' said Biddy emerging from the staircase at a trot, her high boots not inconveniencing her speed at all. 'Come on, Sunday must be starving. For his size, he's got the biggest appetite at Krakow Bond.'

She followed Biddy into the great hall, down to the first floor. Suddenly Biddy veered towards a bridge that looped over the arch. Once they'd crossed this they made their way to the ground floor. After walking past a number of rooms Biddy pushed open a set of carved wooden doors. This space was vast; more banquet hall than dining room. A long table was set for some twenty people but even so it seemed very small in the huge room. The room's moulded ceiling and panelled walls, its sheer scale and sense of history left Alpha feeling totally insignificant.

Sunday jumped up as he saw her. 'Chef Andreyaz asked what kind of eggs we want, but I wasn't sure what you liked, so I said all kinds.' He led her over to the serving tables, and her eyes greedily took in the spread: cereals, bacon, sausages, kippers, corn cakes, beans and toast, bowls of fresh fruit and yoghurt, beef and chicken sandwiches, salads, and seven kinds of puddings.

Sunday filled one of the largest plates with a selection that made her stomach protest. She chose fruit, cereal, and orange juice and was just tucking in when a distant shout filled the air. 'What's she done to get the only student room with its own bathroom? It should be mine... I'm gonna sort her out.'

Alpha shrugged. *This is more like the reaction I'm used to.*

Another female voice with a rakish rasp to it spoke then. 'Leave her alone, pond scum. If you were civilised you'd give her a chance to settle down before you waded in with your size fourteens.'

Alpha wondered who this voice belonged to—she sounded intriguing.

The shouting person, now considerably closer, said, 'Piss off, Janna. It's none of your business.'

'It is if I choose to make it,' Janna's rakish voice called back.

Alpha looked to Sunday, hoping to find out what the hubbub was all about, but his attention was fixated on nothing else but his breakfast.

A door leading to the courtyard burst open and in came a wide-shouldered teenager, her acne heightened by the red flush of her face. She marched over to Alpha and poked her in the shoulder. 'You don't need that room. It's mine. I've earned it. You're nothing here until you prove yourself.'

Ah! The shouter, and would-be bully. Wouldn't you know it, another Lauren. I knew this place was too good to be true. But where's the girl who told her to leave me alone?

Suddenly Dr Scott appeared as if from nowhere, marching across the room, his face a thunderous mask. He slammed his hand down on the table. Alpha almost jumped out of her seat, but Dr Scott's anger was directed at the wide-shouldered teenager.

'Enough Rhodene,' he demanded. 'I won't have you upsetting our new student.'

'Why's she been given that bedroom? I've been here the longest, except for Howie, and he doesn't count because he's wacko. It should be mine.'

'I've made more than enough allowances for you recently, this time you will not get your own way. The room is Alpha's,' Dr Scott said. 'You'll have your own bathroom eventually but only if you behave and certainly not if you refer to Howie like that again.'

Rhodene stood her ground for a few minutes, glaring at Alpha. Alpha slid down into her chair, trying to escape the sour thoughts that were spilling from the bully's mind: *Just wait you worm. I'll get you, and I'll get that bitch Janna for telling on me. She'll keep her nose out of my business from now on.*

Finally, Rhodene gave Alpha a last hard stare, before turning on her foot and stomping off.

'She can have the room, I don't need it,' said Alpha. *Don't want it either!*

'No, she can't!' Dr Scott glared at the retreating Rhodene, before turning back to Alpha. 'Let me explain. Your bedroom is tin lined; even the windows are coated with a metallic finish. That's to give you a break from all the emotional noise in this place. And it means that Lily's dreamer students won't invade your sleep. We've had one or two cases of that already—even with lesser talents than yours it can be most disturbing. Soon all the student rooms will be lined in tin but, because you're telepathic, I wanted you to have the first one. That way you can tune out whenever you want to.'

And you can keep information from me!

Dr Scott was giving off very little emotional spillage—just a touch of the annoyance he'd directed at Rhodene remained. She collected herself to probe his thoughts but before she could penetrate his mind he spoke. 'There's something I need to discuss with you right away.' He looked very serious. When her eyes slid away from his, he placed a finger under her chin, drawing it up until she was looking at him. 'This is important—we live in a house full of psychics, but most of the students are not telepathic and I need you to promise not to delve into other minds. We only allow that in training, under very strict classroom conditions. If we can't trust each other, we can't trust anyone. OK?'

She nodded, unwillingly. *I can promise not to look directly into other people's heads, but I can't stop picking up their spillage. How can I say I won't do something that I can't stop doing?*

Dr Scott removed his hand from her face. 'Good,' he said. 'We all need some privacy. It makes everyone more comfortable in the long run.'

It won't make me more comfortable. It's like you've stolen my eyes.

Biddy returned then, just as Sunday finished the last of his scrambled, boiled, fried, and poached eggs.

'Grand tour time!' she said, bustling about with the plates, and beaming widely.

Dr Scott stood up. 'I'll take Alpha myself, thanks Biddy.'

Biddy turned away from the plates and raised one eyebrow. 'Fine with me, Doc. I've got plenty to do as it is.' She squinted, looking more closely at Alpha, her own eyes lingering on the dark shadows around Alpha's eyes. 'But if it were up to me I'd let Alpha have a good rest first.'

Dr Scott blinked and looked deeply into Alpha's face. 'Yes,' he said. 'You're right Biddy. Alpha needs sleep. Come on Alpha, it's off to bed for you.'

———

In spite of her weariness, Alpha battled to fall asleep. Her mind stewed with concerns: *If I stop reading minds I'll be isolated, forced to ask questions. That means I'll have to talk to people, and I hate talking.*

Who tried to kidnap me?

Am I safe here?

Did Janna fetch Dr Scott to protect me from Rhodene? And why does Rhodene dislike me so much? She's barely met me. I swear there's more to this than bathrooms.

I need answers! How can I get them if I can't search people's thoughts?

Desperately missing other people's spillage, she got up and was glad to find that the windows opened. A few gentle thoughts floated into her, mingling with the sound of a lawnmower. She lay down again. Eventually she fell into a restless sleep.

The day passed and the moon rose. Harsh whispers filled her mind, making her toss and turn.

'What were you doing grabbing her like that? I told you I'll watch her!'

'She's ours. The organisation needs her.'

'Patience… we must find out what she can do first. That's why you failed before. Remember the others!'

CHAPTER EIGHT

Sun streamed in through the bedroom window carrying Alpha far from her dreams. The buzz of everyday thoughts floated through the open window, amongst them the loud ruminations of Chef Andreyaz (who was ranting silently about the oven burning his bread) and the preoccupation of Biddy (who was climbing the stairs to the second floor swearing silently but fluently in her head about a loose heel on her boots). Alpha chuckled, from deep in her chest. Biddy knew swearwords even the teenagers at the Willows couldn't rival.

Biddy knocked, then hobbled in with a tray of food laden with yet another breakfast, managing the door, the tray, and her broken heel without even the slightest shake of the orange juice in the tall glass. 'Morning sweetheart. Have you caught up on your sleep? You've been head down for sixteen hours.'

She slid the tray onto a large chest at the foot of the bed. 'Eat up! Sunday's going to show you the layout of the place then Dr Scott wants you to meet everyone.'

Alpha dressed quickly but before she'd finished breakfast Sunday bounded into the room and took a bite of toast from her tray. She swallowed her juice hastily.

'Let's go,' he said, with the piece of toast still in his mouth. He drew her down the stairs, taking her hand in the most natural of gestures, his fingers slightly sticky from the butter on the toast.

Her first inclination was to pull away, but she sensed that he would be upset by that, so she left her hand in his, drawing comfort from his closeness as she eyed-up the grand proportions of the house. Sunday chattered all the way. 'This part of the house is called North Block. All the students live here.'

'Don't any of the adults stay in this block?'

'Biddy does. She sleeps next to the sick room.' He pointed to a small sign saying sickbay that led off the main hall on the ground floor. 'She's our nurse, as well as the housekeeper.'

After pushing open some double doors he hurried her out into the gravel-covered courtyard. Alpha scurried behind him, but when he stopped unexpectedly near the fountain she almost collided with him.

He gestured towards the buildings surrounding them as though he was a tour guide. Now that Alpha had a chance to inspect the house properly, the sheer scale of it astonished her. There were four wings each three stories high not including the basements. The wings formed a square around the courtyard.

'This courtyard is the best way to get around,' Sunday explained. 'They've blocked off lots of the passages inside, so it's too hard to get through the entire house.' Alpha tracked his thoughts. *Unless you are a small Zulu warrior*, he was thinking. He pointed left, drawing her eye to the long wing that joined North and South Block together. 'That is East Wing. We have school there. Most of our teachers come over from the mainland but Mr Small, he's chemistry, and Miss Finkle, she's music, they live on the island.'

Next Sunday's right hand swung out towards the West Wing. As Alpha peered at it, she realised that the roof had come off and parts of the wall had fallen inwards. 'We're not allowed in there,' Sunday told her, but Alpha had a strong feeling that any number of rules hadn't kept Sunday from exploring the crumbling remains of that wing.

Alpha heard the gravel behind her crunch. She swung round as Dr Scott called, 'Thanks Sunday, I'll take Alpha on from here.'

Sunday looked disappointed but he gambolled off, leaving Alpha alone with Dr Scott. She felt awkward in his company. She'd learned to distrust anyone in authority. In her experience, they were more interested in their own agenda than in the children they cared for. Take her two sets of foster parents for example: one lot had only cared about the money they got for 'looking after' the kids in the home and the other bunch had feigned concern with their countless efforts to make normal conversation, but were clearly very uncomfortable in her presence. They were pretty sure they'd made a mistake in taking her on but were reluctant to admit that to each other. She'd run away from both homes, returning with relief to the Willows. She bit her lip at the thought of the Willows. *If this doesn't work out, I can't go back there. They'll know where to find me…*

Dr Scott broke into her thoughts by placing his hands on her shoulders and turning her southwards. She flinched as he touched her, but he went on smoothly, as though he hadn't felt her pull away.

'The truly interesting stuff happens in there,' he said, gesturing towards the southernmost block. 'That's where the paranormal classrooms and psychic teachers are based. Mrs Hickelroy and I share the top floor. The entire block is lined in tin, just like your room, to ensure complete privacy.'

South Block had a silent, secretive look about it, probably because the windows were silvered, and she couldn't see through them.

'But for now we'll get the mundane classes out of the way.' Dr Scott led the way into East Wing. 'Were you taking any special subjects … psychology, engineering, hairdressing, music? We'll employ a new teacher if we need to.'

She shook her head at each of his guesses. Schoolwork was one of those things she endured, not enjoyed; they weren't going to need an army of teachers on her account.

She met only two students during this trip around the classrooms. In the languages section, Dr Scott introduced her to Miss Cardemon, (a fine-boned woman with a puckered neck, who taught Arabic and Hebrew) and to a student, Martel Hepplewood. He loped down a long corridor towards them with the powerful limbs of a 5000-meter runner and as he got up close Alpha noticed that he towered over Dr Scott, who was by no means a short man. Martel was a good-looking, tall guy, if you liked mocca coffee skin, powerful wrists, and eyes like dead coals surrounded by brilliant whites. Those eyes skidded across Alpha's face, ignoring her as Dr Scott introduced them. *Typical!* thought Alpha, as Martel left them, his long hair, caught back in a band, swinging with each step. *Someone else who dislikes me on sight. Couldn't even bother to say hello.*

The next room was the science lab. Dr Scott smiled cheerfully at the two people there. 'This is Mr Small, our chemistry teacher, and another of our students, Alex Rhodes.' Mr Small, quite unlike his name, was a large man with bushy eyebrows that bristled from a bulldog face.

'Hi—busy unmaking a nail bomb!' Alex commented, glancing at her before turning back to manipulate the twists of wire and detonator on the table.

She was more fascinated by his dexterous fingers, long and pale, than by the red birthmark creeping across his scalp. *So that's Alex. Poor kid—his father thinks his birthmark is a sign of the devil. Personally, I think it gives him a bit of an edge.*

Dr Scott drew her from the room and continued with the introductions. Six teachers later, he grinned and said, 'enough of this. Let's get to the real action.'

With eager steps he led her through the courtyard and into South Block. Once there, he hurried towards the stairs, tripping over a pair of dirty Wellington boots that had been left lying at the bottom of them.

A voice from the first landing called out, 'Oh my God! I'm so sorry, Dr Scott. I was in a hurry to catch Mrs Hickelroy before History. I left them there because I didn't want to dirty the carpet. I've got to tell her, her idea worked.'

At once Alpha recognised the voice—this was Janna, the girl who'd warned Dr Scott that Rhodene was trying to intimidate her in the dining room. She looked up and realised that she'd seen Janna once before as well, in Dr Scott's memories, when she was trapped in his head at Waterloo station. She almost said hello, but then she remembered that Janna wouldn't know her.

'No harm done,' said Dr Scott, beginning to mount the stairs.

Janna ran down towards them, shaking back the two ginger pigtails of hair that fell to below her waist, and in the process smudging her cheek with mud. As she reached them she stuck out her hand but withdrew it when she saw how dirty it was. 'Oops, sorry Alpha. I haven't stopped off for a wash yet.'

'Been raiding the carrot patch again?' Dr Scott asked, a grin turning up one corner of his mouth.

Janna shook her head and smiled wickedly. Alpha felt amused. Clearly Janna had a liking for freshly picked vegetables. 'Not this time, Dr Scott,' she said. 'Mrs Hickelroy suggested that I plant autumn crocuses in the woods. She said it would be a great way to relax, and she was right. I got so carried away I found a grave where a gundog was buried: he was called Red ... his master was crying over him.'

Alpha didn't understand what she was talking about, but Dr Scott obviously did. 'Well done. Mrs Hickelroy will be pleased.' He turned towards Alpha and performed the introductions.

Janna's grin broadened. 'Hi! I've heard all about you. Rhodene moaned about you all evening, but don't worry, I don't take a word she says seriously. What's your speciality? Mine's spaces.'

Alpha gulped like a goldfish, unable to find the words to talk about her ability to read thoughts.

Dr Scott noticed her difficulty and stepped in. 'Alpha's telepathic. Tell Alpha what you're so good at, Janna.'

Janna thought for a moment, then said, 'I'm a Tactile… that means my sense of touch is a whole bunch better than most people's. In my case, I'm best at reading spaces. Sometimes if I enter a room I can tell you who's been there, who lives there and so on, but a lot of what I read happened in the past.'

This is bizarre. I didn't think I'd ever have a conversation quite like this. Compared to her my trick of reading minds is relatively normal, thought Alpha. She smiled tentatively at Janna.

'Well, we'd better let you get on, Janna, otherwise you really will be late for History,' said Dr Scott.

Janna glanced at her watch. 'Gosh yes! It's great to meet you Alpha…I'll just have a quick word with Mrs Hickelroy first.' She gave a wave then scampered up the stairs, her broad bottom quivering as she ran.

Dr Scott smiled indulgently. 'Now you've met Janna. What a minx! I'm sure you'll be friends. Anyway, she started explaining the way we categorise abilities, so let's go up to my office and we'll go through the lot.'

———

Dr Scott's office had a view right down to the beach. Chalky cliffs lined both sides of the sand—no wonder the beach was private; no one was going walk across those.

'Sight for sore eyes, isn't it?' he said. 'I run down there most evenings, but you may prefer to exercise indoors. There's a small pool and a gym in the basement of your block—just book with Biddy in advance.'

Alpha shook her head slightly. I'll get enough exercise just walking from one end of this house to the other.

Dr Scott settled her in an armchair and stretched out in another. 'If you're comfortable with the idea I'd like to do this with mindtalk. It's how Telepaths pass information to each other, but it does mean opening your mind to allow my thoughts in.'

If he thinks I'm going to let him roam about inside my head again, he can forget it!

But Dr Scott put her at ease. 'The way this works is that I'll formulate my thoughts and you can decide whether or not to let them into your head. I won't be able to read your mind or see your memories because my conscious brain won't be inside those thoughts,' he explained.

'I can stop if I want to?'

'Of course. I promise never to invade your mind without your permission.'

Alpha sensed his emotions—he wasn't lying. *He's genuine, through and through. What you see is what you get.*

'Why thank you, Alpha,' he responded, startling her. 'Yes, I can still read the odd thought that overflows the confines of the mind now and again, but nothing more than that I assure you.'

She felt relieved—she couldn't stop people's emotions spilling over to her no matter what she tried. If it was OK for him to pick up spillage it was probably OK for her to do it too.

Dr Scott closed his eyes. Although Alpha could see no change, she could feel a new energy emerging outside his head, as though a third person had sat down between them. His eyes opened. 'Right, they're separate from me now—waiting for you to invite them in.'

Keeping her mind firmly on the sphere of energy, Alpha drew it slowly to the edge of her brain. She hesitated, glancing at him, and he nodded reassuringly.

———

At once her mind was flooded with images, patterns, concepts. She saw a gnarled old tree with four spreading branches, and she knew without being told that this represented the four categories of psychic abilities. The branches crisscrossed each other, and she understood that the categories often overlapped.

The first branch stood for T.I. short for telepathic indicator: a person who could detect the thoughts of other people. Alpha realised that this was her branch, she was a T.I.

… further down the tree, the branch split into two, Empaths and Telepaths. Her path was the telepathic group. The other half of the branch represented Empaths and she gathered that Empaths worked with crowds rather than individuals. The collective emotions of a crowd drew the Empath in and from there the Empath could separate out a single person's impressions.

Her mind dropped from that branch to the apex where the next branch began. It was clothed in leaves that constantly changed their shape and colour, outlining a host of possible futures. As she followed this upwards she found precognitive skills. Precogs, she learned, predicted what might happen. Sometimes they were wrong because the future was forever reshaping itself, every tiny action and decision creating an ever-changing pattern.

After she'd fully explored the nature of Precogs she found herself on the third branch. It was scaly with a shimmering phosphorescence that symbolised the talents of the Tactile. Janna had said she was one and now Alpha understood what that meant—Tactiles picked up images from touching the physical world: houses, rooms, places where terrible things had happened, or from smaller objects like letters and keepsakes.

The final branch was less substantial and was split into fragile subsections that spilled out everywhere like hunks of hair flowing in the wind. This branch included Kinaesthetic skills: the ability to move things without touching them, as well as many other skills that were impossible to define.

———

Dr Scott's mindtalk, having expended its energy, now popped out of existence leaving Alpha staring at him, her brain whirling.

As her thoughts sorted themselves out, she realised that she'd enjoyed the experience; for once she hadn't felt so alone. *Here I'm normal, or rather, I'm just like everyone else—a total oddball. I fit right in.*

Dr Scott grinned. 'If only all lessons could be so easy.'

'Can we do that again?

'Certainly. Whenever you want to,' he replied.

'Can everyone here do that?'

'I'm afraid not. That particular talent is limited to us Telepaths, although I suspect you may be able to mindtalk with Sunday. He's an Empath, but just lately he's developed other talents and he seems to have a direct telepathic link to you. We must explore the reasons behind that soon.' Dr Scott mulled over this before adding, 'With proper training the two of you could be a force to be reckoned with.'

Huh! And what exactly will proper training entail, wondered Alpha.

Dr Scott continued, 'We have another student called Howie who can also read people's intentions. Telepaths are particularly valuable in our situation.'

She didn't need to ask him why, a new thought bubble spilled from his mind, and she welcomed it directly into hers.

——

An image of a man, intent on murdering a bus full of people with a bomb sewn into the fabric of his jacket.

——

The image ended before the explosion occurred, but it left her feeling queasy though, at the same time, she felt a smidgen of pride that perhaps by working here she'd be able to stop that sort of thing from happening.

'Semtex—plastic explosive,' Dr Scott explained. 'It can be moulded into any shape, and it can't be traced by metal detectors, only by trained dogs or artificial smell sensors, neither of which are in great supply, so it's up to people like us to stop them.'

His next words deflated her a bit. 'But, and it's a big but, we have our limitations. T.Is are usually accurate. We can detect crowd violence before it gets out of hand, or identify dangerous criminals, but we have to be in the right place at the right time. With me so far?'

She nodded. He held her full attention.

'So enter the Precognitives. Rhodene used to be our strongest….' Dr Scott halted and shook his head, as if to shed an unwelcome thought, before going on. 'Unfortunately, precognition is extremely difficult: if Precogs get the what right, they may not know the when—if they're clear on the timing, they can't place where it will happen. Usually what they leave out is crucial, so if they can get us to the right what, when, or where, people like you can help to fill in the missing gaps. Together you become a formidable team.'

So I'm supposed to link up with Rhodene. I don't think he's reckoned on how she feels about it.

But Dr Scott surprised her. 'Precognition is where Howie excels. His dreams are very wide-ranging, but because he's mentally disabled, getting information from him can be a daunting task.' He paused, watching her closely. 'You'll be working closely with him.'

He seemed to be waiting for her to react to something, but all she felt was relief that he hadn't said she'd be working closely with Rhodene.

He went on, 'Janna and Martel are both Tactiles—remember, you met Martel earlier in the corridor outside of Languages? Martel is very good with personal items… photographs, jewellery, things with sentimental value. By the way, he's generally known as Mamba.'

'Why?' Alpha found herself asking.

'It was Sunday's idea—and the name seems to have stuck. Mambas are notoriously dangerous snakes scattered across the continent of Africa, which suits some of Martel's abilities. We encourage students to give themselves nicknames if they feel it helps their special talents. That's why Carl Smethie calls himself Kinetic King. Both he and Alex are Kinetics.'

Alpha remembered Alex from the strawberry birthmark that splashed across his face. Dr Scott went on. 'Kinetic King, Carl to the rest of us, can move objects without touching them, but Alex isn't psychic in the accepted sense of the word. What he has is an affinity to all things metal—metal objects stick to his body or remain in the air close to him, and using repelling force he can hurl them long distances too.'

He rose from his chair. 'Now that we've covered the basics it's time to meet Howie.'

The almost desperate emotion behind Dr Scott's words jolted Alpha. Clearly he was hoping for something special from her in relation to Howie, but without going inside his head she couldn't detect exactly what he'd meant. She hoped she could live up to his expectations… and she hoped that Howie wasn't going to be as bloody-minded as Rhodene.

CHAPTER NINE

On the ground floor of South Block, Dr Scott pulled aside a curtain of crystal beads threaded over a door. 'This is Lily Wade's classroom,' he explained, ushering Alpha inside. 'Lily was born in Jamaica. She's a dream-harbourer, so she teaches dream-catching and interpretive precognition.'

The beads tinkled as Alpha entered a big square room, which was filled with many plants. At the far side of the room, partially hidden between fronds of green, she caught sight of someone dressed in a canary yellow gown with a matching turban that highlighted her rich-brown skin. As they drew closer to her the woman's lovely face creased into a smile, drawing attention to her round cheeks. She rose regally from her armchair and glided over, greeting Alpha with a motherly hug. 'I'm Lily. Welcome to Krakow Bond. I know you're going to be happy here.'

Her warming hug was lovely, as calming as oil rubbed into parched skin, but after too tight a squeeze, Alpha emerged from the padded, vibrant fabric feeling, flushed and out of breath. She backed away, almost falling over the sofa near Lily's armchair. As she righted herself on its arm she jumped—there was a boy asleep on it, all spiky elbows, and knobbly knees. His socks were neatly turned over his trainers, and his shorts had been carefully ironed. Is this Howie?

Lily confirmed it in her soft drawl. 'Howie's a lot like you except, he can't speak while he's awake. But in his dream state. he is capable of much.' She raised one finger. 'Watch now. We've nearly finished this session.'

She snapped her fingers and the boy, who couldn't be older than eleven, began speaking with an adult voice which was completely at odds with his lanky boy's body.

'I've told you, don't call me Howie! My name is Howarth.'

Unperturbed Lily said, 'Yes, Howarth. Continue please.'

'Howie dreams of dragon eyes—they're coming towards him. Its wings brush the air but …' he paused, as though confused by the dream. 'The dragon's not flying… it's bound to earth by twin lines of light.'

Lily cocked surprised eyebrows. 'Howie sees two lines. They weren't in this dream before.'

'The moon shines on something… something terrible...' his voice tightened, went up a notch, '…take it away…'

Alpha saw Howie's body shiver. Suddenly he jerked, elbows and knees flying in separate directions. 'The dragon's in pain… it's screeching… they've hurt it!' He twitched violently and fell from the couch. Dr Scott dived forwards and caught him before he could touch the carpet, replacing him tenderly on the sofa.

Lily snapped her fingers twice. 'Sleep now, Howarth, sleep … Wake refreshed, Howie, clear your mind.'

Howie, stirred, opened his eyes, pushed himself up on one arm then stood up. Alpha saw that his left shoulder drooped down by several inches and that his left shoe was built up, its heel much higher than the right one. His mouth hung open and he licked his lips with a loose tongue. In sleep, his face had seemed mature. Now it appeared vacuous. He stared right through her without noticing her, and for some reason this empty look scared her.

I can't tell what's going on in his head; his spillage is all mixed up. Howie's thoughts were a mixture of numbers, complex equations, actual ruminations on how to set each foot in front of the other, and total unawareness of anyone else in the room.

'You did really well today. Goodbye Howie,' Lily called out as Howie jerked forwards into a lumbering walk. At the door Howie hesitated, then slowly turned his whole body, angling it towards Alpha. He remained expressionless but suddenly Alpha had the feeling that he knew who she was. She couldn't detect how he felt about her, but she knew that Howie, at least, didn't resent her presence here. *I can work with him,* she thought, suddenly pleased at the prospect. *Maybe I can find out what's going on under that blank face.*

Once Howie had left the room Dr Scott said, his voice buzzing with excitement, 'THEY'VE hurt it?'

Lily nodded. 'That's the fourth time he's had this dream, but the first time he's mentioned anyone else. We get a little more each time, but it's not all that clear to him either. It's definitely a prediction and whatever it is, it isn't pleasant.'

'It's beginning to sound like a terrorist act,' said Dr Scott.

Terrorists hurting dragons? Flaming heck—this place is getting wilder by the minute.

Dr Scott continued, 'If only we knew what the dragon is. Once Alpha's up to speed, she'll be able to help.'

If they don't know what's going on how am I supposed to sort it out?

'By doing what?' she asked.

Lily glanced at Dr Scott. 'Shall I?'

He agreed, so Lily began, her underchin shaking as she spoke. 'We're going to let you explore Howie's mind, a little at a time because he's very fragile, and his mind works in unusual ways.'

No kidding!

'We're hoping you'll be able to interpret the images he sees. To get to the root of his problem we'll start with the senses—we all have more than five.'

We do? And what's that got to do with Howie?

'I'll show you,' said Lily. 'Stand on one leg… shut your eyes… stretch your hands out in front of your face.'

Alpha complied, feeling like a stork about to deliver a baby.

'Now touch your left ear with your right hand and the tip of your nose with the other hand.'

Alpha managed all these instructions without actually falling over, though there was a bit of shaking going on in the leg department.

'Think about how you knew where the ends of your hands were, how you found your ear and your nose before you touched them? You didn't use sight, hearing, smell or taste. Other senses, which we use every day, helped you perform that experiment. Mainly these are mechanical senses: acceleration, kinaesthesia, balance, and muscle extension or shortening. But we also have internal senses: a sense of pain, of temperature, blood pressure, blood sugar level, full bladder, a need for oxygen in thin air and so on.'

Alpha opened her eyes causing her to wobble wildly.

'You can put your foot down now,' said Lily.

With relief Alpha complied.

'Beyond these are the extra senses, which you students have in such abundance: a sense of the past, present and future in thoughts and dreams and visions. But all these senses mean nothing without perception. If our eyes see a cat, and our ears hear it mew, but our brain fails to interpret what we have seen, we might as well have seen a camel. Or a racing car. We need to turn what our senses tell us into messages that are useful to us—that's perception. And that's what Howie lacks. He has more than his share of senses: he dreams of dangers; he can read thoughts; he has visions, but while he is awake he can't put this into perspective. He can't make sense of his own world, so he can't communicate with us in ours.'

'But that voice Howie used?' Alpha asked, clearing her hair from her eyes. 'It sounded so grown up. And who is Howarth?'

Lily smiled gently. 'Howarth is an adult persona that Howie has created inside himself who can say what he finds and feels. Howie doesn't know that Howarth exists. Through working with me, Howie's brain has found this other channel to spark what his senses tell him. It allows him to escape his prison of poor perception. His mother is most encouraged.'

'His m... mother?' Alpha stammered, feeling bewildered with this onslaught of information.

'Biddy, our wonderful housekeeper, is his mother. That's why she volunteered to work here. Howie was our first student. Until you arrived, he was the most powerful psychic we had, although it is very hard to get him to talk to us.'

Alpha stared awkwardly at the floor. *Me? The most powerful psychic here?* 'But I'm... I'm not a Precog or anything like that,' she stammered.

'No,' agreed Dr Scott. 'We've seen no signs of that. But you are the most incredible telepath I've ever met. If Howie is dreaming of terrorists, you're the best person to get to grips with what he's trying to tell us.

CHAPTER
TEN

On her way to dinner, Alpha halted in the great hall, trying to work out which of several flights of stairs she should be taking. *I need a map and a compass to find my way around here.*

High-heeled footsteps pattered in the minstrel's gallery above her. 'Hello,' Mrs Hickelroy called out. 'You look a bit lost.'

'Is this the way to the dining room?'

'Yes it is. Well done. Your first days here are bound to be bewildering. The place is a bit of a monolith.' Mrs Hickelroy made her way down the stairs towards Alpha. 'I'm so glad I've run into you. I planned to make time to talk to you earlier, but the hours ran away with me. Paperwork and more paperwork— that's what you get for volunteering to be the vice-principal, even of a school as unusual as this one.' She gave a wry smile. 'But I wouldn't change my job for anything.'

Alpha caught a glimpse that Mrs Hickelroy was pleased that Alpha had joined the school before the woman tucked her emotions back in check with the minimum of fuss. To Alpha, the vice-principal's reserved nature was something of a relief after experiencing Dr Scott's emotion-laden personality all day.

'Pop up to my office after breakfast tomorrow morning. Top floor, south wing. Turn left at the top of the stairs. I'll have your timetable for the next few days. As soon as Lily and Mr Thom have assessed you we'll get together so that we can work out the best routine for you. But now we'd better make haste.' Mrs Hickelroy nodded to herself, adding, 'Chef Andreyaz is a demon if we don't give his dinners their due regard. He insists we're all seated by seven.'

Inside the dining hall all but two of the chairs were already taken. Mrs Hickelroy led Alpha towards the end of the table where the students were collected. 'I won't bother with any more introductions. I bet you've had more than your fair share of those today.'

Alpha pulled out her chair and sat down next to Sunday, trying to ignore the stares from people further up the table, while the chef and his crew passed out a pale but delicious soup. She ate slowly, glancing up the table. Dr Scott sat at the head; Mrs Hickelroy had taken the empty chair on his right. A man with a shaved head and a face as lined as a walnut sat to the left of Dr Scott. As Alpha's gaze slid over him his deep-set eyes caught hers, gripping her with his presence. Alpha's senses told her that this was no ordinary teacher—like Lily, he was a paranormal special. But unlike Lily, there was no hint of warmth in his eyes, only a questioning gleam that scrutinised her like he was examining some new kind of bug.

Between the psi-teachers and the students sat another group of adults. Several of them were dressed in overalls or were wearing aprons over their clothes. *Must be the late shift.* One woman, wearing a scarlet two-piece work suit, scowled as she caught Alpha's glance. She was almost as broad as she was tall and, although her hands were spotlessly clean, her fuzzy hair bore traces of garden clippings. Biddy sat in the middle of this group of what seemed to be domestic staff, conversing cheerfully with those around her. To Alpha, Biddy's fishnet stockings and sequinned blouse looked as out of place as a teapot in a toilet when compared to the work clothes of the others, yet they seemed to respect her, nodding gravely as she made some comment about flowers in the courtyard for Parents' Day later in the term.

Alpha felt a pang of regret—*my parents will never make it to Parents' Day, not unless they're coming as ghosts.* Swallowing down the feeling she turned her attention to the students, only to find both Rhodene and Martel staring at her.

Rhodene spoke quietly, a secretive smile playing on her lips. 'You know Martel's called Mamba? Wanna guess what he can do—to you?'

'Hey, woozlewimp, you're obviously too dumb to think up your own threats, so shut up,' said Janna, her tone lazy and insulting. She turned and winked at Alpha.

Alpha said nothing, pretending to be deeply absorbed in the next course, which proved to be a medley of roast meats, vegetables and salads.

Martel's flint-like eyes bored into Alpha throughout the meal. This evening he wore rings that pierced his nose and they seemed to convey more menace than any of Rhodene's spiteful words, glinting every time Martel raised his head. His earlier grace was still evident in the way his cutlery formed natural extensions of his fingers rather than the unwieldy implements Alpha held in her hands, but his neck and shoulders were coiled as though ready to strike. *Snake! Right. Now I see why Sunday named him Mamba.*

Alpha's gaze moved on down the table. Howie sat next to Janna, making a concerted effort to get his fork into his mouth. Eventually he succeeded.

Beside him, and opposite her, Alpha discovered Kinetic King, also known as Carl Smethie, a mischievous ten-year-old with chipmunk cheeks and a mop of blond hair. He and Alex sat together and appeared to be firm friends, chatting away to each other, and laughing from time to time.

She'd no sooner taken her eyes off them when "The Kinetic King" gave Alpha a demonstration of his talents, lifting her plate from the table just as she attempted to get a forkful of salad. The plate tipped; tomatoes slid onto the carpet.

Alex giggled and suddenly Alpha's knife and fork began to bend in her hands, resembling crudely shaped U's. Alpha blushed, feeling mortified. Even without this incident, she'd been unsure of her manners in this grand room filled with the best of crockery and cutlery.

Rhodene laughed. 'Can't be much of a psychic if she can't even manage her own dinner,' she whispered to Martel.

Carl, "The Kinetic King", grinned at Alpha. 'Sorry. I couldn't resist. It's nothing personal.'

Refusing to give in to her embarrassment, Alpha laid her damaged cutlery down gently so it wouldn't clatter against her plate and then, before anyone could register what she was doing, leaned across the table and whipped away Alex's dessert knife and fork, holding on to them as she bent down to retrieve the fallen salad.

She sensed that the boys were being mischievous and had no real desire to hurt her, but Rhodene and Martel were another matter: trouble of a completely different league. Rhodene resented Alpha's presence, but all Alpha could sense from Martel was cool contempt. She couldn't grasp what was going on in Martel's head without looking inside it—and she wasn't allowed to do that.

For the rest of the meal Alpha kept her head down and focused on her plate except when Alex bent Rhodene's spoon backwards, just as she was about to put a juicy blackberry into her mouth. It shot across the table, missed the napkin folded round Howie's neck, and landed on his shoulder. Howie plodded on with the difficult task of raising his own dinner precisely to the middle of his mouth, taking no notice of the purplish stain spreading across his white shirt.

Biddy glanced over at Howie and a sudden look of tenderness crinkled her eyes, followed by one of anger. 'That is more than enough, Alex Rhodes.'

Alex looked abashed. 'Sorry, Miss Biddy. I should have taken better aim.'

———

After dinner as they got up to leave, Alpha noticed Martel whisper something in Sunday's ear. Sunday beamed and slapped Martel's hand in a high five. Rhodene took the opportunity to glare at Alpha before stomping away. Alpha could feel the intensity of Rhodene's dislike eating away at her insides. She shrugged the sensation away. She'd learned long ago not to let other people's opinions touch her: as long as Rhodene stayed clear of physical abuse she would have about as much impact on Alpha as a stone statue. *Or possibly less,* Alpha thought wickedly, *if it was a statue of a naked young man. At least that would offer artistic interest and I could admire its better bits while pretending to examine it for anatomical accuracy.*

Janna touched Alpha's arm as they left the table. 'Let's go for a walk.'

A grin broke out on Alpha's face but, wary of the concept of friendship, she responded cautiously. 'Are we allowed out at night?'

'Why not? What's going to hurt us? The security here is pheee-nomenal. I'll just grab a jacket from my room. It can get really windy here.'

Janna's bedroom was a tip. 'Excuse the mess,' she said, kicking a few books and a ream of paper under the bed. She lifted a broken CD cover from the jumble of bedclothes and hurled it into a corner of the room. Then she patted the bed, indicating that Alpha could sit down on it. 'The bin's somewhere over there, but I can't find it since Biddy refused to send in any of her staff to clean up. She said if she can't walk in a straight line from the door to the bed, I'll have to change my own linen. That was a few months ago, and I haven't got around to changing it yet.' She harrumphed. 'Well, I'm due to move to a new room as soon as the workmen have finished. No point sorting things out now when I'll only have to do it again.'

Alpha gazed round the room, astonished at the sheer number of Janna's possessions: PlayStation—missing bits; remote control for TV (no signs of the TV itself, but that could be hidden under the mountains of garments piled up around the room); laptop about to slide off the desk; four pairs of sunglasses in various stages of repair, half a dozen-coloured ribbons tied in knots, several with strands of Janna's hair still clinging to them. 'How do you find anything in here?'

'Luck,' replied Janna with a straight face, hitching out a fetching green velvet jacket from under an armchair, and brushing it down to remove the scraps of blackened banana skin clinging to it. 'Or if I'm really stuck I use my talents to call it to my attention. It's my parent's fault this room is so stuffed—they keep sending me presents in the post. Must be some kind of guilt trip. Like who listens to CDs these days? OK, I'm ready.'

Janna tucked her arm into Alpha's as they strolled down the drive together. Struggling to make normal conversation (Alpha couldn't remember when she'd last indulged in that occupation) she told Janna, 'you don't need to jump to my defence with Rhodene. It's not that I'm not grateful, but I can look after myself.' She stared at Janna from the corner of her eye to see if her new friend had taken offence at her words, already kicking herself for opening her mouth and putting both feet in it.

But Janna's face was brimming with laughter. 'Aw! Do you have to spoil my fun? I love winding her up. She's such an easy target.'

Alpha began to relax. 'Martel isn't. Why's he called Snake?'

A shadow crossed Janna's face. 'He's a reptile. He doesn't give much away but, well… there was one time I saw him lose his temper. It wasn't even with me; he was mad at Mrs Hickelroy. I just came into the room, and I could feel these super bad vibes—like I'd just stepped on a rattlesnake.'

Alpha nodded. 'Rhodene's your average bully. But Martel… he's got hidden depths. Anyway, tell me about that guy crying in the woods. How did you know that was his dead dog's grave?'

'I saw their ghosts,' said Janna.

Alpha stopped walking to stare at Janna. Is she serious?

Janna swung back towards her, teeth gleaming in the dark as she gave a crooked smile that flashed across her face before disappearing. 'Yeah! I know, it's always a bit of a shock. I don't blame you if you don't believe me. Even my parents don't know what to make of me.'

'I didn't say I didn't believe you… how long have you been seeing ghosts?'

'All my life, as long as I can remember. The first one was my Nan. She was a knees-up sort of granny—she rode a Harley-Davidson for fun. When she died she waited around 'till after she was buried, then came and sat on the end of my bed to tell me a story. It was so cool… for a long time after that I honestly believed mermaids rode on wave horses and that one day I would see them charging through a rough sea. Of course, I was only four at the time. I never saw her again, but I'll always remember that night.'

'Ghosts don't frighten you?'

'No, why should they? They don't do any harm. Living

people are worse… like Rhodene. She keeps on about my lack of upper body assets, reminding me that Mum couldn't find a bra small enough for me. And she makes jokes about the size of my bum. She tells me I'll have to marry a plastic surgeon so he can rearrange my bits. She's bad news, but I sorted her.' Janna sniggered. 'Kylie, my oldest sister, is studying graphics design at college, so I… er…asked Sunday to "borrow" some photos of Rhodene. There was one she had with Martel, so I got Kylie to stick new bodies on their heads. Now Martel is wriggling his way round the net with a streamlined viper body, and Rhodene has the udders of a cow in desperate need of milking. It's a great look for her. Every time they get on my nerves I turn to that web page, www.wonderworksofart… it's a fantastic tonic.'

Alpha burst out laughing. She felt like hugging herself—the friends she'd had in the distant past had dropped away when Mum had taken to drinking. After that it had been impossible to make new friends; she had far too much to hide. But things were different here—she had a chance at a fresh beginning, and maybe with everything new that was happening she could forget, just for a bit, the role she had played in her mother's death.

She tuned in again as Janna continued, 'But it's about time I found a ghost with useful information. I'm tired of talking to ghostly numbskulls.' Janna twirled, sniffing the air. 'Come on ghosties, bring me one with an interest in current affairs.'

'Dr Scott thinks Howie is having dreams about a terrorist.'

Janna spun towards her. 'Honestly? That's great! No, I mean that's horrible, but it means we can be useful.'

'Yeah, but he's dreaming about a dragon and I'm damned if I can see how that fits together.'

'The trouble is Howie sees everything in symbols.' Janna paused, then went on, 'I hope they're right. This school will be sunk in the water if we don't find something soon.'

Alpha recalled the conversation she'd overheard in the train. Now Janna was confirming that the school was in trouble. She mulled over this, feeling the first stirrings of concern, and was startled when Janna suddenly switched the conversation.

'You read minds, don't you?'

'Uh… yes,' said Alpha. 'But Dr Scott warned me not to look into anyone's mind. He said we all need our privacy.'

'Stuff that! When I find another ghost, you can check it out too; it'll be great if you can confirm what's really going on inside my head.'

As much as Alpha resented not having free reign with her own talents, she was reluctant to disobey Dr Scott this early on. 'The rules…I'm not supposed to...' she said, half-heartedly.

Janna snorted. 'Rules schmules… designed for fools. Anyway, I want to find a ghost who can tell us more about Howie's terrorist attack. Some of them are very nosy about the future. Let see who's out there now.' She closed her eyes and dropped her chin to her chest.

Alpha felt a peculiar reaching then, as though Janna's energy was trying to drag her in. Janna drew her jacket tight around her and called out, 'You're not close enough, I can't hear you.'

'What are you doing?'

'I asked if there were any spirits here who could tell me about Howie's terrorists. I can sense one close by, but it can't reach me. I don't get it! Normally I'm a real ghost magnet.' Janna stuck out her arms like a zombie and began walking back up the drive towards the house. 'It's stronger in this direction.' When she reached the portico over the hall doors she stretched up and placed her palms against the stone as though appealing to some unseen entity. But the building kept its secrets and finally Janna turned away in exasperation. 'This one isn't ready for me yet. Damn!'

CHAPTER ELEVEN

The next morning Alpha hurried across the courtyard into South Block. She climbed the stairs and stood at the door to Mrs Hickelroy's office, waiting for the vice-principal to look up. The woman was nibbling on the end of a pen, deep in thought, but when she noticed Alpha, she put her pen down and hurried over to her. 'Good morning Alpha. I've finished your programme—give me a second to find it amongst this clutter on my desk. Take a seat.'

Alpha stared at the desk that seemed remarkably organised to her, and was as far removed from Janna's layers of clutter as it was possible to be. Then, not wishing to be rude, she withdrew her gaze to stare out of the window at the woods.

Her eyes swung back to Mrs Hickelroy when the vice-principal waved a printed schedule in the air.

'Here it is.' Her beauty dimmed a little as a frown crossed her face. 'There are a couple of issues I must bring up with you.'

Here we go! thought Alpha. Rules of the establishment.

'First, make sure you don't say anything about telepathy to the regular teachers or the staff,' said Mrs Hickelroy. Alpha blinked. *I haven't heard that one before.* 'They believe that the school is an educational experiment—and that our role is to develop superior thinking skills—rather like breeding super-kids with super-brains. I'm not asking you to lie, only to avoid any mention of psychic abilities… you understand? The fewer people who know the true nature of our work, the better for us all.'

Alpha doubted that any teacher in the world was going to find her super-gifted, but she nodded. 'No problem. I'm used to not talking about that part of me.'

'I'm glad,' said Mrs Hickelroy, standing then moving closer to Alpha by perching on the edge of her desk. 'Now on to the second point, the matter of communication with the outside world. I'm afraid we don't allow mobile phones at school. We're not trying to isolate you from family or friends, it's just that mobiles interfere with our exercises at times.'

'OK.' *I won't mind that,* Alpha decided. *I wasn't planning on texting Lauren or anyone else for that matter.*

Mrs Hickelroy's face cleared.

Maybe she was expecting me to argue with her.

'But I want you to feel at home here,' Mrs Hickelroy continued. 'You can get onto the web anytime you want in the student lounge which has full-fibre Wi-Fi, and you can make private calls outside of school hours over there.' She gestured towards a bank of mobile phones opposite her office.

'I won't bother,' Alpha told Mrs Hickelroy. 'I don't text anyone much.'

Mrs Hickelroy looked at her sharply, evaluating the comment. Alpha knew that she'd picked up more than Alpha had intended, and had understood that Alpha hadn't made any real friends over the last few years.

'Well then, it's a good thing you're here—we're a happy bunch. No one's going to eat you, even if the bad news is you've got triple languages later this morning.' She leaned forwards and patted Alpha on the shoulder. 'You haven't met Mr Thom yet, have you? Come on. I'll take you down and introduce you.'

As Alpha walked with the vice-principal she felt an unexpected warm glow inside. She wasn't used to kindness. Mrs Hickelroy chattered on about Mr Thom, explaining how delighted Dr Scott had been to find a teacher as qualified as Mr Thom. 'He's travelled the globe from the Himalayas to the Andes, living with Buddhist monks and mountain tribes. He's a T.I.—a Telepath— just like you, as well as a master of meditation, healing, and aura management.'

She seemed very impressed with Mr Thom's abilities. Alpha listened intently, barely noticing where they were going until they reached Mr Thom's classroom in the bottom corner of South Block. The door opened just as Mrs Hickelroy's hand swung towards the doorknob.

'Ah! Mr Thom, meet Alpha. Alpha, this is Mr Thom.'

Alpha came face to face with the man she's seen at dinner sitting next to Dr Scott. To her surprise, he was only a fraction taller than she was.

'Come in,' he said in a baritone voice that seemed far too deep for the size of his lungs. The harsh neon light gave his shaved head and lined skin a ghoul-like pallor. Her glance slid away from his stern face only to see Sunday, standing in a plastic bath filled with ice, wearing nothing but a swimsuit. Sunday's face was screwed up—he looked like he was in a lot of pain.

His feet must be frozen, she thought, cringing as she watched Mr Thom pick up a jug of ice from the bath and pour it over Sunday's head.

Sunday however, seemed undaunted. He wiped the water from his eyes, blinked, and grinned when he spotted Alpha. 'Mr Thom is showing me how to get warm without a blanket in case I have to sleep in the street again.'

'Don't worry Sunday. There's no chance of that.' Mrs Hickelroy ruffled Sunday's wet hair. 'We're going to take very good care of you.'

Sunday shrugged and rubbed his arms vigorously. Alpha sensed the unpleasant memories of cold nights and lack of food that had haunted him. 'Bad things happen,' he muttered.

'They don't here!' said Mrs Hickelroy.

Mr Thom tossed Sunday a towel. 'You've lost control, Sunday, it's why you're shivering. All right, that's enough for now, but practice every day.' Then he folded his arms and remained silent as Sunday stepped out of the bath and briskly rubbed himself down.

Mrs Hickelroy stepped into the silence to explain. 'Mr Thom is teaching Sunday to raise his blood pressure to fend off the cold.' Then she began to question Mr Thom on a technical detail about the new computer system.

Alpha tuned out and let her gaze wander round the bleak room in an attempt to give Sunday some privacy. Mr Thom's classroom was nothing like Lily's, with its comfortable seating arrangements and its myriad of plants. Instead, it contained several long tables, a few hard-backed chairs and a large ebony desk from his past travels, etched with carvings on its legs and sides of strange half-animal masks and of people with sticks through their tongues or large disks inserted into their earlobes.

She quickly turned away. One wall was covered in posters showing segments of the brain. Several photographs of real brains were included amongst these. Alpha looked at these carefully. To her, one or two brains seemed shrivelled, or misshapen. She moved on to another picture that showed a small girl smiling serenely as Mr Thom inserted a metal probe through her eyelid and into her head. Alpha's blood ran cold. *He'd better not try anything like that on me!*

Having dried himself Sunday came up to Alpha and grabbed her hand. His fingers were surprisingly warm. 'I can't feel you in my head anymore,' he moaned.

She didn't know what to say. This didn't trouble Sunday. He squeezed her fingers. 'I'm glad you're here.'

Now that I've met Mr Thom I'm not so sure that I am.

———

After lunch Alpha saw that her programme had her down for a lesson with Lily. This would be her first taste of psychic schooling and she could feel the excitement bubbling in her stomach. She left the dining hall, edging across in the corridor to allow Rhodene to pass by her. But Rhodene started crowding her and suddenly she was stumbling into a disused storeroom as the door on her left gave way. Rhodene shoved her into a corner. She slammed the door shut with her foot, pushing Alpha to the floor and pinning her down.

'Where's your bloody phone?' Rhodene muttered, her fingers burrowing into Alpha's jeans. 'You can't have surrendered it yet.'

If it hadn't been for Rhodene's elbow grinding into her neck Alpha would have smirked. She hadn't had any use for a mobile in years. But then Rhodene yelped as she scratched her finger on the pin brooch in Alpha's jacket.

Shit, I can't let her take that.

Before her mind-thrust could reach the inside of Rhodene's brain the door flew open and a dash of red flew into the room. Alpha's bemused gaze finally steadied on Janna's hand. She was gripping a metal pencil, pointy end dangerously close to Rhodene's eye, while her other arm encircled Rhodene's neck with considerable force.

'Leave her Rhodene! None of your tricks, or the eye pops,' Janna said, her voice low and cold. Rhodene complied pushing herself up by placing a hand on Alpha's stomach. Janna kneed Rhodene in the backside, thrusting her out of the door.

'Thanks,' said Alpha, shakily.

Janna helped her up. 'Keep your eyes open. I've got to run now.'

CHAPTER TWELVE

Still deeply unsettled, Alpha knocked lightly on Lily's door. As though anticipating her knock, Lily flung it open. She beamed at Alpha. 'Come in. We're going to have some fun.'

Alpha ducked as Lily looked set to hug her again, but instead, Lily extracted a set of keys from around her bust and tripped over to a row of cupboards lining one wall. 'Let's see if I have anything here to help you focus that prodigious talent of yours.'

She pulled out a set of panpipes and began to blow a haunting melody, her fingers shifting delicately up and down the reed stems. Sadness swept over Alpha—Mum was always playing miserable tunes on her piano while Dad was away. This one was something special—though very beautiful it had the ability to turn the whole day grey. That was one of the reasons Alpha barely listened to music of any kind anymore.

Lily shook her head. 'No, that's not doing it.'

She watched, mesmerised, as Lily seemed to dance across the long row of cupboards, her hands hovering over drawers and shelves before moving on in an unpredictable fashion. One hand stopped near a high cupboard and Lily pulled over a small stepladder to reach into it, extracting, to Alpha's amazement, what appeared to be a dried lizard skin of the most enormous size.

'Komodo dragon,' said Lily, waggling one clawed foot at her. 'Deceased, of course.' Halfway down the ladder she changed her mind, reversed her step, and shoved it back into the cupboard again. 'Not in fashion these days, I think. And a bit hard to carry around with you.'

Finally, following a lot more deliberation, Lily unlocked a drawer containing a tray of gemstones. 'Come over here. Hands out, palm up.' Lily held each stone above Alpha's hands. After a while Alpha realised that many of the stones were having a physical effect on her. A piece of rose quartz buckled her knees, a bit of flint made a burning hole in her middle, turquoise made her cough, and a red fire opal created a spot of light on the inside of her eyes.

By the time Lily had opened eight more draws and run dozens of stones across her hands, Alpha had begun to feel really uptight.

'Relax,' Lily said. 'You're getting some strong reactions. We'll find something useful soon.'

The next stone was a flat bit of porphyry, which made Alpha think of a holy relic, but agate, onyx, and basanite all had no impact. The final stone in the ninth tray was rounded to an egg shape. At first glance it seemed a shiny black but, as the light struck it, she saw slivers of midnight blue streaking through it.

As Lily raised it over her hands Alpha's fingers began twitching of their own accord. Lily dropped the egg neatly into Alpha's left palm and she closed her fist around it.

'Well?' Lily asked.

'It feels … weird… it's warm and comforting like it can sort of... protect me.'

Lily was pleased, which she demonstrated, to Alpha's dismay, with a tight squeeze, leaving Alpha struggling for air. 'The blue tiger's eye will magnify your abilities. It's unusual, the more common form is brown, but only the blue has protective properties. For now, just keep it close.'

Once released from Lily's grip, Alpha looked at Lily hesitantly. I'm not allowed to read her mind; I'll have to ask. 'About Rhodene...' she began.

'Is she giving you trouble?'

'Uh... not really, it's just...'

Lily shook her head, and sadness crossed her face. 'Recently she hasn't been herself. She's filled with... well let's just say she's lost herself for a while. If she gets you down let me know and I'll sort it.'

'Thanks,' said Alpha. On the inside, however, she felt less trust in Lily's abilities to curtail Rhodene's offences than in her own. Next time she'd be ready.

———

After Lily dismissed her with a smile Alpha crossed the courtyard for her next lesson. She spotted Alex dashing out of East Wing and Rhodene pounding after him. Rhodene shouted, 'come back here scudball,' but Alex had already disappeared.

Janna came out of East Wing too, giggling so hard she was almost bent over double. 'He got her good... at our IT... lesson,' she explained between explosions of mirth. 'He knows her typing skills are rubbish, so he changed the G and L around on her keyboard... on the test she keyed in Mr Leek's name... it came up as... Mr Geek.'

Alpha recalled the tie-wearing, precisely parted, shiny-booted Information Technology teacher she'd met the other day. She guessed he wouldn't have liked that at all. She grinned. Between them, Alex and Carl had a real talent for mischief.

'What's your next lesson?' asked Janna, making an effort to gain control over the blasts of laughter still erupting from her mouth.

Alpha consulted her programme and pulled a face. 'Music.'

'That's all right then. Miss Finkle won't miss you: whenever we bunk off she thinks the VIPs in South Block are conducting a frightfully important experiment on us. Come on—I've got NEWS for you.'

Intrigued by the emphasis Janna was placing on the word, Alpha allowed herself to be led down a flight of concrete stairs into the East Wing basement.

Janna leaned against the musty-smelling wall and began chewing at a loose nail.

'Get on with it then. What's this hot news?'

'It's you! You're the hot stuff around here—Lily and Mr Thom both cornered Mrs Hickelroy this morning, fighting over which one of them gets to teach you.'

'How do you know?'

'I was phoning home from the booths when they both marched into Mrs Hickelroy's office. It's my mother's birthday, and I sort of felt I had to. After the call I hung about in the corridor listening.' Janna's chin went up in a determined tilt. 'Well, I wasn't going to waste that opportunity, was I? Even if I did get double detention for being late for English.'

'And…?'

'Oh! Well, Lily said that if you're going to be delving into Howie's brain you'll have to work under her because Howie's her student, but Tinky-Tiny-Thom wants primary responsibility for you because you're a T.I. and he's the telepathy teacher.' Barely pausing for breath she went on, 'Lily's my mentor, I'm glad I got her. I don't get on with Mr Thom. He says I make up some of my ghosts—the idiot. Martel's his student, he says Thom's OK. He would. Have you seen that desk of Thom's? He says it was a gift, but if someone had given it to me I'd have burned it when they weren't looking.'

Alpha felt a cold breeze run across her shoulders and down her back. It could have been the draughty basement, but she was much more inclined to think it was the mention of Mr Thom, with his metal probes and his icy water treatments, that had caused her to shiver. 'So what did Mrs Hickelroy say?' she asked, praying that Mr Thom wasn't destined to be her mentor.

'I don't know,' Janna admitted. 'The door to the office closed right then.'

Mr Thom's the telepathy teacher; I bet he knew Janna was there and got up to shut the door.

CHAPTER THIRTEEN

After dinner Alpha went up for a shower. She'd arranged to meet Janna in the student lounge at eight-thirty, but the first thing she saw when she opened her door was Sunday, bottom up in the air, head peering under her bed.

'What…' she spluttered as he surfaced.

He grinned. 'Hello. I've been waiting too long for you.'

'Why… what are you doing in my bedroom… no… don't answer that… just get out.'

Instead of removing himself, he rolled over, then sat up resting his back against her bed. He pulled an apple from his pocket, rubbed it against his shirt and took a large bite. 'You haven't got too many things, have you?'

'Have you been looking through my stuff?'

'Yes,' he nodded, with disarming honesty. 'I found this in your jacket.' He held out the pin-brooch made of jade.

'That's mine.' She grabbed at it, but his quick hand pulled away.

'Eh! I wasn't going to steal it!' He sounded offended at the idea. 'It reminds me too much…' He peered at it once more, then handed it back to her. 'Do you have any nail polish remover?'

Gripping the brooch securely she glanced down at her bare and chewed fingernails. 'What would I do with that? And what do you want it for?'

Before he could answer, without intending to, she found herself inside the limbic region of his brain. *Not again—I've got to stop hanging out with these telepathic types.* This sort of thing seemed to happen far too often when two T.I.s got together, so she was much less shocked to find herself in Sunday's head than she had been when Dr Scott's mind had drawn her in.

But unlike Dr Scott's tidy mind, Sunday's resembled a bowl of Rice Crispies: memories and thoughts went snap, crackle and pop as they flared into existence before disappearing as new ideas hopped into his brain. Before she could make the smallest move to extricate herself one of his memories kicked into action right on top of her, placing her bang slap in the middle of it…

… Sunday had been cold, so cold he'd lost the sensation in the ends of his fingers. He moved the sailcloth away from the layers of cardboard that covered him and served as his bed. As he lifted it the tough fabric disintegrated into pieces. Sunday made a tchlocking sound with his tongue against the roof of his mouth and reminded himself, 'New sail. Must steal one today.'

Sunday knew there was little as good as sailcloth for keeping the cold and the wet from street children—but he also knew that it wasn't going to be easy. Very few boats moored in the harbour in Durban these days, and everyone watched their belongings much too closely.

'How is a small Zulu warrior supposed to get through the winter if he can't steal what he needs?' he grumbled…

Horrified by Sunday's former life, Alpha remained glued to this image as that memory dulled and another sparked in its place… It was night. Sunday hung from a third-floor balcony, waiting for the lights in the room above him to go out. As soon as they were switched off Sunday pulled himself onto the balcony and pushed open the sliding door. Too much stupid—because their room is on the third floor they think the balcony is safe. But the occupants of the room weren't all that stupid. They'd taken their money and had locked the hotel safe before going to eat in the restaurant. Nevertheless, there were valuables: he collected a suit that he knew he'd get a good price for and was delighted to find a can of hairspray, almost full.

Having reached the safety of ground level again, a few minutes later he traded three sprays from the can for the loan of a fire, and sat down next to Mbo. When the can was good and hot he sniffed the rest himself. Slowly his body warmed, his brain went fuzzy, and he fell into a deep sleep.

He dreamed… Alpha, lost in the depths of his memories, followed him into his dream… Four young Indian men were sitting in a pub, minding their own business, daring each other to buy the first forbidden alcoholic drink. But the group around them turned ugly, and they chose to leave. The crowd followed them, streaming onto Marine Parade. Sunday felt the crowd's ugly intentions; they were going to beat up the four young men. He awoke, shouting…

… and found that he'd walked down to Marine Parade in his sleep. There, in front of him, were the young Indian men and the vicious group that had been in his dream. Sunday was inside all their heads at once. 'Run,' he screamed to the Indian lads. 'Run for your life.'…

Sunday's memories jumped to the next morning, carrying her with them… He wasn't sure if these intruders in his head were real. He looked for Mbo, sure that the elder boy could help. The Sotho teenager knew many things and had guided him in the ways of the street since he'd come to live here. 'Do you dream of people when you sleep, then find out their voices are too much real?' Sunday asked, unsure whether he was going insane, or if this was something everyone felt when they grew up.

Mbo laughed. 'Mad dogs and Englishmen go out in the midday sun, but only young black boys hear voices in the night.'

Sunday tried to shake the dream out of his head…had he really been trying to warn those Indian guys or was that a dream of a dream?

His memories flipped again, returning Alpha to the morning when he'd planned to steal sailcloth… It was a long walk to the harbour, and he warmed up a lot on the way. When he reached the palm-lined avenue he sat on the esplanade overlooking the yacht mall. Those rich people could easily buy a new sail, it was no bother for them, though it was going to be a great deal of bother for him to escape that security guard and his dog.

A heavy hand settled on his shoulder, and he looked round expecting to see an officer-of-the-law. But the face looking down at him didn't belong to the police. It wasn't even a man. It was a beautiful woman, wearing a furry hat. In Sunday's experience, white women didn't make a habit of coming up to talk to street boys. His eyes sparkled and he began his begging routine. 'Please missus, give money for food. I'm so hungry….'

'Shut up and listen. My name is Mrs Hickelroy. If you do exactly as I tell you, you'll have food enough for six, warm clothes, and even a bath if you want one.'

There were plenty of bad things that could happen to small boys who went off with strangers, but Sunday reasoned that if he had to he could run much faster than this woman, even though she had long legs encased in black stockings. The more he studied her, the more she seemed quite magical, dropping out of nowhere to offer him the most wonderful opportunity. Imagine that, enough food for six.

He smiled, and his tongue poked through the gap in his teeth. 'Yes, missus. And can I have a hat like yours?' he said, pushing his luck.

'Very possibly Sunday,' she told him, before ushering him into the taxi that would take them to King Shaka International Airport, where a plane waited to whisk him out of Africa, to Krakow Bond…

———

Alpha returned to her own body to see Sunday kneeling in front of her wearing a puzzled look. 'Why can you go into my head, but you don't want me in yours?' he asked.

'I… I didn't try to reach for your thoughts. Your memories rushed at me.' Her knees had turned to water, and she fell sideways onto her bed.

A few seconds later, when she felt less faint, she looked up to see that Sunday was still there. 'Were you looking for nail polish remover to sniff it, like the hairspray?' she asked.

Sunday's dark skin flushed with colour. 'Yes, or magic markers … anything like that. Dr Scott made me promise not to do it again, but I thought if I sniffed something belonging to you I would find the inside of your head again.'

'I don't want you in my head. Anyway, those things are drugs, Sunday.'

'I know. Before, when I sniffed the strong stuff, I had too many blisters in my nose.'

She stared at the small boy sharing his secrets with her. His background was horrifying; she couldn't throw him out now. 'You've got to stop—it's dangerous.'

He nodded. 'I saw my friend Mbo die after he sniffed butane.'

She felt tears prickle behind her eyelids. *That must have been awful—like the day she came home from school and found Mum dead.* She blew her nose then said, with all the authority she could muster, 'You mustn't sniff anything, your lungs will be poisoned—you'll die, horribly!'

Sunday extricated a crumbling cheese sandwich from the inner regions of his shirt and concentrated on munching it, as though dying was not something to be overly concerned about.

'I'll know if you sniff again Sunday. I'll tell Dr Scott,' she said, fiercely.

This threat proved more effective. Sunday threw up his hands. 'Don't tell him. Mrs Hickelroy makes me clean the toilets when she is disappointed with me, but Dr Scott will send me back.'

She nodded. She didn't think Dr Scott would do that, but the idea scared Sunday. Clearly he didn't want to return to his previous life on the street, and no wonder. *And if that doesn't work I'll change his mind forever. I'm damned if I'll let him harm himself; he's had a tough enough time already.* 'Why aren't your parents looking after you?'

'I never had a father; that no-good disappeared before I was born.'

'What about your mother?'

'She died from slims last year.'

'Slims?'

'Most people call it AIDS. But back home, everyone knows that it makes you too much too thin and then you die. So after that, I had to live on the streets. I was happy when Mrs Hickelroy rescued me; she's my Bolla.'

To Sunday, Mrs Hickelroy must have been like a guardian angel. *Thank goodness she'd found him.*

Alpha had no idea why Sunday's plight should tug at her so strongly; no one else had moved her like this since Mum had died. Tentatively she stretched out a hand. Sunday grabbed it and bobbed upwards. He joined her on the bed, spilling happiness, and it felt as though he was welcoming home parts of her that had been lost for years.

They sat together, a cosy warmth spreading between them until Sunday said, 'a bad thing happened to your mother.'

She shuddered. Unbidden, the moment when she'd decided to stop her mother drinking relived itself in her mind. She'd found a trigger in the form of a smell, a lovely memory her mother had of her father smelling of sandalwood and buttered toast. She'd played with this thought until she'd grasped hold of her mother's deepest wish—then she'd forced her mother to believe that if she drank one more drop of alcohol she would never meet her husband again on the far side of death.

The mind change was a bitter success. Her mum decided that she couldn't live without drinking so, while Alpha was at school, she took all her sleeping pills at once, washing them down with milk.

'I murdered her,' Alpha whispered. She began to sob, unsure whom she was crying for—Sunday, her mother, or herself.

Sunday blotted her tears with his thumb. 'No! She killed herself and she left you alone. At least my mother didn't want to leave me. It was too much your mother's fault, not yours.'

Alpha looked up at those words and saw Sunday smile into her eyes. *Not my fault?* Sunday was blaming her mother, not Alpha herself. *But it was my fault—I made her stop drinking.*

'No,' said Sunday, shaking his head vigorously. 'Your mother chose to leave you, she could have stopped drinking by herself, she should have stayed to look after you. It doesn't matter that you convinced her to stop her drinking. It was too much her decision to die, not yours.'

For years she hadn't dared to tell anyone the secret of her mother's death, and it had festered away inside, her guilt growing greater every day. Now Sunday somehow knew what had happened, what she'd done. Even though she hadn't spoken, he'd heard her thoughts. And he wasn't blaming her. The weight of her guilt began ever so slowly to ebb away, and she felt a tiny release of the tension she didn't realise she's been carrying around for years. She'd never stop blaming herself, but the burden had somehow eased, if only very slightly. Tears dropped, and she scrubbed at them and gave a small hiccup.

Most people drained her—but unbelievably, this small Zulu boy had given her a modicum of peace. Not forgiveness—no! She would never be able to forgive herself. But ever since her mother's death her pain had been sealed in tight, never to be revealed to anyone; now she unlocked her emotions as she let Sunday into her heart.

CHAPTER FOURTEEN

No time for a shower. Instead Alpha vigorously washed all signs of tears from her face. Compared to the cheesy odour steaming out of Sunday's socks no one will notice my slightly unwashed smell. She giggled, feeling laughter creep into her bones for the first time in a very long time. Everyone had their personal quirks and Sunday's, it seemed, was that he didn't see the need to change his socks every day. He'd waited for her in her room, lolling about on her bed, so that he could show her the way to the student lounge.

The lounge was gigantic, holding every kind of entertainment a student could possibly want. Martel was hanging out on one of the sofas, his legs stretching out well beyond the end of the cushions, earphones shutting everyone out. Alpha noticed that the tension had left his shoulders and he seemed totally chilled—a dark Adonis, showing no signs of his snake nickname. Carl and Alex were playing table tennis and Howie was sitting on a stool at the juice bar with Janna, near the bowling alley. Alpha was pleased to see that there was no sign of Rhodene.

Janna rose to meet her. 'There you are. I thought you'd decided not to come. Hi ya, Sunday. Want to pin bowl?'

'Uh uh,' said Sunday, catching sight of Howie, whose hands were delving into his pockets. 'You play with the balls that are too big. Howie's got his cards. I'll play poker with him.'

'He can play poker? I didn't think Howie could even hold a deck of cards,' whispered Alpha.

'He's too much clever… but he makes the cards all yuck by licking them. He doesn't talk, but he wins even when I cheat. Don't you Howie? It's my turn to win today.'

Howie didn't respond except to begin shuffling the cards with surprising dexterity. Alpha and Janna left them to it and walked over to the two bowling lanes.

As they neared the end of their game Alpha realised that she was enjoying herself, even though Janna was a far better bowler than she was. Janna completed a smooth delivery, knocking down all but one of the pins. Then, under her skilful handling, the last pin tumbled as her second bowl unerringly hit its target. She swiped her hands together: a gesture she used, Alpha noticed, when she was pleased with her shot. 'It's great to play again, I haven't had a match in ages.'

Alpha watched her own bowl slide hopelessly towards the gutter. 'You don't mind that I'm so bad at it?'

'You'll get better with a bit of practice; you've got a good swing when you concentrate. Take your time.'

Six pins dropped on Alpha's last bowled ball.

'See,' said Janna, as the remaining pins were removed. 'OK, game over. Let's get juice from the bar.'

At the bar, Howie was still dealing the cards and Sunday was pouring himself a glass of cola. As Alpha drifted over to the bar, Martel came up behind Sunday and touched the cards that were face down on the table.

'You're going to lose,' he said to Sunday.

'Again?' He puckered his upper lip. 'Aieee! Howie. You're too much lucky.'

Martel tickled Sunday's neck. 'It's "too lucky" not "too much lucky."'

Sunday squealed, then extended his hand.

'Huh!' grunted Martel in satisfaction. 'Giving in so soon. OK, shake on it.' He stopped tickling and took Sunday's hand instead, and the two of them shook hands with an odd series of twists, changing grip several times with flawless ease.

Alpha could feel the warmth flowing between them. Whatever she thought of Martel, there could be no doubt that he was very close to Sunday. Martel was treating Sunday like a big brother would: one who cared about his little brother a great deal.

After this elaborate performance Sunday smiled, then said wickedly, 'I make you a deal. When your Zulu is too much good like my English, I say too lucky, not too much lucky.'

Martel gave a bark of laughter and pulled his hand away to poke Sunday in the ribs. Then he looked up and his face went taut as he saw Alpha watching.

Janna gripped Alpha's elbow and made a pantomime of sniffing the air. 'Let's go and look for my ghost; the air's a bit foul in here.'

'Wait for me,' called Sunday, scampering behind them. 'I've given up trying to beat Howie at cards. He's too much clever.'

Alpha looked back, catching Martel's sharp and piercing stare which was directed straight at her. It felt like the cut of a sabre.

Once outside, the three of them circled the house, passing between the East Wing and the stable block through an extensive vegetable garden. Janna trailed one hand along the walls as she walked, complaining all the while that her ghost had disappeared, while Sunday stepped along the sleepers retaining the vegetable beds, pretending to be a tightrope walker.

Halfway down the wing Alpha saw the large-boned woman in scarlet overalls who'd been at dinner with them. She had her back to them and was waving a watering can over one of the beds—a sergeant major in charge of her troop of plants.

Janna ducked behind a long row of sheds. 'Over here, quick!'

'That's Miss Gilford, the chief gardener,' she explained to Alpha, when they were safely hidden by the sheds and far enough away not to be overheard. 'She'll be mad if she finds me here again, she went ballistic when I dug up a few carrots.'

'She's been at Krakow Bond too much long—before the school moved in,' said Sunday.

'How do you know that?' asked Janna.

'She's got photographs in her bedroom of herself in the garden with lots of other people who are not here now.'

Janna glanced at him, admiringly. 'How did you get into her bedroom?'

'It was easy. Piece of sponge cake. She doesn't bother locking her door.' His words must have reminded him of food because he fished in his pocket and recovered a lint-covered biscuit, which he then stuffed into his mouth.

Janna gave a burble of laughter. 'You little tea leaf.'

'I am not a tea leaf!' said Sunday, chomping down hard on his biscuit. 'Tea leaves are small, pointy things, with their sap dried out. Me—I am a strong warrior with Zulu blood.'

'She means a thief,' Alpha explained. 'Tea leaf rhymes with thief.'

Sunday brightened and stuck out his chest, obviously much happier with this description.

Janna glanced at Alpha over Sunday's head, her lips twitching in amusement. 'So where else…' she began, but the sound of footsteps startled her to silence. The footsteps grew closer. Rhodene stepped round the corner of the sheds, failing to notice them because she was looking back over her shoulder.

'Here comes trouble.' Janna bulked up her shoulders, filling the path with her presence. But Rhodene, after her initial shock at seeing the three, simply barged past Janna and hurried towards the front of the house.

'Did you see that?' Janna demanded. 'She didn't even say excuse me.'

'To be fair, there would have been plenty of room for her to get past you if you hadn't been standing in the middle of the path,' said Alpha.

'Oh that!' Janna waved away the objection. 'Didn't notice I'd grown so much bigger. You know what it's like at this time of a girl's life, we're bulging out in unexpected places.' As she spoke she snapped the elastic of the spare bra that Alpha had lent her, and Alpha noted that, with the addition of a couple of pairs of socks, she had indeed expanded considerably.

'Yeah,' said Alpha. 'You've grown sixty centimetres rounder overnight in your upper measurements.'

They shared a giggle, while Sunday, uninterested in the delicate nature of female underwear, rummaged in his pockets for tastier delicacies.

'Get out of here!' a voice boomed behind them. 'This area is out of bounds to school children.' The three turned as one, to discover Miss Gilford standing at the end of the alley of sheds. The woman was so wide that her arms, placed on her hips, appeared to be scraping against each wall.

Janna called out, 'Dr Scott says we've got every right to be here. And we're not children,' she paused. 'Well apart from Sunday.'

Miss Gilford advanced, threateningly.

Janna would have stood her ground, but Sunday scampered up to the big woman before she could reach them. 'We're going,' he said. 'We just wanted to see if you were growing seeds with the new moon.'

Miss Gilford stopped, considering the small scrap of boy in front of her. 'Moon-phase-planting, you mean. Hmmm. I've been looking into that, there's quite a lot of evidence to support the idea, even though it seems like nonsense at first glance.' Trapped into discussion, much of the heat left her and she waved her watering can at them. 'Shoo! And don't come back this way. I don't hold with allowing children to wander about at all times of night. It isn't proper. Go on, get out of my sight.'

Giggling, they turned and made tracks around the southeast corner of the house. Janna patted Sunday on the back in a congratulatory manner. 'Moon-phase-planting my arse. Where did you learn about that gem?'

'Book in her bedside table,' he told her, skipping nimbly out of her way.

'You're a proper little mine of information,' said Janna. 'I don't suppose you know the security code to the gate?'

Alpha looked up quizzically.

'There's this guy I met working on the sailing boats last time we were allowed into town. He's delish!'

Sunday thought for a moment. 'I can find out.'

'Great. I'd love a bit more free time in town. He's got abs to die for.' Suddenly Janna scowled as a thought struck her. She turned to look back at the passage between the sheds and the house. 'Hey, I bet Rhodene told Miss Gilford we were there. Why else would she appear round the back of the sheds like that.'

Alpha shrugged. 'No harm done.'

Sunday had scampered ahead, but he skipped back and brushed Alpha's arm with his hand, pointing towards the lake that lay in the hollow in the distance.

They followed the direction of his finger. 'Oh ho!' said Janna. 'There's a crowd out tonight. What will her husband say about that?'

Alpha screwed up her eyes and could only just make out the identity of the two figures walking together on the shore. Dr Scott's arm was round Mrs Hickelroy's shoulder.

'She's not married anymore,' said Sunday. 'She's an empty window.'

'A widow, you mean? A woman who has lost her husband?' said Janna.

'I mean window. Since her man died, she's like a wall with a big empty hole in it, waiting for a window.'

'Ha! Did Mrs Hickelroy tell you he died, or have you paid a visit to her bedroom as well?' teased Janna.

Sunday shook his head. 'No way. I wouldn't go through my Bolla's things. Biddy told me.'

While Alpha marvelled at Sunday's strange set of ethics Janna continued to needle Sunday. 'What exactly did you have to do to get Biddy to tell you that? Blackmail her?'

Sunday tutted. 'I only asked her why she didn't bring her man with her. She told me hers was a useless good for nothing and she'd sent him packing. She didn't tell me what he was packing. So I asked what the other women had done with their men, and she told me Lily wasn't married and Mrs Hickelroy's husband was too much dead.'

Half-listening to the conversation between her two friends, Alpha watched the couple down at the lake… they'd stopped walking and seemed to be staring at the moon's reflection on the water. *I hope Dr Scott doesn't go galloping in and scare her off with a heavy dose of emotions.*

By some trick of the rolling lawns, Dr Scott's voice floated across the landscape towards the three watchers, not loudly, but perfectly clear. 'Are you ready for something more, Vicky? I know how hard it must have been to lose your husband in Afghanistan like that.'

His feelings were clear to Alpha, not only in his voice but also in his emotions that were crossing the night air to reach her. *He does know how it feels to lose someone you love. It nearly broke him to watch his twin die and not be able to do anything to help her.*

Mrs Hickelroy's voice wasn't magnified in the same way as Dr Scott's, so they couldn't make out her answer, but she put her head on Dr Scott's shoulder and left it resting there.

'I suppose how he died made it much worse. First tortured, then shot,' said Dr Scott, his voice filled with empathy. 'It must have been a dreadful time for you. Such a brave man, trying to infiltrate a Jihad training camp.' He paused, and then went on more strongly. 'Don't worry about us, I'm prepared to wait as long as it takes. And in the meantime, I'm sure we'll get results soon especially now that Alpha's joined us. We'll carry on his fight against terrorism.'

A burst of horror erupted from Mrs Hickelroy and the image of her husband leapt into Alpha's mind. He was slumped on the floor wearing an orange jumpsuit, a hood over his eyes, fingers dripping blood where his nails had been removed. A bolt of pain shot through Alpha's stomach... *No wonder she keeps her feelings well hidden. If she let those out, she couldn't possibly function normally—not after experiencing something like that.*

The image disappeared from Alpha's mind as Janna murmured, 'Jeez, what a crap deal she's had.'

It was then that Alpha realised how much it hurt to start caring about other people again—their problems pierced the armour she'd spent years building around herself. 'Let's get out of here,' she said, too filled with emotion herself to stay and witness any more.

CHAPTER FIFTEEN

Alpha peered at her programme and grimaced. Her first lesson was with Mr Thom, and she wasn't looking forward to it one tiny little bit. *If he tries to stick me in a tub of ice water, I'll throw it over him. See how he likes it.*

Mr Thom was waiting in the corridor outside his classroom. As Alpha approached he walked inside and over to the window where he drew the blinds, shutting out the best thing about the room—the view of the woods—before sitting down behind his grotesque desk.

'Take a chair,' he told her. Then he sat staring at her, his eyes twin mirrors into other worlds.

Her neck and armpits began to sweat. She couldn't find any spillage coming from him. *Nothing, nada, no emotion, not even one squeak of a single thought.*

Mr Thom was like no other human she'd ever met. She'd known people who spent very little time in the emotional zone (she hated getting bogged down in there herself) but even they gave off tiny flickers of mental energy now and then.

Risking a lot, she tried to probe Mr Thom's brain, but she couldn't squeeze a drop of information from him. That was impossible—only dead people had no leaks. Her mother didn't have any when she'd found her dead in their tiny apartment, her face all swollen and her lips blue.

'That's right, I won't let anyone inside my head. Now let's concentrate on you.' Mr Thom's flat, even tone made her sweat even more.

He handed her a book that consisted only of blocks of colour, six to a page. 'Flick through that and choose your favourite and least favourite colours on each page.'

As she followed his instructions he narrowed his eyes at one or two choices and made notes on a laptop, but when she tried to lie, choosing bright pink over bottle green as a favourite, he said at once, 'Rubbish. Don't mess me around.'

She couldn't wait to leave his classroom. He felt like a bad itch under her skin, an itch that a nasty maggoty creature might at any moment crawl out of.

———

She spent the rest of the day trying to work out how Mr Thom had known she'd lied. Obviously he'd read her mind without her knowing about it. She hardly noticed when Martel and Rhodene came across her in the great hall.

'Here comes suck-face. Let's buy her a dummy so she can practice kissing up to Sport,' Rhodene suggested, making loud sucking noises.

Martel simply passed by Alpha as though she didn't exist.

'Why don't you disappear into the woodwork like the worms you are?' suggested Janna appearing from nowhere and tucking her arm into Alpha's. They ran up the stairs together, across the arch in the hall, leaving Martel and Rhodene trailing behind them.

'Hey, what's up?' Janna asked. 'You look mizz. You're not letting the cow and the viper get to you, are you?'

'That's not why she's upset. She didn't like her lesson with Mr Thom.' Sunday's words, coming from a hidden alcove, startled Alpha.

'How do you know that?' she demanded.

Sunday whirled his finger in the air between them.

'Hey, get out of my head.'

'I'm not in your head! You're too much spitting out that feeling all over the place,' Sunday grumbled.

Alpha sighed. It was going to be impossible to keep secrets around here. 'Sorry Sunday. I'm not used to other people being able to do what I can do.'

'So what did Thom do?' Janna wanted to know. 'Once he made me wash my hair in mustard; he told me it would stop me fantasising about fake ghosts.'

Alpha shook her head in disbelief. *Mustard, cold water, and needles. The man is mad!* She shared with them the ease with which Thom had read her mind. Janna squeezed her arm in sympathy. 'He's not supposed to do that. Dr Scott will have a fit.'

———

After their evening meal—another culinary collection of wizardry—Carl and Alex beat Janna and Alpha roundly at several matches of table tennis, and all thoughts of Mr Thom slid out of Alpha's mind. But later, as Alpha lay in bed, Mr Thom's magical mind-reading act returned to keep her from sleep.

———

Her eyes flew open, the door handle was creaking. The lock rattled against the frame but held firm, denying the intruder access to her room.

'Alpha?' A whisper came through the door, followed by a querulous demand. 'Open the bloody door will you.'

Alpha breathed a sigh of relief, then slid out of bed and padded across the carpet to unlock her door. 'It's three o'clock in the morning.'

'Best time for ghost hunting,' said Janna. 'Get a wiggle on.'

Clearly Janna was a past master at escaping from the house. She led Alpha into the kitchens then slid open a well-oiled door where deliveries were made. 'No one's room is near here, so they won't hear the latches,' she explained, peering around before stepping outside. 'But keep an eye out for that Gilford gardening woman. Stupid interfering Gillybird. I swear she never sleeps'

They went through the arch, then followed an anti-clockwise route round the outside of the house, with Janna stopping every few meters to place her hands against the stone. Alpha kept patient pace with this slow progress and eventually they rounded the northwest corner. In the distance, the path lay in deep shadow as it ran on into the woods.

'There's a strong resonance here,' said Janna, tilting her head to stare up at the building, 'but I still can't make clear contact.'

Even in the sparse light of the moon, Alpha could see that, although the outer wall of West Wing was still standing firm, the doors of this wing were bricked up. She glanced upwards; broken windows in the centre of the wing glared back at her.

'Hello,' said Janna unexpectedly, breaking the silence. 'Come on, come closer.'

Suddenly Janna's body jolted like she'd been hit by a bolt of electricity, and she cried out, 'Now, Alpha! Read my mind now.'

———

Janna's tissue membrane dissolved without Alpha even needing to touch it and she passed through it into Janna's mind. Except that these weren't Janna's thoughts: they belonged to someone else, a young boy, who was stepping along in a marketplace that was packed full of bustling people. He was carrying a bolt of the finest buffalo skin and he rubbed his cheek against the fabric, relishing the smooth feel of it. Papa will turn this into oil wrestling trousers for me, he thought with pride.

The richest of colours flashed past the boy as he trod along the cobbled paths, nimbly avoiding the market wares that protruded into the narrow streets. Alpha could hear traders calling out, 'moonstone, best quality,' 'fine silk carpets,' and 'marble, we'll ship it home for you.' With practised ease, the boy swung past hordes of tourists, before making his way into a shop with a tented entrance. He stood the bolt of leather on its end in a corner of the shop, turned, and spotted his younger sister serving cups of apple tea to customers. 'Pasha,' he called out, adding additional words to his speech in a language Alpha couldn't understand, which was full of 'sss..shshs' and 'fff..tzzz.' The girl curtseyed to a woman who was fingering a pair of trousers, then backed away, coming over to the boy. Their father, a deeply moustached man wearing a fez on his head, smiled at them both before shooing them away to address his customer.

It was obvious that they now had his permission to run off and play because they skipped out of the shop and into the crowds, making their way past stunted olive trees towards the busy harbour, where several tourist boats were moored alongside the sleek yachts and ocean liners of the very rich.

Abruptly the images in Janna's head dissolved, and Alpha slid back into her own head.

———

'Sod it!' said Janna. 'Just when it was getting interesting. Something … or someone… distracted me.' She peered round, seeking the source of the disturbance but with not even a trace of a breeze, the heavy air was silent.

'Who was that in your thoughts?' asked Alpha.

'Hell, I don't know—he could have been anyone! The only thing I'm sure of is that he's dead otherwise I wouldn't have seen him. He might have died centuries ago. Time is a bit weird in the spirit world.'

'No,' said Alpha, shaking her head. 'Some of those tourists were wearing jeans and trainers. They looked current to me. But that wasn't England, was it?'

Janna replayed the encounter in her mind. 'Somewhere in the Med. Greece, or Italy maybe.'

'That little hat his father was wearing—they wear those in Turkey, don't they?'

'So if he's a Turk, what's he doing inside my head on the Isle of Wight? I'm a Tactile, not a long-distance ghost dreamer. I've got to feel things up close.' Janna puzzled over the matter then flipped her hands upwards and shrugged. 'Anyway, I'm glad you saw him too. I get totally fed up with people who think I'm making them up.'

'You mean Mr Thom?'

'Yeah! Well sort of. I mean he knows I'm legit, but he still reckons a lot of what I tell him is bullocks.' In an uncanny representation of Mr Thom's deep baritone, Janna quoted, "Now Janna, don't let your imagination get the better you." She huffed out an annoyed breath. 'That's what he said when he took a bunch of us to the Tower of London, and I saw those boys locked up in that tiny cell—you know—the princes Richard III was supposed to have killed. Mr Thom said that story never really happened, but I saw them, so someone got to them. Anyway, at least he believes I've got extra sensory perception; my mum and dad don't. They love me, but they think I'm batty. They don't have a clue about what to do with a daughter who sees ghosts.'

'That can't be easy,' said Alpha.

'When I was a kid it was a nightmare. Whenever I talked to my ghosts they used to stare at me blankly. Then I grew up and they decided that my invisible companions had gone on far too long, so they hauled me off to see a bunch of psychiatrists who wanted to lock me up. I guess that's why I became a bit of a rebel. I ran away once, spent a week at a psychic fair helping out this dodgy old faker in return for a bit of dosh and a place to sleep. But then I got bored, so I went home. Things were even worse after that. They monitored my every move. In the end, my parents were glad to pack me off to Krakow Bond.'

There was pain in Janna's voice as she spoke of her parents. Her emotions lay open, and Alpha could feel her childhood bewilderment. By not accepting Janna's abilities her parents had rejected a crucial part of Janna herself.

'I'd rather live here,' said Janna, gruffly. 'Dr Scott showed me that I'm not mad. He helped me to respect myself. It's only since I came here that I've come to terms with who I am. That's why I'm determined to find a ghost who can help the school.'

Janna's words and her emotional spillage, sunk into Alpha. Dr Scott had channelled her friend's energies, turning her from Janna the rebel-raiser into Janna the terror-tamer, though she'd managed to carry her devil-may-care attitude along with her for the ride. Janna's loyalty to the principal spoke volumes and Alpha felt a twist of pride, glad that she'd become Janna's friend. She made up her mind to help find that ghost in whatever way she could.

Janna interrupted her train of thought. 'What do your parents think of your telepathy?'

Alpha hesitated. 'They're both dead.'

'Oh shit! I'm sorry. Car crash?'

'No... My dad died when I was seven from a heart attack and my mum...' After opening up to Sunday, Alpha's guilty about her mother's death seemed to have ever so slightly lessened.

Surprising herself, she found that she could talk about it now without cringing away from her thoughts, though they still drove daggers through her. 'Mum committed suicide three years ago. She couldn't live without him.'

Janna blew up her cheeks then popped them with an explosive, 'Phew!'

'That's tough,' she added, her voice rough and gravel-like.

'It's OK.' Alpha said. Though it wasn't, not really. But... 'Being at Krakow Bond has helped,' she said.

Instead of changing the subject, as most people did when they'd brought up a topic that embarrassed them, Janna asked, 'were they telepathic too? Did they understand about your gift?'

'I never told them about it. I don't think Mum had the slightest idea, but Dad... the night he died I had this dream where he was saying goodbye, over and over again. Now I think that maybe it wasn't a dream, he was talking to me in my head.' Alpha smiled— in a strange sort of way that was a comforting thought.

'Yeah, he probably had it too... these things often run in families. I got it from my Nan... shhh! What's that?'

Janna stepped to one side, pulling Alpha flat against the wall. Then she snuck along to the southwest corner and poked one eye round it. 'I knew it, someone disturbed my contact with the ghost, and guess what? There's Rhodene, sneaking away.'

Alpha peered round the corner too. *Janna must have eyes like a hawk. I can't see a thing.* But then she noticed the dark figure, creeping away from them.

'Let's follow her and find out what she's up to,' said Janna.

'Why bother?'

'Can't resist.'

They stalked Rhodene past the end of South Block and beyond the stable rooms.

'Sheesh!' muttered Janna. 'This is the wrong side of weird. She's making her way down to the beach and she never goes there. She hates the wind, says it's bad for her skin, and it's always blowing a gale through that cove.'

Rhodene had dressed entirely in black, but had forgotten the flash of white on her trainers and that made it easy to follow her along the chalky cliffs rimming the beach. Suddenly she dropped out of sight. As they approached the edge Alpha could see that steep stairs had been cut into the hillside, and that Rhodene was making her way down these. Instead of following her, Janna directed Alpha along the cliff edge until they reached a vantage point where they could see most of the beach. Alpha noticed the flash of white halfway down the steps; Rhodene hadn't reached the bottom yet. She shivered; Janna was right; the wind was gusting up from the sea at gale force.

'Hey, that's Mr Thom.' Janna pointed to a dark shadow squatting on the beach.

Alpha stared. The figure looked more like a large rock than a man, but just at that moment the shadow moved, and she saw Mr Thom extend one hand out towards the sand. A small flame flashed under his hand, and within an instant a fire was burning like a beacon on the beach.

Janna's mouth fell open. 'How did he do that? I swear he never lit a match.'

'Maybe he'd lit it before, and it only flared up now with a gust of wind.'

'No way! That flame jumped from his hand onto the sand.'

Rhodene slid back into their view and made her way onto the beach. She caught sight of Mr Thom, stopped short, then walked over to talk to him.

'I reckon she went down there to meet him,' said Janna.

The two talked for a few moments, then Mr Thom passed his hand over the flames once more. They licked up higher and he hunkered down next to them. His hands seemed to roll around the fire, keeping it boxed in and contained, away from the wind that threatened to steal it. This time Alpha knew that Janna had been right—Mr Thom had some internal mastery over the element of fire, and was controlling that flame as though it was an obedient dog being told to sit or stand. She swallowed, feeling bile rise up in her throat. *What kind of a man can light a fire with his bare hands?*

Rhodene stood staring out to sea for a few moments, then turned and began the steep climb back up the steps again.

Janna's eyes glinted, even in the starlight. 'Come on,' she said, making her way towards the top of the stairs. 'She'll be puffed by the time she reaches the top.'

After a short wait, during which they could hear Rhodene's breathing becoming more laboured, she emerged near the top of the steps. Her face blanched as she saw them.

'Why have you been on the beach at night?' said Janna. 'What are you doing with Mr Thom.'

'None of your business. Get out of my way before I break your nose.'

'Yeah! You and whose army? You haven't got Martel with you now.'

The statement made no impression on Rhodene. Alpha was sure that whatever Rhodene had been up to, Martel knew nothing about it. So Rhodene wasn't as attached to Martel as she made out—she was keeping secrets from him.

'Get stuffed!' Rhodene's broad shoulder rammed into Janna as she climbed the last step.

Janna tottered on the cliff edge, and Alpha reached out to pull her to safety.

As soon as her feet were back on firm ground, Janna hurried after Rhodene, looking set to take her on in a straight fight.

Alpha tugged at her arm. 'Let's go back. I'm tired.' Janna turned away reluctantly. Alpha felt relieved. Rhodene's spillage was filled with fury—whatever she'd wanted this evening she'd been denied it. Tangling with her right now would be like taking on a rabid Pitbull.

CHAPTER
SIXTEEN

The following morning a note mysteriously appeared under Alpha's bedroom door summoning her to Mrs Hickelroy's rooms.

When Alpha arrived outside her office on the top floor of south block, Janna was there too. There was no sign of Mrs Hickelroy, so Alpha knocked on the closed office door. When that produced no results Janna tried the handle, but the door didn't move an inch. They stood staring blankly at each other.

Alpha felt something swish behind her, and Mrs Hickelroy tapped her on the shoulder, causing her to jump. 'I haven't unlocked the office yet. Come into my apartment, I'll pour some fruit juice.'

Mrs Hickelroy had her own private kitchenette, and her fridge housed an extensive selection of juices. She mixed up three cocktails of mango, pineapple and a squeeze of something red before adding a sprig of sugared mint. 'Try them,' she suggested, setting the frosted glasses on the table and smiling as she saw the look on Janna's face. 'It's one of my best mixes.'

Although the glass resembled a child's image of a sunset, it tasted a lot nicer than it looked. But Alpha wished Mrs Hickelroy would get on with it. She had a feeling that things weren't going to remain on this pleasant level for much longer. She was right.

'Now girls, Mr Thom tells me that you were wandering around the grounds in the middle of the night. Care to tell me what it's all about.'

Alpha looked at Janna. This was Janna's story, and she wasn't going to say anything unless Janna did.

The question didn't faze Janna at all. 'I've been following a ghost around for days; he finally got through to me—he's trying to give me a warning.'

'Oh!' said Mrs Hickelroy. 'Whose spirit?'

'A young boy, we think he might be Turkish.'

Mrs Hickelroy's head tilted, and she gave Janna a sceptical look. 'Highly unlikely here in England, don't you think?'

Janna bristled. 'He was there—I saw him and so did Alpha. She watched him from inside my head.'

Furrows creased Mrs Hickelroy's brow. 'I never doubted that you saw him for a minute, though a Turk won't be of much help to us. But Alpha! I thought Dr Scott explained that's not allowed except in class.'

'He did, but I thought he meant for privacy reasons only.'

'I invited her in, so it's not her fault,' said Janna. 'I can invite anyone inside my own head, can't I?'

Mrs Hickelroy's stern look disappeared, and she nodded amicably at Alpha. 'Ah! A small misunderstanding. I'm afraid it's not all right, my dears. It's very important that we control all mind experiments properly. Trust me, things can get completely out of hand if we don't.' She turned towards Janna. 'And Janna, can I ask you to concentrate on your schoolwork. Lily's exercises are aimed at our primary purpose—the protection of Britain. We really have to focus on that to the exclusion of everything else. I can't stress enough how important that is right now, both to our country and to the school itself.'

Mrs Hickelroy was once again emphasising that the future of the school was at stake if they didn't find something soon. Alpha felt as though she had let them down by mucking around, just like she had let down her mother, but she didn't know what to do to help.

'But that's exactly what I was doing. I was looking for ghosts who had links with terrorists,' Janna argued.

'You're not likely to find any of those here. Stick with Lily's programme, please. She'll get the best out of you. And no more late-night walks.' Mrs Hickelroy stood up. 'Now if you don't mind Janna, I'd like a brief word with Alpha before she joins you at breakfast.'

Janna paused at the door. 'Mrs Hickelroy, before you take Rhodene's word for anything you might want to ask what she was doing out at the same time as we were.'

'Rhodene?' Mrs Hickelroy looked puzzled. 'It wasn't Rhodene who mentioned your early morning stroll. Miss Gilford told Mr Thom and he asked me to deal with it.'

'Oh! OK. Well, thanks for the drink. See you at breakfast Alpha.'

Alpha nodded, then turned with trepidation to face Mrs Hickelroy.

But Mrs Hickelroy had sat down again and was smiling warmly at her. 'How are you settling in?'

Alpha shrugged. 'Fine, I guess.'

'Still finding your feet? I want you to be happy here. I'm glad you've made a friend already, but if you need any help, please come to me.'

Mrs Hickelroy seemed sincere, yet Alpha had trouble believing that she couldn't manage for herself. She'd had no one else to rely on for years now. But there might be something the vice-principal could help with. 'I know that the students end up with one of the paranormal teachers as their main mentor…'

'That's right, Lily Wade and Horatio Thom. They're both experts in their fields.'

'The thing is, I really like Ms Wade,' said Alpha, carefully avoiding any mention of not trusting Mr Thom to stay out of her brain with his metal probes.

Mrs Hickelroy frowned. 'Mr Thom is an excellent teacher. I'm sure you'll like him once you get to know him but it's early days yet. You'll be working with both of them until they've fully explored your abilities and in the meantime, you'll fall directly under my guidance. And we'll talk regularly, OK.'

Alpha nodded. *At least Mrs Hickelroy didn't say no, and I've got time to persuade her that Mr Thom wouldn't be my first choice—or even my last.*

The vice-principal seemed satisfied that she'd put Alpha's fears to rest. 'Are you sleeping well enough? I noticed that you leave your window open. Some of our students have violent night-time experiences. Dr Scott was worried that you'd be sensitive to predictive dreams; they can be very frightening—that's why he made sure you got the first tin-lined room. Workmen are lining the others over the next few weeks.'

'It makes me claustrophobic to shut it,' Alpha muttered, hoping they wouldn't force her to close the window.

'Right-O! Well, you'd better make tracks if you want any breakfast.' Mrs Hickelroy stood up.

Alpha rose too, realising that the vice-principal had only been voicing her concern and that their meeting wasn't destined for a bad ending after all. As Mrs Hickelroy escorted Alpha to the door, she brushed Alpha's dark locks away from her eyes and caught her gaze. 'Let me know if you experience any problems, will you? You're so very important to us all, I want you to be truly happy here.'

Alpha left Mrs Hickelroy's apartment feeling considerably better than when she walked in. It seemed impossible to believe that within the space of a few short days she'd already made friends and gained the trust of the adults who ran the school. Her life had turned around completely, and she felt like she was coming out of the shadows to become more substantial: no longer a wisp of smoke, but someone solid who was ready for the important task of searching Howie's mind for traces of terrorism. *Now if only the school stays open, things will be as good as they get. As good as they've ever been since Mum... No! I'm not going down that road again.*

She marched on towards the big hall, her steps filled with determination to be the best student she could.

As she approached the breakfast buffet, Janna shot her a questioning look.

'She only wanted to know how I was settling in—nothing heavy,' Alpha explained, dishing out a plate of muesli and yogurt for herself.

'Well she's not going to stop me finding that Turkish boy again,' said Janna.

Alpha grinned. 'We'll have to keep a lookout for that Miss Gilford. Doesn't she ever sleep?'

'Never!' put in Carl, helping himself to about seventeen slices of ham. 'I reckon she's a vampire, she drains the blood of humans to feed to her plants.'

Alex joined in, forming his fingers into claws and scowling fiercely. 'She's building a new vegetative species to conquer the world. Roots are going pop out of the ground and pull us into man-eating jungles. Thorns'll grow everywhere and they'll be tipped with digitalis and deadly nightshade. We'll end up as stockpiles of sap, ready for all the baby seedlings to eat.' As he spoke his fingers sank into the bacon on Janna's plate, and he redistributed a large portion of it onto his own plate, clearly hoping she'd be distracted by his diatribe and wouldn't notice.

Janna's eyes flashed. In one smooth movement she popped her plate down and wrapped herself around Alex, lifting him from the floor. 'Yeah, and I reckon you should be the first sacrifice.'

Her triumph was short-lived. Carl whirled his arms through the air as though he was conducting an orchestra and mandarins rained down on Janna's head. Some of them burst, leaking their fleshy segments onto her face.

Alpha joined the fray then, grabbing both of Carl's hands. Then her mouth dropped as a three-tiered silver fruit tray lifted from the table. It swung round Alex and Janna in an elliptical orbit, drawing ever closer to Janna's head. Alpha released Carl and dived at Janna, knocking her out of the way just before the tray would have drawn blood. The tray clattered back onto the table, wobbling madly but impressively not dropping any of its fruit.

'Less of this noise in my dining room,' demanded Chef Andreyaz, wielding a hot skillet and striding majestically across the room towards the group who had tumbled to the floor. 'You are to show appreciation for my hours of work by consuming the breaking-of-your-fast in the most orderly fashion. Is that understood? Or you will find yourselves without the dinner this evening.'

This threat was more than enough for the group to stand up, dust themselves down, salvage their respective plates, and retreat to their chairs in as dignified a manner as they could muster. Alpha was still grinning sheepishly when Sunday wandered in yawning. He glanced at the table and muttered, 'Carl, if you've taken all the ham, I swear I will send you too much nightmares for a whole month.'

Alpha finished her breakfast and hurried along to her first lesson of the day.

Both Howie and Lily were waiting for her on the sofa. She was intrigued to see how Lily was able to make Howie fall asleep on her couch with just the flick of her fingers. Also how willing Howie seemed to be to accept this treatment. Beneath Howie's closed eyelids, Alpha could see his eye muscles flickering from side to side.

But Howarth, Howie's alter ego, wasn't nearly as accommodating as Howie. 'Go away!' he mumbled.

Lily winked at Alpha. 'Watch this,' she mouthed, beginning to caress Howie's ear with a blue feather.

Howie opened one eye, then shut it again, snorting as he settled back into dream state. Howarth's deeply petulant voice rumbled out of his lips. 'I'm sleeping.'

'Not anymore you aren't!' said Lily. 'What's Howie been dreaming about?'

'Pigs trotters and porcupines, pumpkins or pillowcases. Take your choice.' Clearly, Howarth wasn't in the mood to be cooperative. Alpha was surprised to discover that Howie's alter ego had a sense of humour, even if it was a rather twisted one.

Lily wasn't giving up that easily. 'What? No blood-sucking leeches or spine-tingling cockroaches? Come on, Howarth, you can do better than that.'

Howarth snorted. 'Actually, he's dreaming of ice cream. Gallons of the stuff, and he's not even eating it. He's counting it and weighing it, the stupid tosser.'

'That's your better half you're referring to,' said Lily. 'Is that it? Really?'

'That's it. Now sod off and let me get some sleep. And take that girl with you.'

Lily sighed. 'I'm sorry Alpha. Waste of time at the moment. But he'd have told me if Howie had dreamed about dragons again. It's interesting that he knew you were here, a good sign I think. Soon he'll accept the idea of you probing around in Howie's mind.'

Alpha felt frustration seep into her body; none of this was helping to keep the school open and Mrs Hickelroy was relying on her to do her best. 'Why can't I look inside his head now?'

'Two reasons: first Howie's mind isn't like other people's, you could easily get lost in there, and second, Howarth won't be happy about it until he gives his permission. Howarth protects Howie like a father. He'll do anything to keep Howie safe. I'll wake Howie up now. No point in prolonging this.'

But just as Lily was about to snap her fingers Howarth spoke again, his voice dulled by sleep. 'Tell her... tell Alpha... watch out! HE wants her.' Howie projected a mind-numbing blast of fear at Alpha. He followed this up by showing her flashes of a shadowy entity. The shapeless, overlarge head and featureless face was even more frightening than if Alpha had seen Howie's nemesis clearly. Whoever "HE" was, Howie was terrified of him. Alpha's blood froze.

'Did you see who HE was?' Lily asked, clearly deeply disturbed.

Alpha shook her head, mutely.

Howie, once awake, said nothing, simply choosing to leave Lily's classroom and wander off on his own.

———

Later, as Alpha and Janna sat at the edge of the pool Alpha told Janna what Howarth had said.

Janna raised lazy eyebrows. 'So who exactly is it that wants you? Other than both psi-teachers and our esteemed principals: in other words the entire paranormal faculty. Have you been holding out on me? Is there a boyfriend in the picture that I haven't heard about yet?'

'No boyfriend. I've no idea who he was talking about. Lily didn't get another word out of him.' The euphoria Alpha had felt this morning with Mrs Hickelroy had now completely disappeared, sinking like water down the drain hole of her swirling thoughts. There was wrongness at the school that she couldn't put into words, as though the sun had sunk below the horizon hours too early.

'And you think it's significant because?' When she received no reply, Janna prodded Alpha who was gazing into the middle distance. 'Hello! You're not taking him seriously, are you? I mean, come on, this is Howie we're talking about.'

Janna's voice jogged Alpha from her withdrawn state to reply thoughtfully, 'So? His disabilities don't make him any less believable, do they?'

'Well no, I'll give you that. But Howie? Everything he dreams is in symbols. Lily explained them to me once: apparently, teeth falling out means someone is going to die and any vessel like a cup or a glass, represents dripping blood. Creepy huh? Leave it to Lily to work out what he means. For the rest of us less-ordinary mortals, we'd get more from smoking wacky-backy than from anything Howie says.'

When Alpha didn't reply, Janna kicked her foot. 'You're really worried?'

'Yes. It ties in with some other stuff too. First, there was that guy at the station.'

'Hold fire! What guy at the station?' Janna demanded.

'Oh! I forget you didn't know.' Alpha explained what had happened to her, adding, 'Dr Scott thought that he might not be your average paedophile, that he might have been after me for my talent. Then the first night I was here I heard voices. I thought I'd dreamed them but now I believe I was telepathically picking up a conversation between two people. They said they had to find out exactly what she could do...I think they meant me... that they had failed before, and that they had to learn more about me first.'

'Don't order a larger size in hats just yet. For my money, the guy at the station just fancied a bit of rumpie-pumpie, and those voices could have been talking about anyone.'

'True, but why would I wake up for any old random conversation?'

'Dur! Because you're a psychic, and that's what we do.'

'It doesn't work like that with me. If I listened in on everyone's thoughts I'd never have room for my own, would I?'

Janna laughed and punched Alpha lightly on the arm. 'That implies that you actually think occasionally. Why'd you want to waste time doing that?'

Alpha smiled. There was no denying it; Janna had already improved her mood by a mile. 'Are we ghost hunting again tonight?' she asked, in two minds about it because of what Mrs Hickelroy had said,

'Too right! Meet me outside at the northwest corner. 11 pm.'

———

That night Alpha crept out of the kitchen door, peering round the corner of the arch. Sure enough there was the bulky form of Miss Gilford, standing sentry on the northeast corner. She waited until Miss Gilford turned to stare the other way, then sneaked into the shadows of the shrubs. By moving cautiously and staying out of the light she reached the northwest corner without being noticed. Reluctant to go any further without Janna, she glanced at her watch. Five to eleven.

But eleven o'clock came and went with no sign of Janna, and even the dark shape of Miss Gilford disappeared as she drifted away from her post. All the lights in North Block were off now, and the front of the house lay in darkness. Alpha kicked at the path edges, lifting the neatly trimmed grass along its side, her eyes wandering over the grim-looking West Wing wall. The sliver of a moon wasn't throwing enough light to reveal much but, in the distance, she could make out the heavy outline of trees in the woods.

An owl hooted and Alpha turned, ready to go back indoors. When she retreated round the corner she heard the clip-clop of a horse behind her. She swivelled, following the sound of the hooves as they trotted, then broke into a canter. She could swear that the horse was only a few meters away, yet there was nothing to be seen. As the hooves came rattling towards her she fell back, convinced that the animal was about to step on her. Yet her eyes told her that she couldn't believe her ears.

Then the coldest touch crossed the back of her neck, swiping from right to left. She reached out to grab at it, but her hand came away empty, and her fingers felt a trace of remaining dampness.

Ripples travelled down her spine. It was all very well looking inside Janna's head and finding a ghost in there, but this was something else. She wasn't equipped to deal with ghosts. The owl hooted once more, and near the outline of the trees in the woods, Alpha saw a white light floating through the air.

As it drew closer and closer the night took on a presence of its own. It closed in around her—determined to smother her. Her throat fluttered as fear swept through her. She broke into a run, speeding back through the arch and heading for the kitchen door. The door flew open just as she reached it.

CHAPTER SEVENTEEN

Janna stepped out, and immediately covered Alpha's mouth with her hand. As a result, Alpha's scream came out only as a muffled cry.

'Quiet,' Janna hissed. 'The Gillybird's somewhere out there.' As soon as she saw that Alpha wasn't going to scream again she took her hand from Alpha's mouth and put her arms around her. 'What's wrong?' she whispered. 'You look like you've seen one of my mutilated ghosts.'

Unable to talk, Alpha could only gasp. Finally, she managed to stutter a few words. 'Invisible horse… lights… in the wood.'

'No! Come with me,' said Janna, grabbing her hand. She marched Alpha back through the arch, pulling hard because Alpha was still shivering, and her steps were reluctant. But Janna wasn't aiming for the woods. Instead, her eyes snapped upwards. She pointed towards an open window. 'That's Martel's room.'

Martel stood there, naked apart from pj bottoms, staring down at them, his mouth twisting into a mean grin.

Alpha, still pumped with adrenaline, swung round towards Janna. 'No way. It couldn't have been him. The lights were right over there in the woods.'

'He's not responsible for the lights but he's the reason you're so frightened. That's what he does. He builds up fear inside you until you think you're going to snap. That's when your heart seizes up. He's well named—snake only just covers the way he can terrify a person.'

'But he couldn't have made the trotting sound...'

To Alpha's surprise, Janna grinned. 'No, but that wasn't a ghost either. Trust me, I'd have known.'

Alpha's pulse was still beating unreasonably fast, and she could feel each beat of her heart thumping through her body. She took a few deep breaths, then a lot more, until she felt some control return and was able to look around with a modicum of common sense. She did trust Janna and if Janna was convinced there were no unearthly spirits then there had to be another explanation. 'It could be Rhodene. They could be acting as a team. Maybe they're trying to keep us from finding out about your ghost.'

'Could be, but this has all the hallmarks of someone else. Come on, let's find out.' Janna bolted away from Alpha.

Feeling immeasurably better since Janna had explained the irrational fear that had built inside her, but still unwilling to be left entirely alone, Alpha ran to catch up with her friend. Janna was no longer in sight. She had disappeared inside the long yew hedge that began near the northwest corner.

'In here, quick!' Janna reached for her arm, pulling her into a hole inside the bushes.

Seconds later two boyish voices could be heard giggling softly. Carl and Alex crossed the grass then stepped onto the path, shoving at each other in self-congratulation. 'The ice block across the back of her neck was best,' said Carl, skipping with excitement.

Alex disagreed. 'No way. Did you see how she jumped when my MP3 player whizzed past her with the trotting sounds?'

Alpha and Janna sprang out from behind the hedge and the boys tumbled to the ground under their weight.

'Thought you tricked us, did you? I'll teach you a thing or two about ghosts,' Janna told them.

Alex tore into Janna with his fist, but she had him pinned and fended off the blows easily.

Carl wriggled under Alpha's firm hold, complaining, 'It was only a joke.'

'Yeah?' said Janna. 'Well get this—any more jokes and I'll get a real ghost to tear up your magic cards. I mean it! Have you got that?'

Reluctantly, the boys nodded.

The girls released the boys and allowed them to skulk back to their rooms. 'I still can't believe I fell for that,' said Alpha.

'You wouldn't have if Martel hadn't interfered with your thinking.'

'What's he got against me?'

'Probably nothing, just the fact that you're alive is enough for him.'

A new emotion added itself to the gamut of emotions Alpha had already been through this evening—blind anger.

I've had enough—Martel needs a lesson, she decided, striding back towards the bedrooms.

'Hey, where are you going?' Janna called.

'To fix Martel!'

'Are you mad? Stop! You can't—listen, he's killed one person already. If he goes crazy he could take you too.'

Alpha swivelled. 'What?'

'Don't go near him! If he loses control…'

'Who's he killed?'

'His father. He died of a heart attack after Martel got into a rage. Quite unexpectedly. Come on… forget about him. Let's go and find us a real ghost.'

'How do you know Martel killed him?'

'His aunt believes Martel killed him; that's proof enough for me. She sent Martel a letter, I picked it up. I get these vibes… I know, Alpha, trust me, I know.'

Alpha swung back towards the open window. It was closed now, and there was no longer any sign of Martel. Though Alpha could just about feel the remains of Martel's presence like a cold leak, she turned away. Like snow in a warm hand, her anger had melted as quickly as it had flared up.

She was glad. Anger was not an emotion she experienced often. It left her feeling out of control—and she didn't like that. She tutted, annoyed with herself. 'OK, let's go find your ghost.'

Heaving a relieved sigh, Janna returned to West Wing and began stalking up and down. Finally, she pressed her forehead up against the wall. 'He's strong here, but I think there's some sort of barrier stopping him from reaching me. I've got to get closer to him and that means getting inside this wall. But there's no way into West Wing that I know of.'

'Sunday's been in there.'

'Are you sure?'

Alpha nodded. Janna wasn't the only one who could read other people's secrets. 'We'll ask him how to get in first thing in the morning.'

'Why not now?'

'It's almost midnight. He's only a boy, he needs his sleep.'

Shrugging, Janna said, 'I reckon he gets less sleep than we do with all that creeping in and out of people's bedrooms.' She looked up at the looming wall above. 'But we'll leave him be for now; we'd better crash ourselves if we're going inside that in the morning.'

Arm in arm, they plodded off to bed.

———

A dragon flew through the night—Alpha could see its eyes

beaming as it rippled across the land, coming ever closer to her. It bellowed: a thunderous noise that made her whole body quiver. She felt terribly afraid; her heart was pounding like it was trying to break out of her body.

The dragon rushed past, leaving her trembling. It was only then that she realised that she wasn't afraid for herself. She wanted to cry stop, but she couldn't speak. She turned her head to watch the long, thin body of the dragon as it vibrated forwards in slow motion. Ahead of it, on shining silver lines, lay a shape she recognised; but she couldn't find the words to name it. It was large but nowhere near as massive as the dragon, yet somehow she knew that it would slay the dragon in its tracks.

She woke up gasping for air, and her brain took several seconds to tell her that it was only a dream. She'd never experienced a dream like that before, more real than everyday life. But if it was a dream it was still streaming in through the open window. The dragon had almost drawn level with the hump. She banged her forehead with her hand, and pinched herself, checking… she was definitely awake.

All at once, she understood that this wasn't her own dream; it was Howie's. Howarth had spoken of a dragon and of the silver lines that she'd seen in her dream. That was when she grasped that they weren't lines at all, and that the dragon wasn't really a dragon. She'd worked out exactly what was happening.

Who can I tell in the middle of the night? She ran into the corridor and down the stairs, aiming for the courtyard to cross into South Block where Dr Scott slept.

But Biddy emerged from a room on the ground floor and hurried to catch up with Alpha. 'Where are you going?'

'To find Dr Scott or Lily. Howie's been dreaming,' Alpha panted, her feet still moving towards the door.

'Yes. I know. Nothing to worry about, I've just come from his room. He's settled down again now.'

'You don't understand. I know something—it was a predictive dream. I felt it.'

'Well, in that case, I'll ring the Doc. Come into my sitting room while he gathers himself over here. I'll make you a cup of hot chocolate.'

A few minutes later, Alpha was sipping the creamy liquid as Dr Scott knocked and entered, peering worriedly at her. 'Are you all right? Second-hand dreams can be worse than the real thing.'

She nodded, though she could still feel her pulse throbbing at her throat. 'It was the dragon dream. Only it's not lines Howie's seeing—they're tracks, rail tracks. And it's not a dragon—it's a train about to come off the rails.'

'Where?' the principal asked.

She shook her head. 'I don't know.' The dream was still vivid in her mind, clearer than the sight of Biddy's homely room, but she couldn't see anything else in it to identify the area.

'How's it going to happen? Who's responsible?'

She shrugged helplessly. 'There's something big on the track; I couldn't tell what it was. The train's going to smash into it.'

'Going to smash … it hasn't happened yet?'

She had to think before she could answer. 'Howie's afraid he can't stop it, but he wants to,' she said. 'It feels like it's still going to happen, but I don't know when. That doesn't help much, does it?'

'Yes, it does. Now I can prime everyone to keep an open mind for a train smash. I'll organise a meeting first thing in the morning. You've come up trumps,' said Dr Scott. 'Biddy, I think we'll get Lily to sit with Howie for the rest of the night if that's OK with you.'

'That's fine Doc. Would you like some company too, Alpha? Why don't you tuck up on the sofa here, with me?'

'Thanks,' said Alpha, extremely glad that she didn't have to be alone for the rest of tonight. Until now she hadn't realised that a nightmare could be so terrifying.

CHAPTER EIGHTEEN

The students gathered in Dr Scott's office, whispering to each other, knowing that a meeting this early had to signal something important. Mrs Hickelroy and Dr Scott stood together talking. Alpha sidled up closer to listen in.

'Surely only the Precogs need to know about the dream?' Mrs Hickelroy asked.

Dr Scott shook his head. 'We never know where the next breakthrough is coming from. Our Tactiles might sense something in the next newspaper touching session. Or the P.I.s might catch something over the airways. Anyway, I'm determined to promote a climate of openness at the school.'

Janna signalled for Alpha to join her in a corner of the room. As Alpha reluctantly moved away from the conversation between the principal and vice-principal, Janna asked, 'Where were you? I came to your bedroom at the crack of dawn looking for you. Well at 7:15 a.m. anyway, which is the crack of dawn for me. Then I went to the pool and the student lounge and all that time I swear the Gillybird's been following me around.'

Before Alpha had a chance to explain Lily and Mr Thom walked in and Dr Scott held up his hand. The room fell silent, and the teachers took the remaining seats.

Dr Scott looked round at all the students before beginning to speak. He could barely repress his excitement. 'It's the breakthrough we've been waiting for,' he confirmed, explaining that Howie had experienced another predictive dream and that Alpha had picked up the dream telepathically. 'Alpha, please tell everyone about it.'

Alpha felt like she was about to stand on hot bricks—the last thing she wanted was to become the main focus of attention. Highly embarrassed, she kept her head down and stumbled through what she knew about Howie's dream. One thought kept ringing through her mind—*all I did was leave the window open; the rest was up to Howie.* As she spoke she glanced at Howie from behind her hair in case he felt she was upstaging him, but Howie spent all his time staring at the wall, seeming not to care that this was his dream, not hers.

'It's crap! No real information,' Martel whispered to Rhodene at the end of Alpha's recital.

'Yeah, it's only Howie,' Rhodene replied, though her bottom lip was quivering.

'It's not much to go on,' Dr Scott said finally, 'but it's a lot more than we had yesterday. Now I know that it's Saturday, but we're going to spend most of the day at work.'

Collective groans followed this announcement until Dr Scott held up his hand once more and they wound down. 'Sorry, but this is important. Focus on trains in every exercise you do today, we're looking for confirmation and details to pin this down. Be particularly vigilant about any stray thoughts that drift into your minds, they may be important. Lily and Mr Thom have prepared a programme for each of you, so we'll get to work immediately. Well done, Howie and Alpha.'

Alpha looked round at the others and spotted Rhodene shooting venomous looks at her. *Why does she hate me so much?* Then Mrs Hickelroy gripped her shoulder, and she was immersed in work for the next few hours.

Mrs Hickelroy's technique involved asking an incredible number of questions while Alpha repeated over and over what she'd seen and how it felt. Yet nothing new emerged as they struggled to find an explanation for the hump on the rail tracks.

'Could it be an analogy for a bomb?' Mrs Hickelroy wanted to know.

Alpha had no idea.

'Is the train driver the hump? Had he been drinking?'

Again Alpha was stumped.

'How about another train on the line? Is that it, do you think?'

Alpha shrugged. 'I don't think so, the hump was smaller than the train.'

'What about the track itself? You said it was shining a silvery colour. Is it defective in some way?'

Alpha could only stare at her, wishing like mad that she could provide more of the answers.

Finally, Mrs Hickelroy took pity on her and said, 'I think that's all we can do for now. But don't blame yourself for a minute that we didn't get any more information. You can only see what Howie himself sees, and if his precognitive talent isn't ready to reveal any more then we're stuck until it does.'

She stood up and gave Alpha a hug. 'Well done for what you've accomplished so far.'

——

At lunch, Alpha and Janna approached Sunday and persuaded him to join the two of them in the orchard. He looked mystified at this sudden interest in his opinion though he came with them willingly enough. But once they'd asked their question about access to the derelict wing of the school he grinned widely, poking his small finger into his ear for a good scratch. 'I'll show you,' he said.

Janna bowed elaborately towards Sunday. 'Thank you oh-great-font-of-illicitly-gained-knowledge. We are forever in your debt.' Then she spoiled the compliment by adding, 'Don't eat your earwax. It's not considered polite.'

Sunday swung away from them with a rude noise.

Alpha grabbed his arm. 'Hang on Sunday, before we go I want you to explain why Martel's so friendly with you and such a bastard to me?'

Sunday gave a big, theatrical sigh. 'Do I have to say?'

'Yes, or I'll read your mind.'

'Huh! If you can.' He hesitated, then said quickly, 'It's because I'm all black on the outside, so he likes me, and he doesn't too much like the white part of himself. He'd rather be all brown. He's half Indian with a bit of Moroccan thrown in, but his father was all white. That's the problem. He too much doesn't trust white people—especially not telepathic white people.'

'Why?' Alpha demanded.

Sunday gathered his thoughts, then said simply, 'White telepaths too much remind him of his father. His father was white and telepathic and too much mean. Things get mixed up in Martel's head, and he can't separate out good telepaths from bad. Some days he hates himself because he gets his talent from his father, and he hated his father. He doesn't know whether to hate his ability because it makes him too much like his father, or whether to accept it and enjoy it. Because I am black, he doesn't get confused about me, even though I'm a telepath. I am the colour of his mother, not his father.'

He sighed, then went on. 'Before Martel's father died he beat Martel too much. And he beat Martel's mother too. Martel was six when he died.'

'Shivers!' said Janna, her face filled with horror. 'And I thought my parents were bad enough.' She paused, then asked, 'But if that's the case, why's he friends with Rhodene? She's white and she's got some kind of psychic ability. '

'Yes, Rhodene is white, but she's not a telepath. Martel doesn't feel like that about all white people—just telepaths. But he's not friends with Rhodene. Martel puts up with her,' said Sunday. 'Rhodene is like …' he searched for a word. 'A skivvy?'

'Yeah, that fits,' agreed Janna. 'But that story about Martel's father—that's extreme. It's almost enough for me to forgive him for all his crap.' Suddenly she laughed. 'Listen to me. Any more sympathy and I'll make myself puke.'

Alpha's thoughts were taking a different turn. *If Martel really hates telepathic white people—if he's killed before—I wonder what he's capable of now.*

———

Sunday's route into the West Wing unexpectedly took them into the basement of North Block. Skirting the pool, they wandered through several underground rooms laden with unwanted furniture and towering piles of boxes. Finally they came to a solid whitewashed wall. 'We're under the arch now,' said Sunday. 'Watch this.'

He pulled aside a rolled rug and clouds of dust rose into the air. Beneath it lay a wooden trapdoor that creaked as Sunday pulled it open. 'Shut it behind you,' he said, climbing down the rickety steps.

Janna clambered after him into the dark hole.

Alpha followed reluctantly, shutting the trapdoor above her. As the wood came down the meagre glow from the basement light wells disappeared, leaving them in pitch darkness. Janna screamed.

A narrow beam flickered, then steadied. Alpha saw that Sunday was gripping a torch, shining the light on the stairs so that they could descend. Once they were down Sunday lit the way ahead. They were in an under-basement passage that smelled dank and musty, as though very little air was circulating through it. Stumbling behind each other in single file, they followed the dim beam of Sunday's light. The roof was barrel-shaped, and Janna had to crouch to walk. Bringing up the rear, Alpha felt grateful that at least she was short enough to avoid bending over. But her relief was short-lived as she saw Janna drop to her knees. The passage had lowered to little more than a crawl space. Janna was giving out regular shrieks as she passed the scuttling spiders. Alpha gritted her teeth and knelt down too, feeling claustrophobia threaten to overwhelm her. The enclosed space was ten times worse than spiders. She was forced to crawl forwards on her hands and knees for several meters. Bile rose in her stomach, and she couldn't decide whether to start edging herself backwards somehow, to safety, or push forwards past Janna and Sunday. A scream rose in her mouth...

Just when she thought she couldn't take anymore, they emerged into a wider space where they could at least stand up. Alpha saw a sliver of light leaking down from above and a ladder leading upwards. Sunday climbed it like a monkey. Above him she could see the sky through the holes in the ceiling; apparently the building above this level no longer had a sound structure. But how she welcomed the open air. Then it was Janna's turn, and finally hers. At last she emerged from the subterranean levels.

In front of them lay a steep-sided rockfall formed from precariously balanced bits of plaster and larger chunks of stone, made all the more dangerous by the fillets of broken wood that were sticking out of the rubble. As they clambered across this the mound wobbled under Janna's feet, and a huge block crashed downwards, falling whiskers away from Alpha. A barrage of choking dust rose from the bottom of the mound.

'Stand still.' Sunday's voice had dropped to a low whisper. 'Otherwise too much more will drop.'

Alpha realised that they'd been climbing steadily upwards on a surface that could have collapsed at any moment. It still might. She held her breath as the dust settled.

Finally, Sunday judged it safe to move on. Following in his footsteps, they stepped cautiously until they reached a solid wall. Looking up, Alpha worked out that this was where the derelict West Wing joined up with South Block.

Janna gave a little burble of excitement, and her hand caressed the stone. 'Let's see what I've got here.' She closed her eyes.

After a while she started speaking to herself.

'Hello little Turkish guy, talk to me, tell me what happened to you and your sister Pasha.'

The hairs on the back of Alpha's neck stood up—Janna's hand was resting on the wall that linked directly to Mr Thom's classroom.

'He's here. The lad you saw in my mind before.' Janna bent her neck to look up, speaking to the air above her. 'What's your name?'

She listened. Then, in a strange lilting voice that cracked as she spoke, she said, 'Eee…waar…di.' She reached out and grabbed Alpha's hand without taking her eyes off that same spot above her forehead. 'He says his name is Iwardi,' she told Alpha, her voice returning to normal. 'At least I think that's his name, it's all I can make out from his speech. He's very agitated.' Suddenly she shuddered. 'Now Alpha. Now! You've got to see this.'

Iwardi held his sister Pasha by the hand, pulling her along the narrow lanes in frantic haste. He kept glancing back over his shoulder, his face white with terror. Suddenly he tripped over a large brass urn that went tumbling across the cobbles. The noise was even more startling as Alpha realised that the marketplace was silent and deserted. A long way away she could hear the Imam's prayer song, and instinctively she knew that everyone would be making their way towards the mosque.

Iwardi looked this way and that, searching for a hiding place. Finally he spotted one in one of the colourful walls. The gap wasn't large enough for either brother or sister but suddenly a stone flew out of the wall and fell to the ground. Iwardi pushed Pasha into the crack, ignoring her whimpering, then turned away. The stone that had come loose from the wall quivered and raised itself from the ground, floating towards the crack and jamming Pasha into the hole.

Alpha gasped. He's like Carl—kinaesthetic.

Iwardi ran on, desperately trying to lead his pursuer away from his sister's hiding place in the wall. The passage ended at the front door of a house. He banged on the door, crying out for entry into this sanctuary. But the door remained sealed, and his pursuer came up behind him. Iwardi swung round and a pot of geraniums flung itself at the man, but it bounced harmlessly off his bike helmet.

His pursuer clipped Iwardi on the back of the head, picked up the dazed boy, and dropped him into a large, wheeled case. All at once Alpha knew that feeling. She shot out of Janna's mind.

Shocked, Alpha stared at Janna. Janna was raising both hands as though to fend off a great weight coming down from above. She was panting, taking deep gulping breaths. Alpha saw her sway.

Alpha grabbed her by the shoulders and threw her weight into Janna as her friend fell back against her, collapsing at the knees. Beneath them the mound shuddered. 'Help me Sunday!'

Sunday's thin arms reached out, and he put his shoulder into the hold. Using all her strength, with Sunday's help, Alpha was able to lower Janna slowly onto the pile of rubble. Janna's eyelids fluttered, her eyes shut, and she went limp.

Alpha darted back inside Janna's head; ready to fight whatever it was that was draining her of her life force.

———

But Janna's thoughts were dulled, filled only with a deathlike desire to sleep. A mist had settled on the landscape of her mind, leaving Alpha with nothing to fight. She turned this way and that. Janna's neurons lay like clumps of dead roots to either side and she shook these, desperate to keep Janna awake.

The mist thickened and Janna fell into the deepest sleep. Surrounded by the low pulsing rhythm of sleeping brainwaves Alpha's movements slowed until she'd lost all control over her muscles. Paralysed, each pulse now forced Alpha closer towards the edge of Janna's mind.

———

Her own body jarred her back into wakefulness, and she found that she was cradling Janna in her arms.

Sunday was crying out, 'Alpha, Janna! Wake up. Are you hurt? WAKE UP!'

Janna's eyes opened, glazed and disoriented.

'I thought you said your ghosts wouldn't hurt you!' Alpha said gruffly, her hand gently stroking Janna's face.

'What?' Janna's eyes cleared and focused on Alpha's face. 'No... don't you see? Iwardi wasn't trying to hurt me, he was showing me what happened to him. He was shut in... I felt everything he did. That man hit me, no hit him, and I saw a lid close down on me/him, like a coffin. Then I couldn't breathe. But I'm fine now, it was his death I was experiencing.'

Alpha took a shuddering breath. 'That's what happened to me at the station. Iwardi was like us, a psychic, only he was kinaesthetic. He could toss things around like Carl can. It's got to be the same man. He's trying to grab psychics and cart them off in that horrible case.'

CHAPTER NINETEEN

Janna's indrawn breath whistled through her teeth, echoing the gusts of wind that were blowing in through the open roof. 'So the guy who killed Iwardi is the same man who tried to kidnap you at the station?'

'Has to be,' Alpha confirmed. Icy fingers welled up her spine and her voice came out in a croak. 'There's something else… that place where you found Iwardi's ghost… it's right next to Mr Thom's office.'

'Farting Frogspawn!' At any other time Janna's response would have been funny. 'Was it Mr Thom who stuffed Iwardi in that case?'

Alpha forced herself to remember the scene she'd witnessed in Janna's mind when Iwardi had been caught and trapped in the suitcase. She swallowed and tried to make herself sound more in control. 'No, whoever it was was a lot taller than Mr Thom. But they could be working together.'

'I'll search his desk and his bedroom,' volunteered Sunday.

Alpha grabbed him by the arm. 'No!' She could imagine the telepathy teacher's reaction if he found Sunday sneaking into his rooms. 'Let's get out of here, then we can decide what to do.'

On the return journey Alpha's stomach churned, matching her buzzing thoughts, and she hardly noticed how small the crawl space was as she navigated it on her knees. Instead of the tunnel journey repeating what earlier, had been a lifetime of hell, it felt like only a minute later before Sunday was flipping back the trapdoor. Fear of death had driven out her claustrophobia.

They clambered out. Alpha, who was next in line after Sunday, froze at what was waiting for them. Mr Thom stood there, arms folded, his face an impassive mask. But his earlobes were tinted a deep and very angry purple.

He spoke in a cold voice. 'You know very well that the West Wing is forbidden territory, but that isn't enough to stop you. So I will. You're all grounded for a month. No student lounge, no TV, no internet, and you stay in your own rooms every evening until I say so.'

'But Mr Thom…' began Janna. Alpha hushed her by standing on her toe. If there was one person she didn't want to tell about Iwardi and Pasha it was Mr Thom. She was pretty sure he knew all about them already, and was involved in the siblings' murder, but he didn't as yet know what they had learned about the dead sister and brother.

Mr Thom wasn't interested in Janna's comments anyway. 'I don't want to know. Lily's waiting for you and you too, Sunday. Alpha, you're coming with me.'

As Sunday and Janna hurried away Alpha stared at their retreating backs, feeling frightened and very much alone. Reluctantly she followed Mr Thom outside, which, to Alpha's surprise, was still bright with sunlight. It felt like a whole day had passed underground.

Mr Thom crossed the grass, aiming for the woods, covering ground with deceptive speed despite his short legs. Alpha found herself running to keep up with him when all she wanted to do was run in the other direction.

Once they'd entered the wood it cut out most of the light from the sun. Beech trees battled for space with sycamores and great oaks pushed up above them all. Alpha made out several well-trodden routes. She could hear small creatures scuttling through fallen leaves.

After walking in front of her without saying a single word for about fifteen minutes, Mr Thom turned down a steep path that carried him into a glade filled with ferns. At the bottom he bent to take a sip of water from a stream. He must have walked off some of his fury, for his ears had returned to their normal nut-brown colour.

He snorted deeply, then crossed the flowing water, stepping on the stones scattered within the stream. When he reached the middle he sat down on a boulder and looked back at Alpha, patting the rock beside him, gesturing for her to join him. 'Fresh air clears the mind and opens the psychic channels, and the water helps to neutralise bad karma,' he told her.

I wish it would neutralise you, thought Alpha, clambering across slimy rocks.

'We're going to find out how powerful you are. Dr Scott believes you're stronger than anyone else he's measured.' His nose twitched and Alpha could see that he found that difficult to believe.

Alpha squirmed, unable to find a comfortable position on the hard rock. 'Aren't we supposed to be working on the train smash?'

But Mr Thom ignored that. 'I want you to reach for Dr Scott's mind.'

'But he said I should never try to get into anyone's head.'

'Don't fret; he knows exactly what I have in mind. In fact, he's waiting for you to find him now. We're going to test your range first.'

Alpha had been inside Dr Scott's head, and she knew his thought signature. She let her mind go, hunting the thoughts that felt like a warm bath. To her surprise the blue/black egg in her pocket began to merge with her thoughts as she spun through the woods, beyond the drive, across grassy plains. It made the journey easier, and allowed her to see the route her mind was taking, which led her down the cliff face. Soon she settled on the sandy cove at the bottom of the stone steps. She tried to frame a mind-talk bubble to connect with Dr Scott but before she could ready her thoughts Mr Thom jogged her hand, demanding an answer. 'Have you found him yet?'

'He's on the beach.'

'Hmm... a range of nearly a mile. Impressive. Now shift your mind into the house. Hunt for surface thoughts only, remember we don't enter anyone's mind unless they give us permission first.'

Alpha let her mind drift again. Though the hill made it difficult, the spillage of the staff at the big house flitted through her consciousness, and she was about to choose one to focus on when she came across a very disturbed mind. Rhodene's!

Rhodene was stuffing things into a bag and her eyes were full of tears. Goodbye school! she said silently. I've lost my chance to be a psychic. I'm not coming back.

'I've found Rhodene. She's packing her bags.'

'That's ridiculous. It's not long since she finished a session with Lily. Try again.'

Alpha felt her blood boil. *How dare he suggest she couldn't read something as simple as a bit of spillage?*

'I am right—she's packing her things, and she's not too happy about doing it.' In her fury Alpha rammed through the tissue barrier of Rhodene's brain right into her mind and the first thought she found there startled her. 'She's running away!'

'What!'

'She's leaving Krakow Bond. She's determined to go, even though half of her doesn't want to.'

Mr Thom sprang up and abruptly leapt right over her, causing her to slide sideways into the water. He raced across the stepping-stones and began pounding up the hill, his legs pumping like pistons.

'I'll tell Dr Scott,' she called out, once she'd regained her balance.

'No time for that,' Mr Thom shouted, already halfway up the hill.

Why doesn't he want Dr Scott to know? Is he going to force Rhodene to stay against her will? Is she leaving because of him? Alpha sent her mind chasing across space towards Dr Scott, hoping she could find him again, knowing that each time she reached out she burned up more and more of her supply of psychic energy.

But the egg came to her aid again, stretching her abilities, drawing her towards the principal like a dart flying true to the bull's-eye. Dr Scott, it's Alpha, she projected, pushing the mind-talk bubble right up against his nose so that he wouldn't miss it. *Get back to the house—Rhodene is running away.*

CHAPTER TWENTY

After sending her message to Dr Scott, Alpha charged up the hill, desperately trying to catch up with Mr Thom. She emerged from the woods only to spot him running towards Rhodene, who was staggering down the drive, burdened with two heavy backpacks. Rhodene hadn't even noticed Mr Thom. She was stubbornly heading towards a motorcycle and rider who was half-hidden by the yew hedge. Although Mr Thom was racing towards her, Alpha realised that he wasn't going to catch her before she could reach the bike.

From the direction of the beach a Land Rover aimed for the drive, chewing up the grass on its way. Dr Scott, thank goodness. Alpha's relief gave way to fear, and her stomach cramped when she saw the rider on the bike draw a gun from his leathers. A shot rang out and the windscreen of the Land Rover shattered. She felt Dr Scott fight the wheel as the Land Rover pulled to the right. He over-corrected and the vehicle spun, dropping towards a ditch where it quivered on the edge, before slowly tipping over. Dr Scott fell from the open roof and the Land Rover dropped on top of him. His spillage died in Alpha's mind.

'I told you not to call him,' bellowed Mr Thom. He changed direction and sped towards the hollow where Dr Scott lay.

Although Rhodene had stopped to look when the Land Rover had crashed, she'd begun inching towards the rider of the motorbike once again. Her thoughts took over in Alpha's head.

———

Inside Rhodene's brain Alpha found a mind reeking of self-pity. Only one thing motivated this girl: the desire to be important. Her dreams of being a famous psychic had dissolved. Alpha was shocked to learn that, without knowing it, Rhodene had cut herself off from her own abilities. But since then, the rider of the motorbike had promised her fame and fortune. Rhodene, she wasn't surprised to learn, was determined to make the most of it. Poor, desperate girl, ready to believe promises from that son of a…

She spilled an urgent message into Rhodene's head: Forget about leaving and I promise you I'll bring back your psychic dreams.

Rhodene kept running. Alpha tried again. Stop you don't want to do this—you want everyone at the school to know how good you are. How skilled you are at predicting what's going to happen.

Rhodene stopped running. She twisted away from the direction of the motorbike rider towards Alpha, before turning back again, still set on leaving the school.

Stop! I can help you get your ability back. I can fix you. He can't.

She could actually hear the click as Rhodene's mind was flipped.

———

Rhodene turned and stared at Alpha, a thousand emotions flitting across her face. Then she dropped her bags and ran back into the school.

The man on the motorbike revved his engine. Alpha caught a brief flash of his anger because his plans for Rhodene were thwarted, though why he wanted her was a mystery, because to Alpha it seemed that he despised her. Then he slammed his helmet back on his head and pulled away in a storm of noise.

Dr Scott? Alpha spun round. Dr Scott was squeezing out from under the Land Rover. He looked round groggily. Mr Thom checked Dr Scott's vision then helped him to stand, propping up the doctor under his shoulder like a human crutch.

Alpha tried to stagger towards them, but she felt drained, and her legs were wobbling. She sat down abruptly and forced her head between her knees, trying to stop herself from fainting.

'Alpha?' Dr Scott stumbled towards her.

She turned her head. She could see Mr Thom urging Dr Scott to go into the house with him, but Dr Scott shoved him off.

'Dizzy.' She was too weary to lift her head from her knees.

'Horatio, leave us for a second, please. I need to talk to Alpha.'

'You're concussed,' said Mr Thom, 'I've got to check you over.'

'Horatio!' The single word was enough—the short man backed away, leaving Dr Scott alone with Alpha.

Dr Scott waited for him to retreat then whispered, 'tell me what you did to Rhodene? It was you, wasn't it? You stopped her leaving with that man.'

She looked up into his face. Blood was pouring from his temple. *If I hadn't called him he wouldn't have been hurt. I've changed another mind—everything's going wrong.* Although she was still sitting down her head swayed as Dr Scott's face blurred in front of her eyes.

Dr Scott knelt down beside her. 'Lie flat on the grass, head as low as you can, that will help.' He tilted her sideways onto the ground. Alpha felt the world regain its balance as her blood flowed back into her head.

'All right now?' he asked a few minutes later when she tried to push herself upright.

'Yes. Thanks.'

Dr Scott gently swept her hair aside before cupping her face in one insistent hand. 'Tell me please... did you make Rhodene turn back, change her mind about going with that guy?'

She nodded, a tiny movement against the pressure of his hand.

A look of incredulousness crossed his face. 'Thank you for telling me the truth. But look at you, you're exhausted! Your blood sugar is unbalanced because you've used up all your energy. Do you think you can manage to walk inside? You need a cup of tea with plenty of sugar, and a chocolate biscuit to boot.'

Alpha nodded wearily. Cup of tea, a rest, and then he'll send me packing. I've broken the rules. Again!

CHAPTER TWENTY-ONE

Alpha lay on her bed, berating herself for changing Rhodene's mind. All her suspicions about Rhodene came rolling back to gnaw at her: *why did Rhodene meet Mr Thom on the beach in the middle of the night? And why is she so hostile towards me? Why does she blame me for losing her abilities—she'd lost them before I got here. Who was that on the motorbike?*

Alpha wished she'd left well enough alone; wished she'd let Rhodene leave. If she had she wouldn't be in this predicament. It seemed like hours since Dr Scott had left her to the attentions of Biddy, who'd made her that cup of tea and arranged for some cake while he went off with Mr Thom. She hadn't seen him since. Biddy had wanted Alpha to stay with her but Alpha, as usual, had retreated into herself when she was worried, and had insisted on going to her room. Alone. She wondered how long she'd have before she had to leave, and was packing her own bag once more. She wondered whether they'd let her take the egg with her.

Her thoughts spun round in circles until there was a rap on her door and Dr Scott came in. His arm was bandaged, and his forehead bore a series of stitches over an egg-sized lump. She jumped off the bed and stood facing him, dreading the moment.

Dr Scott looked very serious. 'There hasn't been anyone like you since Stalin's persuader, ninety years back.'

Alpha kept her eyes on the carpet. *What's a Stalin's persuader? Why doesn't he just put me out of my misery?*

'Stalin was Director of Russia, during the 1920s,' Dr Scott explained. 'He set a psychic named Wolf Messing a challenge: to leave the KGB offices without any of the guards stopping him. Stalin advised the guards to watch out for Wolf and was astonished when Wolf met him outside the building only a short while later. Wolf Messing was a telepath… and far more… just like you. In his autobiography he says he persuaded the guards to believe he was a high-ranking KGB official. I think your talents are right up there with his.'

Alpha shuffled her feet nervously. *He told me not to go inside people's heads, didn't he? So what's he on about?*

'What a good thing you persuaded Rhodene to stay. How did you do it?'

Alpha felt her heart go flip-flop. Good thing? *Isn't he going to get rid of me?* Dr Scott held her shoulder, leading her back to the bed to sit down. He fussed a bit, obviously concerned that she was still feeling like fainting. After she was settled he took up a position astride the chest at the bottom of Alpha's bed. 'You do know how you did it, don't you?' he prompted. 'Can you tell me?'

'She was miserable, she can't dream any more… I mean she doesn't have predictive dreams. So I told her I'd sort it so that she can dream again.'

Shock registered in Dr Scott's eyes. 'And can you really do that?'

She nodded. 'I found out that she's afraid to dream those kinds of dreams. That's why she stopped dreaming. But to fix it I'll have to go inside her head again, and you said not to.'

Dr Scott reached over and patted her hand. 'We'll make sure it happens in a controlled environment. Obviously you won't have the energy for it today but, if you're feeling up to it, we'll go and see Rhodene soon. She'll need reassuring and you're the best one for that job.'

Alpha didn't believe that for even one second. She was still finding it hard to accept that she was going to be allowed to remain here at all. Deep inside of her she felt a flicker of delight—it shocked her to realise how much she'd come to enjoy living at the school in the short time she'd been here. *If Dr Scott wants me to talk with Rhodene, then that's what I'll do—even though I haven't got clue what to say—even though she hates me.*

All at once she remembered Iwardi and came to a quick decision. A jumble of words poured out of her as she struggled to put the ghost hunt and her suspicions of Mr Thom into a sensible frame that Dr Scott wouldn't dismiss instantly. Throughout her tale Dr Scott listened carefully, never once interrupting.

At the end of it he leaned forwards, holding her eyes with his own. 'This is crucially important. Do you trust me?'

Alpha started, alerted by the note of urgency in his voice. She nodded.

'Tell nobody about your ability to change peoples' minds. No one at all, not your teachers or Janna, or even Sunday. I only hope his talents aren't strong enough yet to draw it from your mind.'

Alpha thought about that, then nodded. Sunday could read her spilled emotions, but she could keep him out of her brain if she needed to. She was good at keeping secrets and happy enough not to blab about this one. It had caused her enough grief already.

'Good. And please, stay out of the West Wing from now on—it could all come tumbling down around you. Also it would be better if you three didn't discuss Iwardi with anyone else at present.' Dr Scott didn't elaborate any further—he walked to the door indicating that their discussion was at an end, leaving her wondering exactly how much he knew about what was going on at Krakow Bond.

'I'll be back soon,' he said, 'then we can pop along to see Rhodene.'

———

A little later Dr Scott joined her once more and they walked together down the stairs to Rhodene's room. Rhodene already had a visitor. Mrs Hickelroy was sitting next to Rhodene on the bed in Rhodene's popstar plastered bedroom. Rhodene's eyes were downcast, her neck was drooping, and Mrs Hickelroy had her hands wound protectively around Rhodene's arm.

As Alpha entered with Dr Scott, Mrs Hickelroy looked up. 'Hello Alpha. Rhodene's had an upsetting day. Perhaps you could see her tomorrow when she feels a bit better.'

'Alpha and Rhodene need to have a chat. Let's leave them to it, shall we, Vicky?'

Mrs Hickelroy's eyes narrowed, and Alpha caught a rare thought from her: that she hadn't realised Rhodene and Alpha were close enough to talk privately. However she didn't mention it. 'Rhodene's been telling me about the young man on the motorbike. Apparently, he suggested she could have a career in TV, some sort of soap opera thing.'

'But Rhodene's not an actress,' said Dr Scott.

'Exactly! He had some other objective in mind.' Mrs Hickelroy hovered over Rhodene, seeming reluctant to leave her. Alpha picked up from Rhodene that she was grateful for Mrs Hickelroy's attention; in fact she seemed to be relishing it.

Alpha caught Dr Scott's mind-talk as he threw Mrs Hickelroy a look of concern. *Someone definitely knows about us!*

Mrs Hickelroy's reply wasn't clear to Alpha, she was obviously much more adept at shielding her mind-talk than he was. But her frown seemed to spell out…*this isn't the best place to talk.*

'Let's leave Alpha with Rhodene,' said Dr Scott.

'All right. I've got to pack for my trip to Leeds anyway; I'm leaving before daylight. I think I'm wasting my time though. I don't believe the rumours we've had about that boy's possible gift will hold up to scrutiny.' Mrs Hickelroy stroked Rhodene's hair. 'Will you be OK?'

Rhodene lifted her face and nodded.

'I'll email you while I'm away.' Mrs Hickelroy turned and spoke to Alpha. 'Treat Rhodene gently, will you dear? She's had a rough time.'

Then Alpha felt a bubble of mind-talk close to her head, waiting for her to invite it in. She opened her mind to the private communication from Mrs Hickelroy.

––––

You look a bit (Alpha saw an image of herself pushed to exhaustion). Did Mr Thom (sensation of shoving) you too hard. I'll… (sounds of Mrs Hickelroy talking with Mr Thom). Talents like yours must be… (picture of a mother rocking a baby in her arms.) It's important that you take things easy for now. We don't want you to (tiny flickers of a fire dying in its grate.) Finally Alpha felt Mrs Hickelroy place a smile in her head…

––––

and the mind-talk dissolved.

'Try not to stay long, I think an early night will do you both a great deal of good,' Mrs Hickelroy told them.

The door closed leaving the two alone. Alpha peered at Rhodene, who was staring back at her, pockmarks aflame. Alpha felt herself sway and sat down quickly. If she was to manage this moment she needed all her senses in working order. She had absolutely no confidence in her ability to hold a reasonable conversation with Rhodene.

Conflicting emotions crossed Rhodene's face: fear, followed by anger, tinged lightly with hope.

'I can help you,' Alpha said starkly. Unexpectedly, she was overwhelmed with sympathy for the girl. It was only a few days ago she'd wished her own abilities would disappear so she could be normal, but since then her tin-lined bedroom had made her freak out and had forced her to keep the window open. *That's what it must be like for Rhodene—only Rhodene has no window to open.*

'Can you bring my dreams back?'

'Yes. You haven't lost your talent.'

The silver glint of tears formed in Rhodene's eyes. Alpha blinked, astonished at the change in her. *Is this the same big mouth I've had to put up with since I arrived?*

'Mrs Hickelroy said that when you grow up and become a woman, "Paranormal activity goes into decline",' Rhodene whispered.

'She was wrong. It stopped during one of your lessons with Mr Thom.' A new thought twisted into Alpha's mind. *Rhodene could be Mr Thom's victim too.* The idea raced round and round, making no headway for lack of concrete evidence.

Tired of thinking, Alpha got straight to the point. 'Are you sure you want it back?'

'Yes. Absolutely. I used to dream of things that were going to happen. Some of them were horrible and I'd shake for hours afterwards, but sometimes I'd connect with other peoples' dreams… I'd like flow inside them and that was fantastic. I want to be able to dream again like that, it makes me special. Are you sure you can fix it? Can you do it now?'

'Rhodene you're tired. We can bring you back into action together, but I need you fresh and full of energy because it's going to take a lot out of us both. Also Dr Scott said he needs to set it up in a controlled environment. We'll do it tomorrow.'

'You promise?'

'Yes. Only… don't try to run away again.'

'No…' Rhodene snivelled, reached for a tissue and blew her nose loudly. 'I guess I always knew deep down that Gundrad didn't know anyone in the film industry. But it all seemed so hopeless.'

As Alpha eased out of the door, Rhodene looked up. 'Alpha.' She paused. 'I was jealous of you, you're a T.I. and everyone was so pleased about it. I'm sorry, I shouldn't have been such a bitch.'

Amazed at Rhodene's apology and desperate for some time alone, Alpha crept back to her own bedroom. She felt like she'd emerged from a small car containing sixteen sumo wrestlers. Time spent in other people's heads did that to her: there were only so many of their thoughts she could stand.

———

The doors of her cupboards were open and inside hung rows of brand-new shirts, skirts, jeans, jackets and shoes that had certainly not been there this morning. A note pinned to one jacket said, *I think these will fit until we can make time to go shopping together. I hope you like some of them. Buckets of love, Biddy.*

Alpha's eyes filled with tears.

CHAPTER TWENTY-TWO

At dinner Mr Thom kept watch on Alpha, Janna and Sunday throughout the meal. His eyes repeatedly scanned their faces, searching for something. Alpha knew that he was going to enforce their grounding and that there would be no opportunity for the three of them to get together afterwards.

Janna struggled to talk without being overheard. 'I slipped down to the basement again after our session with Lily. Guess why Mr Thom knew we were down in the basement of the West Wing?'

'He can't have, dah, I dunno, somehow read our minds?' Alpha suggested. 'It's not like he's a telepathy teacher.' She was only half-joking. She wouldn't put it past Mr Thom. Never mind the so-called school rules, he'd already probed her mind without her knowing how he'd done it so secretively.

Janna grinned. 'Good guess but wrong. Martel told him. I picked up his signature presence, near the trapdoor. He was hiding behind one of the boxes watching us when we climbed down into the trapdoor.'

'Has he been following us around?'

'Looks that way, doesn't it? But why? What's he hoping to gain? First the Gillybird and now Martel.' She looked round, suddenly noticing that Rhodene wasn't at the table. 'It's a wonder

Rhodene wasn't there too—it's not like her to miss out on the action. And why's she skipping dinner?'

Alpha gulped. For the first time since she'd met Janna, she felt an awkwardness creep into their relationship. She desperately wanted to tell Janna about Rhodene's attempt to run off with Gundrad, but two things were stopping her: firstly, those were Rhodene's secrets and Alpha didn't feel right sharing them, but more importantly, Dr Scott had insisted that she told no one about her ability to change people's minds. *How am I going to explain that I made Rhodene turn back, or why Dr Scott took me to her room afterwards?*

Finally, she settled on saying, 'Rhodene's not so bad—maybe Mr Thom's got his claws into her too.'

Janna looked sceptical. 'Don't go soft on me now, she's a total jerk even if she's stopped hanging out so often with Martel.'

Alpha glanced up to see if Martel was taking any of this in. For once Martel's thoughts weren't guarded; they were shrieking about his plans to catch Miss Gilford on her own straight after dinner... something about underground tunnels?

Tunnels? What tunnels? More tunnels? I've had enough of bloody tunnels!

But she couldn't resist finding out more.

———

Alpha slid into Martel's mind, following his thoughts about tunnels. The trail led towards a clutch of enormous shells in which Martel's memories pulsed like trapped molluscs. As Alpha walked down the trail a slimy substance oozed across her flesh. Shuddering in revulsion, she slipped inside the largest shell, brushing her hands on her clothes to get rid of the slime.

... It had been twilight in that memory, and Alpha saw Martel running back towards the house from the woods. But then the smooth swing of his coordinated limbs was interrupted when he stumbled and fell. He yelled out loud, unable to stop himself from rolling down the hill towards the lake. Dazed, with every bone in his body jolted, he struggled to stand. Eventually, he resorted to holding onto a clump of long grass to haul himself upwards. But thwarting his plan to get upright, the grassroots came hurtling out of the hill, dumping soil all over him and plonking him back on the ground. He stared at the strange concrete circle that he'd uncovered where he'd yanked out the grass. Ignoring his reeling head, he prodded and pulled at the concrete plug until, with a tug, he was able to remove it to reveal an underground tunnel running back into the hill towards South Block. Despite his injuries and his height, Martel slid easily into the cramped hole, and Alpha was reminded of a soldier on a mission. Martel moved with a fluidity and grace unusual in such a long-limbed person. As he crept through the underground space he used his tactile abilities, running his fingers across the trusses supporting the tunnel. His hands jumped back in astonishment—another person had been in here recently.

Something glinted on the dirt floor, and he reached for it. A metal tab from a cold drink tin. To Martel's sensitive fingers it revealed traces of an intruder; a man. The touch both intrigued and disturbed him.

———

Alpha left Martel's mind, her own head feeling like it was about to burst with all these puzzles.

Another underground tunnel… Martel stalking us… planning to talk to Miss Gilford… Miss Gilford shopping me and Janna to Mr Thom… Martel doing the same thing… Are Martel, Miss Gilford and Mr Thom somehow in this together?

As her gaze leapt to Martel's face, he narrowed his eyes. Pain punctured Alpha's chest, and her lungs felt on like they were on fire, each breath a burning agony of pain.

'And that's just a taster of what I can do,' said Martel. 'Now stay the hell out of my head.'

CHAPTER TWENTY-THREE

Sunday was crouched in a space that was no wider than a broom closet, but only half as tall. Though the space was small there was an abundance of fresh air from the passages that led to this hidey-hole. These avenues had once allowed the chimney sweep's lad to clear the soot from clogged chimneys. The hole where Sunday was hiding had once caught and held the birds and mice nests lodged within the flues as the sweeps brushed down from the roof. The cavity now served Sunday well and any remaining soot did little to blacken his already dark skin.

Below him lay Mr Thom's classroom, locked for the evening but quite accessible to someone who was entering via the chimney duct. Unfortunately, the classroom wasn't empty: through a slanting gap Sunday caught glimpses of Mr Thom, his head bowed over his desk, his fingers deftly manipulating the circuit board that lay on the ebony wood.

Sunday flexed his toes in an attempt to iron out the pins and needles in his legs and wished that he'd brought something to eat. When the phone rang he jumped.

Mr Thom picked up the phone and Sunday heard him say, 'Thom.'

A silence, then Mr Thom said, 'Right. I've got that. Meeting in five minutes—Michael's office. It's late, what's the urgency?'

Another silence, then, 'oh, you're leaving first thing in the morning. Well, let's hope that lad in Leeds amounts to something.'

And finally, after a long pause, Mr Thom added, 'yes, I'm concerned about Rhodene too, but even more so about Alpha. Things will come to a boil soon. We'd better sort out what we're going to do. OK, see you shortly.'

Sunday could barely contain himself as Mr Thom eased himself out of his chair and strode past the chimney towards the door. Suddenly Mr Thom stiffened. He sniffed deeply. Then he returned to his desk where he picked up the circuit board, putting it in his pocket before finally leaving the room.

Sunday aborted his mission to search Mr Thom's desk. Instead, he bolted back up the chimney.

———

The silver clock on Alpha's bedside table was standing, like Charlie Chaplin, at ten past ten, when someone rapped on her door. She got up reluctantly. *Is today never going to end?*

Sunday stood there, beckoning her.

Though tired, she was pleased to see him. 'Come in,' she said, conveniently forgetting about the grounding Mr Thom had issued.

'No time! We must go now.'

'Go? Where? Why? I'm already in my pyjamas.'

'Meeting in Dr Scott's office. The psi-teachers are all on their way—they're going to talk about you. We're going to be bees on the wall.'

'Bees on the wall? Oh, you mean flies. But we won't be able to pick up what they're saying; Dr Scott's office is lined in tin, right? Telepathy won't work.'

'No problem.' He tugged her by the hand.

'Wait, let me get some clothes on and my trainers at least.'

'No shoes, it's too much hard with shoes on.'

She drew on a pair of jeans, tucked her pyjama top into them and slung on a light jacket. 'Let's fetch Janna.'

'No time,' said Sunday. He hurried her halfway down the main stairs, to a tiny door that looked as though even a hobbit would have trouble getting through it. Inside was a flight of stone stairs with such a low ceiling that she had to crouch down to climb them. She was relieved when they came out in a poorly lit passage where she could at least stand up once more. It was so dark she had to feel her way along the walls, helped by the sound of Sunday shuffling ahead of her. 'How do you know about this meeting?' Her voice echoed through the long passage.

Sunday told her that he'd intended to check out Mr Thom's belongings, and about overhearing the phone call.

'No Sunday. No! Let Dr Scott deal with him.' But Alpha knew in her heart that the only way to stop Sunday investigating Mr Thom would be to wipe the idea right out of his head with one of her mind-changing acts. Well, she was quite prepared to do that! Thom was too dangerous to mess with.

'More stairs here,' Sunday warned. 'Quick. We must hurry.'

These were spiral stairs and they led up through a turret. Her footsteps clattered on the metal as they climbed, no matter how carefully she tried to step. Sunday's, however, were as silent as a mouse. He wedged open the door at the top to allow her to go through first.

She blinked as she found herself on the roof. The stars were out, as bright as they ever shone on summer nights made of silk. The air was thick, laden with the smell of the sea and of the jasmine that grew in the shelter of the courtyard.

Sunday took his shoes off, and a sweaty odour found its way into her nostrils, diluting the jasmine. *Not too bad, his socks are only a couple of days overripe.*

Sunday rushed past her. 'This way.'

The area they'd come out on was flat, but then Sunday led her past a slippery section of roof that was as pitched as a Chinese temple. Beyond this lay domes and parapets. Sunday scampered ahead, his small body resembling a living gargoyle. They crossed to the East Wing and clambered all the way along it. Finally, on the southeast corner, they rounded a gilded tower and found a stack of chimneys. Sunday put his finger to his lips and squatted down near one of the chimneys.

As she crouched down next to Sunday she could hear Dr Scott's voice floating up through the chimney. 'It's dreadful. Either someone left the gate open, or the guy on the motorbike managed to break through our alarm code.' His voice sounded strained, as though his windpipe was being crushed and she felt an enormous load of worry creep up the chimney towards her. Her neck prickled—her intuition that things weren't right here at Krakow Bond had been spot on. And what's more, Dr Scott knew it too.

'None of us would leave the gate open,' said Mrs Hickelroy. 'We all know how important security is.'

'Who else knows the code?' Lily Wade's flowing tones were unmistakable.

'Only the four of us,' replied Mrs Hickelroy. 'And of course, Biddy checks everyone's details on the intercom before letting them in. If she's not around, I take over. Even Ernie Small and Sylvia Finkle, who live on the island, aren't given the code. They have to press the button so Biddy can let them in and out every day for their classes.'

Dr Scott sighed. 'We've done everything we can to keep security tight, including hiding the student's talents.'

'At least that's working,' said Mrs Hickelroy, dryly. 'Only yesterday Ernie gave me a wink on the sly and told me he thought our "hush-hush" mind-improvement exercises were working wonders on Carl but that he couldn't keep Alex's thoughts on any lesson unless it involved blowing something up or blasting it to smithereens. I'm sure none of them have a clue about what we're really doing.'

'What about a leak from the Prime Minister's office?' Lily suggested.

'I thought the whole place was the best-kept secret in Government?' said Mr Thom.

'It is.' Dr Scott sounded very sure about that. 'John was adamant, only he and the Prime Minister know about the school. He's told no one, not even the Home Secretary. We're an expensive embarrassment to them. John said it's been very difficult, they've had to lie about our funding and in this economic climate... well, we're on a knife-edge here, so we can't afford any slip-ups. I must admit I'm worried. First Alpha, and now this thing with Rhodene.'

'Do you think they're related?' Lily asked.

'There's a link between the two incidents, although it's a bit tenuous. Vicky, you said the man at the station was wearing a motorcycle helmet, and so was Rhodene's fellow when he drove off,' said Dr Scott, 'although I couldn't swear they were the same person.'

Alpha felt the blood drain from her head. She recalled the obscure, shadowy face that Howie had shown her and warned her about. *That overlarge head—it's Gundrad's helmet. First he killed Iwardi, then he tried to capture me, and today he tried to make off with Rhodene. Why didn't I connect him to my abductor?* The answer came to her slowly. *I didn't see the helmet at the station... I wanted to believe that my running days were over.* Her insides quivered with fear as she accepted that Gundrad had followed her here.

'It doesn't make any sense,' Mrs Hickelroy said. 'They're two completely different situations. Someone tried to make off with Alpha, but from what Rhodene told me, that young man was in love with her.'

No he wasn't, thought Alpha. *He despised her; I could feel it.*

'How did he meet Rhodene?' Mr Thom's bass tones rumbled up the chimney.

'It must have been during half-term holidays, when Rhodene went home,' said Mrs Hickelroy. 'I think we should tell the police.'

'Absolutely not. That's the last thing we can afford. Security's been breached already. We don't need the local bobbies poking their noses in here,' said Dr Scott. 'I've taken Burt Johnson and Larry Dolahan off garden work. They'll watch the gate.'

'The code is changed daily, using a random number selector,' said Mr Thom. 'It's a four-digit code. He'd have to be very lucky to break it by guesswork, but on a one-off basis that's not impossible.'

'Statistically, the odds are highly improbable,' disagreed Dr Scott.

'So either someone was dreadfully negligent,' said Lily, 'or you're suggesting one of us gave him the code?'

'No, Lily no!' said Dr Scott. 'I don't know what the devil I'm suggesting. Has anyone got any ideas?'

Alpha noticed that Dr Scott was carefully avoiding any mention of Iwardi. *Who doesn't he trust? He believed me, I'm sure of it.*

'Apart from the students themselves… I suppose one of them might predict the codes or pick up a clue telepathically… there is someone with access to the codes, someone who knows a lot more about the school than anyone else,' said Mr Thom.

'Biddy,' Mrs Hickelroy confirmed.

Above them Alpha gasped. *Did Biddy really let Gundrad in? Or is Mr Thom trying to pull the wool over Dr Scott's eyes?*

CHAPTER
TWENTY-FOUR

Someone with a ten-pound hammer was pounding on Alpha's door. She dragged herself out of the depths of sleep and opened one eye to glance at the clock. A quarter to six in the morning. She groaned and pulled the covers over her head. Whoever it was could get lost. After her night travels with Sunday she didn't fall asleep until past two.

But the pounding got more insistent. Alpha rolled over and staggered out of bed. *This had better be important.* She yanked the door open just as Rhodene raised her fist to pound on it again.

Rhodene didn't bother with an apology for the early hour. Instead she barged past Alpha, forcing her way into the bedroom. She spat out her concerns, without stopping to breathe. 'Mrs Hickelroy's sent me an email, she's gone off to Leeds and Dr Scott and Sunday left a couple of hours ago as well for another meeting with the Prime Minister in London, she said he told her you're not to look inside my head until she gets back, she doesn't want me to ...'

Alpha stopped listening. She was so tired she couldn't make sense of Rhodene's words, but the girl's emotions were shining through loud and clear: she was pleased that Mrs Hickelroy had emailed her personally, but she also felt jealous because Dr Scott had taken Sunday to London, and not her. Alpha yawned. 'Who said what?'

'Mrs Hickelroy. She said Dr Scott doesn't want you inside my head until she's back. That could take days or even weeks.' Rhodene's next words came out in a gush. 'I can't wait that long! You've got to help me now.'

Alpha averted her gaze, wondering what to do. *If I do I'll get into trouble and if I don't she'll try to leave again. I'm sick of being stuck between two impossible choices.*

'Alpha, please,' begged Rhodene, breathing raggedly. Her hand crept to her temple, and she began rubbing it harshly. 'It's not fair—why can't Lily be the control? She's the dream expert.'

Alpha could feel the desperation behind Rhodene's self-pity. 'OK. Sit down, I'll do it now.'

Rhodene's mouth flopped open. 'You will?' She flung herself onto Alpha's bed, and added an abrupt, 'Thanks.' Her hands kept fluttering together then falling apart as though she couldn't quite bring herself to believe Alpha.

'Breathe slowly,' said Alpha. 'You need to relax. It'll be a lot easier for me to trace that memory if you do.'

Rhodene's face fell. 'You mean... you have to go inside my head?'

'Of course. How else did you think I could do it?'

'I don't know. You'll know everything about me.'

'It's that or nothing. Make up your mind.'

Whatever it was that Rhodene wanted to hide, she wasn't as desperate to keep it a secret as she was to regain her predictive talents. 'OK. OK! Just do it quickly.'

'Fine. Now take deep breaths and blow out to the count of ten.'

A few minutes of deep breathing drained the tension from Rhodene's face and the puffiness around her eyes began to disappear. 'Will it hurt?' she asked.

'Not a bit. I won't do anything without you knowing about it. You can say stop anytime.'

'No... I don't think I'm going to do that. This is the only thing I've ever been good at.'

———

Alpha slid into Rhodene's mind and found that she could read her thoughts clearly. She was surprised to hear Rhodene putting herself down ... *'I'm too stupid for schoolwork, too bulky for sports, too spotty for a boyfriend, and now I've lost the one thing I'm good at. Alpha better not be lying or else...'*

Rhodene's thoughts were spun together in an endless weave of pink candyfloss that crossed and re-crossed itself. Clinging stands of self-interest constantly trapped Alpha, and she had to ease them apart to climb through to Rhodene's memories.

The first memory she came across was of Rhodene's parents... they had been going out for the evening and Rhodene was shouting that she was scared of the babysitter. Alpha felt Rhodene's genuine fear—*that babysitter must have been a real monster.* But Rhodene's mother told her not to be silly; she wasn't going to miss Eric's cello recital just because Rhodene was being a brat. Eric, Rhodene's brother, watched smugly as Rhodene made an enormous fuss...

...There were many more painful memories of Rhodene's parents putting her down to favour her elder brother—*so that's what she didn't want me to know about.*

Alpha's arms ached from the sticky hunt before she finally found what she was looking for...what she had glimpsed yesterday...the half-forgotten moment when Mr Thom had discussed Rhodene's dreams with her. 'They're definitely out of control,' he told her. 'Probably because your hormonal balance is altering as you get older. It'll take a few months for me to teach you to meditate in your sleep. In the meantime, I'll insert a tin plate here, just under the skin.' He touched a spot on Rhodene's head, near her left ear. 'Every time it slides closed it'll shut down your predictive ability. We can link it to your pulse so that it stops your dreams as soon as your heartbeat goes too high. Tin is a very light metal; you won't even notice it's there…'

Alpha was horrified. She broke out of the memory and stood amongst the pink, sticky strands thinking about what she'd just seen. *If Mr Thom suggested messing about in my brain, I'd jump out of my skin. But Rhodene wasn't shaken at all—what was it that scared her so much that her brain shut down her predictions all by itself? And why was Mr Thom so keen to stop her dreaming?*

Reluctantly, Alpha returned to that memory to observe what happened next…

'Will you fit it under an anaesthetic?' Rhodene asked him calmly.

Mr Thom shook his head and told Rhodene that anaesthesia was always the more dangerous option, especially for such a minor procedure. He recommended acupuncture instead, and explained that a few needles in the meridians in Rhodene's neck would prevent her from feeling a thing.

At the word needles, Rhodene gave a mental scream and instantly turned off all thought. A tremor arising from Rhodene's horror made the pink strands quake, stretching them to the point of breakage. Alpha was flung about between them as they catapulted her around Rhodene's mind.

Alpha, stunned but protected by the pink strands from real pain, realised that it was the idea of needles in Rhodene's neck that had scared her so much she'd frozen her talents inside a web of fear. Mr Thom hadn't needed to complete the planned operation on Rhodene's skull because, at that very moment, her talents had withered and almost died.

Once the strands had reduced their violent tremors to a level where Alpha could cling on without being tossed about, she replayed the memory, isolating the exact moment when Rhodene had taken fright. That part of Rhodene's brain was coated with a pale fear, as though skeins of white wool had been woven around and between the candyfloss.

Alpha began the slow process of snipping away Rhodene's anxiety. As the white web was shredded Rhodene's talent began to emerge, shining like a full moon. It was a glorious, beautiful thing. Alpha could understand why it meant so much to Rhodene. *I wonder if my talent looks anything like this?*

Finally the last of the strangulating strands had been cut away, and Alpha stared hard at the dirty mark they'd revealed that was staining the shining moon of talent. *What's that got to do with the memory of Mr Thom and his long needles?* Blotting out the beauty of Rhodene's talent, the mark was like ink dropped into ice. It was incredibly ugly—but worse, it was malignant—its feelers were reaching out to other areas of Rhodene's mind. It moved as she watched it, and Alpha began to believe that it would have no trouble switching hosts so that it could grow on her as well.

She recoiled, almost jumping out of Rhodene's head. Without her being aware of it, back in her real body, her fingers clawed at the blue tiger's eye in her pocket. Strength flooded up her arm and into her brain, stabilising her thoughts. She returned to the dark splodge, careful not to get too close. The mark felt cold to Alpha even from a distance.

She followed the streams of ink leaking from the stain, finding more and more, until finally she traced its beginning back to another half-forgotten memory… Rhodene vaguely recalled Gundrad placing her under a hypnotic trance. Minutes later, when Rhodene's control of her own mind had returned, the stain was deeply lodged in her brain…

… Alpha followed the stain as it twisted into the area where Rhodene stored the memories of her predictions. Suddenly her right foot fell into nothingness, her arms windmilled backwards, and she only just managed to pull herself away from the gaping hole and land on her bottom. *Ow! Who would have thought that candyfloss could be so hard?*

She leaned forwards to peer into the hole and her eyes locked onto a terrifying sight. Here there was no weave of candyfloss or shining ball of talent. Only a blank space remained as evidence of missing information: a void as scary as coming back from holiday to find that your home had been blown up. She stared at the hole for a long time. *He's stolen one of Rhodene's memories.*

Eventually, she tore herself away from the jagged gap. Skirting around it, she discovered that the cold streaks also wound right through Rhodene's self-image, putting her in just the right frame of mind to find Gundrad attractive. *Ugh! He shattered her fragile confidence with his mind-stealing marks.*

She frowned, wondering how best to clear Rhodene's mind of all traces of Gundrad.

The marks are cold, fight his ice with fire! She built a picture of a burning volcano in Rhodene's mind then sent out flumes of lava to melt the ice. As the cold stain started to dissolve it spat at Alpha with an icy hiss, burning her arm. She clapped her hand over the burn and her palm felt as though it had stuck to dry ice. She wanted to run, to hide, to get out of Rhodene's brain, but instead she forced herself to push her lava on, deeper and deeper into the ice.

The battle raged on and on, fire consuming ice, ice fighting back, using the steam it was creating to block Alpha's vision, and surround her in a thick mist. The noise of its transformation was so loud it turned Alpha deaf. Relentlessly she pushed forward ignoring the ice's assault on her senses, a blind and deaf warrior slashing everywhere, radiating a cleansing fire. The lava's light surrounded her with a saint-like halo. Heedless of her lack of sight and the holes in Rhodene's mind she strode on, fighting, using her lava like a sword until every last drop of cold had melted.

———

When she was done, she pulled out of Rhodene's mind and slumped back on the bed, frightened to find that her real arm was burning like fury where the ice had landed on it.

Rhodene stared wide-eyed at her. 'What was that?'

'Er…' She quickly masked the ice burn by covering it with her hand. *Rhodene's so screwed up; she doesn't need to know that she's missing one of her memories or that Gundrad left bits of himself behind in her mind.* 'You were scared of the acupuncture Mr Thom was going to use on you, so you closed down your talents and left a warning inside your head.' *Yeah, and any minute now my nose is going to get longer.*

But the half-truth seemed to satisfy Rhodene. She nodded.

'How did you meet Gundrad?' Alpha asked.

'He saw me walking on the beach one day and came up to say hello.'

'You met him here? I thought Mrs Hickelroy said it was a private beach?'

'It is. You can only get to it through the school or by boat. Gundrad said he was drawn to me across the water.' Rhodene gave a comfortable smile and Alpha knew that she'd moved on with no regrets, and could forget the young man as long as Gundrad didn't return to Krakow Bond.

But Mr Thom was still very much in the picture... she had assumed, because of the inky trail Gundrad had laid, that he was the person responsible for stealing one of Rhodene's precious memories. But it could have been Mr Thom; there was no way of knowing because that information had gone along with the memory. She felt incredibly sorry for Rhodene: both Gundrad and Mr Thom wanted to gain control of her mind.

'Is that it? Will I get my dreams back?' Rhodene asked.

'Yes. I'll make one last check—see that everything's in working order.'

———

Alpha found the pink candyfloss doubly entangled as Rhodene's talents entwined themselves once more within the fabric of her thoughts. They wrapped the shining moon of talent in clouds of pink, creating the most wonderful sunset.

But Alpha couldn't resist finding the memory of the moment when Rhodene had met Gundrad. The day had been blustery; sand coarsened the air. Gundrad, who'd appeared from nowhere, had seemed to Rhodene like a prince walking out of the desert.

Alpha hunted through the memory for clues. Nothing stood out until she realised that it was the absence of something that was important. There was no boat on that beach. The only way Gundrad could have got there was through the school grounds.

Alpha recalled last night's meeting about the motorbike rider. This was proof that the gate hadn't been left open by accident. And he hadn't got in with a lucky stab at the code either—he'd been here more than once. Without a doubt, he was being fed the security code and let in deliberately.

She eased out of Rhodene's brain. 'Did you tell Gundrad the security code so he could get in through the gate?'

Rhodene looked puzzled, as though it hadn't occurred to her to question how he'd been able to get in. 'No. How could I? I don't know it.'

But Mr Thom does.

——

Alpha lunged back inside Rhodene's mind to capture the memory of the meeting on the beach between Rhodene and Mr Thom that Alpha and Janna had observed. At once she found herself sharing Rhodene's frustration. Rhodene had expected to see Gundrad on the beach, and she was furious when she found Mr Thom there instead. *Well, so much for Mr Thom and Rhodene cavorting together. But there was no way that let Mr Thom off the hook. Why else would he have been on the beach if not to meet Gundrad himself?*

CHAPTER
TWENTY-FIVE

Gundrad parked his motorbike near the Willows. He watched the house for the rest of the morning witnessing the inmates leaving for school. At twelve-thirty his patience was rewarded. Lauren was returning home. He caught up with her before she reached the house.

Lauren turned hungry eyes on the good-looking young man, with steel in his eyes, his lips tilting upwards in a half-smile. 'Hi,' she said throatily, her voice box scored from bile raised during her recent vomiting bout. 'Is that your bike?'

Gundrad nodded, turning on the charm by casting an obviously admiring glance over her skinny ribs and super thin arms. Inside his disgust mounted, but he showed no signs of this. 'Do you know Alpha?' he asked.

'What do you want with that freak? Anyway, she's run away,' Lauren told him, fluffing up her hair.

'I know.' Gundrad leaned forward and said in a conspiratorial whisper. 'She's in trouble with the police. My name is Jonathan Battersby and I'm employed to check on her background, so I want you to tell me everything you know about her.' He flicked an official-looking badge at her, which Lauren hardly noticed.

Her eyes glowed with excitement. 'She's a total delinquent— she hardly ever speaks, and she tried to set fire to the bins.'

'Really?'

'I'm sure it was her, but she blamed Bruce. Bruce is only nine—she must've been lying,' Lauren paused. 'After Alpha left, Bruce calmed down. He hated Alpha, said she messed with his head. I reckon she was bullying him.'

'Who's Bruce?'

Lauren fluttered her eyelashes at Gundrad and ignored the question.

He gripped her arm with a force that raised bruises. 'I said, who is Bruce?'

'Bruce Pilkington, he's a bit mad.' Lauren pulled her arm away, not quite so keen now on the handsome face in front of her.

'Where is he?'

'He stopped setting fires when Alpha left, so now he's gone to a foster home.'

———

Bruce Pilkington seemed normal enough although he said very little. His facial expressions hardly changed at all as he muttered short answers to Gundrad's questions. They were getting nowhere until Gundrad asked outright, 'Why did you set fires before?'

Bruce's answer was direct. 'To burn people.'

'Did Alpha tell you not to?'

'Yes.'

'Did she threaten you?'

'No, she went inside my head.'

'Did it hurt?'

'No.'

'Do you know what she did inside your head?'

'No.'

Frustrated with the monosyllabic replies, Gundrad tried his charm on the boy, smiling and patting him on the back, but what worked on teenage girls had no effect on the boy.

Not one to give up, Gundrad had one more question. 'What did she make you feel?'

Bruce lapsed into silence, but just as Gundrad was turning away he added in a low tone, 'She went inside my head and changed me into someone else. At first it was boring, but now…'

'Yes, now?' prompted Gundrad.

Bruce's face relaxed and took on a dreamy quality. 'Now I like the smell of bacon frying. I like eating bananas and ice cream. And I love it when I pedal fast, and my new bike goes zoom.' He paused, and his face tightened. 'But I don't like fire anymore… not even candles. Tell my new mother I don't want any on my birthday cake. They make me scared.'

CHAPTER TWENTY-SIX

After Rhodene had left, Alpha sat scratching her head. She was too wide-awake now to go back to sleep. *Why did Dr Scott and Mrs Hickelroy have to go away just when I need to tell them about Gundrad's regular visits to Krakow Bond?*

What was clear was that someone at the school was giving Gundrad the security code… she was certain that it was Mr Thom but, because she couldn't read his mind, she had no way of confirming it.

A thought struck her, and she straightened her back, coming to a new resolution. *Other people might know more than I do… Janna's right…rules schmules. I'm going to find out what everyone knows.*

———

She ran into Carl and Alex on the stairs. They had nothing more in their heads than a trick involving superglue and toilet seats. Alpha didn't bother trying to change their minds, she just waved a finger under each nose and said, 'Don't.'

'Don't what?' Alex asked, innocently.

'Stay away from the shower rooms. And the toilets.'

'It's not fair! You're not supposed to read our thoughts,' Carl, usually the less aggressive of the two, argued.

'It's dangerous. People get hurt with superglue and that takes it beyond a joke.'

'Bog off,' said Alex, clearly pleased with his pun.

Carl punched Alex's arm, delighted with his friend's comment, but now uncertain whether to continue with their plan. 'OK,' he told Alpha. 'You could be right.' He turned to Alex and said solemnly, 'We don't want to bung up anyone's bunghole, do we?'

Alex giggled. 'They might explode.'

'Where are the shower rooms?' Alpha asked.

Carl pointed up the hallway. 'Fifth door, this floor. But we haven't done anything.'

'Yet,' muttered Alex, running lightly down the stairs.

Alpha walked to the door Carl had mentioned and opened it cautiously, finding herself in a room with lots of individual cubicles. Martel was peering into a mirror inserting his nose rings. He whipped round and glared at Alpha. 'What're you doing in here!'

Alpha's heart sunk and she almost turned and ran out of the room. Of all the people to run into Martel was the second most frightening after Mr Thom. *Or was that the absolute most frightening of all?* If she tried to enter his head and he found out .... Gulping, she steeled herself and used the ready-made excuse the boys had given her to be in the room. 'I caught the terrible twosome planning to superglue the toilet seats. I came in to warn you to check them before you sat down.'

Janna stuck her head out of one of the shower enclosures. 'Hey, thanks. I've just popped in to borrow the boy's shower. The toilet seats are OK for now and the workmen say that the girl's shower room will be finished by this evening. I'll ask for a special coded lock on that. Then the brats won't be able to get in. They're getting worse, those two—we have to watch them like hawks—a few weeks ago they put salt in the sugar shakers and before that they blocked the TV receivers. The only station we could get for ages was Nickelodeon.'

'Yeah, well they're young,' Alpha replied. She caught sight of Martel eyeing her up and down in the mirror and deeply regretted her impulse to come into the bathroom. *Last time he stabbed me in the chest—what'll he do this time?*

No—stuff it! I have to find out what he knows. Alpha deliberately kept her eyes on Janna, using a piece of toilet paper to pretend to be blowing her nose, as she surreptitiously slid into Martel's mind.

———

Martel's thoughts confirmed Sunday's reluctant confession: they were full of stinging tentacles that carried a vicious hatred, though this didn't seem to be directed towards most other people—in fact, a lot of it was directed towards himself. Fending the tentacles off, Alpha discovered that Martel had been lonely when he'd first come to the school, finding it vastly different from the life he was used to on the council estate which, despite the dangers of drug dealers aplenty, had been, for him, a warmer place. Of all the people at Krakow Bond, he only really liked Lily and Sunday though apart from Alpha, Dr Scott, Mr Thom and Mrs Hickelroy—the telepaths—his view of everyone else was simply a cool acceptance. He didn't trust the telepaths at all. This lack of trust was tied up with the early emotions that had developed way back in his childhood rather than through any kind of logical thought process. In that respect, he'd never stopped being a kid—reacting from his gut rather than his brain. But Sunday was the closest thing Martel had to a friend here and he doted on the boy. Talk about a mixed bag of emotions.

Tied up with these complicated thoughts, Alpha neglected to watch where she was walking and suddenly found that she'd wandered right into a nest of tentacles. She slapped at her arms as they stung her repeatedly, finding it impossible to make headway past them. Finally, she discovered that the best way to push them aside was to use a stroking motion like rubbing down the tail of a cat. She managed to clear enough room to wriggle out of the nest, sustaining only a couple more stings in the process. But the tentacles followed her, slipping inside her clothes and winding between her legs. She took refuge inside one of the conch shells that held Martel's memories.

…Martel had been arguing with Mrs Hickelroy, his fury filling the room with unbearable tension. 'There's this girl, Chrissie, she's only fifteen and she's disappeared from my street,' he said. 'Everyone's worried sick. I want to go home—it's useless working on mysteries that are hundreds of years old—I can't do anything about those. I want to help look for Chrissie.'

Under pressure, Mrs Hickelroy remained calm. 'Now Martel, you know what happens to your blood pressure when you get agitated. On in case like that, you could do yourself serious harm. Until Mr Thom finds a way to control your emotions without destroying your abilities I'm afraid you're going to be limited to situations that don't disturb you. I'm sorry my dear, it's for your own good. We really care about you.'

Martel's fury slowly abated, though a small flame of anger continued to burn.

It wasn't easy sifting through Martel's memories. In most minds the memories lay close together, connected by detectable patterns, but Martel had done his best to keep his memories apart, as though he was shutting himself off into separate compartments. The slimy trails that linked these memories lead Alpha to the discovery that Martel was a very complex person indeed. He had varying views on most things, and a complicated, multi-faceted thought process. At one point it seemed that Martel despised all terrorists for their indiscriminate destruction of innocents but at another, he supported anti-war demonstrations and longed to chain himself to Number 10 Downing Street. On the one hand, he relished the skills he was learning at Krakow Bond, intensely proud of his ability to unravel information from objects; on the other hand, he rejected the school's overriding mission of protecting Britain from terror attacks, believing that the school could be doing more in the community itself to stop people turning to terrorism.

With each step, slime clung to Alpha's feet and hands. She carried it with her as she walked so that it contaminated the next thought. This contamination made Martel almost impossible to read. Hatred played with love, despair fought against pride and yet, through it all, Martel managed to project a cool and self-contained image to the outside world.

Exhausted from pushing away the slime-ridden tentacles, Alpha crept inside another memory shell... Here Martel had brushed against Rhodene as they sat down to dinner. His hands twitched in deep suspicion: Rhodene's clothing bore the same sensation that he'd picked up in that underground tunnel, as though Rhodene had been in contact with the person who'd been hiding there...

...Here at least Martel's thoughts were clear: he considered Rhodene too gormless to be involved in a fiendish plot, instead suspecting that Rhodene had been duped. Cleverly, he had worked out that the school had been infiltrated, and he'd resolved to discover who was involved, to turn it to his own advantage...

...Another step showed Alpha Martel's first thoughts on finding out that she was joining the school. Another telepath! He could just about put up with Howie, because of Howie's severe afflictions, and he loved Sunday, but someone new like Alpha, who was completely telepathic, was just bad, bad news to him.

But within a new shell, Alpha learned that time had shown her up in a slightly different light to Martel. His deep-seated hatred had been replaced by a level of curiosity about the slight girl who was such a powerful mind reader. He didn't trust her— but at least he no longer disliked her because he was wrongly basing all his perceptions about her on his memories of his father. He'd somehow broken out of the trap that every white telepath was his archenemy.

… In the next shell, Martel's stony eyes kept tabs on many people. He became highly interested in Alpha and Janna as he observed their ghost hunting antics, suspecting that at least one of them was connected to the infiltrator… For Alpha, it was the oddest sensation, watching from Martel's suspicious eyes as he followed two people, realising that she was one of those people. She seemed different when seen through Martel's eyes: a mysterious and sinister influence on the school. *Is this what he thinks of me? How strange—we both suspect each other.*

…Soon Alpha was able to recover the moment when Martel reported to Mr Thom that the three students had entered the trapdoor leading into the West Wing. In this memory Martel's thoughts were filled with fear for Sunday, his acute senses detecting that the sub-basement was unsafe. Alpha gave a guilty start. *Martel's right; I should never have made Sunday lead us into the West Wing…*

…Another shell showed Martel's next stop had been Miss Gilford. Martel was sure that, as head gardener, she had access to the original plans of the gardens. He accosted the woman, demanding to know about tunnels leading through the grounds or under the buildings. Miss Gilford literally bristled. Her bushy hair stood straight up, and she used every inch of her large muscular body to try to intimidate Martel. She denied the existence of any such tunnels and ordered Martel back into the house, but Martel stood his ground, forcing the woman to walk away. A fleeting smile crossed his lips…he already knew about two underground tunnels, there were bound to be more. He decided to keep a careful watch on the gardener…

Alpha thought she could feel Martel becoming aware of her. She slipped out of the conch that enwrapped Martel's recent memories and took refuge in a shell from Martel's distant past… In there a small, dark-skinned Martel, surely no more than six, cowered in front of his father, a white man with the palest skin who towered over the child with a weighty strength and a swinging leather belt. She could feel Martel's absolute terror at what would come next and knew that the whole of Martel's life would be shaped by that moment. No wonder Martel hated white telepaths so much.

The memory was so full of pain that Alpha couldn't shift to another until this one had played itself out. She stood there silently, powerless to help the small boy as the big man pushed fear into his mind, seeking to control the boy in the same way he controlled the mother, using both brute force and mental torture.

'*I can read your mind,*' the bully that was his father said, forcing the unsaid words into Martel's head. '*You're pooping yourself, you little black bastard. You're right to be scared. I've got something special planned for you.*'

But as tiny as he was Martel himself wasn't helpless. A fusion of steaming emotion shot towards his father, like a pressure cooker blasting off its lid. As the man stepped closer and raised his arm with the belt, the bolt of panic hit him between the eyes, causing his eyebrows to lift and his eyes to flip back within his eyeballs. He reeled, then crashed into a wall and dropped to the floor, where he lay, arms and legs twitching as a result of the heart attack brought on by his drink-ridden body and the extreme fear Martel had pushed back into him.

The muscles around Alpha's heart clenched. Intense pain spread through her chest, and her breath caught inside her lungs. The panic she'd felt when the boys had played their horse trotting trick on her was magnified a hundred-fold—the entire world had become her enemy. She spun out of Martel's thoughts, buckled and fell to the floor.

———

'Alpha?' Janna knelt next to Alpha, naked apart from a hastily grabbed towel, splashing drops of water everywhere.

Alpha's eyes fluttered open, and she glimpsed Martel in the corner of the room, pinning her to the floor with his eyes alone. She knew without any doubt that Martel was controlling her heartbeat with an unbearable dose of fear.

Long seconds passed before Martel brushed a hand across his face, cutting off the contact. 'You finished, girl?' he muttered, now avoiding looking at Alpha.

'Y…Yes.' Alpha stammered. She pushed herself up onto her elbows. 'I'll go now.' But getting up was another matter, and Alpha felt too weak for that.

Janna tossed her clothes on inside out, shouting all the while at Martel. 'What have you done to her, you bastard!'

She knelt down next to Alpha. 'You look like death. I'll call Biddy.'

Alpha waved off her concerns. 'I'm fine.' *Now that Martel's stopped.* She gripped Janna's hand and stood up unsteadily. 'I'll see you later, Janna.' She tottered from the bathroom, her breath still rough and catching in her throat.

Martel had known that she was inside his head, and he had reacted like a snake, filling Alpha with fear, just as he'd struck at his father so many years ago.

Gradually Alpha's heartbeat lost its spiked rhythm, leaving room for pity for the young Martel to squeeze in alongside her fear. She took a deep breath, then exhaled slowly. Other people's secrets were as bad as her own. Just as he was beginning to lose his distrust of her, she had to bring it all back again.

But, on the plus side, she was now certain that Martel wasn't involved with Gundrad, however radical his mixed-up views were. *It would be good to work with Martel on finding out what is going on,* she thought. *If only he would be willing to.*

The next moment she'd changed her mind. *Na! It's never going to happen, Martel isn't that trusting, especially of me. Especially not now!*

She bit her lip as she realised that she couldn't talk to Janna about this either. *I can't go splashing Martel's deepest secrets around, confirming Janna's suspicions that he murdered his father. Janna doesn't even know Gundrad's name, let alone his connection with Rhodene… how can I explain that Martel isn't on Gundrad's side, that he's also trying to find out what's going on at this school?*

And that leaves me nowhere.

Except…. maybe I should try Miss Gilford… or Lily… or Biddy. Damn! I wish I could read Mr Thom's thoughts. This problem is a mythical beast with too many heads: no sooner do I shoot down one suspect than another rears up to take its place.

CHAPTER TWENTY-SEVEN

Alpha's target was Mrs Gilford, but the woman had disappeared, doing whatever it was a head gardener did when she wasn't spying on students. She didn't even make an appearance in the dining room for breakfast but during the morning tea break. Alpha caught up with Janna for the first time since their early meeting in the shower room. Their newly arranged schedules had kept them apart including over breakfast. Alpha suspected Mr Thom of doing his best to separate them.

'Are you OK?' Janna asked. 'You looked worse than some of my ghosts.'

'Thanks a bundle. I'm fine.' Alpha racked her brains to find a way to tell Janna about everything she'd discovered without sharing anything she wasn't supposed to, but all too soon break was over, and they were obliged to part. Mr Thom's beady eye let them know that they had little choice in the matter.

Alpha decided that Lily would be next on her list. *I can't believe it's her, but Dr Scott wouldn't let her act as the control for me to fix Rhodene's dreams. He wanted to wait until Mrs Hickelroy was back. Does he suspect Lily?*

———

At her next lesson, which was with Lily, it was easy to enter Lily's mind—she allowed Alpha to dive right in.

'Find anything interesting in there?' Lily asked after a few moments, a smile creasing her ample chins.

'No, sorry. I was… ' Alpha turned red behind her curtain of hair.

Absolutely no guilty thoughts had come to the surface of Lily's brain. Her prime concern was that she be given responsibility for Alpha's training rather than Mr Thom.

Alpha also knew from her exploration that Lily was worried about Howie's health. But she hadn't had time to explore all Lily's thoughts before the teacher had let her know that she was fully aware of Alpha's unauthorised entry in her mind, so she left the lesson still in two minds about Lily.

––––

Alpha had a free period next, so she went looking for Biddy. Biddy was a dark horse and might know more than anyone suspected.

Alpha caught sight of her stepping into the courtyard, bustling towards East Wing, rolls of paper towels in her arms. Alpha was just about to approach her when she saw Mr Thom creeping down a flight of stairs into the basement of North Block. She dashed across the courtyard. Below her, through one of the basement light wells, she spotted movement. She bent down and stuck her nose to the grid. *Yes! There he is.* As she observed him he clicked on a switch and the area he was in flooded with light. *All those rows of electrical switches—that must be the electricity board and meters.*

Mr Thom opened one of the boxes, flicked a large red switch then snipped a wire. He spent a few moments adding a piece of circuitry to the system, before rejoining the wires, turning the switch on and closing up the lid.

Alpha stared at the markings on that box—it was labelled security system. Mr Thom put the pliers in his pocket before leaving the small room. He was definitely determined not to be seen because he peered round the door before going through it and she could feel his extra senses testing the air for onlookers. She tensed, but he didn't glance up at the light well.

Then she realised why. The egg in her pocket had become warm and she could feel its presence surrounding her with an invisible glow, a sort of psychic screen that hid her from his telepathic search.

At last Mr Thom was satisfied. His senses shrank back into him and as they did Alpha felt the glow from the egg dim. She took it from her pocket and stared at it. It looked just like a normal stone egg, except that the bands of blue were sparkling in the sunlight. She knew, though, that she hadn't imagined its shielding properties. *Fantastic!*

But however interesting the egg was, she was still dead keen to find out what Mr Thom was up to. Instead of following him down the basement steps, she went into the hall. If she used those stairs to get down to the gym she could pretend to be checking out the facilities as a reason for being 'lost' in the basement, although what she knew about electricity boards and their workings could be written on the head of a pin.

But as she entered the hall she caught another glimpse of Mr Thom. He'd obviously climbed back up the basement steps because he appeared outside of North Block. Within an instant, he had slipped behind the yew hedge. Now, screened from the view of anyone in the house, he could walk towards the gate without being seen.

Alpha frowned. *Has he been disabling the security system?* Her nerves fluttered. H*e might be on his way right now to let Gundrad in.*

There was no way she could follow him; she'd be far too visible. She dragged her feet as she considered what to do next until she heard a car screech into the courtyard. She hoped it was Dr Scott, but instead she saw Mrs Hickelroy get out and take her suitcase from the back seat. Earlier Alpha had gained the impression that Mrs Hickelroy would be away for quite a while. Now she guessed that Dr Scott had ordered her to return because he didn't like to leave the school rudderless for too long.

On impulse, she ran towards the car. 'Mrs Hickelroy,' she called out.

The vice-principal turned and put down her case. 'Hello. You look a bit flustered.'

Alpha regarded her shyly, not sure exactly what she should tell her. 'It's Mr Thom…'

'If it's about who'll be your primary tutor, I've been thinking… the last thing I want is for you to feel unhappy, so I'm going to take on that role myself.'

Alpha felt a flush of relief but her worries about Gundrad and Mr Thom overrode that almost instantly. 'No… it's… well I've just seen Mr Thom messing around with the electricity circuits.'

A touch of surprise crept out from Mrs Hickelroy's mind, but her face remained calm as she said, 'Mr Thom often deals with repairs around here. You're not scared of the dark, are you? Don't worry, whatever it is he'll have fixed it by nightfall. He's very handy, you know.'

That's what I'm scared of. The man has his hands everywhere, including inside people's heads. 'No, but…'

'Leave it with me. I'll find out what's gone wrong now.' She sighed. 'We could do without any more problems—we've got to focus on that train smash. First thing tomorrow I want you in my office. We'll plan how to get Howie to open up to you.' The frown left her face and she smiled at Alpha. 'We're going to do good work together, you and I.' Then she turned away and bent to pick up her suitcase.

Part of Alpha basked in a warm glow but by far the largest section of her gave a guilty start. *Howie's dream!* She'd all but forgotten it with everything that had happened since. She couldn't concentrate with Mr Thom at the front of her thoughts. If only Mrs Hickelroy would listen—but she was far too nice to believe bad things about anyone. 'Can I carry your case?' Alpha asked in a last-ditch attempt to spend a little more time with the vice-principal persuading her that Mr Thom was dangerous.

'It's kind of you, but I'll manage. I don't want you to be late for lunch. Andreyaz's temper must not be frayed.' Mrs Hickelroy grinned and walked away.

Alpha's shoulders slumped. Clearly, Mrs Hickelroy didn't think that Mr Thom's actions were anything to be alarmed about… *or if she does, she isn't going to tell me about it.*

It seemed like whichever avenue Alpha explored she was destined to discover no more than she already knew—and they were no nearer to solving the mystery of when and where the train smash would happen either.

CHAPTER
TWENTY-EIGHT

Uncertain of what she should do next, Alpha plodded towards the dining hall.

'Why so miz?' Janna asked, running to catch up with Alpha at the sight of her in a deep funk.

'Don't tell me, now you can read my mind too.'

'Don't be dim! It's your face I'm reading, it's so long it's trying to say hello to your shoes. Come on. We've got ten minutes, let's hit East Block basement. It's just the place for your deepest, darkest confessions—as long as they don't involve Howie's mad predictions again.'

'What about lunch?' warned Alpha.

'Doesn't matter if we're a bit late. I'll tell Andreyaz we've been in the woods hunting for mushrooms for him. I've even got some for him. He's a sweetie under all that bluster—he'll forgive anything if it involves food. Come on, I'll race you. Last one down sits opposite Rhodene at lunch and gets the full effect of her farts. They're something wicked since she gave up her diet and started munching chocs again.'

'You're evil—just as bad as Sunday, twisting everyone to your will,' called Alpha, running to catch Janna who'd already shot down the steps.

'Me? When did you ever see me breaking into bedrooms?'

Alpha chuckled to herself as she skidded down the concrete stairs. Janna always managed to improve her mood.

Janna had already settled back against the dusty wall when Alpha caught up with her. 'Come on slowpoke, tell Mama all about it.'

'I don't know what to do next,' Alpha confided. She explained how she'd caught Mr Thom in the act, but couldn't prove anything. 'Mrs Hickelroy thinks I'm neurotic about him, which doesn't help. And I'm worried that we still don't know any more about that train smash. What if it happens today?'

'There's no point worrying yourself to death over that. You can't force psychic skills, either we'll pick up a trace or we won't.' Janna dug her foot into a crack in the wall and hoisted herself onto the window ledge, perching her bottom precariously on it. 'Tell you what, if we can't get to tinkie-winkie Thom directly, the best thing we can do is to follow Rhodene and Martel. Especially Rhodene—why did she meet Thom on the beach?'

Alpha hung her head, forced into biting her tongue to stop herself from blabbing. *Damn Dr Scott and his promises.*

Janna brushed Alpha's shoulder in a friendly but questioning gesture. 'What happened in the bathroom this morning? You went inside Martel's mind, didn't you? What did you find in there?'

Framing her sentences with care, Alpha explained that Martel had discovered an intruder, though she left out the fact that the intruder was connected to Rhodene and the memories in Martel's mind about his father. 'You see,' she concluded, 'Martel's suspicious of us, so he can't be involved with Iwardi's killer.'

'That's not necessarily true,' disagreed Janna. 'This intruder of his might not be connected to Pasha and Iwardi. One of the staff could have a secret lover.'

Alpha swallowed the lump in her throat. Explaining about the link to Gundrad would mean explaining about Rhodene, and then she'd have to tell Janna how she got Rhodene to change her mind about leaving the school, and she'd be breaking another promise to Dr Scott. Only this promise, she knew, was much more serious than her promise not to look inside people's heads. She was caught up in deceit; her very silence breaking down the friendship she'd developed with Janna.

And Janna knew it too. 'What aren't you telling me?'

Mutely, Alpha shook her head.

Janna stared at her accusingly. 'You've been checking out people's thoughts and you won't even tell me about it.' She hesitated, then demanded, 'Mine too?'

'Only when you invited me in to see Iwardi and Pasha.'

Janna kicked at the corner with sharp little thrusts. 'Well if you don't trust me then sod you.' Suddenly she slid off the ledge down the wall and ran out of the basement, slamming the door behind her and leaving Alpha gaping behind her.

Over lunch Alpha tried to apologise to Janna but, without giving away her promise to Dr Scott, her excuses held no substance. And with both Rhodene and Martel within earshot this was mission-bloody-impossible!

Janna looked sceptical as Alpha concluded by whispering that Rhodene really wasn't all that bad. 'She's only been such a misery-guts because she thought she'd lost her talent.'

'Why didn't you tell me that before?' Janna hissed, her eyes showing the hurt she felt that Alpha hadn't trusted her.

'I'm sorry, but it wasn't my secret to tell.' Alpha was already regretting sharing this much. 'I wasn't supposed to read Rhodene's thoughts at all and Dr Scott said I shouldn't talk about it.'

'Huh!' Janna retreated into her meal to avoid further conversation. Alpha hunched over her plate, desperately trying to find the words to tell Janna how bad she felt about keeping her in the dark.

But before she could say anything else Mrs Hickelroy rushed into the room and began causing a stir at the far end of the table. Both girls' eyes were drawn to her as she bustled up and down, asking questions of the staff. It seemed that Biddy had vanished sometime in the last half an hour or so. Unable to gain any information, Mrs Hickelroy moved on to the students, and eventually, her busy questions established that Alpha was the last person to see Biddy.

'She was in the courtyard just before you drove in,' said Alpha, 'about to go into the East Wing. Hasn't anyone seen her since then?'

Mrs Hickelroy shook her head.

'Why's Sunday gone with Dr Scott?' Rhodene asked the vice-principal, her jealousy leaking into the atmosphere.

Mrs Hickelroy's lips tightened into a thin line. 'The Prime Minister insisted on it. He wants Sunday to tell him what the Saudi delegation will be willing to settle for before he commits himself one way or the other.'

If he wanted someone to read minds why didn't he take me? Alpha wondered. *Doesn't he trust me?*

Martel's eyebrows drew together darkly. 'They're exploiting that boy!'

'Dr Scott is furious,' Mrs Hickelroy let slip, walking away.

Alpha sensed that Janna was still feeling argumentative and, having decided not to talk to her, Janna wanted someone else to vent her anger on. 'We should be grateful,' Janna told Martel. 'Sunday is the only one offering the government a service at the moment. Without him, they'd close us down.'

Martel snorted. 'So,' he drawled, 'you think you're the queen of psi just because you were invited up to the House of Lords once?'

Normally Janna would have a retort on the tip of her tongue, but today she simply blushed and looked upset. 'I wasn't any use, was I? All I could sense was Mrs Thatcher's enemies trying to chuck her out decades ago.'

'Exactly. Waste of oxygen, that's what you are,' Martel agreed.

Mrs Hickelroy, already halfway up the table, turned smartly on her heels to reprimand him. 'Martel! I won't put up with that kind of talk. Apologise to Janna at once.'

She waited until Martel had mumbled an ungracious 'Sorry', then left the table again.

'Bitch,' muttered Martel under her breath, glaring at Mrs Hickelroy.

Alpha shook her head at Martel's obvious dislike of Mrs Hickelroy and his mean comments to Janna. She tried to console Janna, apologising once again for not telling her everything but Janna only gave a tight smile and turned away.

Alpha bit her lip and sat staring at her plate for the rest of the meal, having lost her appetite. She wasn't the only one not eating; Mrs Hickelroy hadn't sat down at all. Why she should make such a fuss about the housekeeper skipping a meal was a mystery, but Alpha had to admit it was a bit unusual that Biddy wasn't keeping a motherly eye on Howie.

Howie sat at the long table, aiming spoon after spoon of jelly at his face and taking no notice of the discussion about his mother raging around him. When the bowl was empty, he sat quite still with drops falling from his cheeks. Alpha realised that every other time she'd seen Howie eat, someone had tucked a napkin into his collar and draped it across his lap. That must have been Biddy.

Janna turned away at the end of the meal, muttering that she had to revise the news scanning technique that Lily had taught her. Alpha gazed after her, her mood sinking even lower.

Then abruptly, she firmed her mouth, deciding that now was as good a time as any to tackle Howie's brain. She went up to him and tapped him on the shoulder. 'Let's see if we can get those spots off your trousers.'

Howie allowed himself to be led away from the table and she coaxed him up the stairs to her bathroom. At the basin, she wiped Howie's cheeks and dabbed at his trousers making a moderate improvement to the mess on his knees. He stood there complacently until she had finished, opening his mouth to poke his tongue out through his teeth.

———

Inside Howie's mind, she found herself in a maze. Normally she didn't enter the parts of the brain that did little reasoning or remembering, but in Howie's case she had no control over where she was going—his sense of balance was jumping from one side of his head to the other, creating a treacherous path that caused her to slip from side to side. His brain simply did not work like other people's. She navigated through channels that moved like open lifts, swinging wildly in unexpected directions. She found memories that should have been stable but that had become expectations of the future. Feelings were pushed to the back of the brain with little chance of escape. Lifts whizzed back and forward, jolted, then swung her around so that she was travelling at speed in every direction. At times she was dropped off before another lift came by to pick her up again. When she landed it was as though she was standing on a series of crazy, shifting rooftops, seeing other buildings around her that kept moving in height and in angle. Some even revolved upside down while others shot off into the distance. One came hurtling towards her and she ducked, almost falling.

Lily had said that Howie wasn't able to interpret the things his senses told him, but she found that wasn't true. On the contrary, Howie had rather too many interpretations for anything his senses fed him. His brain was filled with thousands of images, thoughts and equations. His problem was choosing what was real or important.

Bizarrely, the one sense Howie could rely on was his tongue. His tongue appeared not only to taste but also in some strange way to see. He used it to find out what was going on around him, like when she caught a glimpse of a memory of Howie licking the packs of cards he and Sunday had been playing with. Instantly his head had filed all the suits and numbers of every card in the order they'd been shuffled into. *Amaaaaa...zing! No wonder he won so often.*

She was unaware that at that moment Howie was trying to get close enough to lick her face. But Howie's balance was whipping around in his head, and he was staggering from foot to foot on the perfectly stable bathroom floor.

She slid through a bunch of sums—Howie's way of making connections with things. Everything was measured: mass of jelly, length of spoon, distance to his mouth, room size, number of steps up to her room, paces to the door, her weight, her height, distance to her face. Howie had equations for everything.

Howie's brain threw her from side to side yet again. She tried to map where she'd been and where she had yet to be twisted into, but nothing inside Howie's head remained in the same place for very long. Howarth lived somewhere in this muddle, and she wanted to find him.

Howie lurched forward, succeeding in finding her face with his tongue. Unconsciously Alpha took a step backwards in Howie's mind. As she did she slipped downwards through a dark chasm and into a deeper layer underlying the chaos—a layer filled with tall pillars of flame, burning with the unmistakable smell of sulphur. This, then, was Howarth's hideout.

Howarth had his own mental image of how he looked, and he was a solid, chunky man. He was also furious. He came at her; an enraged bull determined to remove this intruder.

She ducked to the side and Howarth ran right past her. He whirled but she sped behind one of the flaming pillars.

A mad game of chase followed with her darting and weaving while Howarth lumbered around looking for her. Howarth had none of Howie's abilities with numbers and he failed to find a way to trap her into a corner.

Endless minutes passed until Howarth snorted, gave a last backwards glance, then retired once more to the dark corner where he'd been slumbering earlier. He seemed worn out as he sank to the ground.

Moving silently, she stepped out from behind the pillar. Howarth was fast asleep.

She knew that she had no chance of finding a trigger inside Howie's disturbed head, everything was moving too fast. Even if she found one, how could she get Howarth to talk to her? He did his own thing inside Howie's mind.

Then she remembered that Howarth did speak; he spoke to Lily when Howie was asleep. *So how does Howarth hear her questions?*

She edged through Howarth's quarters, trying not to wake him as she sought the spot that was a link through to Howie. Apart from the flaming pillars that had died down to half their previous size, this part of Howie's brain was asleep. Neurons hung above and below her like transparent multi-limbed spiders, empty and waiting. None of them was fired up with information.

Then she found what she was looking for: an irregular hole above her head that acted as a funnel for passing information back and forth between Howie and his alter ego, Howarth. She squeezed into a corner near the hole then projected a small portion of her attention back into her own body.

Now to pretend to be Lily…

————

Alpha was unaware of Howie's probing tongue now licking her arm as she copied Lily's rolling Jamaican accent. 'When I snap my fingers, Howie, you will sleep. Wake when I snap them twice.'

Obediently, Howie fell asleep at her snap, slumping sideways into the wicker armchair Biddy had so thoughtfully provided in her bathroom.

————

Inside the lower chamber she saw Howarth stir. 'I'm looking for Howarth. Answer me, Howarth,' Lily's voice, as well as Alpha could imitate it, instructed.

Instantly Howarth became fully awake.

'Tell me about Gundrad,' Alpha demanded.

The bull-like man bared his teeth. Then, in a deep man's voice he said, 'He and his partner walk in the night when the moon sleeps and the sky is darker than Hades.'

Yes! 'Tell me about his partner.'

'They're related by blood and cord; joined by purpose.'

I get the joined by purpose bit, but what does he mean related by blood and cord? Mr Thom and Gundrad can't be blood brothers; Thom is much older than Gundrad. Icy fingers crept up her back. Had they committed murder together, tying their victims with cord before slicing them up? Or was that only her imagination getting the better of her? *For heaven's sake Howie, talk sense.* 'Who is his partner? Is it Mr Thom?' she asked, her put-on Jamaican accent slipping.

A different, lighter voice answered her now, as though reciting a children's rhyme. 'Who…is the monkey who lives in the Zoo. Tom, Tom the butcher's son.'

Oh Howie, don't go iffy on me now. She tried a different tack. 'What do Gundrad and his partner want?'

The man's voice was back. 'To bind Alpha in a coffin lined with silver and cloth—the cloth of blood.'

Alpha shivered. *Coffins again. First Iwardi in his coffin case and now Howarth is going on about one for me. Where did he learn to talk like this? Apparently, he's swallowed a couple of Dr Zeus books then stayed up late watching Dracula reruns.*

'Why this girl Alpha?' she asked, doing her best to copy Lily's melodic tones.

'She must join the FBFBA to serve their cause. The FBFBA, FBFBA, FBFBA!' Every repeat of the acronym made Alpha shiver.

The FBFBA—Dr Scott mentioned them before. 'What's their cause?' she asked impatiently, almost forgetting to use Lily's accent. Howarth hesitated, his brow creasing in puzzlement as he decoded Howie's information. Then, at last, he answered a question directly.

She wished he hadn't; the answer chilled her to the bone. 'They're a terrorist organisation. They aim to kill every fucking moderate freethinker in Britain. Alpha is a weapon—Gundrad wants Alpha,' he paused, 'wants you, as their instrument of death.'

'W…weapon? Weapon to do what?'

'To bring down the government.'

Shocked to her core it was all she could do to whisper, 'How?'

The boy's voice echoed down the funnel. 'Gundrad's back… he'll hear me… don't make me talk… they're both here at Krakow Bond… I'm afraid.'

'Don't be scared, Howie,' rumbled Howarth, showing by the volume of his voice that he, at least, wasn't afraid. He stood up and thrust his fists in front of him. He flailed and fought with unseen foes, missing Alpha but charging around the lower chamber of Howie's mind at speed.

No, Howarth no! she screamed, trying to regain control of the raging bull-man.

Then his huge fist swung out past one of the flaming pillars and caught her brainwaves. He grabbed and squeezed, and she shot out of Howie's mind.

———

Her head spun dizzily, and from the corner of her eye, she caught sight of Howie nuzzling and drooling as he turned his face towards her. Then she fainted, falling sideways, banging her arm on the tap in the shower before crashing her head against the tiles and falling to the floor.

Everything went dim just as Howarth added three more words. 'Mother will die!'

CHAPTER TWENTY-NINE

Alpha lay on a cold, hard surface, slowly becoming aware that she was wet. Her head was throbbing, and her eyes stubbornly refused to open. Warm liquid splashed onto her face.

Sounds filtered through to her. She sensed people around her.

Someone leaned over her. The drips stopped but her clothes continued to soak up the surrounding wetness.

Lily's voice floated through the air, as though from a great distance away. 'How could this happen, Horatio?'

'I don't know yet,' Mr Thom said, his tone flat and even. 'I'll find out when I examine Alpha's mind. Vicky, can you check that Howie hasn't been hurt? And has anyone found Biddy? She should be here.'

'There's still no sign of her.' Mrs Hickelroy's voice swam in and out of Alpha's awareness.

Someone pried her eyelids open. The light hurt. 'Pupils look fine, no dilation.'

Her eyelids were left alone to close. Her mind drifted. Darkness closed in.

Touch. A pressure against her left leg. Slowly, Alpha worked out that someone was squatting down next to her. Her head was grasped between two firm hands, and she felt fingers push hard into her temples. She heard a deep, male grunt—Mr Thom—and suddenly one of his hands was behind her neck, and the other was grabbing her throat and squeezing.

'Stop! You're choking her,' Lily cried.

'No. I'm threatening her body so that her mind will respond.'

Liar! Liar! Help! He's strangling me to death. But she couldn't speak; the air was being squashed from her windpipe. Her eyes flew open.

Beyond the squatting figure of Mr Thom, Alpha could only just make out the hazy image of Mrs Hickelroy. The vice-principal was frowning anxiously as she bent over Howie, totally oblivious to what Mr Thom was doing. Alpha tried to scream but the hands around her neck stopped all breath, allowing only a shallow gasp to emerge. Her eyes flew towards Lily Wade who was shaking her head and wiping tears from her eyes with the ends of her flowing sleeves, all her focus on Howie. Alpha flapped her arm feebly, trying to attract her attention.

The hands around her neck loosened and she coughed. Lily's stricken face loomed above her. 'My dear, dear child. What happened?'

'Mr Thom. He's trying to kill me,' Alpha croaked.

'Rubbish! She's been messing about inside Howie's mind.' Mr Thom twisted Alpha's face until she was looking directly at him. 'What have you done to Howie?'

He can't kill me in front of everyone—can he? As though in line with her thoughts, Mr Thom relaxed his harsh grip. Alpha transferred her blurry gaze to Howie, who lay sleeping peacefully in the wicker chair. 'He's OK. I just have to wake him up.'

'Do it!' Mr Thom barked, propping Alpha upright from behind.

Alpha's limbs still felt paralysed. With an effort, she raised one hand until she could see the blurry outline of her fingers in front of her face. It took several goes before her damp fingers managed to snap twice but as soon as they did Howie stood up abruptly and took five short paces to the door, stepping round Lily and ignoring everyone. He stuck his hand out and tugged at the handle until the door opened, which allowed him to shuffle forwards into the bedroom. He repeated the exercise with the door into the corridor, then left without a backwards glance at those assembled there.

'Child! What have you done! Testing your teachers is one thing, but messing with students … ' Lily shook her head, sadly. 'It's so dangerous inside Howie's mind. You can cause untold damage, both to him and to yourself.'

'Has she tried to read your thoughts as well?' Mrs Hickelroy asked.

Lily nodded, looking reproachfully towards Alpha.

Alpha tried to speak, spluttered instead and coughed several times before finally managing to say anything. 'I…I'm sorry, Miss Lily… Howie's fine… I didn't hurt him… Please don't let Mr Thom…' Mr Thom's hand tightened on her back. Somehow she wrenched herself away from him.

Mrs Hickelroy's usually unruffled face was flushed in anger. 'Alpha, I'm bitterly disappointed—you've broken the most important rule we have here. Psychics can't learn together if they can't trust one another. You'll remain in your room until I've decided what to do with you.'

Alpha looked up into Mrs Hickelroy's cold face. *I've let her down*, she thought, feeling sick about it. She had to persuade the vice-principal that she'd done no harm to Howie. 'Howie…'

'Is not your concern,' Mrs Hickelroy interrupted.

'I'm going to check on Howie, then I'll come back and examine Alpha to make sure there's been no permanent damage,' said Mr Thom, rising effortlessly to his feet.

Alpha's heart lunged. 'Don't leave me alone with him!' she pleaded.

Mrs Hickelroy looked her up and down before replying. 'Very well Horatio. But Alpha is restricted to her room and must not leave it. Lily, get Miss Gilford to stand guard outside her door.'

'If you say so, Vicky,' Lily agreed. 'I'll just see to Howie first, his mind is so very fragile.'

Mrs Hickelroy drew herself up to her full height. 'Fetch Miss Gilford at once, please, before you go after Howie. I'll wait in the corridor myself until she arrives.' She stalked out, followed by Mr Thom, leaving Alpha lying on the bathroom floor.

Alpha grabbed Lily's trailing sleeve, but before she could beg Lily to stay with her, Lily pulled herself away, saying crossly, 'Not now Alpha. I must see to Howie.'

Alpha watched her glide out into the corridor, closing the bedroom door firmly behind her.

Janna, Alpha's mind screamed. *Help, Mr Thom is coming to get me.*

But the workmen had finally finished Janna's new bedroom, and, like Alpha's, it now was lined in tin. Alpha knew that Janna was in there; she couldn't find her mental signature anywhere else in the building or the grounds. *She probably wouldn't come even if she could hear me, and I don't blame her.*

She dragged herself up from the bathroom floor, staggered to the bedroom window and gazed down to where safety lay three floors below. There were no creepers or drainpipes to help her down. In desperation, she called out to Sunday, crying his name again and again, knowing that even if he could hear her, Sunday was many miles away in London, with Dr Scott.

CHAPTER THIRTY

Alpha staggered to the bedroom door and flung it open. Outside stood the chief gardener, her scarlet overalls ironed into neat stripes down the leg, her hair scattered with grass clippings. Miss Gilford had gigantic muscular arms, weighed in at around sixteen stone, and was built like a bus. There was no way Alpha was going to get past her.

If she's in league with Mr Thom and Gundrad, I'm sunk, thought Alpha. 'What's the code to the security gate?' she blurted out. Miss Gilford folded her massive arms across her belly and glared at Alpha—her spillage easy to read. *She doesn't know it! She thinks I want the code so I can run away.*

Alpha tried a more direct approach. 'Are you working with Gundrad? Is Mr Thom his partner?'

The Gillybird stepped closer, filling the door frame. Astonishment was written all over her face. It was obvious that she had no idea who Gundrad was, never mind his partner. Her thoughts showed that she was beginning to believe her prisoner was a basket-case. 'Flaming kids—nothing but trouble,' she said, under her breath.

Alpha slammed the door in her face. *If I can't get out myself maybe I can keep him out.* She flicked the key, and the lock tumbled into place. The door would hold for a while and unless they were working together she couldn't see Mr Thom chopping through it with that battle axe standing guard outside.

A dreadful thought occurred to her then. *Mr Thom's telepathic! He doesn't need to get in.* She ran across the room and shut the window, glad for the first time that her room was tin lined. Next, she pushed the painted chest in front of the door. It was filled with bed linen and made her puff. She added the wicker chair from the bathroom to the barricade, jamming it under the handle and hunted round for anything else that would keep that monster out. *The desk.*

As she began shoving it towards the door she heard footsteps outside in the corridor. The lock clicked open by itself, the knob turned, and the door was pushed inwards. The heavy chest stopped it immediately. She ran to the chest, stood on it, slammed her weight against the door, and reached across the chair to twist the key, gripping so hard with her fingers that they hurt. She heard footsteps moving away from her room.

For a long while, still standing on the chest, she stayed glued to the spot, but nothing happened. Her fingers cramped.

Then lighter footsteps ran along the corridor outside her room.

The chair flew up into the air narrowly missing her head. It fell to the floor, breaking into bits. The chest she was standing on tilted until she tumbled off. Taking on a life of its own, it danced smartly away from the door into the far corner of the room. The lock clicked again, and Mr Thom strode in, wearing a thunderous look on his face. Behind him she caught a glimpse of Carl, his mouth forming a startled 'O', before Mr Thom slammed the door and turned towards her.

She backed into the corner, fell over the chest that had come to rest there and landed on her bottom on top of its lid. There was nowhere else to hide so she pulled herself into a ball and hid behind her hair, for all the good that was going to do.

'Now,' said Mr Thom, 'tell me what is going on or I'll switch off that prodigious talent of yours for good. I swear it.'

He stood with his legs spread wide apart and, though he was short, he seemed grounded to the floor. Like a stone buried deep in the earth. 'For goodness' sake—why are you behaving like this? Come on, talk.'

She remained mute, tucked tight into her corner.

In the silence that followed, Mr Thom unfolded his arms and his shoulders slumped. He walked over to her bed and sat down on it, putting his face in his hands. She stole a quick glance at him; suddenly he looked less like the world's most vicious man and more like a tired and worried teacher.

Finally, he raised his head and spoke to her, openly and honestly. 'Alpha, I think someone is trying to sabotage us by making off with our students. It wouldn't take much to close the school; we're very vulnerable at the moment. Now I'm sure you know something ... please... tell me. Otherwise, I'll have to shut you down, truly I will. Mrs Hickelroy's right about that. We can't take the risk that you'll be taken by them. You're simply too powerful. Unless we can sort this out, your ability will attract them like flies to honey. Whoever they are, they're very dangerous, to you and to others.'

Gundrad. He wants me as his weapon.

Mr Thom's eyes, which moments ago had been hard marbles, were now soft and liquid just like their old Labrador, Jake, had looked, all those years ago before Alpha's dad had died. 'Look into my mind,' he pleaded. 'I'll let you in. You can check that I won't hurt you.'

She shook her head. This could be a trick; as soon as she entered his mind he would warp her thoughts just as Gundrad had bewitched Rhodene.

'You are scared, aren't you? That's what this is all about?'

This time she nodded.

He peered at her intently, then hazarded a guess at what was wrong. 'You touched someone's mind and found shreds of evil?'

Her startled look confirmed it.

'Howie's?' he asked, his voice puzzled and rattled.

She gave a quick shake, then risked a few words. 'Gundrad left his thoughts in Rhodene's mind. They hurt me. And I think he stole one of her memories.' *Or you did!*

'Gundrad?' He thought for a moment. 'Is he her motorcycle man? The one she was planning to run away with?' To Alpha, whose senses were very finely tuned at this moment, he seemed genuine, and he definitely hadn't connected the name to the man on the bike before now.

When she nodded, his eyes crinkled as his gaze softened. 'Right! Now I understand.'

'I can help you protect yourself,' he went on.

Mr Thom had always been so distant, and she'd never felt any spillage from him before, but now she could tell that he was shocked that she'd been hurt. *He can't be acting, can he? His emotions feel so real.*

'Did you learn anything else inside Rhodene's thoughts?' he asked.

She decided to give him a little more rope to find out if he'd hang himself, and possibly her, in the process. 'Gundrad is the same guy who tried to abduct me at the station. He belongs to a terrorist organisation—and he's been here before—I mean before that time he came on the motorbike. It wasn't a lucky guess or an accident that he got in, someone's feeding him the code.' The words she'd left out—*and I think it's you*—hung in the air between them.

Mr Thom nodded. 'I suspected as much, but I'm glad you've confirmed it. Are you certain he was your abductor at the station?'

'Yes,' Alpha whispered. 'Howie said he wants me as his weapon.'

Mr Thom's fingers gripped the bedpost, his knuckles whitening as he did so. Alpha could tell that she'd given him bad news, but she wasn't sure whether the bad part was that they were the same man, or that she knew about it.

He stared at the carpet as though searching for answers then looked up at her. 'As soon as Dr Scott returns we'll get to the bottom of this but right now I'd like to teach you how to keep other people from harming your mind. Will you let me do that? I need your permission to get to the top layer of your thoughts. I always ask first; it's only courteous. And I promise I won't go any deeper—I can't anyway. I can't match your skill.'

Alpha shook her head, violently.

'Please. You need protecting,' Mr Thom begged.

'You're lying. What about those colour cards?'

'What about them?' Mr Thom looked baffled. 'They're personality indicators. I use them to find out a little more about students before I start doing any serious work. They're helpful, but they're just indicators. They can't tell me everything about you.'

'So how did you know I was lying when you asked me to choose my favourite colours if you didn't read my thoughts? I'm sure I wasn't leaking any spillage.'

'No... I didn't need to read your mind. Your other choices told me that bright pink was way off. You couldn't choose that colour if you tried; it's not in your nature. You're silent and secretive, not outgoing and forward, and you have a lovely caring nature that you strive to keep hidden. Also, you've had rather too much pain for one of such tender years. That's all I know about you.' Mr Thom smiled wryly. 'I take it you think I'm the person who has been letting this Gundrad person in? May I ask why?'

A dozen reasons flickered through Alpha's mind, but she struggled to put any of them into words now that the floodgates of doubt had opened in her mind. Eventually she launched an accusation. 'You've got that picture in your classroom, the one of the girl with the probe in her head, and you were going to fiddle about in Rhodene's head and put in a metal plate.'

'And that scares you?' His face cleared, as though the solution to a major mystery had been unearthed. 'Well, I suppose it would if you don't know anything about my medical skills or that girl's background. That's young Luwuth; one of my former students. Her family breeds Andalusian horses.'

A mind-talk bubble formed in front of Alpha. As it touched her brow she could see an image of the young girl riding a grey stallion with a long, flowing forelock. The girl was a few years older than in her picture in his classroom, but Alpha could tell that it was the same person, and she could see that Luwuth was now full of life. The vibrant, moving image was a strong contrast to the placid, disturbing look the girl had worn when the picture was taken.

'Luwuth is a horse whisperer; she hears them talk to her. Before my acupuncture she thought she was going mad, she could hear so many of them at once. Now she can focus on one at a time and it's an invaluable asset to the family business. They tell her when they're in pain, when they're ready for breeding, when they're angry about something, or simply when they're comfortable and content. She sends me postcards every so often…' He paused, then the corners of his mouth twitched in gentle amusement. 'Tell Sunday they're in my desk, top drawer, you can read them anytime he's up to the job of removing them, but be sure to warn him to change his socks next time he comes calling. They do waft a bit down that chimney. And as for Rhodene, well I'm sure she told you I never did a thing to her, it simply wasn't necessary, after…'

'After she stopped herself dreaming because she was so scared of your needles.'

Mr Thom looked flabbergasted. 'So that's it—you are unbelievably good! It's baffled my brain trying to work out why she stopped having her predictive dreams and here you are giving me the answer just like that.' He waggled his head. 'If only I'd thought to ask you. Now is there anything else I can explain that will help you trust me?'

'That circuit board—Sunday saw it and so did I. You went to great pains to stop him taking it off your desk and then you attached it to some wiring in the basement. I'm sure it's got something to do with the security code.'

Mr Thom nodded. 'Dr Scott and I had hoped to keep that a secret. I've added a few security precautions of my own, a surveillance video that will tell us exactly who's used the entry code and at what time.'

Sounds plausible, but… he would have answers at the ready, wouldn't he? And yet… I'm picking up strong spillage from him and it's telling me he's telling the truth—Dr Scott did ask him to set a trap. So Dr Scott trusts him more than anyone else.

But there were still unanswered questions. 'Why were you waiting for Gundrad on the beach?'

'Waiting for Gundrad? I didn't even know about Gundrad until you told me about him. I'd seen Rhodene make her way down to the beach at night, and I was worried about her. It was most uncharacteristic behaviour. Normally she avoids the great outdoors. I was frightened she'd try to drown herself in a fit of depression, she was so miserable after her dreams shut down.'

Once more Mr Thom's words had a ring of truth about them, but Alpha didn't stop probing. 'What's your connection with Miss Gilford?'

'Miss Gilford? The head gardener?' The overriding emotion shining through Mr Thom's emotions was confusion. 'I don't have a connection with her. Mrs Hickelroy decided to keep her on when we took over the school. Miss Gilford reports directly to her.'

Unwilling to give in Alpha tried one more rather lame effort. 'Your desk…'

Mr Thom actually chuckled; giving a series of deep ha-ha-has that transformed him from ghoul to kindly uncle. 'It's a bit much, isn't it? But I couldn't refuse it, to do so would have been indescribably rude. And it's not as frightening as you might think; those faces represent fertility in central Africa. During the tribal dance, in early spring, the masks are worn to invoke the spirits into giving their blessing for the year ahead and to make the soil rich for good crops.'

Another mind-talk bubble waited for her to invite it in, and this one demonstrated the fertility dance in all its bizarre glory. The masks, worn by real people didn't look quite so frightening as they whirled and stomped and whirled again. Mr Thom, obviously an honoured guest, sat cross-legged on the ground near the chief, wearing only a loincloth and clapping loudly in time to the beat. *Is he really Gundrad's partner?* she asked herself. *He's celebrating this dance to life with so much joy; can he really be following a cause that wants to kill all free-thinking?*

No, he isn't the traitor, she decided, deeply disturbed. She felt a hollowness enter her soul because this threw into question her ability to read people. She'd always relied on her mind-reading to tell her the truth. Now her abilities had led her thinking astray. She was no longer who she'd always believed she was, and she found herself in a frightening vacuum.

How could I have got it so wrong?

But Mr Thom's next words helped her understand how she'd lost her way and ascribed all sorts of sinister motives to him when he hadn't actually done anything to deserve them.

'I'm sorry,' he said. 'It's my fault you didn't trust me. I should have realised that someone who relied so heavily on her extra senses to read people would feel shut off if I didn't produce any stray thoughts. I isolated you from me; it's no wonder you're finding it difficult to accept that I only want to help.'

He's right. If I'd been able to read what he's letting me read now I would never have blamed him for everything. But if he didn't let Gundrad in, who did? I've got to find out—before they find me, and use me as that weapon. Her mind circled those questions but found the answers impossible to pin down. She could feel fear eating into her, making her weak and indecisive.

'OK,' she finally agreed. 'Teach me how to stop Gundrad from getting to me again.'

Mr Thom's brown eyes stared into hers. She felt a rush of heat as his mind merged with her own, and for a moment she panicked, but then she realised that he hadn't entered the thinking lobes at the front of her head. Instead, he'd eased into the muscles at the top of her neck (which felt like mallets beating on the ball of her brain.) He became a comforting hot water bottle. Soon her thoughts softened, and her brain waves changed from conscious thought into smoother sleep-like waves. Her breathing mirrored her relaxed brain, and she felt her chin tuck down towards her chest.

'Hold that feeling, Alpha, that's how to defeat intruding thoughts. If you change your brain's electrical frequencies to

Theta waves there's nothing to grab hold of. Any intruder is forced to slide away.' She felt nothing but drowsy sleep. 'I'm going to try an attack on the frontal lobes now. Just hold the waves steady and I won't even be able to find any stray thoughts leaking out.'

A soft stroke whispered over her brow, but nothing reached under the skin until she thought of what Howie had said. *"Gundrad's back… they're here now at Krakow Bond."* Her eyes flew open, her agitated brainwaves spiking into activity.

Mr Thom's mind slid right into her thoughts, though it withdrew urgently as soon as he realised she'd lost her defences.

'Howie said Gundrad's returned, that he and his partner are here right now,' she confided.

His brow wrinkled. 'Impossible. Burt and Larry have been watching the gate round the clock. We've also got a video record of all entries and exits, no one's sneaked in.'

Was Howie wrong? He does interpret things in peculiar ways; he turned a train into a dragon. She remembered that he'd said something else just before she lost consciousness and she tried to recall his exact words. They came to her in a rush and trembled on her lips before she dared to speak them out loud. 'He also said, "Mother will die."'

'Biddy?'

What else could Howie have meant? Reluctantly, she nodded.

Horatio Thom stood up and seemed without moving to be at the door.

'How do I hold onto the Theta waves?' she cried.

'No time for that now. Stay in your room until we've sorted out this mess. The school isn't safe.'

'But I ….'

'No buts, Alpha, no buts at all. I'm sorry, but it's necessary for your safety. Stay here!' he ordered, slamming the door.

CHAPTER THIRTY-ONE

After hours locked up in her room Alpha was fuming, and pacing the carpet threadbare. *How dare he keep me in my room? What use am I in here? There's a traitor on the loose and I'm the only one with any chance of finding out who it is.*

She had to get out, preferably with no one knowing about it. It would be much better if the traitor thought she was locked up, out of the way. *Think, girl, think.*

She forced herself to calm down and sat on the bed, her nostrils flaring, her breath erupting in furious huffs. Her ears caught the sound of a knife and fork scraping against a plate: obviously Miss Gilford was still outside, eating dinner. *Are they planning on starving me to death?*

Not that I could eat anything anyway. Her stomach curdled as her thoughts returned to Howie's warnings. *A weapon! What do they want me to do—persuade the cabinet to withdraw troops? Force the prime minister to resign? Or something much, much worse? And what have they already done to Biddy?*

This school had taught Alpha to take pride in her abilities, but now they were haunting her, leaving her wishing that she was just an ordinary person.

Another thought forced itself into her mind. What they wanted was one thing—how they were going to force her to do their bidding was another. What would they do? What would it take before she agreed to do something so horrible she couldn't even imagine it?

She tried desperately to think of a plan of escape, but short of physically or mentally punching her way past the gorgon outside her door, her brain failed to come up with a solution. She discounted both ideas: Miss Gilford weighed a tonne and would be more than a match for her. Plus, after her encounter with Howie, she was pretty sure she wasn't up to the mind-punching bit. She needed to restore her mental energy, but right now rest was the last thing her brain was willing to give her.

Her thoughts fixed on the traitor, and she ran over the information she'd gleaned so far. *Howie has confirmed that Gundrad's partner is here at Krakow Bond. I'm looking for a person with regular access to the code.*

Miss Gilford doesn't know the security code so she couldn't have let Gundrad in.

It isn't Rhodene; I've practically turned her brain inside out.

I checked out Carl and Alex's minds too, it's not them, and there's no way it's Sunday or Janna.

In frustration she hurled a pillow across the room; it would have been such a neat solution if Martel had been the one, but Alpha was certain he couldn't be linked to Gundrad. *And anyway, there's something about Martel,* she caught herself thinking. *He's not really a monster, he's been through something terrible. He's a bit lacking in trust, that's all, and I know how that feels.*

Howie doesn't fit the bill either. Though he had the ability to lift the security code from his mother's head, Howie was terribly afraid of Gundrad.

Dr Scott then. She was about to discard him as a suspect when a sneaky thought crept into her mind. He'd insisted she talk to no one about her mind-changing abilities. What if that wasn't for her own protection? Her heart fluttered with anxiety. *Not Dr Scott, please not him.*

Suddenly, with enormous relief, her thoughts flashed back to her extraordinary encounter with Howarth. *He said Gundrad's partner is here right now, but Dr Scott is in London with Sunday.*

At that thought, the horrible fear swept out of her, and she was able to reason things out. *I can't be sure with Howie what's now and what's next week, but it's definitely not Dr Scott. He let me go all over his mind at the train station; he wasn't shielding his thoughts from me.*

So moving on... since his visit to her room earlier she no longer believed that Mr Thom was involved either. His feelings had been crystal clear; he wanted to catch whoever was doing this.

'Biddy?' she chewed at her thumbnail as she continued her solitary debate. Biddy had a deep love for her son and Alpha didn't think she'd leave Howie here on his own. *I think something's happened to her... something bad. Howie believes his mother is in mortal danger.*

'Well, what about Lily?' She rolled the name around her tongue as if tasting it for possibilities. 'Dr Scott was very clear when he told me not to tell the teachers about my mind-changing abilities.' She nodded slowly. This was beginning to add up.

But doubt nagged at her mind—she'd been wrong before— so she played devil's advocate. 'On the other hand, I couldn't find any guilt in her mind when I touched it.'

But I wasn't in there for long so maybe... Her eyes widened—there was one more piece of evidence that could be held against Lily: Mrs Hickelroy had said that Alpha wasn't to explore Rhodene's mind with Lily in charge—in fact, she'd ordered Rhodene to wait until she returned from her trip to supervise it.

Suddenly Alpha's leg tingled as she felt a patch of skin near her hip grow warmer. The egg in her pocket was heating up. She took it out—it was warm to the touch but not hot—and placed it on the bedside table, staring into its bands of blue, hoping for inspiration.

'Oh!' she exclaimed as a thought struck her. *Lily can't be the traitor. She gave me the blue tiger's eye.* Alpha recalled the three occasions when the stone egg had come to her aid: in the woods when Rhodene was running away it had made finding Dr Scott a walk in the park even over all that distance, then it had shielded her from Mr Thom's psychic search and finally, of far more importance, it had helped her fight Gundrad's brain stain. *It makes no sense that Lily would give me a tool that helps me fight off her own partner.*

'But that only leaves….'

Alpha jumped up from the bed, her thoughts spinning. 'No, no and no… it can't be!'

Her heart contracted, trying to squeeze out the pain that her thoughts were churning up inside her. It couldn't be Mrs Hickelroy, the woman who'd placed her trust in Alpha, who'd said that they were going to do good work together. No! It couldn't be her.

Yet that cynical voice of hers insisted she examine the evidence. As she did she found several things that pointed to the totally organised vice-principal. *What did Dr Scott say? "We're not getting the sort of results I expected…" Mrs Hickelroy didn't let Martel look for a missing girl. Then there was that time when Dr Scott wanted me to be alone with Rhodene, but Mrs Hickelroy told me Rhodene needed to rest—was she frightened I'd pick up traces of Gundrad? Or didn't she want Rhodene to get her dreams back?*

Now the very same clue that had pointed to Lily pointed even more strongly to Mrs Hickelroy—*she told Rhodene that Dr Scott had instructed her that I couldn't go into Rhodene's brain unless she was there. But what if Dr Scott had nothing to do with that? She could have lied, not because she wanted to keep Lily out, but to make sure I didn't probe Rhodene's memories too deeply and find out about Gundrad's work.*

Alpha's brain raced as an image tumbled into her mind: the view of the woods she'd seen from Mrs Hickelroy's office. *Her rooms are two floors above Mr Thom's classroom on the southwest corner.*

That's right where Iwardi's ghost came to roost. Why didn't I realise that Janna looked up at the ghost? Up… towards Mrs Hickelroy's apartment.

But Mrs Hickelroy's husband had been killed—tortured— wasn't that why she was working here? The cynic in Alpha had an answer to that too: Mrs Hickelroy had probably lied to Dr Scott about her background to get a place at Krakow Bond.

Her thoughts clicked into place with a dreadful certainty: *when I left the Willows only Dr Scott, Mrs Hickelroy and Sunday knew that the train I was on would end up at Waterloo station; who else could have told Gundrad where to find me?*

And one final thing clinched it: Howie's timeframe. She'd seen Gundrad ride out of the grounds when Rhodene refused to go with him. Since then, Dr Scott had put guards on the gate and Mr Thom had erected a CCTV camera; if Howie was right about Gundrad returning, how did he get in? *The only way he could have escaped notice was in the boot of a car… Mrs Hickelroy got back from Leeds this morning and parked her car in the courtyard.*

Tears squeezed from Alpha's eyes, and she blinked them back fiercely. Sealing up her emotions she slowly came to terms with the idea that Mrs Hickelroy could be Gundrad's partner. It left a sour taste in her mouth. She felt let down and desperately hurt— the woman who'd been a surrogate mother to her had been manipulating her all along.

And what about Dr Scott: if Mrs Hickelroy had been her mother, Dr Scott had become her father. How would he react to this betrayal by the woman he loved?

But worst of all was the effect this would have on Sunday: Alpha's heart went out to him, how was he going to feel when he found out his "Bolla", who had rescued him from a life on the street, wasn't a guardian angel after all?

And while I'm locked up in here I can't do a single thing to prove that I'm right, she thought bitterly.

CHAPTER
THIRTY-TWO

A loud knock put a stop to her dreadful thoughts. She looked up abruptly as the door opened a fraction and Janna's voice called out, 'I've brought you dinner.'

Alpha's heart leaped. *Has she forgiven me for keeping her in the dark about Rhodene and Martel?*

Alpha said a heartfelt, 'thank you,' even though food was the last thing on her mind. The pleasure of seeing Janna was unbelievable. She'd thought that Janna may never speak to her again.

'You can't stay,' yelled the Gillybird as Janna edged her way into the bedroom.

Both Janna's hands were occupied, carrying an enormous tray laden with several starters, a main course, and two puddings, so she wiggled the door shut with her bottom. 'Just dropping off dinner,' she shouted to pacify the witch outside the door.

Then she went on, speaking to Alpha in a low tone. 'I didn't know what you'd like so I brought you a bit of everything. Things are a bit mad downstairs. We haven't found Biddy, but Chef is still making miracles.' Janna put the tray down. She eyed the broken chair without comment and waved airily at the door. 'I bet you're having a horrible time with her outside.'

Warmth rushed through Alpha at Janna's friendly words. 'I'm sorry, Janna. Sorry about keeping you in the dark like that.'

Janna reached for Alpha to squeeze her arm. 'Forget it. It's my fault, I'm such a hothead. I totally understand. When Dr Scott tells you to do something, you do it… he's like that; you don't want to let him down. Anyway, I wouldn't want you blabbing about my secrets to other people, so it's only fair you don't spread theirs around either.'

Alpha dropped her voice to a whisper. 'Can you get me out of here?'

'Give me a bit of time… I'll think of something. Mmm… maybe I can organise a distraction. Be ready to move fast.'

'Thanks, it's really, really important.'

'It's not fair that you're locked in—I bet Dr Scott will let you out when he gets back.' Janna shook her head as though trying to puzzle it all out. 'Mrs Hickelroy is so nice most of the time, but just occasionally she's evil.'

You don't know how right you are!

Miss Gilford stuck her head around the door. 'You're not allowed visitors.'

'I'm going, I'm going,' said Janna, winking at Alpha.

———

Minutes turned into hours, and hours turned into nightfall. Alpha paced restlessly round the room. Ages ago she'd stuffed pillows under her bedclothes, creating a reasonable image of a girl fast asleep in the hopes that the gorgon outside the door would peak in, find her sleeping and go off to her own bed, but Miss Gilford was taking her duties seriously. Obviously, she'd spied on the students for her boss, Mrs Hickelroy, for a long time. Alpha wondered what else she'd been willing to do for the vice-principal.

Where was Janna?

Thump, thump.

She looked round. The bangs were coming from Sunday's room, next door to hers.

Thump, thump.

Now she could hear water gurgling through the pipes and more thumps.

Heavy footsteps sounded outside her room. The battle-axe was on the move.

Her own door flew open. 'Quick,' mouthed Janna.

She followed as Janna ran down the corridor. Suddenly Alpha turned and dashed back into the bedroom.

'Come on!' Janna mouthed.

Alpha grabbed the tiger's eye egg that was still sitting on her bedside table and hurtled after Janna, just managing to twist onto the narrow back stairs as Sunday's door opened and Miss Gilford marched out of the room.

Alpha crept down the edge of each stair to reduce the squeaking of the floorboards, saying silent *Halleluiahs* that Miss Gilford was looking the other way.

'How did you manage that thumping trick?' she asked when they were out of earshot, on the first floor.

'I got the boys to help,' Janna explained. 'They created a poltergeist effect in Sunday's room from the floor below.'

'That's brilliant. Thanks. You're sure Carl and Alex won't say anything?'

'Not a word. They're happy to get even with the Gillybird. She stops them playing football in case it damages her precious lawn.' Janna giggled, then turned serious again. 'Where are we off to?'

'I'm sorry, I have to go alone.'

'I'm coming and that's that,' said Janna.

Alpha stared at her friend. *Please don't let me have to change her mind.* 'Janna… trust me. Look, I need a backup. If things don't go according to plan and I'm not back by morning I want you to contact Mr Thom.'

'Mr Thom?' Janna's voice was incredulous.

'Yes. He's not involved; he's trying to figure out who is. Tell him…tell him to look for me above him.' That should be enough of a hint, without revealing too much to Janna. Alpha was dead certain that she didn't want her friend to know about Gundrad. Gundrad was the most dangerous person Alpha had ever encountered—she wouldn't risk Janna's life just to prove Mrs Hickelroy was connected to him.

For a long moment, Janna didn't say a word. Then she clasped Alpha's hands with her own. 'Tell him to look for you above himself. OK. I hope he's better at riddles than I am.'

'You're a real friend.' Alpha wanted to hug Janna but felt uncertain about how to initiate such close physical contact.

Janna gave her a tight hug anyway. 'Be careful,' she said, unable to mask the flash of concern in her eyes before she turned away.

Alpha waited until she was sure she was alone, then found her way to the door meant for midgets. Entering it, she was able to retrace the route she'd taken with Sunday onto the roof. She emerged from the turret and looked across to the southwest corner of the building, where Mrs Hickelroy had her rooms. As she'd hoped there was a chimney over them too, matching the one on the corner over Dr Scott's office. If she got close enough, she could read the vice-principal's mind through the gap in the tin.

It was the *getting close* that was going to be a problem because the path she and Sunday had taken to reach Dr Scott's office wouldn't do. A rounded dome lay in the centre of South Block, yet another notion of the mad architect who'd designed this building. There was no way she'd be able to climb over that.

With a sigh, she turned towards the decrepit West Wing. She had to know, and this was the only way. The roof of this wing had collapsed inwards, but the outside wall remained. She hitched across a tumbled down parapet, felt it move under her feet, and swung herself hastily onto the wall. It was made of blocks of stone that were wider than her shoulders, but she found it impossible to forget that the drop on either side of her was three storeys deep. She decided to kneel and crawl forwards rather than walk across, but bits of stone dug through her jeans and her hands began to bleed. She shuffled around and continued on her bottom wobbling from one cheek to another, every movement taking her just fractions along the wall. Her legs hung over the edge, and it felt like her body was about to follow them. Despite the cool breeze, sweat dripped from her brow.

She started as lightning flashed overhead and thunder growled nearby. This was hard enough without a storm to add to her difficulties.

Eventually, she reached the roof on the southwest corner and was horrified to find that it sloped steeply. But if she wanted to pick up any voices from Mrs Hickelroy's apartment there was no alternative; she had to climb it. Holding her breath, she pushed the toes of her trainers into the cracks between each tile and edged herself up... ten, eleven, twelve... her fingers found the chimney and she flung her arms around it, drawing herself onto the crest of the roof.

She braced herself, lowered her chin to rest on the chimney, closed her eyes and sent her mind floating downwards.

Her mind sprang back to her as Mrs Hickelroy spoke. 'There you are!'

She almost fell off the roof. *Is she talking to me?* But then Mrs Hickelroy went on...

'What a week! You won't believe the trouble I've had with Alpha! I've had to think on my feet to keep her from exploring Rhodene's thoughts—I've had that old fool, Gilford, watching her for days. But can you credit it, now Alpha is convinced that Thom is up to no good? How ironic is that?'

Sadness flooded through Alpha as the loss of her mentor was confirmed.

'Oh, what a tangled web we weave when first we practice to deceive. I warned you you were getting in too deep here.' The new voice—a man's voice—was identical to the young man in Rhodene's memories. It belonged to Gundrad. Alpha's skin crawled with loathing for him.

Mrs Hickelroy spoke again. 'Hmmph! Well, that's not all I've been up to. It took some doing to get those backers in Leeds to release the funds, but I've done it. We're poised to take over the school and not a moment too soon. Scott's throwing in the towel—his scruples have finally got the better of him. He sent me a text saying he's told John he won't allow Sunday to read the cabinet's mind again. Says its unethical… or some such rot.'

Alpha felt elation float from the chimney, an airy emotion that smelled like a cake rising in the oven. But underlying this cake was a putrid base: its ingredients weren't wholesome—there was a whiff of rotten eggs.

The bad cake smell flitted away as the woman's mood changed. 'Anyway, I'm glad you made it up here without being spotted. I was worried. Scott's pepped up the security. And now Biddy is missing. I only hope she hasn't seen something suspicious and gone to the cops.'

Gundrad laughed, a dry, cold sound that set Alpha's teeth on edge. 'Oh! She did.' Alpha couldn't see what was happening in the room below, but then she heard clicking sounds.

Mrs Hickelroy gasped. 'You fool! Couldn't you leave well enough alone? Why did you have to tackle the housekeeper?'

Biddy! He must have taken her just after I followed Mr Thom.

'I had no choice. She saw me getting out of the car, so I knocked her out.'

Mrs Hickelroy spoke accusingly. 'How could you be so stupid! I told you to lie low until lunchtime—of all the times to get caught. The PM would have jumped at our offer to take over the school at no cost to the budget. And other things were slotting into place too… Howie's been dreaming of a train smash and Alpha's confirmed that it's no accident… we could have found a way to use that, but with Biddy missing Scott will insist on a full-scale investigation.'

'Clever kids these are—able to read the future like that. That's why I extracted Rhodene's dream about the train… very neatly though I must say so myself,' Gundrad said.

'Rhodene had the same dream?' Mrs Hickelroy's voice edged up a notch. 'You didn't tell me.'

'It wasn't necessary for you to know. You were right though, Rhodene's predictions could have been useful to us. Still, that's water under the bridge, we've got a better option now—your girl, Alpha.' He went on, his tone confident and brimming with future plans. 'The train smash is icing on the top—when it happens I'll prepare a statement—we'll declare ourselves Muslim radicals and claim responsibility for the incident. Things have been too quiet on that front recently.'

Mrs Hickelroy's reply was bitter. 'It's too late for that now—you know my background won't stand up to serious investigation. The whole of England would have been primed for our actions. With the talents at this school we could have done wonders, and you had to mess it up.'

Alpha's heart hammered wildly—*Howie was right, Mrs Hickelroy isn't just a traitor to the school; she's a terrorist.*

'Your plan was taking too long,' Gundrad said. 'Anyway, we don't need them all anymore—not since you got this new girl.'

'What do you know about the situation? You're out of touch.'

Alpha heard the sound of breaking glass. 'Don't speak to me like that!' Gundrad exploded. 'I'm in charge since Dad died.'

'Stop breaking the furniture. I know those bastards murdered your father, but that doesn't mean you shouldn't respect me too. I'm your mother!'

Related by blood and cord. An image flashed through Alpha's mind: Baby Bruce with the cord wound round his neck. *Of course, umbilical cord. Chalk another one up for Howie. But please, let him not be right about Biddy dying.*

'Yeah, OK.' Gundrad's voice was filled with rancour. 'But you're not in charge. What do you know about wiping out these damned immigrants—the animals that breed like rats, and tell us how to run our country? You married into the cause; you weren't bred to it.'

'You ungrateful little swine.'

Alpha's head flew back as Mrs Hickelroy's emotions barrelled up the chimney towards her. *Damned immigrants? They aren't Muslim radicals—what the hell are they?*

Mrs Hickelroy wasn't finished with her son yet. 'I taught you everything you know. How to get inside a girl's head, how to make a favourable impression and play on her fears. How do you think we got all those recruits? Without me the Free Britain for Brits Army would have only two members—and we wouldn't have any backers putting up money either. You think you could have persuaded those big corporations we were the answer to their prayers?'

'All right. You have your place in the FBFBA,' Gundrad agreed, 'but I want our plans advanced now. We can do much more with this girl. We don't have to discredit the scum anymore, we can force them out of the country, kill them without repercussions.'

It sank into Alpha then that terrorists didn't have to be Islamic fundamentalists. Gundrad was as bad as any of those horrible acts that were happening all over the world—only his motives were different, the politics of the extreme fascist right, just as nauseating as Hitler's.

'I don't know what you expect from Alpha—she's only a girl with telepathic ability.'

'She's much more than that. I know what she can do, I spoke to this boy Bruce… she turned him from a warped little psychopath into a boring brat. Now he gets his kicks from riding a bike instead of trying to char his carers on a blazing barbeque. She changed his personality entirely.'

'So she can actually turn people 180 degrees. Unbelievable! I wonder if Scott knows. He hasn't said anything, but then I've been away in Leeds. Wow! That puts her powers well beyond ours, but we can't get her to work for us if she isn't willing. I need a bit more time… Michael's falling under my spell, his eyes follow me everywhere, but he's not hooked yet. He'll be invaluable, he's got a wealth of information on how to train these kids.'

'Don't be stupid, they don't need training. They need persuading, with a gun to their heads.'

'Psychic talent doesn't work like that. The more relaxed they are the better.'

'So I'll charm her into it. Look, we don't need the whole school now. Think about it. With Alpha on our side, we can persuade the Prime Minister to throw out all the refugees and immigrants. We can force him into war with any country harbouring terrorist training camps. We can stop all overseas aid. He'll be our puppet.'

The words hit Alpha like a wave of icy water. She gasped out loud—she'd never felt so vulnerable. The sense of exposure was so strong she almost missed the prickle of warning.

Before the egg could shield her presence, she heard Mrs Hickelroy say, 'Someone's up there! On the roof.'

'How the devil did she get up there?' Gundrad shouted.

CHAPTER
THIRTY-THREE

Alpha let go of the chimney and slid down the roof. Her foot hit the West Wing wall but buckled underneath her, causing her knee to bang into the stone. She clutched at the remains of the cast-iron guttering, almost passing out as pain shot through her leg.

When her vision eventually cleared—she looked down and saw Mrs Hickelroy peering out of a window directly at her. Alpha staggered upright and started running across the wall that just a short while ago she had edged across in fear of falling. With each step her knee sent pain zinging up her leg and she stumbled like a drunk.

Phut!

What was that? She looked back over her shoulder—Mrs Hickelroy was holding a gun. She doubled her speed, scrambling dangerously across the stones. Thunder crashed above her, and rain began to fall in massive drops. She cursed as water sloshed into the gaps in the mortar, making the stones even more slippery.

Phut!

The bullet whisked past her shoulder. She flinched. Suddenly she was teetering, and her right foot could find no support. As her body fell towards the collapsed interior of the West Wing her fingers clutched at the stones. Microseconds before plummeting to her death she found a small chip that protruded from the top of wall. She gripped it desperately, but her weight pulled her down and her hands tore away from their anchor.

Then the ball of her foot slammed into a solid base. Her eyes dropped—she was balanced on one of the joining blocks that had once held roof timbers: a sickeningly small perch, suitable for birds, not humans. She wobbled and threw herself forwards into the wall, clinging to the uneven blocks with frantic fingers. Her other foot sought a crack, and her toes dug in. Heart pounding, she used reserves of strength she didn't know she had to push herself upwards. Her hands reached up, her foot followed, and tiny crack by crack she inched upwards, like a climber challenging a vertical mountain face.

Finally, finally, she pulled herself up until she was back on top of the wall. Then she lay there, on her stomach, panting.

Phut. The bullet whizzed past her ear, deafening her ear drum.

That was too close!

She crawled on her belly, ignoring her throbbing knee and the bite of stone against her skin. At last the broken parapet appeared before her. She scrambled round it, back to the relative safety of the north roof. As quickly as she dared she made for the door in the turret, limping down the spiral stairs—taking them slowly, far too slowly, because her knee couldn't bare her weight. She dropped the last few steps into the dark corridor.

And there Gundrad was waiting, clutching a sawn-off shotgun. Her bowels knotted in fear. She tried to muster the strength to enter his mind, but he tossed a large, hard object at her, interrupting her concentration. It slammed against her chest, bounced off and rattled to the floor.

'Pick it up and put it on, or you're mincemeat.'

He meant it. Her knee gave in, and she fell to the floor. Her hand touched her leg: blood was gushing from it. With sticky fingers she felt all over the floor, until her hand came to rest on a round surface. She picked it up. It was his motorbike helmet.

As soon as she put it on she understood its function: it blocked her access to other people's thoughts, turning her powers blind. It had to be lined with tin.

'You're coming with me,' Gundrad ordered.

'I can't walk.'

'Then crawl. Not a single sound.' He jammed the shotgun into her ribs.

In the end he half-carried her, slinging one arm under her shoulder while the other held the shotgun to her neck. He pushed her down the stone steps at the end of the corridor, following easily in spite of his height. At every point along their route into the basement, past the swimming pool, and through the East Wing basement she was aware of the barrels of the shotgun prodding her head, her neck, her back.

They met no one until they entered South Block though a door that previously had always been locked tight. At that point Mrs Hickelroy joined them, smiling thinly, her lips looking less inviting than the open jaws of a crocodile.

'Don't do this,' Alpha begged. The helmet muffled her words.

'I've no choice,' Mrs Hickelroy told her, propping Alpha up by holding her arm. Between them they got her up into Mrs Hickelroy's apartment then dragged her down a short passage into the lounge.

Gundrad snatched the helmet from Alpha's head—she caught sight of two extra-large wheeled suitcases—like coffins, just as Howie had said.

'Help,' she screamed at the top of her voice, no longer caring if they shot her. She couldn't stand being shut in one of those again.

'It's pointless screaming, my dear. These rooms are sound-proof and tin-lined,' said Mrs Hickelroy, genuine pity in her tone. She eased Alpha to the floor, then opened one of the cases. 'I'm sorry it's come to this. I hoped you'd agree to work for us willingly.'

Deep red silk gaped from the case: the cloth of blood lining the mouth of a hungry T-Rex. Gundrad shoved Alpha into it.

'Be gentle with her,' Mrs Hickelroy ordered.

'Please, don't shut me in!'

Ignoring her plea, Gundrad slammed shut the lid of the suitcase. A stifling redness closed in around Alpha as silk filled her eyes, nose and mouth. She punched and kicked and clawed in a frenzy that made things worse because the motions caused unbearable pain to shoot through her knee. She gasped, drew in a mouthful of material and blacked out.

CHAPTER THIRTY-FOUR

Alpha came round slowly. Nausea was slewing around in her stomach. She couldn't see, couldn't move, could barely breathe. All at once, it came back to her, Gundrad had shut her in a case. Again! She heaved dry sobs that came right from her gut and almost tore her apart.

Gundrad's voice floated towards her as though from a vast distance. He was talking to his mother. 'Wear the other helmet when we take her out of the case. We can't risk her getting to you.'

The smallest dose of relief flooded through her—they weren't going to leave her in here forever.

She could barely make out Mrs Hickelroy's reply. 'I suppose so. You've left me no choice; I'll have to go with you now. We could have explained Alpha's absence, said that she'd run away, she was always a bit troubled. But with Biddy disappearing as well...'

Gundrad snorted. 'It's time for you to go, you've been here too long.'

Silence followed, then Mrs Hickelroy said, 'Are you sure she'll be OK in there. Remember Iwardi and Pasha?'

Alpha's stomach cramped, agonisingly. *Iwardi! He died in this case. And Pasha—they'd taken her too.*

'That was years ago. How was I to know they'd suffocate? We had to act quickly; the Turkish police were after us, so we had to get the brats across the border somehow. Anyway, after that, I had holes chiselled into the bottom of the cases and covered them with a tin mesh. They let in enough air to breathe. Just.'

I'm lying in a coffin. A coffin that killed those children. Alpha pushed her mind to the edge of the suitcase, but it slammed into a solid barrier and refused to go any further. Panic rose, spilling acid up her throat. *I've got to get out.*

She felt a strange touch then, as though someone was stroking her hair. She could feel fingers weaving through the strands, and it almost drove her over the edge. *It's impossible, how can anyone be in here with me?*

No one can…except… a ghost.

'Iwardi?' she whispered.

The movement stopped.

'Pasha?' Alpha felt the ghostly fingers begin their delicate winding again.

Warm air kissed her ear and a breathy little voice said, 'Tell papa. Tell him we're in the far-off land now. We're together, and we love him.'

The touch on her scalp continued, almost soothing now, leaving Alpha feeling less alone. She swallowed down her fear and, as her panic subsided, she was able to spare a thought for Janna. *These are Janna's ghosts. Janna will tell Mr Thom in the morning—he'll save me.*

Mrs Hickelroy's voice started her. 'Are you sure she can't influence our thoughts through the case?'

'Absolutely. Yesterday I had the case lined with a tin-coated membrane. Air permeates through the mesh at the bottom, but it'll block her thoughts. It cost a fortune, but I'm sure.'

Gundrad went on, speaking of a boat that was soon due to land on the beach, but Alpha's mind stuck on what he'd just said. *Tin-coated membrane? Something about tin. Someone mentioned it before, what did they say? Concentrate!*

Concentrate? I'm shut in a suitcase, a death trap... how am I supposed to concentrate?

She applied every ounce of focus she had running over the conversations she'd had recently...

Nothing!

Maybe it wasn't something she'd overheard; it could be a memory she'd explored.

She replayed Dr Scott's memories, then Sunday's, Martel's, Janna's, Rhodene's...

At last Mr Thom's words came back to Alpha. "Tin is a very light metal," he'd told Rhodene when he'd discussed putting a tin plate in her head.

Light metal? Her spirits rose marginally, and she tested her ability to move. She could wiggle her arms, but her legs were tightly confined. Her hands clawed at her jacket, seeking the jade brooch that was always pinned under her collar. She pushed it through the fabric lining the case and felt it press into a solid surface. *I've only got to puncture the tin skin,* she reminded herself, praying it was true.

She stabbed the pin into the case, but the point slid off. No matter how hard she pushed, she couldn't break through the tin. *At least the brooch isn't bending,* she thought, trying to ignore the pain in her knee that was screaming at her to stop moving. *I need something to hammer it with.*

The tiger's eye egg.

She wiggled herself into a position where she could reach for the egg in her pocket. Without giving any thought to what would happen if she missed the brooch and hit her hand, she bashed the brooch soundly. Her touch was dead accurate, but her fingers lost contact with the pin.

'What was that?' Gundrad said.

'She's trying to get out. Keep still Alpha,' Mrs Hickelroy called out. 'You'll be in there for some time, but we will let you out. Get some sleep.'

'I'm not letting her out until we're on that boat. We'll wheel her in the case, the dark will give us cover.'

The dark...Gundrad's taking me away on a boat tonight! Janna will be too late! Her fingers clawed at the silk, seeking the pin. It was worse than finding a needle in a haystack. The fabric twisted itself into folds that masked the sense of touch in her fingertips.

'I'll go down to the beach and see if the Moonrider has arrived,' Gundrad declared.

'Lily and Thom are dangerous. They'll sense you.'

'Not if I wear my helmet.'

'Be careful, Gundrad. Thom's set up surveillance cameras.'

'I won't take the direct route. I'll take the tunnel down to the lake and slip round that way.'

Alpha heard a door close. She reckoned she had about half an hour before he came back. *Where was that damned brooch?*

Finally, she felt a sharp stab as the jade tip gouged into her, tearing at a cut in her hand. She didn't care about the pain. She grabbed at the pin, frightened that she'd lose the spot. Her fingers closed around its shaft. It was stuck in the wall of the suitcase. She yanked; it came loose and flew out of her hand. She felt it spin, and struggled to retrieve it, but it had gone below her knees, and she couldn't reach into the bottom of the suitcase.

One hole, she thought bleakly. *One hole. Will it be enough?*

She sent her mind out, consciously squeezing it through the tiny hole. The room, lined in tin, sent her thoughts spinning around and around with nowhere to go. There was only one option now.

Mrs Hickelroy didn't notice Alpha sliding into her temporal lobe, but almost instantly Alpha came up against a membrane that was shielding the woman's inner thoughts. *So this is how she stops her emotions from seeping out. Sunday described it as a dirty window, but it's more like a skin around her mind.* She prodded the sausage-like skin, but it refused to give, and she knew that if she punctured it Mrs Hickelroy would know she was there. She stayed still, desperately worried. *Gundrad will be back soon.* She was about to lunge through the sausage skin and take the consequences when a tiny thought bubble pushed its way out of the membrane—Mrs Hickelroy's concern for her son had begun to leak beyond the skin. As the emotion squeezed out, Alpha hurried through the gap it left, sliding into Mrs Hickelroy's inner sanctum just as the hole closed.

———

Now she could slink through room after room of memories. She forced herself to move slowly to avoid alerting Mrs Hickelroy to her presence… She found a young woman, bored with her ability to attract any man she wanted at university. It was there that Mrs Hickelroy met a man who finally intrigued her, a lecturer who was immune to her charms. As the past unfolded, Hunter Montgomery, Monty for short, shared his cause with her—a cause that had long since left peaceful protest behind. To him immigration was the root of all evil, sucking away at the pure blood of the white European nations—and so, across time, Mrs Hickelroy became a white supremacist. Jews, Muslims, Romanians, anyone with dark skin, anyone whose family hadn't lived west and north of Italy for generations—they were all hated equally.

Alpha shook her head, careful to keep her thoughts to herself. *You stupid woman, couldn't you see he was using you, just like Gundrad used Rhodene.*

...Mrs Hickelroy was thrilled with her skill in persuading young people to join FBFBA. Unlike Alpha, she manipulated people by unlocking their inhibitions, working her best magic on young men, using sex as a tool to allow their wildest thoughts to roam free. Across Europe she built a cadre of youth all focused on a Nazi dream.

Alpha sneaked into memories of the next decade... Mrs Hickelroy hid her relationship with Monty, keeping their marriage in Germany a secret, which became important when the police started questioning him... She was delighted when her son was born and even more so when she discovered that his abilities equalled her own... They played mind games together, penetrating each other's thoughts until Gundrad's strength grew greater than his mother's.

... But as Gundrad grew into a teenager Mrs Hickelroy's enthusiasm began to sour. Room after room showed her arguing with Monty, furious that he was putting Gundrad in danger. ... Then the unthinkable happened. Monty was murdered trying to penetrate a Jihad training camp... and Gundrad took his father's place at the helm of the FBFBA, a new unstoppable force who worked tirelessly to place the blame for both real and manufactured terrorist atrocities on immigrants and their children.

...Mrs Hickelroy worried as Gundrad placed himself in life-threatening situations every day. She proposed another approach and persuaded Dr Scott that she should join his team... In the next few memories, Alpha sensed that Mrs Hickelroy had begun to change, to stop blaming others for Monty's death. In some ways, his death had released her from the cause that had become her prison. At Krakow Bond she found an inner peace; just as she trapped Dr Scott in her net, he, in turn, charmed her with his honesty. She began to fall in love with him, her mind torn between two desires—two philosophies—two people.

Alpha pounced—*choose Dr Scott; let go of the cause.* She felt her snare click into place. *Quick, open the suitcase, let me out.*

———

Alpha sat up wincing as the lid opened. Mrs Hickelroy was staring aimlessly round the room wearing a dazed look on her face.

'Get into the other suitcase,' she told Mrs Hickelroy, hoping to get rid of at least one of her enemies. She struggled to climb out of her own case, and stand up.

Mrs Hickelroy opened the second case, but it was already occupied. Biddy lay sideways, her shock of hair spilling all over the interior, her legs bent awkwardly and pulled up to her stomach like they'd been squashed in with a shoehorn. Alpha stared hard, but there was no sign of her chest moving up and down. *Is she dead?*

'What have you done to her?'

'She hasn't come round yet. Gundrad must have hit her very hard.'

Alpha gulped, only partially reassured by that answer. Her knee wouldn't take her weight; she stood on one leg, balancing precariously. *I can't carry Biddy; I can't even walk. How am I going to get out of here? Janna, please don't wait until morning!* She looked round frantically. A revolver was lying on the floor near a smashed glass table. *If I can hold them off until Mr Thom comes...* 'Pick up the gun. Give it to me.'

Mrs Hickelroy walked over to the table, stooped, lifted the revolver and dangled it carelessly. Then she twirled it round her finger, examining it as though she wasn't entirely sure what it was.

'Bring it here.'

Even as she spoke the door opened and Gundrad came in. He was carrying something heavy. Alpha saw with horror that it was Janna. Her body was floppy, her apricot hair hanging in wet strands around her still, pale face. *Nooo! He's killed her.*

Alpha's bowels felt loose; her thoughts went into free-fall. All her hopes, her fight and her strength drained from her. *I brought this on Janna.*

Gundrad kicked the door shut, slinging the helmet from his head. 'I saw lights, the boat's there. Look who I found sneaking around by the lake.' He paused, turned, then dropped Janna, staring down the passage. 'What's she doing out of the case?'

Alpha hobbled towards Mrs Hickelroy, but her knee gave in. As pain shot up her leg she suddenly felt a wave of burning anger towards this pair. With it came the strength to act. Her mind thrust out towards the vice-principal, filled with revenge. More than anything she wanted Mrs Hickelroy to kill her own son. *Shoot him, shoot him.*

Mrs Hickelroy's hand twitched, almost imperceptibly. 'Shoot him,' Alpha screamed. The arm raised itself as though it was entirely separate from the woman. Slowly, it targeted Gundrad, and the finger tightened on the trigger.

Suddenly the image of Alpha's dead mother spilled into her mind, shutting down her hatred, thrusting her anger into the cold, hard face of death. *I can't!*

'No! Stop! Don't shoot,' she shrieked.

Mrs Hickelroy's arm dropped slowly until the gun was pointed at the floor.

'Bring me the gun,' shouted Alpha, feeling control slipping away from her.

Gundrad lunged towards Alpha. He grabbed her by the shoulders and twisted her round to face him. She tried to shove him off, but his mind bored into hers, trapping her like a fly in a spider's web. The spider commanded her attention—demanded that she give in to him. With some revolting part of her, she wanted Gundrad to throw his arms around her—to kiss her.

She struggled to raise her hands to push him away and found that she couldn't move. He held her in thrall. She tried a mental attack, pressing into his brain, hoping to deflect his thoughts.

He laughed at her weak attempt and shot ice through her frontal lobes, into the temporals on each side, then on to the back of her brain. She fought the attack, but the ice splintered into further shafts and began stealing her mind. All of her was becoming him, and his mind was a war zone.

———

… She could hear the rattle of gunfire. A grenade exploded nearby and the ground shook. The air stank of smoke and dust. She tried to turn, to go back, but she was pushed forward by the thousands upon thousands of soldiers behind her. They were advancing mindlessly: an all-white army, marching, she realised, because she'd forced them to follow his orders.

Enough! She slammed the brakes on in her mind. She didn't know how long she stopped thinking before she allowed one tiny image to enter her mind in a pattern of waves. Theta waves. She tracked them endlessly through her thoughts, over and over, until she was almost asleep on her feet.

———

A noise jerked her from her defences, but Gundrad's concentration must have dropped too because she found that he'd left her mind. Biddy was pushing herself out of her case. Alpha twisted from Gundrad's grasp, dropping to the floor as her knee buckled completely. She watched, fear washing through her, as Biddy stood up, staggered, then launched herself at Gundrad. He skipped neatly out of the way.

Mrs Hickelroy swivelled and raised the revolver, cupping the barrel with one hand, nudging the trigger with the other. Biddy wobbled unsteadily, squinted as she saw the gun, changed direction, took three stumbling steps towards the vice-principal, then made a great and clumsy leap. Mrs Hickelroy's finger squeezed, very gently. Noise blasted through the room and Biddy fell down. She didn't get up.

Gundrad pushed Alpha into the open suitcase, slung the lid down and flipped the catch, sealing her inside. She gasped; all thought suspended as she struggled for air.

'Now give me that damn gun,' he ordered his mother. 'And put your helmet on, that will protect you from her. I'll kill that silversmith—the membrane isn't working. She's spun her spell on you through the air holes. When we take her out of here I'll cover them with metal tape. I don't care if she can't breathe—she'll have to take her chances.'

CHAPTER
THIRTY-FIVE

Willpower alone stood between Alpha and madness. Three times she'd been shut in this case, twice she'd survived the experience, but this time… this time she knew that they were going to cut off her air. *Iwardi and Pasha had suffocated to death before they drilled the air holes.*

Janna dead, Biddy's dying, and I'm going to die too. I'm going to die, to die, to die, to die, to die...

Those thoughts drove her insane, spinning round and round in her mind, absorbing every other thought, robbing her of her will. Her windpipe began to close up, her bladder gave way and a trickle of warm liquid sloshed down her legs.

Maybe it was the embarrassment, but there was no one to see her or to smell the urine. Or maybe it was the shame. Whatever it was, somehow the sensation of wetness drew her briefly out of that world of panic and brought her back to herself.

This way lies madness!

Alpha held herself rigid. She made herself stop breathing until she felt her lungs would burst.

Then very, very slowly she let out a tiny bit of air. Her chest eased, and she let out a little more air, forcing herself to think of nothing else. After many more controlled breaths in and out, she was finally sure she wouldn't go crazy. At least, not yet.

At last, she allowed herself to think, and her thoughts led her to the pinprick she'd made in the case. *If Gundrad and Mrs Hickelroy are wearing those helmets I can't do a thing to them, but I can try to reach beyond this room.*

Lily and Mr Thom lived in South Block—her heart dipped as she realised that they would be sound asleep behind the tin walls of their own bedrooms at this time of night.

It was also hopeless to try to contact anyone without psychic abilities. Her chances of influencing a sleeping mind weren't good at the best of times (that's why Mr Thom's Theta waves worked so well). Even if she could make contact with any of the staff in the stable block they would only think they were dreaming.

Her only hope lay with the students, far away on the north side of the house.

If only Sunday was here, he'd wake at my lightest touch.

Taking a deep breath, she gathered her remaining energy, determined to reach out right now before her air ran out. Her thoughts squeezed out of the coffin and spun around the room, but she couldn't find the chimney—it was like searching in the dark without touch, or sound, to guide her. Her mind kept slamming into tin-lined walls. She felt bruised and battered even though her body hadn't moved out of the case. Again and again, she sought the chimney, trying various methods. First, she circled the walls and then the ceiling in horizontal arcs, next she tried zigzagging from side to side. Finally, she chased corners hoping, praying one of them would lead her to the chimney. No escape. Her brain, exhausted now, remained trapped in the room just as her body was trapped in the case.

Eventually, more by accident than design, after resting for a second in an alcove, her thoughts travelled upwards. To her surprise, they kept going up, and up, into the passage hidden within that sheltered spot, only to break through a narrow opening to the night above. She felt freer in the open air and her thoughts soared before zooming in on the student's rooms. The first floor of North Block yielded nothing. The workmen had been busy over the last few days, lining the bedrooms with tin. The boys and Martel were all sealed off from her.

She dropped to the ground floor and found Rhodene's room. Rhodene's quarters hadn't been touched but her mind was engaged: she hadn't experienced a predictive dream in months, and tonight she was making up for it.

————

Rhodene hurtled through the night, captive in a car driven by a man. His bald head shone in the moonlight. His passenger was drinking vodka and popping pills. Alpha tried to shake Rhodene's mind awake, but nothing could loosen Rhodene's hold on that dream world. *Why did I agree to free her mind?*

Alpha banged about inside Rhodene's other memories to wake her up.

Nothing.

Alpha returned to the dream and watched as they drove through town and countryside: past houses and sleeping villages; past traffic lights on amber; past closed corner shops with morning newspapers flapping their messages at her.

And still, Rhodene dreamed on and on...

————

Alpha felt despair creep into her bones. There was only one mind left. One that frightened her almost as much as this suitcase without any air holes.

She bit her cheek so hard that she drew blood, then plunged into Howie's room and into his mind.

————

His thoughts were asleep—as she suspected Howarth was in charge during the wee hours of the night, stamping through his hellish quarters. Howarth, who had followed Mrs Hickelroy's evil for months but who couldn't talk of it; Howarth, whose bullish strength had squeezed her brain into darkness.

Howarth, it's me, Alpha. Mrs Hickelroy has shot your mother. Wake Howie, your other half, fetch Mr Thom, take him to Mrs Hickelroy's rooms. Please, there's a chance you can save her.

Howarth turned towards the girl hiding behind a pillar of flame. As soon as he located her he charged. She stepped aside and projected her thoughts so that they sounded like Lily. *Howarth listen to me, this is Lily. Stop this fighting now and hear what Alpha has to say. It's about your mother.*

Howarth stopped in his tracks, his head tossing this way and that as though trying to sniff out where his enemy was standing.

Alpha spoke again as herself. *I am not your enemy, Mrs Hickelroy is. She's Gundrad's partner. Wake Mr Thom now. Your mother's life depends on it.*

————

Before she could repeat her message Gundrad's next words jolted Alpha from Howie's mind, back into her own body. 'Too bad if she can't breathe—it's done. The tape will stop her psychic tricks.'

'What about these two?' Mrs Hickelroy asked.

Gundrad grunted as he lifted the case. Alpha's body slid sideways, thumping against the base of the suitcase. 'I was going to take Biddy as a hostage for Alpha's good behaviour, but I think she'll bleed to death before daylight. Leave her here; it'll be morning before they find her. Pack the other girl in the case, she'll do just as well when she comes round. One way or another, if Alpha does somehow survive the lack of air, she'll work for us. If not, we'll just have to find a way to use the other one instead.'

CHAPTER THIRTY-SIX

It was as though a candle had been lit inside Alpha's dark prison. *Janna's alive*, her heart sang. But her next thought extinguished the light, filling Alpha with despair. *I can't save her; I can't save either of us.*

She tried to send her mind out again, but she didn't have either the mental or the physical strength to travel beyond the case. She sobbed helplessly, convinced that Howie would do nothing, certain that when Gundrad had what he wanted from her he'd kill them both... if she didn't die from lack of air first.

'That's right, shove the big one in the case. It doesn't matter if you break a limb or two squashing her in. Let's go,' said Gundrad.

Alpha felt her body rise into the air as someone picked up the suitcase she was in. She counted twenty-three paces, then the case was lowered again. She heard the sound of a door easing open. Through her exhaustion, she barely registered that this was the door leading into the corridor outside Mrs Hickelroy's suite of rooms.

'What is it, Howie?' Mr Thom's deep voice rattled up the stairs.

'Damn. Get back inside quickly. We'll have to wait until he's gone,' Gundrad whispered.

Alpha began to kick and scream as loudly as she could.

'Shut up! That won't do any good. I told you these rooms are soundproof,' Mrs Hickelroy said, banging on the side of the case. The thump almost took Alpha's head off. 'Peel off the tape, Gundrad, we could be here a while. She'll die without air.'

'No way. I'm not taking any chances—she could influence anyone coming in. Put your dressing gown on over your clothes. If Thom knocks, slip outside into the corridor to talk to him. I'll take the cases back into the lounge so he can't see them.'

As her case swayed again Alpha pushed the fabric as far from her mouth as possible, hoping to gain a little more stale air. Then she tried to keep absolutely still. The less energy she used, the longer her air supply would last. *I've got to stay conscious—wait for the right moment.*

Alpha overheard Mrs Hickelroy speaking. 'Blast it. Scott's back,' she said.

Alpha's heart skipped a beat. With Dr Scott and Mr Thom, they had a chance. Maybe she could reach Sunday if only Mrs Hickelroy would take the tape off. But then she remembered the guns. Whatever happened she couldn't risk Sunday running into Gundrad.

There was silence for a long period. Her air supply was drying up. She began to gasp.

Through the foggy haze that had become her thoughts, she heard Dr Scott shout and bang on the door.

'I'm coming.' Mr Thom's cry penetrated her confusion.

Now Dr Scott sounded much closer. 'Victoria!' he said, the single word full of disgust.

'Michael,' Mrs Hickelroy implored. 'Join us. We can give you the world. It's what you want; you know it is. No need to bother with ethical constraints, you can capture the very essence of these kids' talents. I tell you; we've gone way past your experiments, you'll be delighted.'

The door to the lounge clicked open.

'Stand still Thom, or you're dead,' said Gundrad.

Alpha heard thumps and bangs—the sharp intake of air—
the squeal of a body hurt. A hard thing clattered to the floor and
the case she was in skittered across the floor. Her knee felt like it
was exploding, and it brought her round from her semi-conscious
state.

'What have you done to Biddy? Where's Alpha?' Dr Scott
demanded.

'Never mind Biddy. She's nothing compared to what we could
be,' said Mrs Hickelroy. 'Stop moving, or I'll shoot.'

'She's not nothing; she's a wonderful human being,' cried Dr
Scott.

'No! You'll not shoot the Doc…' Biddy's shout was cut off as
Alpha heard the sound of a bullet. Someone screamed, then the
shriek turned into a gurgle that sounded like a throat filling up
with blood.

The stale air inside Alpha's lungs failed to provide enough
oxygen for her brain. She passed out.

———

The case opened. She breathed, coming round slowly.
Groggily, her eyes focussed on Mr Thom. He stared down at her,
his face a mask of shock.

Oxygen filled her lungs, and her thoughts cleared. *Who has the
guns? Who screamed? Where are Gundrad and Mrs Hickelroy?*

'Janna! In the other case,' she panted.

Mr Thom turned to flip open the lid of the second case.
Then Alpha heard Dr Scott say, 'Biddy, no my dear, no. Howie
told us where to find you. Please, you've so much to live for, don't
die now.'

Alpha went cold with this new shock. She struggled to sit up,
succeeding only in raising her head above the level of the case. Dr

Scott was kneeling next to Biddy. She looked so pale against the dark blood pulsing from her mouth. 'Is she dead?'

Mr Thom felt Biddy's wrist. 'She's got a pulse, but it's very faint.'

Janna moaned. Alpha turned to look at her—she was gripping her head. As she spotted Alpha she whispered, 'Sorry babe, I messed up. Ow! Talking hurts.'

Alpha's vision blurred with tears. As her tears spilled she saw that, behind Janna, Dr Scott was gripping the shotgun. He turned to round up the prisoners but discovered that they had fled. 'I'll call an ambulance. And the police.' He fumbled for his phone.

Mr Thom began to pound Biddy's heart. Then he looked up, his eyes shadowed with pain. 'She's gone.'

Dr Scott's cry tore into Alpha. 'No. No, Biddy. Not now.'

'Go after them, Michael. There's nothing you can do here,' Mr Thom said.

He breathed into Biddy's mouth and thrust at her chest again. Shook his head. Carried on. Between pumps of Biddy's heart, he said, 'It's too late for Biddy. But Alpha and Janna are safe. Go get them.'

Alpha saw Dr Scott take a shuddering breath, then his face tightened with determination as he gripped the shotgun, and went out into the corridor.

Alpha shook her head, trying to clear the muggy haze that was her thoughts. 'They've gone to the beach,' she yelled after him. Then she put all her energy into rolling out of the suitcase and shuffling across the floor on her bottom to reach Biddy. Mr Thom sat back from Biddy's chest, his face stiff and silent. 'Don't stop now, please!' Alpha begged.

Taking Biddy's hand in hers, she slid inside Biddy's mind.

———

It felt empty, like a decrepit old house that was falling down, but Alpha refused to believe that Biddy had really gone. She chased through chamber after silent chamber until she reached the motor functions right at the back of the brain. There she found what was left of the Biddy's mind. It was busy carrying a few simple signals to shut down her entire body.

In those few remaining synapses, Alpha spoke to Biddy, telling her of Howie's actions, telling her that somehow deep inside his damaged brain he'd interpreted the message she'd sent, that he understood exactly who his mother was, that he knew her and loved her, and had tried to save her. Over and over she poured words of Howie into the dying woman. 'He loves you; he needs you, he loves you, he knows you, he loves you, don't go. Please, for Howie's sake, stay. He loves you...'

———

Biddy's heart fluttered. Mr Thom, still pumping her chest, looked up with hope and amazement in his face. 'She's back,' he said.

CHAPTER THIRTY-SEVEN

Alpha woke in her own bed and opened one eye, astonished to find herself still alive. The first thing she saw was Sunday, sitting on the chest in her bedroom, pulling the skin from a banana.

'Er... hi,' she said, feeling bewildered.

Sunday stood up hastily, grabbing a glass filled to the brim with brown stuff. 'Here! Mr Thom said you have to drink this the minute you wake up.'

She smelled its bitterness before it got to her face and glared at Sunday. 'I'm not drinking that!'

'You have to. Mr Thom said so.'

Alpha sighed then held her nose and gulped down the offending liquid.

'Hey! It doesn't taste as bad as it smells. A bit like minty chocolate.' She watched Sunday pop the entire banana into his mouth and felt like hugging him. Reluctant to shift her dodgy leg, she settled for stretching out her hand to rub his arm. 'I'm so glad you're back.'

'So am I,' he mumbled, chewing furiously. 'Dr Scott and John fought like dogs all day yesterday. Dr Scott told John he'd had enough, that he wasn't going to let them use me like that again, but John said I had to keep working. In the middle of everything I felt you call me. I told Dr Scott and he said we were leaving. John said we mustn't go, but Dr Scott said he didn't care, he would tell the newspapers about the school if John tried to stop him.'

She felt Sunday's hand tremble in hers. She sensed that he had been told what Mrs Hickelroy had been up to and that he was furious about her treachery. *I was still in my room when I called out for him… that was back when I thought Mr Thom was the traitor… I almost wish he had been. Sunday wouldn't be feeling so bad.*

Then the whole of last night came back in a rush and her heart lurched. 'Biddy? Janna? How are they?'

Sunday shrugged. 'Janna's too much OK. Biddy's in hospital but nobody's telling me anything. What happened?'

Before she could answer the door half-opened, and Lily popped her head round it. 'Hi. How's your knee? Mr Thom worked his magic on it while you were asleep.'

Alpha got out of bed and stood up, putting very little weight onto her leg because she expected it to give way under her. She couldn't believe it. There was no pain at all, and the knee bent easily without giving in. 'It's good to go. What about Biddy?'

'Dr Scott and Howie have only just got back from the hospital. Biddy's out of surgery. Coffee in Dr Scott's office in ten minutes, he'll tell us all how she's doing.'

Alpha dressed as quickly as possible then raced across the courtyard, marvelling at the way her leg had recovered, but at the same time feeling all churned up on the inside. She couldn't wait to learn about Biddy, but she also dreaded the news that Dr Scott might be bringing. She ran into Janna in South Block and threw her arms around her friend. 'Sunday said you were fine, but I wanted to see for myself. How are you?'

Janna winced and rubbed the back of her neck. 'I'll live, apart from a stinking headache. Mr Thom said it'll go soon—he's given me one of his bloody-awful draughts. Hey, I'm so sorry, I should have waited until morning like you said but I was worried, I couldn't stay in my room for another minute.'

Alpha clutched her hand. 'No, in a way you were right. The morning would have been too late, they were planning to ship me out last night.'

They climbed the steps together. In front of them, Howie shuffled into the office, his face staring ahead blankly just as though he hadn't spent much of the night in a hospital on the mainland waiting for his mother to come out of surgery. Alpha sat down on the carpet next to him, tucking her arm through his.

Dr Scott was perched against his desk, his long legs stretched out in front. Despite his apparently relaxed stance, she noticed his jaw muscles bunching up. She shut herself off from his thoughts, too frightened to pluck them out of the air. *Let Biddy be alive*, she prayed. *If I'd forced Mrs Hickelroy to shoot Gundrad… if only I hadn't told her to open that case… Biddy wouldn't have been shot.*

Dr Scott glanced at Mr Thom and gave a quick nod. Then he stood up to address the students. 'Biddy is seriously ill. The surgeons have taken a bullet out of her lung, but she's come through the operation well. She's still on the critical list, but the doctors think she'll recover.'

Alpha heaved a sigh of relief and the twist of guilt inside her eased a little. She couldn't have born it if Biddy ended up like her mum.

She squeezed Howie's hand, sure that on some level he understood about his mother. His head turned slightly towards her, then away again.

A steady stream of feedback was coming from the other side of the room, and she realised she could pick up Martel's emotions from amongst the flow of spillage. He too was feeling a wave of relief at the news about Biddy. It was odd, she hadn't realised he cared about the housekeeper, but his emotions were clear to her.

All around her the other students were emerging from their initial shock, and bursting into a gaggle of questions. Dr Scott coughed, held up his hands, and waited for everyone to settle down. 'Right. For those that don't know all the details, this is what happened. Late yesterday afternoon Sunday told me that Alpha had called out for him. We returned from London as fast as we could. Early this morning, long before sunrise, Howie took the keys from his mother's room, used them to open the door, crossed the courtyard, woke Mr Thom, and insisted that Mr Thom follow him to Mrs Hickelroy's rooms. Sunday and I got back at about the same time. Mr Thom and I broke into Mrs Hickelroy's rooms where we found that she and her son, Gundrad, had captured Alpha, Janna and Biddy. In the kerfuffle that followed, Biddy was shot. Our thoughts and our hopes are with her. Janna and Alpha, we're so pleased you've come through that ordeal safely.'

As several stunned faces stared at him he said, 'Let's give Howie and Sunday a round of applause for their actions.'

Lily led the clapping, standing and cheering as well. Alpha patted Howie's hand. 'You got my message and passed it on. You were fantastic,' she whispered.

Howie's mouth firmed up at the corners and seemed to smile, though his spillage was still garbage to her—full of numbers, keys, hands of stud poker and for some odd reason the stock inside the pharmacy at the hospital—an image of which he held onto like a photographic memory. She was glad she had been inside Howie's mind, though she wasn't going back in a hurry. She understood him much better now and wondered whether one day Howarth and Howie would become one.

She glanced towards Sunday. Comically, he was on his feet, taking a bow. She knew he was doing his best not to dwell on Mrs Hickelroy by forcing her right to the back of his mind.

As the clapping died down, Dr Scott went on. 'First, I want to tell you how sorry I am that I exposed you all to Mrs Hickelroy's influence. Krakow Bond has been under a dark cloud but today is a fresh beginning, in more ways than one. This morning we're going to discuss many things that come under the heading of national security, and I believe it's crucial that we're honest with each other. Ask questions about anything you like. And Alpha/Janna, chip in if you've got any further information to add.'

Rhodene shifted from side to side and rearranged her legs for the fifth time, full of wound-up energy. 'I can't believe it—Mrs Hickelroy? She was always so nice.'

'No she wasn't,' said Martel. 'She had a proper mean streak. I could feel it every time she came near me. Has she been arrested?'

Dr Scott ground his teeth together. 'By the time I went after them, they'd disappeared. The police have checked her rooms but there are no clues as to where they've gone. John, our contact within the government, has put out a search warrant for them. There's some evidence that they belong to a group called the FBFBA.'

'The Free Britain for Brits Army,' said Alpha, relaying to everyone what she had learned from being inside Mrs Hickelroy's thoughts. 'She and her dead husband started it. She's a traitor to Britain.'

Martel grunted, casting a glance at Alpha which she couldn't interpret, then tilting his head to listen intently as Dr Scott went on.

'John's very interested in the FBFBA. MI5 have picked up rumours that they've been recruiting students and John thinks that they're funded by some heavyweight corporations. He's down from London to interview you, Alpha. He'll need to speak to you soon.' Dr Scott sighed and rubbed a hand across his eyes. 'In the end, Mrs Hickelroy has actually done us a good turn.

It seems that the FBFBA is a fascist right-wing terrorist group and we've discovered more about them than all John's spooks have uncovered in over a year. The Prime Minister is pleased, even though I made it clear that I won't let our students become political footballs.' He gave a tired, half-baked grin. 'You're worth so much more than that. And you'll be pleased to know, Sunday, that I won't be dragging you to those endless meetings again.'

'Good,' said Sunday. 'The food in London is horrible. It's all small salmon sandwiches, raw-fish sushi and fizzy water that smells like peppermint but tastes like dog's breath.'

'What's this FBFBA thing all about?' asked Martel.

Dr Scott shrugged. 'Alpha?'

Alpha's mind rewound Gundrad's words. With her help, they'd intended to make the Prime Minister their puppet. She wasn't ready to share that. 'They want to keep immigrants out of Britain and they're willing to do anything to accomplish that. Anything at all.' *Including turning me into a monster war machine.*

Martel glared at her, taking Alpha's words personally. 'You mean they hate Black people and Asians?'

Alpha held her gaze. 'Not exactly. Just anyone whose parents and grandparents and great-grandparents weren't born here. Jewish people, anyone not white, anyone Muslim or Hindu, people from Eastern Europe—all sorts of people who can't be classified as fifth-generation Brits.'

'That must be half of England,' Carl chimed in.

'Yeah!' agreed Alex. 'I'm OK—my folks have been farmers in Yorkshire for generations, but you lot are going to have to take your chances against the dark forces.'

Martel's fists clenched and his eyes turned on Alex. Alpha could feel the temperature in the room rising. Mr Thom squatted down next to Martel. 'Chill. No one here agrees with them. Now that Mrs Hickelroy's gone, we're all on the same side.'

Martel's thoughts flew towards Alpha, almost drowning her in their fury. *So he wasn't an effing news reporter—he was Hickelbitch's son. How could I have got it so wrong? It's my fault, I should have said something to Scott before.* His leakage spilled out, allowing Alpha to learn that Martel had desperately wanted to find the intruder whom he had imagined to be a journalist. He had hoped that bringing the intruder out into the open would expose the school to public news, and he had reasoned that the police would have to accept his help if the newspapers splashed the story of a school full of psychics funded by the government. Then he'd be free to go home and look for Chrissie, the missing girl from his neighbourhood. He planned to help look for her in any way he could, even though his family had wanted him to stay at this school. They strongly believed that he would be able to make something of himself if he didn't come back to a drug-ridden estate.

It's so sad. No wonder he gets so angry from time to time—he's trying to please everyone except himself.

Janna's motion, as she suddenly stood up, placing her hands on her hips, drew Alpha's thoughts from Martel.

'How did they get off of the island?' asked Janna. 'I mean, they can't still be here, can they?'

Alpha and everyone else contemplated this thought with some horror, but then she remembered the boat.

At the same time, she felt Martel cool down instantly, his quick mind considering the point. 'Of course, they're not still here. This island is pathetically small—the police would have cornered them by now, they'll have done a house-to-house search,' he said rationally.

How does he flip his emotions so quickly, Alpha wondered? *It's that iron control he's got over himself.*

'It's easy enough to leave by boat,' said Mr Thom.

Alpha nodded. 'Gundrad called it the Moonrider.'

Dr Scott raised his eyebrows. 'Another important detail for John.'

'You should have woken me. I'd have wrapped them up in handcuffs,' said Carl.

'I'd have beaten them over the head with a metal pole.' Alex mimicked a rod coming down on the back of Sunday's head in a mock fight.

A shiver ran up Alpha's spine as she envisaged these two boys coming across Gundrad last night. 'No! You can't mess with them. Gundrad and Mrs Hickelroy are powerful telepaths. I don't think any of us could stand up to a direct assault by them. And they had guns.'

Dr Scott nodded. 'I knew Mrs Hickelroy was telepathic; she was always better at finding psychics than I was. But you say her son has it too?'

'He's much stronger than she is,' said Alpha.

Lily shook in outrage. 'As long as they've gone for good. That dreadful woman—I can hardly believe anyone could be so heartless.'

'I can,' whispered Alex to Carl. 'Good riddance to the bloody blister queen. She never let me have enough time on the Internet. Or on the games consoles.'

'Right-on!' Carl smacked Alex's upturned hand. 'We're well rid of her!'

'They might have left part of their auras behind,' said Janna, her eyes sparkling with excitement, and Alpha wondered what new mischief was going through her friend's mind.

'They're well and truly gone!' Mr Thom said. 'They won't risk coming back.'

Alpha, who had sunk into Gundrad's putrid mind, thought otherwise. A cold fear washed through her at the thought of facing him again.

Then, to add to her misery, Dr Scott's thoughts blanketed the room. He was blaming himself for everything that had happened, his emotions so heightened that the negative atmosphere was spilling over to everyone, creating a melancholy silence.

For long moments no one spoke.

Then Alex held his nose. 'Are you farting Sunday?'

Sunday shook his head vigorously. 'No food inside, no farting. I told you, the food in London is all sushi or thin slices of salmon in tiny triangles of bread. It goes through me quicker than you can blink. That's my belly you can hear. I'm so hungry it's making creak-crack-grrr sounds all the time.' As he got up to help himself to yet another plate of bacon and egg sandwiches, his stomach agreed with him, grumbling loudly.

'Creak-crack-grrr pop-pop-pop-pop-pop,' said Carl, making exploding noises with his mouth, clearly not buying into that no-food/no-farting story for a minute.

'Machine gun Sunday, filling up with more ammunition,' added Alex, and the two boys curled up in laughter. Sunday merely looked bored. Talking about food wasn't nearly as good as eating it.

'OK boys, that's enough!' Dr Scott ordered, trying to hide the boyish grin that was pulling up the corners of his mouth. Alpha felt his spirits lighten. 'By the way, Mr Thom found this inside one of those dreadful suitcases. Does it belong to you?' he asked her.

The pin on the jade brooch was bent, but Alpha was very glad to get it back.

As she pinned it onto her shirt she shuddered, reliving her experiences inside the case.

Seeing Alpha's reactions, Janna gripped her shoulder. 'Iwardi and Pasha have moved on. They're at peace now—that's something,' she told Alpha.

Lily looked up. 'More ghosts?' she asked Janna. 'You didn't tell me about them.'

'That's because we…' Uncharacteristically, Janna lapsed into silence.

We didn't know who to trust, Alpha realised. *We knew Gundrad had killed them—but we didn't know who else was involved.* Those ghosts had kept her sane. She owed them an enormous debt of gratitude, and now, in a small way, she could pay it back. She explained to the others, 'Gundrad trapped two children in those cases in Turkey—Iwardi and his sister Pasha—they suffocated. Pasha wants me to tell her father they've gone on to a better place.'

'Good heavens!' said Dr Scott. 'John will want the cases examined for forensic evidence. We'll find their father, Alpha, and make sure he knows. Right, any more questions?'

Rhodene raised her hand.

'Yes, Rhodene?' Dr Scott asked.

'Why did you tell Mrs Hickelroy that I had to wait for her to get back before Alpha could fix my dreams?'

Dr Scott looked blank.

'He didn't,' said Alpha. 'He only said he wanted a control in place—it was her who insisted we wait—she wanted to keep me out of your memories in case I found out about Gundrad. Oh yes, and Gundrad, Mrs Hickelroy's son, is the guy you nearly ran off with.'

Rhodene paled.

Dr Scott shook his head as if he still found it hard to believe how Mrs Hickelroy had deceived everyone. Then he straightened up. 'If we've finished discussing Mrs Hickelroy, I've got a very important announcement to make.' In the silence that followed, he looked round the room and Alpha sensed that he was choosing his next words carefully. 'Last night Rhodene dreamed, and yes, Lily has classified it as a P1 event. Rhodene's bedroom showed massive levels of paranormal energy. The dream confirms Howie's prediction of a train crash and it's no accident. Rhodene—over to you.'

Rhodene stretched her neck and wiggled her shoulders importantly. 'It was dark,' she began. 'I was in a car, a Ford Mondeo, with two guys—I sort of flew in through the rear window and they didn't know I was there. The driver frightened me, he seemed familiar, I think I might have had a scary dream about him before, but I can't quite remember.'

You did, but Gundrad stole that memory right out of your head. He didn't want your predictive dreams to get in the way. He wants that train to crash to create an anti-Islamic climate of fear.

'How'd you know it was a Ford Mondeo?' demanded Alex.

'Because my uncle's got an old one. It was red. They didn't talk … they looked at each other… grinning. I hated those smiles… I knew they were up to no good. The bald one started the car and drove off. The other one with tattoos on his arms kept hitting the dashboard with his fist… he looked a bit spaced out. Anyway, they drove and drove, and I was sort of time-out for a while… I nearly lost the dream. But then it began again… they stopped the car and got out, leaving the doors open. The baldy one was laughing fit to bust a gut. The other one just kept saying, "Chill man, chill." They climbed a hill and sat down on the grass. It was wet with rain or dew.'

Rhodene's face drained of colour, and she wiped her forehead. 'That's when I saw the lights. They were a long way away. The driver of the car saw them too and he poked the other one.'

Howie gave a loud cry and clasped his chest as though in pain. 'They're killing the dragon!' he screeched.

Lily shifted her vast bulk over to him in an instant and hugged him to her.

He stopped screaming and began to whimper instead. 'Carry on Rhodene,' said Lily, her eyes wide with alarm.

Rhodene's breathing became laboured. 'I heard this rumbling noise... the lights came closer... it was a train. It got nearer and nearer the car... the driver shouted... then the train rammed into the car. It carried the car a long way in front of it, and the train sort of crumpled, the back swung round, and the middle carriages collapsed over on their side.' Her hands waved vivid patterns in the air, showing them exactly how the tragedy would happen.

She paused. Mixed with her excitement at being centre stage, Alpha could sense the pain she was feeling. To Rhodene this crash had already happened, and she'd been there witnessing it. 'Lots of cars came... ambulances and stuff... and I could hear people screaming. It was horrible. I saw those two guys run up to the train so they could see the damage they'd caused. Then I woke up, and I knew it was going to happen soon... unless we stop them.'

Rhodene swallowed, stuck her thumb in her mouth, took it out quickly when she realised what she was doing, then looked round the group expectantly.

The challenge came from Janna. 'What use is that, it doesn't tell us where or when or who or why, so what are we supposed to do about it?'

'Don't be negative Janna,' said Lily, gently stroking Howie's hair. He was still shivering against her shoulder. 'We know a great deal more than we did before last night.'

'Did they speak English?' Mr Thom asked.

Rhodene thought for a moment. 'Yeah! They were born in England, somewhere up north.'

'What makes you think they're from Northern England? Could they be Scots?' Dr Scott asked.

'They didn't sound Scottish, more English. The baldy one said he wasn't stopping at no garage for petrol. He said … "Gah ritch"… to rhyme with itch, not "Ga raaj" like you all say here.'

'Well spotted, Rhodene. That's great,' said Dr Scott.

Rhodene blushed at the praise, which made her acne blend into her face. She looked pretty and interesting and happy, thought Alpha.

Martel put a damper on Rhodene's smile. 'The north is a big place. And just because they were born there, it doesn't mean that's where it's going to happen.'

Dr Scott's brows drew together in a formidable glare. Martel shut up. 'What about clothing? Anything to go on there?' Dr Scott asked, turning to Rhodene.

Rhodene screwed up her eyes in an effort to remember. 'They had dark clothes: the passenger wore a hoodie and boots. I remember dirty black boots. The other one wore trainers and a jacket with a green stripe on the sleeves.'

'Tattoos—can you describe them?' Mr Thom put in.

Rhodene put her fingers to her temples. 'I don't know…' her fingers zapped outwards into sharp points, as she remembered the details. 'There was a lion on one wrist, and a square sort of cross on the other.'

'Could you draw them?' asked Lily.

Rhodene nodded.

'What are the terrorist squad going to do about it?' Mr Thom asked Dr Scott.

'I've told John about the dream, but of course, he wants more detail. It's impossible to police every siding and level crossing in England for months on end. I'm certain Rhodene's right—this will happen soon—but it's up to us to find out when and where. Normal lessons are suspended until we have a breakthrough;

we're going to work at it until we come up with some usable data. Let's pray that we find it in time.'

Everyone stood up to go. Alpha gasped as her memory of the time she'd spent in Rhodene's dream flashed into her mind. She had to tell them right away. 'I… went…' with difficulty she raised her voice until her words broke through the hustle and bustle. 'Last night I went into Rhodene's mind looking for help, but I couldn't wake her. She was dreaming of two men in a car. They stopped at a roundabout, near this corner shop. There were newspapers in the window. The date on them was the 15th June.'

'That's tomorrow,' said Dr Scott. 'It's going to happen tomorrow night.'

CHAPTER THIRTY-EIGHT

Dr Scott held Alpha back as she was about to leave the room, allowing everyone else to file out before speaking. 'I'm sorry Alpha. When I promised that you would be safe here, I had no idea I was leading you into the lion's den.'

She nodded. 'It's OK.' She was certain that he would never have brought her to Krakow Bond if he'd suspected Mrs Hickelroy.

Dr Scott looked grim. 'It's not OK, but right now we haven't much time. John's here already. Andreyaz is delaying him with some coffee and cake while I talk to you.'

Alpha looked up, startled.

'I know you persuaded Howie to go to Mr Thom's room, but I said nothing at the meeting because I don't want anyone else to know what you can do. I'm sorry you didn't get the credit, but the fewer people who know how far your talents go, the safer you'll be. Say nothing to John about your ability to get people to change their minds. He knows you're telepathic—let's leave it at that.'

Stunned at the idea of hiding something from MI5 she hesitated. Before she could reply a middle-aged man walked uninvited into the office. 'I'll take my coffee in here. We've got plenty to discuss,' he said, nodding pleasantly.

'Hello John. This is Alpha, Alpha Moore.' Dr Scott smiled wryly. 'Alpha meet John. Apparently, he doesn't have a last name.

Now, most importantly John, we've established that the train smash will occur tomorrow night.'

John flipped open his mobile, hit quick dial. '15/6. At night,' he said economically, to whoever was on the end of the line.

Alpha looked closely at him. She could barely recognise him from Dr Scott's memory of his first meeting with the Prime Minister. He'd altered his appearance slightly but significantly. Today the tie was missing, his stance was more relaxed and there was nothing at all memorable about either his face or figure. He was of medium height, medium build, average colouring, hair neither long nor very short, body language unobtrusive, no distinctive features. She could have walked past him a dozen times and never noticed him.

'Good quality for a spy,' John said, putting his phone away and allowing one corner of his mouth to tilt up in a smile.

Her thoughts reeled—is *he telepathic too?*

John explained. 'No, I can't read your mind. When people learn that I work for M15, they all think the same thing. Lack of memorability is a quality I cultivate, a sort of invisibility cloak that's been very useful to me in the past. Now about that date?'

Dr Scott told John what had happened during the meeting, and how Alpha had intruded into Rhodene's dream. 'Alpha can tell you more about the FBFBA and you'll want to get those suitcases forensically tested. Alpha overheard them speaking about two children who'd been imprisoned in Turkey. They died.'

John grimaced.

Alpha, reminded once again about Pasha and Iwardi, swayed on her feet. *What a horrible way to die—and it nearly happened to me too.*

Dr Scott gripped her shoulder with a steadying hand. 'Go easy on her,' he told John. 'She's been through a great deal. Sit down, Alpha.'

John looked at her quizzically. 'Are you up to talking about it?'

She nodded.

'Before I start, I need to establish for myself that you really are telepathic so that I can trust any information you've picked up mentally.'

Dr Scott smiled. 'Still think I don't know my job? Will you trust standard psychic cards?' He walked over to his desk, withdrew a pack of black and white cards from a drawer and placed them on his desk. Then he joined Alpha on the other side, indicating that John should take the seat behind the desk.

John shuffled the cards, picked one at random from the middle of the pack, looked at it briefly, then held it close to his chest, staring questioningly at Alpha.

'It's a diamond, but you thought I was going to say circle. Most people say circle first.' John raised one eyebrow and pulled another card.

Forty-two cards later she'd correctly identified each card as bearing a diamond, a square, a circle, a rectangle or a set of wavy lines.

From there they progressed to pictures. John asked her to describe what kind of scene he was looking at while carefully hiding the picture from her.

It was easy work so soon she was able to drift beyond John's surface thoughts into his memories. John's life was interesting: he'd been many people and played lots of roles but now he was tied up in administration as the Prime Minister's direct link with MI5. She surfed through his mind; he'd been born Ebenezer Thrups. No wonder he'd chosen something simple like John as his contact name.

Half an hour later John put down the picture cards. 'I can't believe it; you go far beyond statistical significance. You missed the ducks on the pond, but everything else was correct. You're 98% accurate.'

She'd seen the ducks but hadn't bothered to mention them, because at that moment John's memories had been revealing an interesting period when he'd been pretending to be a woman.

'Only 98%.' Dr Scott grinned. 'Busy doing other things Alpha? Or are you just a bit tired today?' He turned to John. 'Will you take her word now?'

John picked lint from his jacket, trying to hide the look of amazement that was written all over his face. 'Yes.'

She told him everything she'd heard and extracted from Mrs Hickelroy's mind, carefully avoiding any mention of how she'd persuaded the ex-vice-principal to release her from the case. John insisted she went over and over the details and she began to feel very frustrated—none of this was going to stop the train smash.

'There's something you're not telling me,' John said finally.

Alpha gulped. Even if he couldn't read minds he was used to interrogating people. *How am I going to deflect his questions? Dr Scott said I mustn't mention my attempt to change Mrs Hickelroy's mind.*

One of John's earlier memories came to her aid—a shameful moment that he'd hidden from others when he'd been held captive without toilet facilities. 'I…I…was so scared I wet my pants,' she muttered, hiding behind her hair. That was true, but it wasn't the whole truth.

John was silent for a long while. 'I'm sorry I pushed you,' he said eventually. 'But it's crucial that I know everything. These people are dangerous, I'll do anything I have to in order to catch them.' He stood up to leave. 'Goodbye Alpha. You've been a great help. Thank you for your services to the Crown and to Britain.' He held out his hand.

'Goodbye Mr Thrups,' she said, shaking his briefly.

John's jaw fell open at the mention of the name he'd kept secret for so many years. He looked at her as though she was an alien species, though he declined to comment directly. Instead, he turned to the principal and said, 'Take good care of her, Michael. She's priceless. And don't worry; the entire police force is on high alert about that train. Now if only you could tell me which crossing?'

Dr Scott shook his hand then led him to the door. 'Best let us get to work on that.'

As the door closed behind John he asked, 'Is that his real name?'

'It's the name he was born with, but he's got lots of others.'

A quick smile played across Dr Scott's lips. 'You definitely persuaded him to take us seriously.'

———

All afternoon Alpha's frustration grew. She sat with Howie and Lily for hours, trying to pick up any random thoughts, but Howie was so exhausted that Howarth was asleep too.

———

Then it was Mr Thom's turn with her. He made her lie down on one of his long tables and placed his fingers on the back of her neck, twisting and turning her head until she was almost asleep, except that she could feel energy pulsing through her body and down into her knee.

When he finished she stood up, annoyance creeping past the lethargy his manipulations had produced. 'What about the train crash? This isn't helping.' Her hand flew to her mouth, surprised that she'd dared to address him so boldly.

He responded calmly. 'Predictions are not your forte—leave them to others. I've been getting you fully charged with Reiki. I don't think it will be long before we need your particular talents.'

His words didn't stop her from feeling helpless. She was certain that the only place she was likely to find any information was right inside Rhodene's head, but Rhodene had been tied up with Dr Scott since John had left.

———

Over dinner, she found out that no one else had been successful either. The table was unusually silent—everyone conscious of time ticking away. After the meal, she caught up with Rhodene, who was heading off towards her bedroom on the ground floor. 'I can help you remember more about your dream. Let me read your mind.'

Rhodene raised weary eyes to meet Alpha's probing stare. Alpha could see that she'd spent herself during the day in her efforts to find out more about the train smash. 'No.' Rhodene tapped her head. 'Dr Scott's tried everything, even hypnosis. There's nothing more in here.'

Alpha sensed her disappointment.

CHAPTER THIRTY-NINE

Sunday hovered about in the student lounge, flitting from chair to chair. Unable to settle he skittered across the room from bowling lane to console, considering how best to spend his evening. Mr Thom appeared to have forgotten about his grounding order, but that was of little use when everyone else had drifted off to bed, worn out by the day they'd had.

Deep inside, Sunday was nursing his torn emotions; they kept threatening to erupt into outright anger. *Mrs Hickelroy, I too much hate you*, he thought, kicking the sofa soundly.

'Where's Alpha?' asked Janna, creeping up behind him.

He swivelled, stamping his foot, crossly. He could sense that Alpha wasn't too far away, but he didn't know which room she was in. 'She's here, somewhere.'

'I know that but where exactly?' Janna demanded.

Girls! thought Sunday. *Why do they too much want details?* He shut his eyes and allowed his senses to expand beyond his body. Alpha was easier to track now, he knew her signature sensation well, and it was only a matter of time before he pinned down her location. 'She is with Rhodene, near that girl's bedroom.'

'Damn!' spat Janna, her eyes fuming.

Sunday turned away, feeling an urge to escape before Janna started to rant and rave; knowing that he was angry enough for the two of them. He didn't need Janna blasting away about the Alpha spending time with Rhodene.

But the torrent of jealous words he expected never came. Janna merely tutted. 'She's probably working on the train smash. Everyone's doing everything they can, except me. How can I use my talent at reading spaces when we don't know *where* it's going to happen?'

Sunday picked up a small measure of her frustration, knowing his own was even worse. 'It's no better for me. Today's a wipe-out.'

'A washout, you mean. Listen, I've got an idea… I was going to ask Alpha to help, but since she's busy… and you're here?' She let the question hang in the air.

'OK,' said Sunday. Anything was better than facing an empty room when his thoughts were filled with betrayal. *My Bolla*, he thought, for the umpteenth time that day, *I curse you*.

Janna led Sunday across the courtyard to South Block and up the stairs towards Mrs Hickelroy's apartment. But there they could go no further.

'Occupationally-challenged-orangutans!' exclaimed Janna, eyeing the police tape wound across the entrance to Mrs Hickelroy's quarters.

'Huh?' said Sunday.

'This place is filled with psychics, but the damned cops aren't going to let us through to her rooms.'

'Oh! Well if that's where you want to go, that's not the only way in,' said Sunday, waving a hand breezily at the striped tape. 'If you too much want to get inside?' he queried. Janna wasn't going to like his alternative.

'Yeah! There'll be vibes in there that will tell me where she's gone. I've got to get my psychic teeth into something.'

Sunday shrugged. 'You better be too much sure,' he said, hiding the doubts he was harbouring about Janna's reaction to the method of entry he was about to propose.

———

Wedged into a tiny hole above an even tinier funnel that formed the chimney flowing down into Mrs Hickelroy's apartment, Sunday raised his eyebrows at Janna's vast range of swear words. Most of them were aimed at him, though she'd saved a savoury few for the spiders along their route. She was even using words he'd never heard of before. He filed them away for future reference, pleased that his knowledge of English was improving with every second. Janna concluded with, 'Stuff it sludge bucket, you're out of your tiny mind. How do you expect me to fit through that gap?'

'Here.' He pulled out a stained dishcloth from inside his trousers. 'I've soaked this in olive oil. Rub it on your bum, it's your widest bit.'

Janna recoiled from the piece of cotton in his hand, as though he'd withdrawn a vicious ferret instead of a harmless oil-soaked cloth. 'Dung beetle! I'm not touching my skin with that. Heaven knows where it's been.'

'Do you want to get in there or not?'

Janna grabbed the lint from his hand. 'OK, OK. Turn around dinglebat, you're not watching this.'

Sunday swivelled obediently, completing a full circle just in time to see Janna's skirt flop down. She leaned over and peered once more into the gloomy narrow hole beneath her. He sensed her reluctance to enter it, so he raised his knee and bumped her gently on her rear end. She teetered on the edge of the hole, then shot down the first two meters, giving a pig-like squeal. He grinned with satisfaction, but then the whooshing sound stopped. He looked down—her skirt had ridden up above her waist, and her hips were plugging the gap near the bottom of the chimney.

An ear-splitting yell rose up the shaft. 'Sunday… Sunday! I'm stuck.'

Sunday sighed, before replying calmly, 'Stop screeching and pull in your stomach.'

Breathing raggedly, Janna tried to follow his instructions and managed to wiggle down two centimetres before getting stuck again.

'Sunday? Sunday! It's not working. Help!'

Mumbling about hysterical females Sunday positioned himself carefully at the edge of the hole, then jumped, landing with his feet placed neatly, one on each of Janna's shoulders. After a moment's resistance, he felt her drop below him, felt her feet touch the fire grate and her legs buckle beneath her. She collapsed in a heap, and he rolled from her shoulders into the room, adroitly avoiding both the lip of the mantelpiece and Janna's body.

She extricated herself from the claws of the fire grate, but instead of voicing her gratitude, she crawled out of the fireplace, glaring at him. 'What have you got for brains? Sheep guts? We could have both ended up stuck in there.'

Sunday felt she was being unreasonable. 'Stop complaining—you said help, so I helped. We're here, aren't we?'

Janna shot him another stinking look, then stood up and brushed at her hair frantically, as though it was covered in cobwebs—which it probably was. Muttering 'never again,' under her breath she began to wander from one side of the lounge to the other, following a path that made no sense to Sunday. Suddenly she stopped at the broken glass of the coffee table, kneeling down to press her fingers against the shards. 'How dare she? I'm in charge, not her, why doesn't she listen, she never trusted me, stupid bitch.' Janna ranted on in a sulky, masculine tone of voice that didn't sound at all like her own silver-tongued insults.

For a moment Sunday thought she was talking about Alpha, but then Janna stood up and raised her chin, taking up a pose that reminded him of Mrs Hickelroy. 'You ungrateful little swine!' she said, in an uncanny representation of Mrs Hickelroy voice. Sunday realised that she was taking in the room, reading its messages, and playing out conversations as though the owners of those voices had taken over her mind.

My Bolla, he thought as the memory of the woman he'd trusted returned to boot him in the stomach once more. *How could you do this to Alpha? Why did you let me down?* The mule kick of the image was so powerful it almost floored him. He pushed down his feelings with a hard swallow. *I believed in you, but you were too much a tokoloshe wearing angel's wings.*

For a while he watched Janna step around the lounge, shaking her head in frustration. Then, tired of the inactivity, he wandered into Mrs Hickelroy's bedroom and opened her extensive wardrobe. He fingered the pockets and jacket linings of the clothes within it. He could hear Janna moving through the rest of the apartment, talking to herself at random intervals. Finding nothing to interest him in the wardrobe, he gravitated towards the antique dressing table, taking out each of the drawers to inspect its underside, and peering into the gap each drawer had left to look for hiding places.

Janna's footsteps sounded lightly at the doorway. 'What on earth are you doing?' she asked.

He glanced at her—it was more than obvious what he was doing—he wasn't going to bother answering.

Janna sighed, then lay down on the bed, stretching out on the pillows. 'I can't feel a thing,' she moaned. 'It's like Mrs Hickelroy left years ago, not last night.'

Sunday flipped back the heavy rug on the floor and extracted a pencil torch from his pocket, running it along each crack between the floorboards.

'It's no good, let's get out of here,' said Janna. 'I don't care if we get into trouble for cutting the tape, I'm not going back up that chimney.'

'Have you got a hairpin?' he asked.

'Hairpin? What do you think I am—a flaming geriatric?'

'There's something in here. I can't get it out.'

Stirred from her depression Janna rummaged through the drawers in Mrs Hickelroy's dressing table. 'Here, will this help?'

Sunday jiggled and poked about with the pair of tweezers she passed him, and ever so slowly the blue stub came within his grasp. Triumphant, he pulled it out and handed it to Janna.

Her face fell. 'It's nothing but a ticket with a hole punched in it. I don't see what good this…' As she reached out to pluck it from him, she reeled, her eyes rolled back, and she fell to the floor in a trance.

She looked dead lying there on the floorboards. Alarmed Sunday grabbed a facecloth from the bathroom, soaked it in water then shot back and smothered her face with it.

She still didn't wake. He patted her cheek. 'Janna, Janna what's wrong?'

He was just about to go for help when she opened her eyes and stared dreamily at him. 'This ticket... Mrs Hickelroy's son was on that train—the one that's going to smash. He was testing the route.' Suddenly she pushed herself up. 'Come on, we need to get out of here and find Dr Scott. We must tell him about this.'

CHAPTER FORTY

Alpha felt like punching Rhodene, but she could tell that the girl wasn't being deliberately obstructive. Rhodene looked exhausted and a quick reading of her emotional leakage showed that she honestly thought there was no more to be found inside her head. Rhodene was certain that she had done her best, and was bitterly disappointed that her best hadn't been good enough.

Alpha gritted her teeth and insisted, 'I can get at more of your memories than you can.'

'Forget it. I'm going to bed. With any luck, I'll dream again tonight.'

'If we find anything, I won't take the credit. You can tell them you remembered.'

Rhodene looked suspicious. 'Why'd you want to do that?'

'It doesn't matter about me. It's the people on the train who are important. They're going to die. Come on Rhodene, please.'

Rhodene considered the matter, balancing Alpha's argument against her own feelings. 'OK. But only because you helped me get my psychic dreams back. I don't think you'll find anything, but if there's the smallest chance...'

In her bedroom Rhodene pottered about, changing into pyjamas, setting up her three teddies on the bottom of her bed. 'Don't take long about this. I'm very tired.'

As Rhodene climbed into bed, Alpha slid inside her head. She found the train dream at the surface of Rhodene's thoughts. She spent a long time in Rhodene's dream. Rhodene's head slumped sideways, and she began to snore gently. Finally Alpha found something, though it wasn't directly connected to the dream or the two who were planning the train crash.

——

She gave Rhodene a gentle shake and Rhodene snorted awake.

'You've got to tell Dr Scott about your gran.'

'What?' Rhodene grunted. 'But it's nothing... it's just a feeling.'

'No! You're concerned that your gran will be unhappy because...'

Rhodene had a sudden revelation. 'Because... because her neighbour... Mr Peterson... he'll be on that train. Gran thinks the world of him, she'd hate him to die.'

'And your gran lives where?' Alpha prompted.

'Manchester. The train's leaving Manchester, and Mr Peterson, that nice man who always fixes Gran's sink when it gets blocked, will get on it.'

CHAPTER FORTY-ONE

The entire party took the ferry off the Isle of Wight at first light, then caught a plane and flew northwest. Dr Scott, Lily and Mr Thom sat in front of Alpha, pouring over maps of Manchester and the area north of Manchester.

'Manchester has its own underground. That narrows our search—the smash is almost certainly beyond the tube lines,' said Dr Scott.

Lily nodded. 'Rhodene described the scene as though she was in the countryside at night.'

Mr Thom pointed to the map on his lap. 'There's this line through Bury or the one to Bolton. No further—beyond that and it'll be daylight.'

'Have the anti-terrorist squad been advised?' Lily asked.

'Yes. And John's arranged for the emergency services to be put on high alert. Even the rail police are in on the act,' said Dr Scott, his jaw tightening. 'At least he has faith in our predictions.'

'So they haven't been told why?' asked Lily.

Dr Scott lowered his voice, but Alpha could sense his bitterness. 'No. The PM still refuses to divulge our existence. He's terrified of looking like an idiot—he hasn't even told Home Office about us.'

'Bah! Even if going public stops another attack? I can't believe that man!

'I'd tell the press myself except that they wouldn't believe me,' said Mr Thom, his ears lobes changing colour in anger.

Dr Scott glanced at him, the glance conveying a stern warning. 'I'm under strict orders to instruct everyone to say nothing if we run into the police. They're doing what they can—they've stationed people at the crossings and they're chasing up owners of Ford Mondeos.'

Mr Thom grunted. 'Lot of good that will do—the criminals will probably steal a car.'

A worried look crossed Dr Scott's face. 'True, and there's no insider information and no phone traces for them to go on. We're all they've got.'

After the flight, at the airport car rental, Dr Scott signed up for the two biggest vehicles available, while Lily attempted to split the students into two groups. She wanted Howie, Carl, Janna and Sunday to travel with her. But Carl wanted to travel with Alex.

Lily heaved an impatient sigh, turning to Dr Scott, but he simply nodded and rearranged the groups: Howie, Sunday, Janna and Martel with Lily in the 4x4; Alpha, Rhodene, Carl and Alex travelling with Dr Scott and Mr Thom in the estate car. Carl and Alex sat together in the boot, on the spare seats. Their hired vehicles drove out beyond the city, heading in different directions.

'We're going toward Bury,' said Dr Scott, twisting the steering wheel to get off the main road. 'The other team is heading for Bolton.'

Alpha sat in silence, listening as Dr Scott and Mr Thom discussed the roads. Rhodene, placed next to her, had slumped against the car door and closed her eyes. Alpha could feel Rhodene's disappointment that she hadn't dreamed more of the same dream in the few hours of sleep they'd had.

Alex pulled out a pack of magic cards and he and Carl began a complicated game involving the forces of earth and fire. They started squabbling almost at once, until Rhodene shouted, 'Shut up, will you? Just shut up!'

'We're all tense, Rhodene,' said Mr Thom, his phrasing sensitive to all their needs. 'The boys are trying to keep their nerves under control with the cards.' He turned to peer at the boys sitting in the rear of the vehicle. 'Pipe down, lads.'

As the boys quietened Dr Scott said, 'Listen—you need to know this.' At once there was utter silence from the rear of the car, broken only by the purr of the engine.

Dr Scott went on, 'Janna's uncovered a connection between the train smash and Gundrad. If he or Victoria Hickelroy turn up, stay back. They're armed and dangerous. You're not to go near them. Is that understood?'

A core of cold entered Alpha's body, freezing her from the inside out. *I knew we hadn't seen the last of him.*

She jumped as Dr Scott turned his head to roar at them. 'Is that understood!'

She felt herself sitting up straighter as she replied, 'Yes, Dr Scott,' amidst a mass of similar agreements. She had no problem with his instruction. She knew exactly how dangerous Gundrad was. *I should have made the connection—Gundrad was so full of himself when Mrs Hickelroy mentioned the train dream. He's responsible for the smash. That mad bastard is going to kill dozens of people just so he can lay the blame on Muslim radicals.*

The tension in the car grew tangible—no one wanted to say what everyone was thinking—that there were only a few hours left before dark.

More to calm herself down than with any real hope of finding new information Alpha asked, 'What does the driver of the car have to do with Gundrad?'

'No idea,' said Dr Scott. 'John's been trying to trace the tattoos on the driver, but he's had no luck. Gundrad has a very secretive past. After he left university, he fell off the radar.'

Alpha lapsed back into silence; worrying like a dog over a bone about any scrap of information she could remember. She went over and over the night he'd captured her, seeking a clue as to where he might be now.

Mr Thom switched on the radio—her breath caught in her throat as they listened to the news. Nothing about a train smash. He turned the radio off again. *Why aren't they telling people to stay off the trains from Manchester?*

Mr Thom's phone rang. He spoke briefly, then closed it. 'That was Lily. Howie's been raving about his dragon, but she can't get directions from him.'

Alpha saw Dr Scott's fingers tighten on the steering wheel.

Darkness drew in around them. Then they were back on the A56, checking every conceivable place where the road passed anywhere near the railway track. Alpha's eyes ached as she stared into the gloom, willing herself to sense something.

Rhodene's thoughts spilled over, showing Alpha horrible images—she replayed her dream over and over in her mind: the cries of the victims who were still alive but hurt, the two monsters running down the hill to revel in the gory details. She could hear a baby crying and this disturbed her more than anything.

That plaintive cry of the baby in Rhodene's spillage drilled through Alpha until she wanted to scream at Rhodene. She swung towards her but stopped short of saying anything as she caught sight of the state Rhodene was in. The girl was sitting forwards in the car; her face in her shaking hands, unable to control her ragged sobs. Alpha rubbed her arm, awkwardly. *It's not her fault!* she thought.

Mr Thom turned on the radio again.

Political row about misused money…

Captains of industry speaking out against energy prices…

Rain predicted…

And nothing… absolutely sod all about terrorists.

The baby wailed in Rhodene's mind again.

Stop it. Stop thinking about it.

'Where next?' demanded Dr Scott of Mr Thom. 'Come on. We must keep moving.'

'Left, then right at the roundabout.'

A phone rang. Its ring startled Alpha.

'No, nothing Lily,' answered Mr Thom. 'What about you?'

He listened, then hung up, shaking his head. His shrug as he turned towards Dr Scott said it all. He bent down and opened the bag at his feet. Then he tossed wrapped sandwiches over his shoulder. 'Eat, guys. Keep your strength up.'

Alpha's chicken, lettuce and mayo sandwich went down her throat like sandpaper—even the cola couldn't wash it down properly.

Mr Thom leaned forwards—turned the radio on. Nothing new. Time was locked into a cruel cycle—managing somehow to both drag and fly.

Ring tones again. John this time. Alpha's heart almost stopped. *Is this it?*

She held her breath until Mr Thom said as he shut down his phone, 'There's no change. And my battery's giving out.'

Alpha's shoulders tightened—they'd be able to use her as a table soon, she so was so rigid with tension.

Dr Scott reached into his shirt pocket and tossed Mr Thom his phone. It rang just as he caught it. Rhodene twitched violently. Mr Thom switched the mobile to speakerphone, and they could all hear Lily saying, 'Janna's been walking up and down the same piece of track for ten minutes. She says it's vibrating—an accident of sorts—but she doesn't know if it's from the past or the future.'

'Describe the scenery,' said Dr Scott.

'It's a straight piece of track—splits into two at a set of points,' Lily said, her voice sounding tinny and far away.

'No,' said Rhodene, shifting to the very edge of her seat. 'The line was curved.'

'Go on, Lily,' said Dr Scott.

'Travelling south, there's an industrial building—a smoking chimney.'

'What about hills? Hills…' Rhodene shrieked, her voice filling with hysteria. Alpha put her arm around her. Rhodene flinched, then seemed to take some comfort from the gesture. She went on, her voice cracking, 'They drove down a private road… across a field. They got out …walked up a steep hill.'

'No hills here,' Lily reported.

'Wrong place. Get out of there now.' Dr Scott banged his fist against the steering wheel. 'Blast it!'

Rhodene collapsed against Alpha's shoulder, crying. Alpha longed for something to bang too.

CHAPTER FORTY-TWO

'We've learned something.' Mr Thom's map crackled as he refolded it to peer at a new area. 'It's not going to happen on a level crossing. Rhodene said they drove onto a private road.' He stabbed at the map with a pen. 'Let's try here.'

But no one felt anything as they got nearer to that point. No one said anything either. Meanwhile, Alpha's neck tied itself in yet another knot.

Mr Thom broke the silence by calling the other team. 'It's on private land. Ignore everywhere else,' he told them. Then he shuffled the maps on his lap and pulled out a hand-drawn one of a much smaller scale. 'The line crosses private land here, here and here.' He circled the areas in red

They tried two of the markers. By the time they'd driven to the third area, it was three o'clock in the morning.

Nothing again.

Stony-faced, Mr Thom directed Dr Scott down a minor road.

Alpha's thoughts filled with despair. *It's too late. We've failed.*

Lights from an oncoming vehicle flashed them, and a 4x4 pulled up on the other side of the road. Lily stuck her head out of the window and shouted, 'I've been trying to call. I gave Martel the aerial maps to try. He sensed something on your patch. Follow me.'

Tyres screeched in complaint as Dr Scott swung into a U-turn.

Lily drove recklessly, braking then stopping at a place that seemed just like any other. She twisted the 4x4 onto a dirt track. Dr Scott followed, the estate car shuddering wildly.

Invisible from the road, there was a tiny, hand-painted sign, saying private property, some way up the track. The 4x4 turned at right angles along a route that was never meant to be driven on by anything other than a tractor. They followed, the estate car bumping and swaying terrifyingly. The undercarriage scraped on a rock—Dr Scott changed gears and ground the engine. They lurched forwards with a jerk.

Now Alpha could see the red gleam of the Ford Mondeo in the light of the half-moon. The doors were open, and it was parked across the train tracks.

Dr Scott grabbed his phone.

Mr Thom jumped out and ran over to the red vehicle. 'No keys,' he cried.

'No phone signal,' said Dr Scott. 'I'm going to ram the car. Everyone out.'

They scrambled out, falling over each other to clear the estate car. The principal drove straight into the boot of the Mondeo, but it was the front of his car that crumpled, while the Mondeo stayed fixedly on the rail.

'My turn,' Lily shouted. The team in the 4x4 clambered out and Lily brought her heavier vehicle into play, ramming it into the red car. But the Mondeo was going nowhere. She reversed at speed, ready to try again.

'They've put metal stuff in the boot,' Alex screeched. 'It's too heavy.'

'I'm going to …' Carl shut his eyes, his brow furrowed in concentration. Beads of sweat broke out on his forehead and slithered down his cheeks, but the red car stayed right where it was.

Then Alex's hands lifted, waving through the air like a magician casting a spell. Suddenly the boot popped open, and pieces of junk flew out in all directions.

'Don't drop it on the line, boys,' Mr Thom cried.

Dr Scott threw his phone at Mr Thom. 'Take the car—drive to where you can get a signal—call the police. Tell them to stop all trains on this line.'

'The dragon's coming,' shrieked Howie.

Rhodene dropped to the ground and began pounding her head on a rock. 'Get out—I can't take any more!'

Janna lifted Rhodene from the ground and held her close, wiping away the smear of blood on Rhodene's forehead with her sleeve.

Dr Scott grabbed Howie and hugged the boy to his tall frame. 'Get ready to ram the car again, Lily, as soon as the boys have cleared the junk.'

Alpha was certain that the only way they were going to move that car in time was with the keys. Clutching the blue egg in her hand she let her mind stream out into the rolling landscape, searching... seeking... finding the culprits. The two men were sitting on top of the tallest hill.

———

She entered the bald head of the driver. His mind was awash with a slimy substance—an oil slick on a dark sea. This slickness was filled with a sick delight: with this act, he'd wiped away the boredom of his life. He laughed at the small figures far below trying to move the car—he was God—he held death in his hands.

Shaken by his thoughts, Alpha faltered. She'd have to swim through them to make any headway. Hesitating only briefly, she dived into the oily liquid, feeling it swill around her. Waves washed past her—damn, she felt her mission disappear, the other one had grabbed the keys, chuckling insanely.

'Train!' Janna screamed.

Alpha barely heard the shout, but the high-pitched clamour of the train got through to her. She shot out of Baldy's head.

―――

Her eyes picked out the lights that were just pinpricks in the distance. Yet, as time spaced out in unbearable fractions, the train came towards her like a dragon in full flight.

Her brain screamed at her. She had nanoseconds to force the passenger to drive the car off the track.

She dropped inside his mind, but it was a lunar landscape— empty—a dead zone. It could not have been more deserted. His brain cells had disappeared into whatever drug he had chosen to destroy himself with—there was nothing left to work on.

―――

She tore back into the bald man's mind. His oily thoughts were hard to grasp; even the pleasure he felt at his trick was slippery. *Oil slick mind; sick trick mind.*

The train was now less than eight hundred meters away.

Trigger. I need a trigger. But his sick sea of a mind was sloshing her around, filling her mouth with oily waves, choking her. She was tossed randomly between his memories. Childhood—poor but normal… Parents—bully boy father, cringing mother… Pain—Baldy shrugged it off… Nothing to move this monster who was growing up just like his dad.

A wave washed right over her head, and she swallowed in the moment when Baldy had first opened up to Gundrad; his desire to commit mass murder easy to read. Gundrad only needed to steer him in the right direction, provide the idea, formulate the plan. Baldy lapped it all up.

Drowning, gasping for breath, she managed to kick herself away... *none of this would move that car.*

Six hundred meters. The train was drawing closer at frightening speed.

Using long, desperate strokes she swam into Baldy's childhood memories. Aged nine, he'd explored a deserted building, an infested building. Ah! A tiny seed, but workable. He feared rats like Janna hated spiders.

Alpha filled Baldy's mind with a million rodents. They nibbled at his face, his armpits, his softest tissues. He stared at one that was poised to pierce his eye with its sharp teeth.

Get up, she screamed inside his head. *Grab the keys—drive the car off the track. Run... run before the rats take you.*

The man snatched the keys from his senseless friend's hand and ran.

———

Pain dammed in Alpha's head as her thoughts were wrenched from the oily ocean into a war zone: a grim and wretched place that she knew all too well. Now she was back inside Gundrad's mind.

CHAPTER FORTY-THREE

Alpha twisted this way and that frantically trying to find a way out of Gundrad's brain, but there was no way out of this maze. Rifle-fire shuddered behind her; a rocket zoomed overhead. Dust and fumes filled her lungs. Suddenly armoured vehicles were engulfing her—Gundrad's army everywhere she looked. Faceless drivers and crew sprang out, grabbing her and pinning her arms behind her back. Gundrad's face appeared above her, enlarged a hundredfold. 'Meddling witch. You're too late,' he gloated.

'No!' She hurled herself away from him. Hands grabbed her, connecting with her wrists, her clothes her throat. Her arms felt like they were being torn from her torso; her neck lashed in excruciating agony as her hair was yanked backwards.

Gundrad's laughter echoed while her world exploded into pain. In a distant part of her mind, she knew that those hands had nipped right inside her head, and were tearing chunks from her mind, in the same way that Gundrad had stolen Rhodene's memory. Soon they would leave her with no more mind than an advanced-stage Alzheimer's patient.

Abruptly Gundrad stopped laughing and his face contorted into a hideous mask. The soldiers around Alpha fell back and Gundrad's thoughts dissolved around her.

———

She dropped out of his head, spinning across the hills to return her own body. She felt ill. Bile was burning a hole in her throat. She spat to clear it from her mouth, but her body forced her to drink most of it where it continued its assault on her stomach.

She shoved the nausea down as her eyes caught sight of the figure on the hillside. Bald guy was still two hundred meters away from the track. He slithered down the hill, picked himself up, ran again. She turned her head; the thundering train was almost on top of the car—there was no way Baldy would reach it in time.

All hope that Gundrad had failed fell away. She waved her arm weakly in the direction she had felt him. 'Gundrad… over there,' she said, the words catching in her throat.

Then Janna shrieked, 'Sunday! He's in the car.'

Alpha homed in on the small figure in the driver's seat of the Mondeo and her heart wept.

CHAPTER FORTY-FOUR

A few minutes earlier...

The sky rained hammers and rocks and steel bars on Sunday as he slithered on his stomach towards the red Mondeo. He ducked his head when a rusty hubcap spun towards him. The wheel skimmed his shoulders before rolling away into the grass. 'Aaiee! Too much vooma, Alex.' He shook his head, marvelling at the young kinetic's skills. *What a fine warrior Alex will make.*

He reached the track and risked a quick look backwards—everyone's concentration was on the train—*good!* He maneuvered himself into the passenger seat of the Mondeo and from there slid across into driving position. He bent over the dashboard, his right hand pulling and twisting, probing where no adult's fingers could reach, hot-wiring the car. The car belched and shivered, and smoke came from the exhaust.

He pushed his foot onto the clutch. 'Eh-he! Now what did Mbo say about how to drive?' he muttered.

A plaintive cry filled the air. 'The dragon's here.'

Sunday tried to block Howie's words from his thoughts. He had to concentrate.

Then an ear-shattering scream drew the others' attention towards him: Janna was shrieking, 'Sunday! He's in the car.'

'Get out now!' Dr Scott thundered.

Sunday almost jumped to attention; he was much in awe of Dr Scott. 'Go away...' he said. 'I must think...gears, which one first?'

He felt Alpha whisk through his head, but he ignored her plea to get out.

Suddenly he was reliving a memory—*Alpha was pushing his car-stealing lessons with Mbo to the front of his mind*—his hand grazed the gear lever, and somehow pushed it into first gear. He released the clutch as his other foot rammed down on the accelerator.

The car bumped forwards, then stalled as the handbrake kicked in.

Martel's voice spilled into the night. 'You've left the handbrake on!'

The sound of feet, pounding towards the car, chopped into Sunday. But then a much louder noise. He looked up and saw the train bearing down on him, saturating the inside of the car with light. He heard brakes: their screech blasted into his head, petrifying all thought, all action.

Instinctively he ducked and as he did his gaze flashed over the handbrake. As though raised by unseen hands the handbrake was unlatching itself.

The movement broke through the shock that had solidified his thoughts. 'Thank you, Carl,' Sunday murmured, his mind snapping out of the paralysis caused by the roar of the train. He twitched the wires, restarting the car. Once more he released the clutch, simultaneously pressing down on the accelerator. With a blast of sound, the Mondeo leapt away, and then began to inch forwards—but not far enough.

The train struck. Sunday's head jerked onto the steering wheel, and he knew no more

CHAPTER
FORTY-FIVE

Alpha saw the train hit the rear bumper of the red car, wrench it free and carry it along the track with the horrible sound of tearing metal. Train wheels pounded over it, corrugating it until it crumbled. Her eyes remained glued to the train as it rumbled past, separating her from Sunday whose thoughts had gone black.

Nooo! You can't die on me.

Way down the track the train drew to a safe halt and the red Mondeo came into view.

She ran towards the car. Sunday's bloody head was resting against the steering wheel. Her stomach heaved.

———

Suddenly she was back inside Gundrad's war zone of a mind, pulled by an inescapable force. But the war was no longer raging around her—it was inside her.

'You!' His voice rattled, machine-gun-like, into her brain. 'You've destroyed my plans.'

She felt his fury, bent on revenge, bent on ripping her sanity to shreds. Still in shock, she could only endure as her mind was stretched. Her emotions, raw and bleeding, were pulled into one another becoming a ball of cruel energy.

'You put all your efforts into the driver... and he still didn't get there on time,' Gundrad taunted. 'You left it up to that little black bastard.'

She saw her failures… her mother, Biddy, Sunday. Her guilt was too much to contain within herself; too much to hold in. It imploded, fracturing her mind.

Desperately she tried to regain some sense of who she was; to retain some tiny essence of herself. She made herself remember Janna—twirling in the night air—her look mischievous as she said, *'It'll be great if you can confirm what's really going on in my head.'* She forced Dr Scott's words into her head, *'You are the most incredible telepath I've ever met.'*

Her determination firmed as her memories shored up the remnants of her identity. *No! I won't let him drown me in guilt.*

But then she could no longer shut him out: he was speaking right inside of her in a terrible voice that told her to face what she knew. And now there was Sunday, his head covered in tight curls, lying twisted and lifeless against the steering wheel. *Precious Sunday—closer to her than she'd ever dreamed. Dead.*

Her final resistance against Gundrad shattered. She was one with him—a conduit for his foul thoughts. She could not resist, she had to obey, to control—to kill.

Yes—yes! Kill. Make them fight to the death.

A veil came down over her mind as she gazed at the group around her, each of them caught as if in slow motion. Dr Scott was running towards the Mondeo… Lily had leapt towards Howie… Janna was clinging to Rhodene. Martel stood frozen, staring into space.

Gundrad's orders rung through her mind. The urge to blast out at these meddlers became unbearable. *Who first?* Her gaze swept around, choosing…

Within the space of a heartbeat, she'd shot into Martel's mind, searching for the memory that would turn him into a lunatic. The memory that had changed Martel forever… had marked him a killer once… and would mark him again.

Martel's tentacles reached out, but she spun past them, dancing like a ghostly wreath, avoiding them all. Martel's early memories, protectively enclosed inside a shell, lay ahead of her.

She swivelled inside the shell, whisking through Martel's childhood, returning to Martel's father. She braced herself, ready to force Martel to see everyone around her as his father. Her throat opened, filling with the harsh whisper of the father's voice as he tormented the young Martel. *'Think yourself clever, you small piece of black shit.'*

Martel reacted, fast as a striking cobra. The words were barely uttered when Alpha's chest burned with fear. Her joints became loose, and her knees turned to jelly. She'd never imagined so much pain… so strong it blanked out everything, blessedly killing Gundrad's control.

———

Gundrad was clutching at her thoughts, he wouldn't let her die, and he dragged her back into his head.

'You're dead, bitch,' he told her, but she knew that already. She lay passively within his mind, twisted and broken, dully staring out at the world through his eyes.

She heard a loud click: vaguely she registered that the doors of the car were now shut, locking them both in together. The windscreen shattered. A metal bar flew towards Gundrad's head, striking him in a clean blow to his temple. The bar swung itself round, hitting him again and again in a frenzied attack until his face was a bloody mess.

Good, she thought dimly as she felt him lapse into unconsciousness. *We'll die together.*

CHAPTER FORTY-SIX

This was hell. Her mind wouldn't rest, wouldn't stop. *Sunday's dead—it's my fault. My fault! My fault! My fault! My fau...*

...Voices. The words were jumbled up... running into each other... whispering.

Sunday's face pressed down on her. Her heart ached with loss and with guilt. Then, blessedly, her thoughts became too heavy to hold.

———

'Alpha, Alpha! Come back to us.'

She felt a twitch begin deep down in the soles of her feet.

No more... let me sink back into emptiness.

The pain of remembering hit her again. *Sunday—he's gone—he died.* Loneliness drenched her soul.

'Alpha? Come on, numbskull. Wake up, will you?'

Alpha felt a momentary anger at the voice. *Bugger off.*

But the voice wouldn't let her go. 'She's awake! I saw her head move.'

'It's easy to imagine movement. You've been at her bedside a long time. You should get some rest.'

'Listen you stupid nursy nitwit... she's awake, I'm telling you. Look!' Janna's voice shouted. 'Her eyes are flickering.'

Alpha felt her arm being lifted over her head. She was so tired, she longed for the relief of the blackness again—*leave me alone!* Her arm dropped towards her face. At the last moment, she flicked it weakly away from her nose, so that it landed on her chin. *Ow!*

Her eyes opened and travelled round the room, taking it in. A blur of pale blues and greys… curtains round her … bars at the side of the bed. Her head was throbbing.

'Where?' The word was furred, as though her tongue had forgotten how to form words.

'Hospital… you've been really poorly,' answered Janna frowning, then leaning forwards to gently touch her brow.

'No. Where's….' Alpha tried again, but the words wouldn't come.

Across Janna's shoulder, Alpha caught sight of Dr Scott rushing through the door, closely followed by a man she didn't know and a nurse.

'Hello,' said the stranger. 'I'm Dr Marriott. I'm going to examine you, then you can spend some time talking to your friends. But only ten minutes Nurse Williams. She needs her rest.'

Alpha endured the indignities of examination, answering in monosyllables where she could, and otherwise passively watching Dr Scott and Janna watching her. Their faces were drawn… pinched almost.

Sunday! Despair washed through her as she considered that there might be yet another death on her hands apart from Sunday's. Had Martel survived Gundrad's attack? *No—not Gundrad's*, she reminded herself. *Mine.* She hoped so. Martel had been brilliant. *I manipulated him, forced him to feel that huge rage again—he'll never forgive me, but he broke Gundrad's control over me and stopped me from making everyone kill each other.*

As soon as the doctor and nurse left the room she turned to Dr Scott her throat scratching out the dreaded word. 'Gun... drad?'

'In prison.'

Her heart sank. 'He's...' she swallowed, forced herself to say, 'not dead?'

'No, but he can't get at us now. His capture was quite an event. Carl locked his car doors kinetically, while Alex tossed a metal bar through his windscreen. It knocked him out.' Dr Scott patted Janna on the arm, then reached for Alpha's hand. 'Thanks to Janna's warning that he was involved with the train smash John had circulated his description. The police arrested him while he was still groggy. Otherwise, he might have got clean away. Oh! And they've taken in both occupants of the Red Mondeo too.'

Janna poured a glass of water for her. Alpha took it gratefully, sipping slowly because her throat hurt. 'Martel?' she croaked.

'Martel?' Dr Scott looked surprised. 'He's fine. He alerted us as to where Gundrad was parked—that's how the boys knew where to find him—somehow Martel was able to follow his thoughts through your mind.'

'I...talk...to him.'

'There's plenty of time,' said Dr Scott soothingly. 'Carl, Alex and Howie have gone back to school with Lily, but the rest of us are staying in Manchester until you're well enough to return. John's been giving us a thorough grilling; you'll be glad to have missed that.'

'Talk to Martel... now. Alone.'

Janna glanced at Dr Scott. Both of them looked set to argue with her.

'Please?'

Dr Scott must have registered her determination telepathically because he gave in easily. 'OK. I'll fetch him from the hotel.'

Before he could leave Nurse Williams bustled into the room, saying, 'Time for a rest, Alpha. Your friends can see you later.'

Alpha sat up in agitation. 'Martel.'

'Sleep now,' said Nurse Williams, trying to push her down again.

Alpha ripped the tape from her wrist and began to extract the needle in her arm. 'Martel. Now.'

'I believe I must insist,' Dr Scott told the nurse. 'You've no idea what she's capable of once she's riled.'

———

Fifteen minutes later Martel dragged out the visitor's chair, twisted it around, slung his legs over the seat and sat. He draped his long arms across the chair back, and rested his chin on them, his cold gaze alighting silently on Alpha.

'I'm sorry,' said Alpha, trying to hold Martel's gaze. Her whole body was shaking with the effort. 'I didn't know what else to do.'

'You tried to get me to hurt everyone.'

'Yes…no. NO! Gundrad had me under his control… he ordered me to kill you all… the only chance I had was to take you first.'

Martel sat, stony-faced.

Desperate for Martel to believe her, Alpha continued. 'Because… because I hoped you would kill me before I could get to the others.'

Martel's eyes flashed … Alpha looked away, biting her lip. 'I'm sorry. I don't know what else to say… I'm glad you were able to track him down.'

'Shit!' said Martel, eventually. 'I wish Alex hadn't stopped short of beating him into oblivion.'

'Me too.'

Martel stared at Alpha and Alpha wilted under his gaze. Eventually Martel said, 'That doesn't excuse what you did— those memories you dredged up out of my head were terrible. I never want to remember that… but it was worse to feel that I wanted to kill. The fury… it was red hot. I don't think I'll ever forget that feeling.'

He paused, then went on. 'But now, thinking about it, in some way I feel good knowing that I don't really have a killer's instinct— no matter my past. I didn't kill you, or the others. I couldn't. It's changed my perception about myself. And you helped Sunday get that car off the track. In my book that counts, so we're even.' He stood up and turned away.

To her astonishment, Alpha felt waves of guilt radiating from Martel. He was blaming himself for not working more closely with Alpha and the others. He reasoned that if he'd worked with everyone they might have been able to get to the car in good time, and Sunday wouldn't have needed to get into it.

Alpha's eyes brimmed with tears, and she couldn't stop the sob that burst out from her heart. 'It's not your fault. If I hadn't tried to go after the driver, I could have stopped Sunday from climbing into the car.'

'If you'd done that all those people on the train would be dead.'

'But Sunday would still be alive!' The injustice of having to forfeit Sunday's life for a train full of unknown people was too much for Alpha, and she crumpled back into the pillows, totally drained.

Martel swung towards Alpha, an odd, startled look on his face. Then he strode out of the door and gave a piercing whistle. Seconds later footsteps bounded down the corridor, and a black face peered around the corner. The rest of Sunday's body entered the room, and Alpha saw him fly towards her, before his arms wrapped around her.

Her thoughts spun out towards him, showering him in a flurry of emotion that contained every ounce of her earlier misery. She could barely believe he was alive.

'You're hurt!' she whispered, fingering the bandage strapped across his forehead.

Sunday drew back from her, grinning hugely. 'Aaiee! Don't worry about me. Zulu warriors have too much hard heads.'

CHAPTER
FORTY-SEVEN

Alpha and the other students were finally allowed to fly back to Krakow Bond. Bored and tired after a long flight delay, they chatted together until it was time for their plane to leave.

Alpha cocked her ears as she overheard Martel question Dr Scott about Mrs Hickelroy.

'No, they haven't caught her yet, but it won't be long now. John says they're closing in on her,' Dr Scott told Martel. 'They're hopeful that Gundrad will provide them with information about her whereabouts but so far he's said nothing at all.'

Alpha saw a sliver of satisfaction in Martel's eyes then she caught Martel's thoughts. Martel was hoping that Gundrad would be forced one way or another to tell the truth.

'When they catch her they'd better throw away the key,' Martel said to Dr Scott.

Suddenly Martel's thoughts slammed shut as he swivelled towards Alpha. Alpha slid backwards, trying to hide behind Dr Scott, but somehow Martel's finger appeared under Alpha's nose. 'I'm warning you, keep out of my head.'

Then, just as quickly, he turned away as though nothing had happened.

Alpha blinked, stunned by Martel's rapid threat and retreat. Martel was something else... he had such control over his intense emotions that he scared Alpha, even though Alpha could understand him much better now. Clearly there were still issues to be addressed between them. *And Martel has this thing about telepaths*, she remembered.

Sunday slipped his hand into Alpha's and insisted on sitting next to her on the plane. As they sank into their seats Alpha put her head back, feeling drained and exhausted. Behind her she could hear Janna chatting to Rhodene in a friendly if forthright manner. 'Pull yourself towards yourself, girl,' she was saying. 'You're the big heroine here, without your dream we couldn't have done a damn thing. Now stop moping around and give yourself a fat pat on the back.'

Alpha's lips curved into a little smile. It had taken a near-disaster to bring Janna closer to Rhodene.

Sunday opened his paper bag to disclose the food he'd nicked from the hospital (three biscuits, two yoghurts and an orange.) Alpha declined any of this feast, so he scoffed the lot then lay back his chair and closed his eyes. His head drifted onto her shoulder.

Alpha squeezed her knees tightly together: *Is now the time to find out if what I thought I saw in Sunday's head was real?* Slowly, she allowed her mind to merged with Sunday's memories.

———

A nugget of jade… twisting between Sunday's tiny fingers when he was just a toddler. It was carved into a barrel shape and was surrounded by a set of miniature mice that ran up and down as he spun it. The moment she'd glimpsed it, while she was searching for some way to force him out of that car before the train struck it, she'd known there was something very important about it. The barrel was hinged and could be opened, but it was the shape of it that was most fascinating. Alpha remembered how interested Sunday had been in the jade pin-brooch her father had given her mother. She was certain that if she plunged her pin into the centre of that barrel—it would fit exactly into the gap.

Hesitantly, she eased through his life… yes… there was his mother before she'd shown signs of illness. She was singing a soft lullaby and was stroking Sunday's head as he fell asleep in the small room they shared. Candlelight lit the room and threw up shadows on the woman's face.

Alpha gulped. She'd been right. Sunday's mother was a stunning black woman, whose face was identical to the image she'd seen inside her father's head on her fifth birthday.

———

Roused from sleep by her start Sunday murmured, 'What is wrong?'

'I… nothing. Go back to sleep.'

'No. Tell me,' he insisted, yawning loudly.

Alpha couldn't speak her thoughts out loud. They were too big, too important, and much too fragile. She slid back into Sunday's mind and whispered without words. *I'm your sister, at least, your half-sister. I think we shared the same father.*

'Mmmm,' mumbled Sunday. 'That is too much good.' Then he promptly fell asleep again.

Alpha couldn't sleep after that. She felt a wellspring of bitterness rise up inside her against her father. Though she often wished it had never happened, she'd accepted his death, and had always blamed her mother for choosing to drown herself in drinks. But now she blamed him for not providing for Sunday.

As soon as Sunday woke up she asked him about his mother.

'She used to live in Egoli, South Africa's golden city. She worked too much too hard in a hotel,' he told her. 'Then my father, he disappeared. I was a too much small baby still in her belly. After that, she took me back to her birthplace. She said he never saw me…never even came back after I was born.'

Alpha sighed. 'He died. It happened on one of his flights to South Africa. On his way to see you. I think he loved your mother and mine, and he left them both alone. And you. I'm so sorry.'

Sunday patted her hand, leaving a citrusy smell all over it. 'It is OK. I am not sad. I am too much glad I found my sister.'

Alpha mulled over that for a few seconds, then gave up thinking. The sudden flare of anger she'd felt towards her dad died away, and she smiled contentedly. Sunday's pragmatic approach to life seemed like the perfect way to accept that she was no longer alone against the world.

CHAPTER FORTY-EIGHT

The following day Alpha begged to be allowed to visit Biddy. She still felt rotten about Biddy being shot. Mr Thom accompanied her, taking her into the subterranean depths of the hospital, through doors guarded by nurses, where was she required to don a surgical mask and latex gloves before she could enter Biddy's room. She found Biddy propped up on several pillows breathing in short, painful breaths. She looked small and frail; nothing like the vibrant young housekeeper Alpha had learned to care so much about.

'I'm sorry,' said Alpha. 'I could have stopped her before she shot you.'

Biddy put out her hand and clasped Alpha's weakly in hers. 'Hey, what rubbish... is this? You saved my life. It wasn't... your job to stop her... it was ours. We failed... I failed.' She paused for a pain-ridden breath then continued. 'I'm... so proud of you all... stopping that train crash.' An even longer pause, then Biddy whispered, 'tell Howie I love him. You... you can...talk to him.'

Alpha nodded as hard as she could. She couldn't speak, her throat was filled with tears.

———

The next day the whole house was spruced up in preparation for parents' weekend. In deference to Biddy the house staff was cleaning with renewed vigour: in the great hall, the golden oak of the banisters gleamed; sunlight, pouring through newly polished windows, covered the floors with dancing colours and the chandeliers sparkled like diamonds. Miss Gilford herself had placed bunches of peonies and roses throughout the common rooms and had seen to it that the garden was a picture of outdoor order with not a twig out of place. An air of excitement buzzed amongst the students, particularly when they learned that a party was planned in their honour later that evening.

John flew in by helicopter, landing on the flat grassy plain near the West Wing, and delighted them all by inviting them to share trips around the island in the chopper. Alpha looked down in wonder on Krakow Bond, so large on the ground, so tiny from this high up. It was the school that had become her home—a home she never thought she'd have. At her side Janna grimaced, pointing out the broken roof of the west wing that Alpha had traversed such a short time ago.

Later, dead on seven o'clock in the evening, the students and psi-teachers converged on the student lounge all at once, where Chef Andreyaz presented them with a buffet that exceeded even his own superior standards.

'They've invited some of the locals to join us, including, to paraphrase Lily, " a selection of the island's youth". And Andreyaz tells me there'll be dancing in the ballroom,' said Janna, shimmying her way up and down a bar stool before plonking her bottom on it. 'I hope they've included that dishy guy who works in the boatyard. He's all suntan and sinew. I wouldn't mind a peek at his six-pack.'

Alpha grinned.

Dr Scott walked in with John and clapped his hands for their attention. Then he invited John to have his say. John cleared his throat and looked very serious for a minute, before breaking into a huge smile. 'The Prime Minister is delighted,' he told them. 'You've proved yourselves worthy of all his expectations.'

'Does that mean he's going to keep the school open?' asked Janna.

'Without question,' agreed John. 'However, I must warn you, Krakow Bond will still be taking a low profile—there aren't going to be any names splashed across newspapers. But make no mistake, you're valuable. Enormously, fantastically valuable. Britain needs you, more now than ever before. What a champion team you make.'

Dr Scott nodded. 'That's the most important point. You've shown how good you are when you work as a team. Remember, you stand and fight together, not as a bunch of separate individuals, but as a force with a formidable repertoire of talents. Please would you all fill a glass? Your efforts deserve to be toasted.'

As she listened to his words Alpha felt a new emotion fill her. *A team? One part of the whole.* The idea was unfamiliar territory to her. *I've never been part of a team before.*

Suddenly she realised that Martel was echoing her thoughts. *Teamwork?* he was thinking, deeply suspicious of the concept. Then she saw Martel shrug, and smile across at Sunday. Sunday gave him a thumbs up, downed his fruit punch in one gulp and began to heap up a plate with goodies, stuffing every third handful into his mouth.

Here goes nothing, thought Alpha, sidling over towards Martel. *I have to try, even if he bites my head off.*

For once Martel was unaware of his surroundings as his thoughts continued to plug away at the strange idea of being part of a team.

'Tell Dr Scott about Chrissie,' Alpha whispered. 'He'll want you to help, and maybe some of us can join in the search too.'

Martel flinched, then turned, his eyes blazing. Alpha shook in her boots. Then suddenly his hand dipped into his jacket. Alpha half expected a knife, but instead, Martel withdrew a letter. He held it out towards Alpha in such a way that Alpha could only read the bottom of it.

Hope you're enjoying that school of yours, and they're not treating you snotty-like. It's taken years of worry off your mother that you don't have to go to the local anymore. All our love, Aunt Fell. See you soon at Parents' Day.

P.S. By the way, Chrissie's home. She's five months pregnant, but the old girl's so pleased she's back she's forgotten to kick off about it.

Alpha just had time to absorb the spidery handwriting before Martel snatched the letter away and placed it carefully back in his pocket. Without a word, Martel reached towards Alpha, grabbed both her arms, pulled her towards him and kissed her on the mouth, his lips as warm as his spillage. For long seconds there was nothing but the heat between them and the taste of Martel on her mouth, turning Alpha's whole being into an indescribable tingling sensation. Then abruptly he released her, pausing to look deeply into her eyes, before turning rapidly and stalking over to the punch bowl.

Alpha let out the breath she'd been holding. *It's a start,* she thought. Holding close the warmth of her emotions, she slowly sipped her own glass of juice.

Dr Scott jumped onto a chair. 'Have you all filled your glasses? Well now, students of Krakow Bond, I salute you,' he said, raising his glass in a toast.

'To you,' repeated John. 'Our psychics. Nothing is going to hold you back now.'

Maybe! thought Alpha, ever cautious. Then she too shrugged as she felt her heart well with happiness. The future could take care of itself; for now, the present was good enough for her.

About the Authors

T Rose

T Rose is the daughter of S Rose, her co-author. T is an accomplished writer, having obtained a degree in English and History from the prestigious Queen Mary University of London. While at university, T earned five academic prizes for her writing. Over the years she has worked with various charities, focussing on promoting reading as well as organizing events and activities to help children and adults in need. She was born in England and now lives in a rural town surrounded by trees and nature, but which also lies only twenty-five minutes by train from the bustling metropolis of London. She describes it as, 'having the best of both worlds'. Her particular literary interests include the genres of psychological thriller, horror, and science fiction, focussing on the ways in which they reflect personal and societal anxieties. T Rose is the character and dialogue designer in this writing duo, bringing youth and freshness to their stories, which is needed to offset the miserable world of terrorism.

S Rose

S Rose was born in South Africa, but partially schooled in Germany and the UK. S now lives in London and has published a gardening story for young children, as well as a fantasy tale for young adults. Her career as a town clerk, working for the good of the community, keeps her exceptionally busy, so writing takes place during stolen moments just before bed. She has lived in many places around the world including an enjoyable period in Kissimmee, Florida in the USA, and has held an eclectic variety of jobs such as running a leadership training school, and owning a restaurant where she was front-of-house manager. She experienced in person the peaceful transition of power from the ruling white government in South Africa, through democratic voting, to the ANC, and passionately believes that, instead of violence, there is always another way. She creates the intricate plots that are a feature of the writing duo.

Apprentice
House Press
Loyola University Maryland

Apprentice House is the country's only campus-based, student-staffed book publishing company. Directed by professors and industry professionals, it is a nonprofit activity of the Communication Department at Loyola University Maryland.

Using state-of-the-art technology and an experiential learning model of education, Apprentice House publishes books in untraditional ways. This dual responsibility as publishers and educators creates an unprecedented collaborative environment among faculty and students, while teaching tomorrow's editors, designers, and marketers.

Eclectic and provocative, Apprentice House titles intend to entertain as well as spark dialogue on a variety of topics. Financial contributions to sustain the press's work are welcomed. Contributions are tax deductible to the fullest extent allowed by the IRS.

To learn more about Apprentice House books or to obtain submission guidelines, please visit www.apprenticehouse.com.

Apprentice House
Communication Department
Loyola University Maryland
4501 N. Charles Street
Baltimore, MD 21210
Ph: 410-617-5265
info@apprenticehouse.com • www.apprenticehouse.com

www.ingramcontent.com/pod-product-compliance
Lightning Source LLC
Chambersburg PA
CBHW051331020726
47501CB00007B/2034